Also by HEATHER GRAHAM

THE UNSPOKEN
THE UNHOLY
THE UNSEEN
BRIDE OF THE NIGHT
AN ANGEL FOR CHRISTMAS
THE EVIL INSIDE
SACRED EVIL
HEART OF EVIL
PHANTOM EVIL
NIGHT OF THE VAMPIRES
THE KEEPERS
GHOST MOON
GHOST NIGHT
GHOST SHADOW
THE KILLING EDGE
NIGHT OF THE WOLVES
HOME IN TIME FOR CHRISTMAS
UNHALLOWED GROUND
DUST TO DUST
NIGHTWALKER
DEADLY GIFT
DEADLY HARVEST

DEADLY NIGHT
THE DEATH DEALER
THE LAST NOEL
THE SÉANCE
BLOOD RED
THE DEAD ROOM
KISS OF DARKNESS
THE VISION
THE ISLAND
GHOST WALK
KILLING KELLY
THE PRESENCE
DEAD ON THE DANCE FLOOR
PICTURE ME DEAD
HAUNTED
HURRICANE BAY
A SEASON OF MIRACLES
NIGHT OF THE BLACKBIRD
NEVER SLEEP WITH STRANGERS
EYES OF FIRE
SLOW BURN
NIGHT HEAT

* * * * *

HEATHER GRAHAM

THE
UNINVITED

ISBN-13: 978-1-62090-351-3

THE UNINVITED

To the great city of Philadelphia,
and to my favorite Pennsylvanians in the world,
Gail Spence Crosbie and Ann Spence—
and to Jimmy, Megan, Spencer
and Anthony Crosbie

Prologue

It was a beautiful time of day, close to dusk, at a beautiful time of year, early fall. Philadelphia's Tarleton-Dandridge House sat back from the street, majestic and stately, in the light that had just begun to fade, as fine and poignant as an old building could be, a proud remnant of an era long gone, yet ever remembered.

Julian Mitchell almost felt guilty. Almost. He couldn't quite manage guilt; he was too ecstatic over his day, still pumped with enthusiasm and the beat of the music he'd been playing. He enjoyed being a guide at the Tarleton-Dandridge, but today he'd had to ditch it. The audition had been important and, much as he loved his job, he loved the idea of working full-time as a guitarist more. Sure, it was great dressing up and playing with the band in Old Town, but he had dreams of being a real rock star. Now, however, he had to slip back into the house—and suck up to Allison. She was their unofficial leader, head of the guides or docents at the Tarleton-Dandridge, and if she forgave him, the others would, too.

He saw that one group of guests had already entered the house with their guide and that another, the last group of the day, was assembling just outside the main door. He could see Allison Leigh to the side of the house near the gate, welcoming those who were gathering for the final tour. Allison was dressed in the typical fashion of the Revolutionary era—the typical *high* fashion of the Revolutionary era, since female guides wore clothing along the lines of that which would've been worn by Lucy Tarleton, the martyred heroine of the house. The male guides dressed as Lord Brian Bradley, the British general known as "Beast" Bradley, who had occupied the house.

They all looked pretty cool in their clothing, he thought. But especially Allison. She was beautiful to begin with, even if she *was* kind of a nerd. A real academic. But she did bear a resemblance to the heroine she played, Lucy Tarleton. They'd all remarked on her resemblance to the painting in the house and those in various museums, but there was no evidence that she *was* a descendent of the woman. And if anyone would know, Allison would, since she was a historian. Maybe it was the clothing that gave her the look.

Allison wasn't even glancing his way, so he quickly jumped the old brick wall that surrounded the house.

He was still in his period clothing from the morning shift; he hadn't sneaked out until after lunch. Luckily, his band's audition had been to open for the new "it" group—rockers who liked to dress up like Patrick Henry and friends—which meant he hadn't had to worry about auditioning in his work outfit.

Of course, he hadn't asked for the time off. He'd decided that in life it was generally better to *do* and ask forgiveness later than it was to beg for permission and get a big fat *no!* What guilt he did feel was because one of his colleagues had to take the tour group *he* should have led.

Still, he had a plan. He'd wait until the last group

had gone through, and Jason and Allison had finished for the day. He winced; he realized Annette wasn't at work. She'd made an appointment for a root canal. But he knew his fellow docents as well as they knew him. Jason would leave before Ally. Julian just had to wait until Jason had left and Allison was alone, checking as she always did that the doors were locked and the alarm system was on. She would come down to Angus's study—ye olde study, where that poor bastard Angus Tarleton had died, supposedly of a broken heart—to make sure no kids were hiding under the desk to spend the night in the "haunted" house. He'd wait for her there. When Ally showed up, he would beg and plead and he could honestly tell her they'd probably get the gig, and he'd do anything to compensate for the time he'd missed. And he'd promise her backstage passes to the first concert.

He tiptoed to the front door and listened. Once Jason's tour had moved into the social rooms to the left, he hurried up the stairs. But when he reached the second-floor landing, he heard conversation and footsteps coming down from the attic. He dodged into Lucy Tarleton's room. He'd forgotten the board was meeting at the house that day. He'd have to wait until they were gone.

At last, they were. He heard the foursome going down the main stairway. As usual, they were bickering among themselves.

"Cherry, you may be a descendent of the family, but this place is owned by Old Philly History now. We're only the board." She started to speak, but Ethan Oxford interrupted her. "Yes, it's privately owned and operated, but there's a charter. The house was donated for the preservation of history."

Old Ethan Oxford was the senior member of the board. Cherry's mother had been the last of the Dandridge family. Cherry would probably have eschewed her own father's name to take on Dandridge, Julian was certain, except that her husband, George Addison, was becoming a very well-known artist, and she liked the prestige that came with being Mrs. Addison.

"No one knows this house like I do," Cherry insisted.

"Really? You never lived in it. It was handed over to Old Philly History long before you were born."

Julian smiled. That voice belonged to Nathan Pierson, who loved to listen sweetly to Cherry and then zing her.

"Hush!" Sarah Vining said. "There are tour groups in here!"

A moment later, even their voices faded away as they left the house.

Julian started toward the attic but paused. For some reason, he had the odd sensation of being held in the room and he turned around, curious. He saw nothing there. Nothing except the painting of Beast Bradley. The *nice* painting of Bradley. "They say you were a brutal bastard. Glad someone saw the good in you!" Julian said. Giving himself a mental shake, he dashed up to the attic to hide. He sat at the desk there, glancing at the piles of paper around the computer and the countless file folders. Some of the information here was pure business—schedules, events planned at the estate, programs planned, money collected. But most of the piles belonged to Ally. Professor Allison Leigh. "You would have to be a brainiac!" he said aloud. He was a year or two younger than Ally, but he'd had a crush on her since he'd taken his position here. And she wasn't *all* work and no play. He knew because she'd dated another musician for a while, an acquaintance of his.

"You may have brains, Ally, but your taste in men isn't so great." It was one thing to have a casual friendship with a drug addict; it was another to date one. Ally's romance had ended when she realized she couldn't compete with his cocaine habit.

Ah, well, history seemed to be her true love. He picked up the nearest folder and began to read. "Huh!" he murmured. Apparently, she'd found a new lead on an old subject.

To his own surprise, he became interested in her notes. Ally definitely seemed to be on to something. He set down the folder and listened carefully. It was safe to go down to the second floor, he decided, since Jason's tour group had departed.

Julian hurried back to Lucy's bedroom. There was a beautiful rendering of a young Lucy on one wall. She was dressed in white and had a look of open excitement in her eyes, as if she loved life, and the whole world. It had been an eighteenth-birthday gift to Lucy from Levy Perry, an artist killed at Brandywine. Naturally, it was painted before either of them had learned about the horrors of war.

He turned from the image of Lucy and stared at the painting of Beast Bradley again.

"Charmer, were you?" He laughed softly. "Well, that's not what history says."

As soon as he could, he'd go down to Angus's study and wait for Ally. If she gave him any grief, he could tell her he'd read her notes about Bradley and Lucy, and they were brilliant, just brilliant.

Interesting that the painting of Beast Bradley in the study was nothing like this one.

He smiled. He'd have the chance to stare at *that* one for a while. Because he wanted to be in Angus's chair when Ally found him. He was dressed as Beast Bradley—why not play the part completely as he begged her to forgive him? It was the perfect way to convince her that he was serious about his job here. At least until his music career was well and truly launched...

Leaving Lucy's bedroom, he reached the door and thought he heard a noise behind him. But that was impossible.

Unless it was good old Beast Bradley himself, roused from the dead to rummage through the research papers?

Tiptoeing down the stairs he laughed. He opened the hall closet on the first floor to pick up the reproduction muzzle-loading musket and bayonet that went with his uniform.

He heard a noise again and frowned. It *couldn't* be coming from the attic. No, he told himself, the rustling was probably outside.

"'I ain't afraid of no ghosts!'" he muttered.

And yet, it was with great unease that he waited.

He felt he was being watched.

And followed.

1

"Are you Dolley Madison? Or, like, Martha Washington or something?" one of the boys edging toward the front of Allison Leigh's tour asked. He was about nine or ten, still awkward, but obviously determined to create some havoc—no doubt to avoid embarrassing himself in front of the few other teens and preteens on the tour.

A taller, older boy, maybe twelve, who might have been his brother, nudged him. "You idiot, they're both dead, and she's alive. And she's hot, buddy. She's way too hot even in that getup to be one of *those* old ladies." The second boy tried to look mature. He reminded Allison of a very young Adam Sandler. The boys were part of her tour, which included a mix of ages. Summer was just drawing to a close and families were still on vacation.

She heard someone behind her choke back laughter; it was Nathan Pierson, longtime board member for the nonprofit organization that now owned the Tarleton-Dandridge House. They'd had a meeting in the attic, where a small office was located. Cherry Addison, the remaining descendent of the Dandridge clan, had already moved on, spike heels clicking. Ethan Oxford, their eldest member, had politely made his way through the crowd. Nathan and Sarah Vining were the last of the four board members to leave the house.

Nathan grinned and winked at Allison as he approached. Sarah hurried to catch up with him. She was a wisp of a woman who had given herself frown lines worrying about the board's every move, while Nathan was the opposite, always certain things would work out. He was a slim and stately man in his forties, not exactly a father figure, more like a cool-uncle figure. And he was amused.

Ally shot him a warning glance, but he kept grinning as he stepped past her. When he looked back and winked again, she forced a smile to her lips and turned her attention back to the group.

"Well, thanks, I think," she told the boy who'd spoken. There was nothing like having a few young kids on the tour, giggling and not the least bit interested in the history of the Tarleton-Dandridge House—or the nation, for that matter. They didn't want to be here and were going to be thorns in her side if she didn't do something quickly. Ghost tours were the answer in situations like this.

To most kids an old house just seemed stuffy and boring. She understood how they felt, even though she'd always been the odd kid out herself—a history nerd, as Julian liked to call her. She was from Philadelphia; she'd gone to Boston for her bachelor and master's, and to New York for her doctorate, but she loved her own city almost as if it were a friend with whom she'd grown up. From the time she was little, she'd gaped at Independence Hall and marveled that she could stand in the same place where some of the greatest men in American history had stood.

She surveyed the crowd and concluded that the two boys were indeed brothers, dragged along on a historical jaunt by their parents, the attractive couple a few feet back.

"Actually, my name is Allison Leigh, and the person I'm dressed to portray is Lucy Tarleton. And," she added teasingly, "she's supposed to haunt the place, so I'd be careful if I were you." She took a step closer to the taller of the two brothers. "She wants you to know your history."

He grinned and struck a swaggering pose. "I wouldn't mind meeting up with a hot ghost," he said. "And I know all about her. Lucy Tarleton, that is. We went on a ghost tour last night! She was a *spy*. Like a Hairy Mata."

"Mata Hari!" his dad whispered, shaking his head in amusement but setting a hand on the boy's shoulders. "Sorry!" he murmured to Allison.

"It's fine," Allison assured him. She turned back to the boy. "Great, then you're in the know," she said gravely. "You could meet up with Lucy today. Or maybe the ghost of Lord Brian 'Beast' Bradley, who is said to have murdered several patriots in cold blood, among them Lucy Tarleton."

"Ghosts? Bring 'em on!" the boy shouted.

"Todd," his father chastised. "Keep it down."

"It's all right. Everyone loves historic ghost stories," Allison said. She did like kids and understood that they were going to be, well, kids. She just wished people would recognize the human toll of war and what history could teach them.

She stepped back to welcome her entire group of fifteen. "Good evening," she said loudly, "and welcome to the Tarleton-Dandridge House, here in historic Philadelphia!"

Trees swayed gently in the breeze, and the air had taken on a sweet chill that might have been the promise of rain or merely the slow descent from summer into fall. Dusk was coming, and with it, a soft fog. They hadn't shortened their hours at the mansion yet, but the last tour was usually out while there was still a glimmer of light in the sky.

Watching the sky and feeling the breeze, Allison Leigh thought she didn't mind the long days at all, even if she was tired tonight. Of course, a lot of what she did was by rote and she could do it in her sleep, but she was fascinated by history, and adored the old historic house where she worked as a guide when her teaching schedule allowed. Summers generally meant full-time guiding. She liked people, too, especially children and young adults, and valued the opportunity to show them where the fate of a nation had been decided and to discuss both the Colonial era and the Revolution itself.

On most busy days the other three guides did their share of the tours. Annette Fanning, a good friend as well as coworker, had left early, scheduled for a root canal. Jason Lawrence was leading the tour group just ahead, dressed in the manner of the British dandy, Lord Bradley, who'd resided in the house when the patriots had fled. Julian Mitchell, the fourth guide employed by the private nonprofit corporation that owned the house, had disappeared around lunchtime. He was an effective guide, but he was also running around auditioning with his band, and had a tendency to show up late or disappear early. With the last of the school-age crowd going through at the tail end of summer, his lack of responsibility was irritating, but this tour was it for the night—and then she'd be ready to close up and go home. They all liked Julian; he was just driving them crazy.

"Watch out! A ghost's going to follow you home," a young man in the crowd whispered to the boys. He smiled, looking at the young woman with him, his wife or girlfriend, as if watching the boys because he might want a few of his own one day.

"I don't think ghosts follow you home," the younger of the two brothers said bravely. "I mean, they're supposed to haunt a *place,* right?"

"Maybe they *can* follow you home!" his brother teased. "They can go through walls, can't they?"

"Stop it!" the younger one said.

His brother made chicken sounds.

Allison clapped her hands to draw their attention back to the tour. "The Tarleton-Dandridge House is open to help you understand the Revolutionary War and the occupation of Philadelphia, not to send ghosts home with anyone," she announced. "So, we'll start with a brief history, although I'm sure you know most of this. Philadelphia was the first capital of the United States. And the Declaration of Independence was written and signed here. But by that time, shots had been fired in Boston—and the British navy was occupying Staten Island. What you may not realize is that the First Continental Congress worked here before they decided on independence. At first, they were seeking a means to achieve…can someone tell me?"

Oddly enough, it was her swaggering young beau, the older brother, who raised his hand. "No taxation without representation!" he said.

"Very good. So, since it looked like the royal foot was coming down to punish the colonies for their revolt against taxes—and they'd already risked being hanged for protesting lack of representation, the next step was to go all the way. Make the stakes worth the consequences, in other words. But it wasn't the citizens of Philadelphia who were eager for war, or at least not all of them. Remember, this area was settled by the Quaker William Penn. He granted the city its charter. Those who believe in the Quaker creed are and have always been antiwar and antiviolence, but by the time of the American Revolution, this was a city of about thirty thousand, all mixed in their beliefs and backgrounds."

"Yeah! They were ready to fight for freedom!" the older boy said.

She nodded. "By then the colonies had formed the Second Continental Congress, so a fight for independence it became. But Philadelphia would pay the price. The British wanted the capital. According to their logic, if you took the capital, the rest of the upstarts would fall apart and surrender. However, General George Washington had learned from his Indian wars, and he waged a different kind of warfare. Still, we lost many battles and, as I said, Philadelphia and her residents paid a heavy toll."

She seemed to have won over the boys, which pleased her, and they were looking at her intently now rather than gawking.

"Gentlemen, if you will?" she asked the two brothers.

They actually seemed nervous as she walked back to the podium by the gate. She took out two mock Colonial muskets and gave them to the boys. The male guides carried exceptionally accurate reproduction muskets, but to entertain young adults before entering the house, the guides used mock-up plastic muskets.

"Now, how would you feel if I put you twenty feet apart and told you to shoot at each other? Do you think it would make a lot of sense?"

"You shoot enough and…I guess we could hit each other," the taller boy said. "Eventually."

"Maybe," the younger brother added.

She nodded. "Muskets of the day weren't great on aim. For every shot, a man had to load his powder, tamp it down and hope the enemy wasn't upon him before he could fire again. What are your names?" she asked the boys.

The younger brother was Jimmy, she discovered, and the older one was Todd. She had them perform and they followed her instructions, demonstrating a manner of fighting in which they walked toward each other, and then another manner, in which one of them hid behind a tree.

"George Washington had learned well, don't you think? He knew the British could outman, outpower and outdiscipline him. So if they wanted the city, he'd take to the countryside. Back in the 1770s, for about a hundred miles all around Philadelphia, there was nothing but wilderness. Washington could abandon the city, let the British move in for a while, and the Revolutionary government could keep trying to sway the French to join us, which happened in 1778. And the British knew they could become locked in, trapped. So they in turn had to abandon the city."

Allison checked the little watch she wore on a chain around her neck, and saw that she'd given Jason plenty of time to take his group through.

"Shall we enter the house?" she said, opening the gate that led up to the handsome brick house.

"Let's go!" Todd blurted out.

She arched a brow at him. He grinned, and she smiled back.

As she led her group into the small but beautifully manicured yard, Allison told them, "The house was built in 1752 of brick and stone, in what was known as the Flemish style, with alternating longer and shorter bricks. It was built for Lucy Tarleton's father, an Irish immigrant who rose to success and attained great riches as a merchant—and had no love for the British King George."

"Mad King George!" Jimmy said.

"Yes, so they called him." Allison paused on the porch, waiting for the stragglers to catch up.

"King George never set foot here, of course," she went on. "The days of kings leading their men into battle were long gone. But as for King George's war," Allison said, "there were two English brothers in control of the war effort here—Admiral Richard Howe on the water and General William Howe on land. One thing they hoped, of course, was that many citizens would be loyal to Britain and start coming out of the woodwork when they arrived."

"And there *were* citizens loyal to Great Britain, right?" Jimmy asked.

"Yep. There were citizens loyal to Great Britain, although many moved to Canada—the United Empire Loyalists—when the war began. But this city was a prize to the British, harder to obtain than they'd expected."

"The rivers weren't deep enough for the Royal navy!" Todd said. "I know that because we've been on so many history tours already!"

"Exactly," Allison agreed. "And there were numerous unseen obstacles under the water. It was difficult!

But eventually they made their way here." She continued the story she'd told so many times before. "Philadelphia fell to the British, and was held by them from September 26, 1777, through June 18, 1778. General Washington deprived them of greater victory by seeing that the city was abandoned and the Continental Congress moved to New York City. The British set up a puppet government in Philadelphia for that nine-month period. Meanwhile, the British soldiers enjoyed the warmth and comfort of some of these splendid homes, while Washington's men froze at Valley Forge. And so here, at this beautiful mansion, Lucy Tarleton stayed behind, pretending to be loyal to the Crown, throwing parties, and even feigning a romance with Lord Brian Bradley—soon to be known as 'Beast' Bradley, and soon to execute—without trial or king's command—the lovely patriot, Lucy Tarleton. Lucy was indeed passing British secrets to General Washington down in Valley Forge. She was passionate about her cause and she was to die for her efforts, in a rare but tragically vindictive incident. Follow me."

The front door led through a tiny mudroom with cut-glass windows and then into a grand foyer. "In the city, you'll find that many businesses were on the first floors of what are now historic buildings, while the living quarters were upstairs. But here, a servant would greet guests in the foyer, and determine where they'd go. Mr. Tarleton's study was to your right, while the salon was the first room to your left," she said, gesturing in those directions. "The kitchen is still a separate house out back, which prevented a cooking fire from reaching the main house. Beyond the salon is the dining room, and it gave the servants easy access to the kitchen. The left side of the house as you face me was the entertainment area, you might say, and to your right were the family rooms. In back of the study is the ladies' parlor, and behind that, the music room. You'll see an exquisite harpsichord there that actually belonged to the Tarleton family. Upstairs, there are five bedrooms and the attic, which contained storage space and rooms for the servants. The Tarletons had five household servants who lived in the main house and a number of gardeners and grooms who lived over the carriage house, which is also preserved."

"Servants! I could use a few!" the boys' mother said, ruffling her younger son's hair.

Allison grinned and went on to describe various objects in the house. Then she explained that because of tight spaces and narrow hallways, they should go by themselves and look into the rooms on their own, respecting the velvet cord barriers. "So, please go ahead and walk through the first floor, and I'll be here to answer any questions. Don't forget to note the dumbwaiter at the rear of the dining room! It's still in perfect working order."

She stood in the foyer, in a central area so guests could question her. She was surprised when Todd came up to her. She suspected some kind of sexual innuendo, but he seemed oddly quiet and awed. "Miss, can you come here for a minute?"

"Sure, Todd." She followed him to the doorway of Tarleton's study. The room held his large carved maple desk, reproduction ledgers, quills, ink pots, study chairs and wooden shelves, some covered with glass doors. There were two paintings that dominated the walls in the room, one of Angus Tarleton himself, painted when he was a young man with shiny dark hair and bright blue eyes, traits he'd passed on to his daughter.

But Todd was staring at the other painting. He pointed at it.

"Who is that?" he asked in a whisper.

"Oh, that's the man they called 'Beast' Bradley," she told him. "Brian Bradley. Remember? We talked about him." She stared at the painting, too. Bradley was a young man in the portrait, with a narrow face, high cheekbones, and dark, brooding eyes. Allison had always thought that although the portrait was certainly flattering, the artist hadn't liked the man. The cruelty for which he would one day be known seemed painted into the sharpness of his features and the look in his eyes. He was elegantly dressed, in the fashion of his day. And while he was a general in the king's army, she'd seldom seen him depicted in uniform. She assumed that wearing anything that might be rank and file—even with elevating insignias—would have been, in his eyes, beneath him.

Todd shivered, still pointing at the portrait.

"And a ghost will follow you home!" he said, and his words weren't light. He was truly unnerved.

"He was a horrible man, but he's long gone," Allison said, surprised that the would-be "cool" preteen now seemed more like a scared schoolboy.

"He isn't gone," Todd said. "He...he looked at me."

Despite herself, Allison felt a chill. She tried to tell herself the boy was trying to tease her, play off the situation and get her to slip an arm around him.

But he wasn't playing any games. He appeared really frightened.

"It's the way the portrait's painted," Allison assured him, but she found herself staring up at Bradley again. She never came into this room when she was alone, locking up and setting the alarms for the night. She always stood in the doorway, glanced in and moved on. While the house was equipped with a modern alarm system, they were supposed to make sure no visitors tried to stay on to defy the ghosts of the mansion.

Legend had it that Beast Bradley had thrust his knife straight into the heart of Lucy Tarleton in the grand salon; he'd killed her there while her father had wept for her life and been forced to watch. To add to the cruelty of the act, he'd left Angus Tarleton alive to hold his dying daughter. According to history—in this case, the accounts that were handed down by the survivors—Brian Bradley hadn't killed Lucy for her patriot escapades. He'd killed her because he'd discovered she was false to him, that she wasn't in love with him at all.

Before the arrival of the British, Lucy was about to become betrothed to another patriot, Stewart Douglas, who had fled the city with other American soldiers. It was a sad tale, one Allison would share in a few minutes when she'd gathered her people in the foyer again.

"Todd, this is a creepy picture of a man who was apparently a monster, which had far more to do with him than with the fact that he was British. Horrendous incidents, beyond any code of warfare, have taken place during just about every conflict in history. But the British *weren't* monsters, and neither were the colonists. Most of the evidence we have says that Bradley did behave abominably, and—"

"How did he die?" Todd asked her.

"Actually, no one knows, but it's presumed that he was killed in the fighting soon after the British abandoned the city. Howe was furious with him for his brutal actions in Philadelphia. They argued before the

Battle of Saratoga, and he disappeared from history," Allison said. "A few letters that mention him have been preserved, and some suspect he might have been killed by his own men. Those letters suggest he was a brutal commander, as well. Way, way, way back, he was related to the Royal House of Hanover, and he seemed to think he was entitled to his behavior through the divine right of kings—even though he was certainly not a king and never going to be one."

"He's still here," Todd whispered. "He's still here."

She did set an arm around his shoulders. Allison was about five-ten in her two-inch Colonial pumps, giving her a bit of height over him. "Todd, that was then, and this is now, and you need to see the rest of the house, learn about the history, and have fun with your family tonight. The historic tavern restaurants, where they serve in Colonial garb and entertain with flutes and old jokes, are really fun. You'll enjoy that."

He shook his head, gazing at the painting as if drawn to it.

She led him firmly from the study. "What happened to the house after the British left?" he asked.

"Angus died a year after his daughter. She had a younger sister, Sophia, who married a fine American soldier, Tobias Dandridge, and they inherited the house. It's now owned by a private corporation called Old Philly History, and there's still a descendent on the board of governors. The house stayed in the family until 1930, when the owner formed this corporation. That's why so many of the original family pieces have been preserved."

She'd managed to get Todd back into the foyer, and she smiled at him as she related the history of the house she'd just given him.

"Now, the upstairs. We'll go up together and I'll wait in the hall while you look in all the rooms," Allison said cheerfully. "The master bedroom is at the far end of the house, but the one everyone finds most interesting is Lucy's room, on the right side of the staircase. She and her sister both had grand rooms with large dressing rooms. There's a 1700s tub in Lucy's room, which is authentic to the house."

She sent them off and waited, watching Todd. He ignored all the rooms except for Lucy's.

He came back to stand by her. "I saw her picture on the wall. Lucy's picture. You look like her."

"I think a lot of women do when they're dressed like her," Allison said.

Todd nodded solemnly. "Maybe. But you mostly." He studied her for a moment and then whispered, "Someone else died in the study, right?"

She shouldn't have been surprised. After all, the family had gone on a ghost tour last night. Though the house itself was closed to these ghost tours, they all walked by it and embellished the tales that went along with it. Personally, she thought the truth was far more haunting than anything they could make up.

"A lieutenant who fought in the War of 1812 came here when he was wounded, and he died soon after. Another soldier on the Union side in the Civil War also died in that room. And yes, one of the Dandridge girls died there in 1890—she took poison to commit suicide."

"And a few years ago, one of *you* was found dead in the room, right?" Todd asked her, wide-eyed.

"I'm going to give all this information when the tour gathers again," she told him.

"Right?" he persisted. She felt acutely uncomfortable. Every old house had its history. Naturally some of it was sad and even distressing.

"Angela Wilson did die in that room. She had a heart attack while locking up one night."

Todd regarded her solemnly. "She died sitting at Angus Tarleton's desk, didn't she?"

"Yes, Todd, she did. She sat down—she must have been winded. Like I said, she died there of a heart attack."

"And somebody else died in the house, too," Todd said. "A couple of years ago."

She inhaled a deep breath. "Yes," she admitted. "It was really a tragedy. A young college student decided to hack into the alarm system. The police believe he was pledging for a fraternity. He tried to break in and did something wrong with the alarm, and he was electrocuted. Everyone involved with the house was appalled, but—"

"And there was another guy. The woman on our ghost tour told us. One of the curators or guides or whatever you're called."

"That was in 1977. He fell down the steps and broke his neck," Allison said.

"Fell? Or was pushed? I bet Beast Bradley pushed him!"

"Oh, Todd. Beast Bradley's been gone for over two centuries. He's not hanging around here trying to kill people." Allison shook her head. "The house has been here for a long time, and over time, bad things happen."

Todd frowned at her. "I think he is. I think he wanted to stay in Philadelphia, and he wanted to marry Lucy Tarleton, but she hated him. So he killed her, but he still didn't want to leave the house. It was supposed to be *his* house. So he came back here when he died. And now he kills people!"

There was something about the boy's insistence that made Allison uncomfortable. She loved the house, and she loved working here. She didn't need this job; she'd gotten her degrees in history and was a college lecturer who also wrote articles and was currently doing research for a book. She worked at the house because she loved the people part of history, loved understanding the realities and nuances of everyday life far more than dates and figures. She'd grown up farther down on Chestnut Street and had admired this place all her life, and as a result she could answer questions that few others could. She'd respected the house, and she'd never wanted to sensationalize it by writing ghost stories. Like any historical place, it had an aura about it. She felt that same aura standing next to the Liberty Bell or when she went into Independence Hall, or any of the sites around the world where people had once lived and passionately taken part in the shaping of destiny. She couldn't believe that Todd was suddenly making her afraid of *this* house.

"Like I said, bad things happen, Todd, and they happen everywhere. That's why we go through life trying to drive properly, cross the street only when the light is green and take care of our health—because human beings are fragile." She smiled. "I work here three days a week, and sometimes more, and nothing has *ever* happened to me. I usually close up by myself, too, and I'm just fine. And I've never seen a ghost."

Todd looked at her oddly. "He *likes* you. He might not always like you, but he likes you right now. He likes women."

The way the boy spoke was unsettling, and she told herself he was heading back toward being a raunchy preteen, acting in a manner that was natural for his age.

His mother walked up to them a moment later. "I'm Todd and Jimmy's mom, Haley Dixon," she said. "I'm so sorry if the boys have been bothering you. As you've probably heard, we did the ghost tour last night. There are all kinds of stories about this place, and they're boys, and..." Her voice trailed off.

"Mrs. Dixon, Todd's been asking me about the house, and he's a good listener," Allison said.

Haley Dixon smiled at her son. "Todd, I'm glad you're curious, but we have to leave Ms. Leigh alone and allow her to give everyone her information at the same time."

She seemed a pleasant woman, and a good parent, slightly at a loss as to what to do with a couple of boys. Her husband, viewing some of the portraits on the wall, turned. Grinning, he came over to join them, slipping an arm around his wife. "Artie Dixon, Ms. Leigh. You do a wonderful tour. Forgive my sons, please, if they're too inquisitive."

"No such thing in this house," Allison assured him. But she stepped back to include her whole group. "All right, everyone, gather around and I'll give you all the grisly details on some of the sad and tragic occurrences here, since it seems the ghost story guides are beating us to it."

She told them about the soldiers, then reminded them, "In the past, many women died in childbirth. It was the norm to have your baby at home, so several of them died here. Many family members died of illness or simply of old age. Remember, all human beings are mortal and leave this world in *some* fashion!" She tried to speak lightly, looking at Todd. "Now, we're going down the rear steps to the old food preparation room, and then we'll head to the back to see the outbuildings."

Allison managed to get her group out to the yard. The property still consisted of about an acre, with the majority of the grounds in the back. The kitchen stood off to her left, behind the dining room, with a covered path between them. It was a one-room kitchen, large with a massive hearth and spit and a multitude of rafters from which pans and cooking utensils hung. Glass-frosted cupboards showcased the family's fine china and several sets of silverware, and one of her group murmured that it was probably the most complete example of an upper-class Colonial kitchen she'd ever seen.

They went across another, broader path to the carriage house. There were no horses now, but there were stalls and tack and three eighteenth-century carriages. As Allison let the group look at them more closely, Haley Dixon came up to her.

"There's a ghost horse here, too, or so they said last night," she told Allison, sounding a little apologetic.

Allison sighed. "Firewalker. He brought Stewart Douglas racing back to the house, heedless of the British after he heard that Bradley had threatened Lucy. Stewart was the man she really loved. She'd urged him to take the horse after he snuck into the city to see her once, because Firewalker was such an exceptional stallion he could sail through enemy lines. Firewalker was born and bred on the property, and carried Lucy Tarleton on many of her journeys in the middle of the night, when she rode out to bring information to the Revolutionary troops. He survived the war and lived to a ripe old age, then died here in the arms of Lucy's sister, which means, of course, that we have a ghost horse. We have a ghost hound, too. With the imaginative name of Robert. He was Lucy's, and when Bradley went to kill her, the hound tried to kill him. Naturally, the dog died, as well. We probably even have haunted squirrels," Allison said.

Haley Dixon laughed. "I guess. It's strange. The house is strange because so much happened in it. I'm not sure I could hang around here alone at night."

Allison shrugged, smiling. "You get used to it, really."

She announced to her group that she'd show them the graveyard next.

The family burial ground was a popular destination. Lucy Tarleton herself lay in a handsome private Tarleton crypt in a beautifully sculpted tomb. Allison described the workmanship and explained that it was common for wealthy families to have their own graveyards. She noted that Todd didn't want to be in the cemetery; she was shocked to realize that she was anxious to end the tour herself.

It was finally time to usher her people out, but Allison was still disturbed by the way Todd looked at her as he left with his family. They were the last ones out the back gate, and he lingered. "A ghost can't follow you home, can it?" he asked in a whisper.

"I don't think so. I mean, if we do have ghosts, I imagine they'd just hang around here. Have fun tonight! Pinch a tavern wench somewhere, okay?"

He grinned at her. "You don't mean that."

"No. She'd slap you. But go forth and have fun and be a kid!"

When they were gone at last, she hurried into the

house through the back door. She found Jason Lawrence in their small employee quarters behind the main pantry.

He had removed his Colonial garb and was wearing jeans and a T-shirt that promoted his favorite band.

"Hey, you holding up okay?" he asked her.

"Yes, but it's nice when four people actually work on the busy days," Allison said. "We could've used Julian. I understand why Annette had to go—poor thing. She looked like she was in so much pain."

Jason was an attractive young man, about three years her junior at the ripe old age of twenty-four. They'd been friends since they'd met, and although they had great chemistry together, it wasn't sexual. They were friends. He raised his brows and let out a sigh. "We may all love him for being a clown and a prankster, but Julian can also be a total pain in the ass," he said. "He thinks he's going to get rich and famous—and that we're all going to be grateful just to have known him. But you have to speak to him or to Sarah or someone else on the board, because this isn't fair."

"I'll try talking to him first," Allison said. "And then, if he doesn't start acting more responsible, I will talk to Sarah."

Jason nodded. "Mind if I scoot?"

"Hot date?"

"I hope so."

"Go."

"I hate to leave you alone…"

"I'll make a run-through and set the alarm as I head out."

"I'll lock the back door. The back gate's locked, right?"

"Yep. I can just hit the alarm and dash out the front."

He gave her a kiss on the cheek and she heard his footsteps on the hardwood floor as he went to lock up. She heard him as he moved through the house, and she heard the front door close as he left.

To her annoyance, she was suddenly frightened in the house. She silently chastised herself. Todd was at the age when he wanted to be a sexual lothario one minute, and a kid spooked by a campfire tale the next. She wanted to rip off her dress and stomacher and change into her comfortable jeans; instead, she decided to hurry up and check the house, then get out of there.

She glanced over the room and went out, locking the door. She walked past the dining room and the grand salon and returned to the foyer. Looking up the stairs, she knew she wasn't going up to make sure she'd left no scared toddler or would-be ghost hunter in the house. She knew that every man, woman and child on her tour had departed through the back gate.

A sense of something dark and evil seemed to have drifted over her, and she wished she could call Jason back. As she crossed the foyer, she stopped.

She'd heard a sound. A ticking or a...scrape or...

It was coming from Angus Tarleton's study.

She didn't want to look. She wanted to rush to the front door, hit the alarm and run home, run out of the house screaming....

How ridiculous!

It might have been an air-conditioning vent or... wood settling. There were probably dozens of technical or architectural things it could be.

She closed her eyes, shaking her head, annoyed again that Todd had managed to unnerve her like this. She was a sensible and responsible human being, a historian.

She walked to the room and looked in.

And a scream, shrill and horrified, tore from her throat.

Julian Mitchell *had* returned to the Tarleton-Dandridge House.

2

Tyler Montague's first impression of Allison Leigh was not a good one.

But then, the woman had apparently been at the house where a friend had died—either accidentally or through a very bizarre form of murder—for hours before coming down to the police station to deal with more paperwork.

She hadn't been *accused* of murder, not yet. Probably because the police and the pathologists couldn't quite figure out how a woman her size could have managed it. Julian Mitchell had been big, tall, well-muscled. For her to have dealt with the weapon *and* the man would have been a nearly impossible feat.

She had dark hair, so sleek and deep a brown, it appeared black. He assumed she'd started the evening with her hair neatly tied back but now it was tumbling down around her shoulders beneath an eighteenth-century-style mobcap. Allison was dressed in the daily wear of an upscale Revolutionary-era citizen—*a robe à l'Anglaise,* he believed they called the gown—and looked exhausted. She was seated at a table in one of the interrogation rooms, a cup of coffee in front of her, and when he arrived, she had her head down on one arm.

"Ms. Leigh knows you're coming to talk to her," a quiet voice said at his side.

Tyler turned to look at Adam Harrison. Adam had to be close to eighty, but he walked with the ease of a much younger man and stood straight as a poker. His eyes were a very gentle blue, showing signs of a smoky color that might have come from his age. He had snow-white hair, and his suit was casual and in impeccable taste. He'd arranged for Tyler's Krewe to be called in because of Ethan Oxford, an old friend of Adam's with whom he'd served on many philanthropic boards over the years.

Adam Harrison was the reason Tyler had left a career with the Texas Rangers to join this extremely unusual unit of the FBI.

Tyler didn't know *everything* about Adam Harrison; he didn't think anyone did. But Adam seemed to have friends everywhere. A call from him and a rough road could be easily traveled. But then, years before Tyler and his Krewe had ever met the man, Adam Harrison had been putting the right people in the right circumstances. And while other government agencies might consider the Krewe units as something completely separate and even an embarrassment at times, they were respected for their prowess. They had yet to fail when it came to finding the truth in any of their investigations.

"And she knows who I am?" Tyler asked.

Harrison shrugged. "She knows you're FBI."

"She must be ready to crawl the walls. It took me a little over three hours to drive in from northern Virginia, and we didn't receive your call until an hour or so after the body was discovered." He checked his watch. "It's after midnight."

Harrison sighed, shuffling his feet slightly. "The police were left with no recourse, really. There was the dead man. There was the woman who called it in. Tour groups had been at the house all evening, along with a couple of other docents, and when Ms. Leigh dialed 9-1-1, she was the only one on the premises. She was shaken when they got there. With a death of this nature, you have to be suspicious of anyone in her situation. The sad thing is that I believe she's entirely innocent. *And* she's just lost a colleague."

Tyler saw that Harrison's empathy for the young woman was strong.

"Did she suggest a ghost killed him?" Tyler asked skeptically.

Harrison didn't look at him; he continued to look through the one-way glass at the young woman. "No. Ms. Leigh—technically Dr. Leigh—is a professor, historian and scholar. She teaches history at the university, except that she's off for the summer. She also writes papers. Even when she's teaching, she gives tours at the house, but the point is—she does not believe in ghosts." He spoke with a grimace. Her feelings on that might change in the near future.

"I'd like to see her, get her out of here and then read up on everything that's happened in the house," Tyler said. "They aren't charging her, are they?"

"No, but they made the right call in asking her to come down here," Adam told him. "I'll bring you over and introduce you."

"You know her? Or you just met her?"

Harrison smiled. "I've made it my business for many years to meet and greet politicians and those in law enforcement and, thankfully, many remain grateful for help they've received. I was here when the house hosted a dinner for up-and-coming men and women in the city, sponsored by municipal leaders. Ms. Leigh was very charming and of great assistance in arranging the evening. I think you'll find that she can tell you more than you'll read in most history books. So, we're not best friends, but yes, I know her."

The door to the observation room opened just then, and a middle-aged man with fine, intelligent eyes and a bloodhound's weary jowls walked in. Tyler had already met him; he was Detective Jenson, assigned to the "suspicious" death.

"All the paperwork for the evening is complete. Ms. Leigh may leave whenever you're ready. Agent Montague, you wanted to go to the house tonight?" Jenson asked.

Tyler nodded. "I'd like to get in while the evidence is still fresh."

Whatever Jenson thought of the "special" FBI unit that had been brought in, he didn't let his feelings show. "The crime scene people have just finished up," he said. "They've been in there for about six hours collecting everything they can, but, of course, the house is a tourist location so they have hundreds if not thousands of prints. I'll get you Ms. Leigh's key to the house and the code to bypass the security system," he told Tyler. "And, needless to say, we'd appreciate it if you shared any findings with us immediately."

"I can't find anything without the help of the police," Tyler said, "so, yes, of course."

Judging by his quick smile, Jenson seemed to like that. "You're free to speak with Ms. Leigh." He glanced at Adam. "And get her home."

Adam thanked him. They left the observation area and entered the interrogation room.

Allison Leigh sat up stiffly, regarding Tyler with

narrowed eyes that gentled as she looked at Adam Harrison.

The man just had a way about him.

"Allison, I'd like you to meet Agent Tyler Montague. He's here to investigate the situation—and the Tarleton-Dandridge House," Adam said.

Allison Leigh gave Tyler a long cool assessment. "The *house?*" she asked skeptically. "The *house* caused Julian to slit his throat on his bayonet?"

"There've been a number of incidents at the house, Ms. Leigh," Tyler said.

Allison turned to Adam. "He believes he can arrest the ghost of a Revolutionary soldier?"

Tyler answered. "No, Ms. Leigh. But the number of strange occurrences at the house, especially in recent years, suggest that someone who's alive and well is playing deadly pranks. Actually, we're here to see you home if you'd like."

She frowned, and Tyler thought her hostility toward him had relaxed somewhat. "You're not going to ask me to go through everything that happened again?"

He shook his head. "I'd rather you went through the house with me. If you're up to it, that is. Otherwise, we'll take you home, as I said."

She stared at him, then blinked. He could see her mind working, and it was fascinating to watch the emotions that flashed through her beautiful if red-rimmed eyes. She'd been up for hours; she'd just lost a colleague, possibly a friend. She'd been in the interrogation room forever. She wanted a drink or simply to collapse for a while and forget the horror she'd witnessed.

But he also knew that she understood why he needed to see the house now, as quickly after the event as possible. She didn't *want* to go back and see where her friend had died, but she understood that anything that might be discovered would be most easily found before too much time had elapsed.

She lifted her hands. "Of course," she said with a nod. "Are you coming?" she asked Adam, her voice hopeful.

"If you wish, my dear."

"Please."

Tyler admired the effect Adam had on others. He knew that Harrison had once had a son, Josh, and that Josh had been killed in an accident at a young age. Josh had apparently been born with a sixth sense, and when he'd died, Adam had spent years trying to reach him. Tyler had recently heard that the father could finally talk to the son, although Adam didn't usually have the ability to communicate with the dead.

What he did have was an uncanny ability to connect with the living.

Tyler definitely wished he had a little more of that ability himself. He wasn't sure why he seemed to lack it. Maybe it was his height, which people often considered intimidating, since he stood at about six-five. From the time he was a kid, he'd wanted nothing but to be a Texas Ranger and now, although he loved the change in what he was doing, he wondered if he carried some kind of aura from the years he'd spent working in tough areas of Texas. He didn't know if it was his appearance or his no-nonsense demeanor, but people seemed to find him imposing, and it always took him a while to convince them that he *wasn't* a swaggering, gun-toting cowboy.

"Well, then, let's get going," Adam said. "I know

you must be emotionally drained, my dear, but we'll get you home soon."

"That's it? I can just walk out?"

"That's it."

She stood, a bit clumsily. Tyler saw that she was a respectable height for a woman, maybe five-eight or nine, and that she wore the historic dress exceptionally well. She seemed fragile for a second, as if she'd been sitting too long and couldn't quite find her feet. She didn't shake him off when he touched her, but she said regally, "Thank you. I'm fine."

He released her elbow and they exited the station. Detective Jenson was waiting for them at the precinct door. "Thank you, Ms. Leigh. Thank you for your patience with us. And please accept my deepest sympathies."

She nodded. "If I can do anything, provide any more information..." She paused. They'd already kept her long enough to glean anything she was likely to know.

Tyler's SUV was just outside the station and he nodded toward it. "We'll get you home as quickly as we can," he promised.

Adam politely ushered Allison into the passenger seat and took the rear himself, insisting that even at his age, he'd show courtesy to a lady until he keeled over.

Although he was silent during the drive, Allison began to speak. "It seemed like such an ordinary day," she murmured.

"There were a lot of tours?" Tyler asked her.

"Yes, it was busy, which is good. We work hard to make the tours interesting and informative, and to keep the house sustaining itself."

Tyler asked a few questions about historical tours

as he drove, trying to put her at ease. They reached the house, parking in the adjacent lot.

Maybe it was fitting that there'd be a full moon that night. The house seemed large and alive in the light, encased by the shadows surrounding it.

By day, he thought, it was probably a handsome Colonial house, built to withstand the ages. But now...

Now it seemed as if it were waiting.

There were warnings posted by the police. No Trespassing! Invasion of the Premises in Any Manner Will Result in Immediate Arrest!

The warnings covered the sign beyond the podium that usually advertised the property's hours of admission and the prices of tours.

"There's—there's tape all over the house." Allison spoke blankly, obviously too tired to be shocked.

"Yes, your chairman has ordered the house closed for a few weeks, long enough for a real investigation," Adam said.

Tyler slipped a knife from his jacket pocket to cut through the tape. He keyed in the code on the gate alarm.

"A real investigation?" Allison repeated.

"Yes," Tyler said. "We're trying to find out if the security's been breached and determine whether there's another access. Also, if there's someone who knows the code and has dangerous concepts of history, dangerous beliefs about this house. That's why it merits investigation."

Allison's eyes narrowed again as she studied him. "You're a ghost hunter."

"I'm not a ghost hunter—I'm an agent," Tyler said. "*Hunting* ghosts would be a rather useless effort." He forced a smile. "They only appear when they choose to. Inviting conversation—now, that's another thing."

Leaving her to Adam, he strolled up the walkway. He wanted to spend some time in the house alone.

At the front door he once again slit the tape before typing in the alarm code and using the key he'd received from Detective Jenson to let himself in. When he entered the foyer, it felt as if he'd stepped back in time.

Tyler stood there for a minute. You didn't need to be a Krewe member to "feel" a house, a battlefield or any other historic place. He'd seen the most skeptical, steel-souled Texas Ranger take on a look of grim reverence when standing at the Alamo. It was a feeling that touched most people on the battlefields at Gettysburg or in the middle of Westminster Abbey, Notre Dame or other such historic places.

This house had it. That feeling. It was a sense of the past, a past that was somehow still present. Perhaps the energy, passion and emotion of life that had once existed here lingered in these rooms.

This was a beautiful house and maintained in a period manner that no doubt added to the *feel*.

Tyler didn't stay in the entry long. He could hear Adam and Allison following behind him, Adam explaining that what they investigated was history rather than ghosts.

He knew that Julian Mitchell's death had occurred in the old study, and he strode down the hallway toward it. He stared at the old maple desk; blood stained the wood and the Persian rug beneath it where the deceased man had been found. A few spatters lay on the reproduction ledgers and account books covering the desk. Initial contact with the blade had caused a spurt, and the blood had drained straight down. A lot of it.

Tyler tried to picture the scene as it had been described to him—the young man seated in the chair, the musket between his legs, the bayonet through his throat and mouth as if he'd used it to prop himself up. He had bled out quickly, according to the pathologist who'd first examined him. He hadn't appeared distressed and he didn't appear to have fought with anyone. He had simply sat down, set his chin upon the bayonet as though to rest on it...and skewered himself with it.

Who the hell *accidentally* put a bayonet blade through his own chin?

But he hadn't cried out. Tourists leaving the premises would have heard or, at the very least, Allison Leigh would have as she locked up for the night.

Tyler remained near the entrance to the room, noting its location. There was the door that opened off the entry hall, and another that led from the study to the next room. This meant there were two points of access, as well as a way to exit.

But how did you get someone to die on a bayonet in such a position and leave no sign of a struggle? *Talk him into it?*

He looked at the paintings on the wall, which were authentic period pieces. Two men had been depicted at somewhere between the ages of thirty and forty. Beneath one, he made out the name Angus Tarleton; the other was labeled with the description Brian "Beast" Bradley.

The eyes of the latter seemed to have an unusual power. The artist had managed to depict a handsome man—and also a cruel and cunning one. He'd read that the Mona Lisa's eyes seemed to follow her viewers. Bradley's did the same, apparently focusing on him as he moved about the room.

He turned to the hallway. Allison Leigh was pale as she stood next to Adam, who watched and waited for Tyler to take the lead.

"Allison, can you tell me exactly what happened leading up to your discovery of Julian?" he asked her.

She winced. "I should've written it down earlier, I've had to repeat it so many times," she muttered. She was hostile again, he thought. Hostile and angry, but that was good. If she'd fallen apart, broken into tears, she wouldn't have been much help.

"I didn't run into a bloodthirsty ghost," she told him.

"I would've been surprised if you had," Tyler said. "I'm sorry, but you do want to catch the killer, right?"

She stared back at him with eyes that were as clear and beautiful as a summer sky.

"I don't think there was a killer," she said. "Julian could be a clown. He was full of himself, an entertainer. He had a tendency to piss the rest of us off with his unwillingness to accept responsibility, but he also made us laugh and…he was a friend." She took a deep breath. "It looked as if he sat down, started fooling around with the musket and set his head right on the blade. Yes, we use real muskets and bayonets, and never, ever, have we had a problem. The costumed interpreters don't carry bullets or gunpowder and no one's ever gone crazy and tried to bayonet a tourist. Who'd imagine that anyone could die on one?"

"He wasn't in any way suicidal?" Tyler asked.

"Julian? He was convinced the world was waiting for him," she said. "No, I don't believe he committed suicide." She hesitated for a moment. "We were all angry with him, figuring he'd had some kind of great offer and decided just to disappear."

"He was supposed to be working—and he wasn't?"

"Yes. Well, he showed up for the morning tours. He took off after lunch, probably for an audition."

"But you found him in his period costume?"

She nodded. "He was with a bar band that had higher aspirations. They did a lot of auditioning and sometimes they had permits to play in the historic areas, so it wasn't uncommon for him to stay in his work clothing."

"But none of you saw him after lunch?"

She shook her head.

"Are there places in the house where he could've been and you *wouldn't* see him?" Tyler asked.

She glanced at him. "A closet?" There was a hint of sarcasm in her voice. "Or," she said, her tone serious, "the attic. We don't go up to the attic with any of the tour groups."

"May I see it now?"

"If you want."

"Shall we?" Adam suggested.

Allison seemed to go back into tour-guide mode as she led the way. She pointed out the ladies' parlor, the music room and, across the entry, the dining room and parlor. As they walked up the first flight of stairs she talked about the owners of the house and the bedrooms used by the family—and by the British invaders.

Tyler paused at Lucy Tarleton's bedroom; from the doorway he'd noticed another painting of Beast Bradley.

It was different from the one in the study. The light of cruelty wasn't apparent in the eyes. He'd been depicted in a more thoughtful mood, his eyes conveying wisdom and strength rather than cruelty.

"One more floor to the attic," Allison said. "If you'll—"

"I'm curious about this painting," he interrupted.

"It's Beast Bradley. I don't really know why the painting's in here. Bradley took over the master bedroom while he was in residence at the house."

"This is a nice painting of him."

"I'm sure he had friends."

"It's interesting that the foundation chose to keep the painting here, since he moved into the master bedroom," Tyler commented.

"The house was owned by the family until it was turned into a nonprofit institution," Allison said. "That's where the painting was. The board determined to keep everything as it was, getting rid of modern additions and buying a few authentic pieces to bring it back to the Revolutionary period. But in the 1930s, when the work was being done, the painting was in Lucy's bedroom and the board at the time decided to keep it there."

"Adding insult to injury for poor Lucy. The original family must be rolling in their graves," Tyler said. He tried to keep any irony from his voice.

A derisive sound escaped her. The expression might be a common one, but in her world, people did not roll in their graves.

Some old houses had stairs that were pulled down for access to the attic. Not the Tarleton-Dandridge House. At the end of the upper hallway he saw a staircase leading to the door; a sign on it read Staff Only! He assumed the door was usually locked, and he was right.

"The front door key opens the attic, as well," Allison explained.

He used the key and pushed the door open. It led to a few more stairs. He climbed them and found himself standing on the attic level of the house. It was dark up here, but the moonlight and streetlamps offered some relief from the black shadows as his eyes grew accustomed to the change.

Someone had been there. Someone had tossed the place, rummaging through the old boxes and trunks and the modern equipment that had sat on a desk. A computer lay on the floor, along with a printer. Letters and correspondence were everywhere and, scattered among them, posters for special events and other paraphernalia.

"My God!" Allison breathed.

Tyler turned to Adam. "We need to get the crime scene techs back here. I doubt we'll find fingerprints other than those that belong here, but you never know."

Adam nodded and pulled out his cell phone.

Allison continued to stare at the mess. She seemed almost punch-drunk, as if the day itself had just been way too long. He empathized with her, even if she considered him an oversize caricature of a slime-seeking ghost buster.

"They'll be here shortly," Adam said.

"Ohhhh." Moaning, Allison sank down to the floor, her period dress drifting in a bell around her.

It was natural that the death of Julian Mitchell drew headlines across the country.

He had died in a historic home—a "haunted" house, according to just about everyone—and whether or not people believed in ghosts, it was undeniably a house riddled with tragic history.

Allison saw the headline minutes after she woke the next morning. She still had a newspaper delivered each day. She loved flipping leisurely through real pages while she drank her coffee.

As she picked up the paper, she felt tears stinging

her eyes again. Julian had often been a jerk, but he'd still been a coworker and a friend. She blinked hard and realized how exhausted she was. She'd spent most of the night with the police. She was still horrified that they saw Julian's death as "suspicious" and knew that any suspicions of murder certainly included her. After all, she'd found him. She couldn't believe the number of hours she'd spent at the station and then at the house when the crime scene techs had arrived again.

She glanced over at the clock—it was already eleven, and she still felt exhausted. It was a good thing the house was closed down until it had been "investigated." She couldn't begin to offer a tour today, and she was glad she didn't have a crowded schedule in the coming semester, just a few lectures. She felt numb about history, even though it was the love of her life. Rich and giving and...

Taking. It had somehow taken Julian's life. She didn't understand how or why, but she sensed that the past had something to do with it. She'd claimed that his death *had* to be an accident. And yet...

Allison set the paper on the counter of her small house on Chestnut Street and walked over to the coffee machine, popping a pod in place and waiting the few seconds for it to brew.

The coffee tasted delicious. She figured she needed about a gallon of it. She'd been at the Tarleton-Dandridge until nearly 3:00 a.m., when one of the officers had driven her home.

She wished she could've slept the entire day, and then thought she should just be grateful she hadn't had horrible dreams, considering how Julian had looked....

A shower seemed in order, although she'd taken one

the night before. A psychiatrist would probably tell her she was trying to wash away what she'd seen but she didn't care. It might make her feel more human. Or at least more awake.

While the water streamed over her, she thought about Julian and let her tears flow. She thought about the many times they'd been ready to smack him for his lack of responsibility or for leaving one of them in the lurch. It didn't matter. He'd still been a friend. Worse, it was such a *ridiculous* way to die.

When she'd first found him, after the initial horror and disbelief, she wondered if he'd sat there to play a prank on her, maybe planning to apologize for disappearing. Maybe he'd tell her he'd gotten the gig of a lifetime because he'd taken off that afternoon.

It had never occurred to her that anyone had *killed* him. His death had looked like a tragic, stupid accident. And that was terrible enough, but...

Why would anyone kill Julian Mitchell, and why would that person go up to the attic and trash everything there?

And how had it happened with her and Jason in the house, not to mention the thirty or so people in their tour groups?

She'd barely dressed and her hair was still dripping when her doorbell rang. She cringed, not wanting to see anyone, but curiosity got the better of her and she walked to the door to look through the peephole.

It was the Texas ghost buster.

She watched him as she ignored the buzzer. He rang again.

He didn't go away.

She considered it bizarre that the police had called in

the FBI—and that they'd called in *this* unit. Allison had to admit she didn't know that much about the FBI or the "Krewe of Hunters," but she'd checked the internet when she first met Adam Harrison and read that they were a special unit sent in when circumstances were *unusual*. Unusual meant that something paranormal might be going on, or seemed to be going on, and it appalled Allison that a historic property like the Tarleton-Dandridge House could be turned into a supernatural oddity. Of course, the ghost tours in the city loved the house and the tales that went with it, but those tours were for fun. And that kind of fun was great as long as it didn't detract from the *real* wonders of Philadelphia.

All the information she could find about Adam—or his Krewes—seemed to have plenty of read-between-the-lines suggestions that there was something out of the ordinary about them. From what she could gather, the Krewes were well acquainted with the paranormal and made use of strange communications in solving crimes. No way could she buy into that!

Peering out at Tyler Montague seemed to make it all the more ludicrous. He looked as if he should be in a barbarian movie; he was tall as a house and built with pure, lean muscle. How could such a man believe in ghosts?

He had waited a respectable amount of time. He rang the bell again.

With a sigh, Allison threw the door open. "What?" she demanded.

"I need your help."

She turned and walked back through her house toward the counter that divided the kitchen from the living area. "With what? Do you need a cup of coffee?

That I have. Do you want to know about the Tarleton ghosts? Can't help you there. I've never seen them. Oh, and I suppose I should mention this—I don't believe they exist. We have a shot at life, then we die. Period. I believe in God as an entity seen by different people in different ways, but I don't think He has an open-door policy in heaven, saying, Hey, come and go as you please. But coffee? I've got that."

"I could use a cup," he said mildly, following her inside and closing the door. He walked to the counter as she placed another pod in her coffeemaker. She turned to look at him, hoping—to her surprise—that her house was clean and neat. She had the feeling that, ghost hunter or no, he was observant and perhaps judging her character through her living space.

"Things might be a bit messy," she said, sweeping out an arm that indicated the sections of newspaper strewn on the table and her shoes and cape thrown on a chair. "Sorry. Long night."

"Looks pretty good to me," he commented.

"What do you like in your coffee? Oh, and what are you doing here?"

"I told you. I need your help."

"That doesn't answer my question about the coffee. What do you want in it?"

"Just black, thanks."

"Of course. A fed from Texas. Black coffee." She handed him the cup, asking, "What do you need from me?"

"Information about the people you work with."

"Everyone fills out an extensive form in order to work at the house, and then has to pass an oral exam. Guides have to know what they're doing. Believe it or not, the place gets a lot of applications. When the board hires, they want people who not only have a good grasp of history, but really love it. So they ask personal questions, as well."

"I'm aware of all that. What I want to hear is more about what *you've* seen. What you, personally, have observed."

She paused, eyes narrowing. "You think one of my coworkers had something to do with this?"

"I don't think Julian Mitchell went crazy, trashed his workplace, then sat down and killed himself on a bayonet—no."

Allison shook her head. "I've been through it and through it, with you and with the cops. I don't know what else I could possibly tell you."

"Start with your day," he told her. "Tell me about it again."

She sighed. "It was pretty much like any other day," she said.

He took a sip of his coffee, smiling. "I was looking for a little more detail than that. Were any of the tours unusual? Did anything stand out to you?"

"Yes, I found the body of a friend in the study," she said curtly.

Before he could respond, his cell phone rang. He excused himself and answered it, frowning as he listened.

Allison felt a chill; she knew it had something to do with whatever was being said.

A moment later he hung up. "You took a family with two boys, Todd and Jimmy, on your last tour."

She nodded. "Yes, why?"

"Their father's in the hospital. He woke up in the middle of the night, screamed and fell into a coma. One of the kids was so hysterical when they reached the hospital that someone on staff called the police."

"*What?* Why? That's terrible, but—"

"The boy, Todd, wants to talk to you. He said that you'd understand. According to Todd, a ghost did follow them home."

3

The hospital was cold. Outside, the late-summer heat was beginning to wane and the day was still beautiful, but inside the hospital, Allison shivered against the chill that seeped into her bones.

She didn't want to be there; she wanted to run away. But Todd wanted to see her because for some reason he believed she could help.

And she *wanted* to help.

The two boys were seated in an otherwise empty waiting area. Todd's mother was in with his father, and an attractive woman of about forty was sitting with the boys. Seeing Allison, Todd leaped to his feet and came running over to her. She was startled when he threw his arms around her but she comforted the boy, embracing him and stroking his hair.

"He followed us home! He followed us home. That awful man followed us home. The beast—Beast Bradley. He killed your friend and he made my father sick!" Todd said, his words muffled.

Allison looked helplessly at the woman in the room and then at Tyler Montague.

"Todd," she said gently. "Ghosts can't do that. Really. They're just...inventions, something we make up in our own minds. Your father—" She paused, praying this wasn't a lie. "Your father's going to be fine. You're in an exceptionally good hospital and the doctors will find out what's wrong with him."

The woman who was with the boys had risen and come toward her, a hand extended. "You must be Allison Leigh. I'm Rose Litton, Todd and Jimmy's aunt. I'm sorry you've been asked down here. I know you're dealing with your own loss. But Todd was nearly hysterical and insisted that he see you."

"It's all right. It's quite all right," Allison assured her. But it wasn't. She didn't know how to make this better for Todd.

She could only be glad that—as far as she knew— the ransacking of the attic's office space had not been divulged to the media.

"What do the doctors say?" Tyler was asking.

"So far they can't identify the physiological cause," Rose Litton said. "Not yet, at any rate, but they're doing a lot of tests. Early this morning, while he was still in bed at the hotel, Artie jerked up, screamed—and fell into a coma. It was as if he saw something in his sleep...or in his dreams. They believe he might have ingested some kind of hallucinogenic, which made him see something that terrified him, although they can't tell what it is or how this might have happened. They just don't know."

Allison touched Todd's chin to get him to look up at her. "The doctors here are the best. They'll find out what's wrong with your father," she promised again.

"Who are you?" Rose Litton asked, frowning at Tyler. "Forgive me—that's rude. I just knew the nurse had called the police station, asking about a way for Todd to see Ms. Leigh."

"Not rude at all," Tyler said, reaching into his jacket and producing his credentials.

"Special Agent?" Rose Litton read, her voice worried.

"I'm here to discover what went on at the house," he told her. "Please, don't be alarmed. We don't suspect any kind of true toxin. Allison would be ill, too, if there had been, and so could a hundred-plus other people who were in the house yesterday. I'm not a doctor, but I do know there are many reasons for a coma, and the doctors here *will* get to the root of it." He hunkered down. "Did you see what happened? Perhaps, earlier, your father knocked his head? Was he agitated, stressed out about anything?"

Todd shook his head. Jimmy stood and came over to join them. "No, my dad doesn't get stressed," Jimmy said. "He's a good guy. He yells sometimes, but not much. We had fun after we left the house. We went to a tavern for supper and Dad was okay when we went to bed."

Todd nodded vigorously. "Yeah, he was fine. He let us watch TV for a while in the hotel. Then we fell asleep and woke up because Dad screamed. He just screamed in the middle of the night. We were scared 'cause Dad never screams and suddenly he did." He looked proud for a minute. "My dad is really brave. It had to be something awful, a monster like Beast Bradley, to make my dad scream like that."

"Thank you," Tyler said gravely. He stood again. "You know, sometimes we have monsters in our minds, in our imaginations. I'll go speak with one of the docs," he said. "In the meantime, you shouldn't worry." He smiled at Rose and set his hand on Todd's head. "Excuse me. I'll be back."

He left them, and Allison felt more awkward than ever.

She tried to smile at Rose. "It's great that you could be here."

"I'm only over in Hershey," Rose said. "Not far at all. And I'm glad to be with the boys." Her expression was pained, her eyes on Allison. Her silence seemed to say a lot.

I don't know what's the matter with Todd. He's convinced it's something from the Tarleton-Dandridge House. I hope you can reassure him....

The realization that this might have been a bad time to bother Allison seemed to come back to her.

"I really am so sorry!" Rose said. "You lost someone last night. Tragically. It's...it's all over the news. And they're making it sound—" she glanced at the boys "—like a...well, paranormal event."

Allison nodded. "Of course. People love ghost stories."

"There *is* a ghost," Todd insisted.

Jimmy gasped. "We saw that a tour guide died at the house. It was on the TV news when we got back. My parents were worried. They hoped it wasn't you!" he told Allison. "Dad turned the news off. He says we'll get to know enough about the real world when we're older." He frowned. "I'm sorry. I mean, I'm glad it wasn't you, but I'm sorry about your friend."

Todd took her hand and squeezed it. They *were* sorry, but Julian was an abstraction to them, a news story, while their father was lying here in a no-man's-land. "Yeah, we're really sorry," he said.

"Thank you. I'm the one who found him, and it was heartbreaking for me. I'm going to miss him very much. But, Todd, like I was telling you, bad things just happen sometimes, even to good people. Listen, you have to trust the doctors here, and you can't get upset about the house or believe you have a ghost with you. Okay?"

He looked at her stubbornly. "The ghost likes you.

You can talk to him. You can get him to leave my dad alone."

As Allison struggled for speech, Rose Litton shrugged apologetically.

"All of us, every one of us, will do whatever we can for your dad, okay, Todd?" Allison finally said.

Todd whispered a solemn "Thank you."

A moment later, Tyler returned. He offered Todd an encouraging smile. "They'll keep at it, young man. Meanwhile, you stay calm and help your mom and little brother."

Todd nodded. He studied Tyler, and then apparently decided to trust him.

"I will. I'm going to help my mom and my family," Todd said. "Please, help *her,* though," he said, glancing over at Allison. "The ghost likes her."

Rose moved closer to Allison. "I am so sorry," she said again. "He was just crying and going crazy, and the idea that you might talk to him was the only thing that worked."

"We'll do everything we can from our end, Todd," Tyler said.

Allison noticed that the boy seemed to respond to him. He nodded. "I can reach you if I need to, right?"

"We'll be here," Tyler promised firmly. "I'll even give you my personal cell number. You can call me anytime."

Todd gestured at Allison. "She doesn't understand," he said. "But she can help us, and you can help her. Please?"

"I'll do whatever I can, buddy."

He wrote down his cell number and handed it to the boy, then took Allison's arm to lead her from the hospital. She steeled herself not to wrench her arm out of his grasp.

When they exited, she moved away from him. "That was wrong," she told him.

"What was?"

"You made that poor boy think we could help him by convincing a ghost to leave his dad alone!"

"I didn't say that."

"But you believe they exist!"

They'd reached his car. He leaned against the roof, looking over at her as she waited by the passenger door.

"I went in and spoke with Mr. Dixon's doctors. There is absolutely nothing physiological causing his problem—nothing they can discover. Of course, they're still testing. And he may come out of it himself. One of the theories his primary physician has is that he put himself in the coma to avoid some horrible fact or illusion he'd seen in his own mind. Whether you want to believe I'm a quack or not, you have to admit that the power of the human mind can be incredible. Maybe if we look into this and find something to say to the kid, the family or even Mr. Dixon himself, we can reverse the situation."

"If *we* can find something?"

"You know the history and the house better than anyone else."

Allison lowered her eyes, remembering the way she'd felt when Todd was in the house yesterday, so convinced that something evil was still alive there.

She looked back at Tyler. "I'm an academic. I believe in the power of men and women to do good or evil. I don't believe in spirits."

"But you believe in history?"

"Of course. You can't *not* believe in history," she said.

"Ah, but what about the famous saying: History is written by the victors. And sometimes the victors might exaggerate or lie or leave things out. Sometimes history has to be rewritten. It isn't an unchanging, monolithic entity. Attitudes change, and they change history. So do new facts as they emerge."

Allison sighed, wondering how the granite Texan could be so ethereal in his statements.

"History didn't kill Julian Mitchell," she said. "Or put Mr. Dixon in a coma."

"Belief is everything," he countered. "And, Allison, I do believe it's obvious that *something* is going on. Even if by some remarkable chance Julian accidentally killed himself or just decided, Hmm, let me think of a really gruesome way to kill myself, it still wouldn't explain what happened in the attic."

"Maybe Julian trashed the attic."

"Why would he have done that?"

"I don't know! Why would he have sat down with his rifle—and then leaned his head down on the blade?" she asked wearily.

"Those are things we have to know. Other people could die," Tyler said.

"You mean Mr. Dixon. He wasn't at the house when he went into a coma."

"No. But he'd *been* at the house, and you found a friend dead there a matter of hours earlier. Dixon saw the news about Julian's death before going to sleep."

"So, he dreamed a ghost had followed him home and it was so real and frightening to his sleeping mind that he slipped into another realm," Allison said. "I don't know the answers to any of it. I just know that it's real and horrible and I'm so tired I can't think. Will you take me home, please?" she asked. "I'd just like to be alone."

He looked over the top of the car at her and Allison saw that his gaze was filled with disappointment. Of course. He wasn't going to get what he wanted. But it was more than that; it was disappointment in *her,* and somehow that was disturbing.

"Certainly. I'll take you right home."

Allison had no idea why his reaction bothered her. It just did.

"I really need some time!" she said, almost pleading. "Julian is dead. Not in a coma. There's no coming back from that."

"I completely understand. Really."

She slid into the passenger seat. He was silent as they drove and she watched him, feeling a clash of emotions. Life had become so painful and intense overnight. It was still hard to fathom that Julian was dead. She was still tired from last night. She'd discovered the body of her friend. Then she'd dealt—for the first time in her life—with the police, and with crime scene techs trying to find out what she'd touched and what she hadn't. Later Adam Harrison and this man had shown up... And today she'd spent time with a heartbroken child. She was mentally and physically exhausted, and dismayed because she was disappointing a *stranger.* And now, she was staring at that stranger, wondering how someone with such a strong jawline and intense eyes, such a tall, powerful build and compelling presence, could be part of a team of *ghost busters.*

Yesterday she'd been herself—a teacher who loved history and brought that love to costumed interpretation. She loved her life, and she had good friends, a great family. And this morning...

She looked straight ahead. She wasn't being selfish. She needed to go home. To speak with her coworkers and friends from the board and— Good Lord! She had to call her parents and let them know she was all right.

He drove to her house and stopped the car. Turning to her, he said quietly, "I'm very sorry about your friend, and truly sorry that you were the one to find him."

She nodded. "I just need some time," she said again.

"Call me when you feel you want to get back into it."

"Of course."

He was watching her so intently she wondered if she had food on her face.

"You'll need my number," he reminded her.

"Oh. Yes." She gave a deep sigh. "I do want to help the kids. I do want to help you, even though it did look like a horrible accident." Allison took out her cell phone as she spoke.

"The trashing of the attic wasn't an accident." He removed his phone from his pocket. "I'll dial you," he said.

He already had her number. Of course. He was an FBI agent.

She clicked on the call and added his number to her phone. Then she realized she'd asked to be taken home and they'd arrived, but she was still sitting in his car.

"I'm not sure what I can do for you," she told him. "You're here, Mr. Harrison is here, the police have been through it all. I don't know what I could contribute."

"I doubt that anyone is as familiar with the house or its history as you are." She caught herself studying the color of his eyes. They were a mixture of blue and green, a kind of aqua she'd never seen before. He was a very striking man.

She blinked, suddenly aware that she was staring and that she needed to reply.

"There *have* been some tragic and terrible incidents at the house, but I don't think something that happened years ago could have any bearing on what happened yesterday."

He shrugged, smiling wryly. "That's what we'll find out." He exited the car and walked around to open her door.

She remembered that she was supposed to get out. "Thanks," she mumbled.

"Are you sure you'll be right alone?"

"Yes, thanks. We'll, um, be in touch."

"Thank you," he said with a nod.

Awkwardly, she started up her front walk. She knew he was watching her, and when she fit her key into the door, she turned around to wave. He waved back, then got into his car and eased out onto the street.

Inside the house, she closed the door and leaned against it for a moment. She'd wanted to be alone.

Now she didn't.

But she walked in and dug out her phone before tossing her purse on the sofa and sitting down next to it. She had to start returning calls.

But even as she decided that she had to call her mother first and then the board and her coworkers, the silence in the house seemed to weigh down on her. She got up and turned on the television. A news station was playing, with a reporter standing in front of the hospital. Mr. Dixon's strange fall into a coma was being added to the tragic news about musician and tour guide Julian Mitchell.

She changed the channel. The speculation on the "evil" within the house on *news* stations struck her as overkill.

With a comedy repeat keeping her company, she

looked at all the calls she'd ignored while she was with Tyler Montague. She called her parents, who'd gone to their home in Arizona for a few weeks, and made a point of being calm and sad and completely in control. As much as she adored her mom and dad, she didn't want them coming back here because they were worried about her.

They'd met Julian a few times and offered their condolences, but when they questioned her safety, she made it sound as if the media were going wild—which they were—and described what had happened as a tragic accident. She assured her mother that as a Revolution-era woman or even as Lucy Tarleton, she didn't carry a musket with a bayonet.

Next she spoke to Nathan Pierson. She told him she was fine, and he promised he'd be there for anything she needed with the police or the house. He'd talk to the rest of the board, too. She didn't have to call anyone else, he said; she should just relax.

Nathan was the easiest member of board to deal with. He was a good-looking man who had never married. She wasn't close enough to ask him if there was a long-lost love for whom he pined, but if so, it didn't seem to affect his dating life. At various functions, she'd seen him with different women, all of them beautiful and elegant. He was unfailingly polite and courteous to her. Sometimes he teased her, claiming that he was waiting for her to notice him and ignore the age discrepancy; he teased a lot of people, though, and he had a way of making his words sound like a compliment rather than licentious.

He was the solid rock of the board, in Allison's opinion. Ethan Oxford was like a distant grandfather, Sarah was like the family old-maid aunt—even though she'd

been married. She was high-strung. And Cherry was...
Cherry. She always considered herself a cut above the
rest of the world.

Allison was grateful that Nathan was going to speak
with the other board members, but she did have to call
Jason Lawrence and Annette Fanning.

Jason still seemed stunned by the whole thing. She
told him about the attic but said they were keeping that
information from the media.

He, too, wanted to make sure she was okay.

After that she called Annette.

Annette was smart and fun and usually logical, so
Allison was shocked by the tremor in her friend's voice
and the view she seemed to be taking of the situation.

"It's not surprising, is it? Oh, Allison, I thank God
for that root canal, and I never thought I'd say that.
I wonder what happened. Did Julian freak out? One
toke too many? But he's never been out of it at work.
That's just the heavy-metal image he likes to portray.
It's the house, Allison. It terrifies me! I can always feel
it when I'm there, like...like the house itself is breathing. I mean, when you're out on the street, the windows
seem like eyes, watching you. Maybe so much evil did
happen there and it continues, on and on. Like something malevolent that waits and—"

"Annette! No! The house is a pile of brick and wood
and stone. It's a *house*. Horrible things take place everywhere. We go through life grateful when they don't
happen to us, and either sad or broken when they do."

"Well, I for one am glad they're closing it down.
No, wait—do we get unemployment or anything? I'm
out of a job! I don't think they'll be able to pay us—
there won't be any money coming into the house without the tours."

"We're not out of work, Annette. They're closing it temporarily for an investigation. I'm sure they'll provide us with some kind of compensation."

"The house needs an exorcism!"

"No, Annette, it doesn't. The house isn't possessed. Or evil. And if the house could feel anything, it would be grateful to us for keeping it alive. Annette—"

"Ohhhhh," Annette broke in. "You have another job. I don't. In fact, you have a cool job, a real job. You're a professor."

"Annette, you *do* have a real job. The house will open again. It'll just be closed for a few weeks. They'll shore up the alarm system, and we'll be bombarded when we reopen because people are ghoulish and they'll want to stare at the place where Julian died. Besides, you work at the tavern as a singing waitress sometimes."

"Yeah, thank God! I was there last night. I went for a drink after my root canal and to hang with some of my friends. I can ask for a few more nights."

"The house won't be closed that long."

"Are you alone? Oh! You're not still at the police station, are you?"

"No."

"I saw some government guy on the news—not an interview, just a shot of him talking to the police. The U.S. government is in on this, Allison. It's scary, scary. But, hey, have you met him? My God, he's gorgeous! Whoops, excuse me, Barrie heard that. Barrie, he's not as gorgeous as you, just, um, pretty gorgeous!"

"Annette, pay attention. Those guys are here because of Adam Harrison. You know, the nice elderly gentleman who's been to a few functions at the house."

"I remember him. Maybe there *is* going to be an exorcism! I heard that his people look into strange stuff. Like paranormal events."

"Annette, if Barrie's there and has the day off, please go and spend some time with him."

"What kind of friend do you think I am? I'll be right there—"

"No, no, please! I'm fine by myself. I'm going to try to get some rest. Okay?"

Annette was silent. "I'm not sure you should be alone."

"Annette, I'm fine. I promise. I'm going to curl up on the couch and try to doze off."

"Call if you need me, Ally. I can be there in five minutes."

"I will," Allison said. "Thanks."

She was able to hang up at last. Setting the phone down, she rose and headed into the kitchen to make a cup of tea. She really hoped she *could* doze off for a while, and hot tea and an inane comedy on TV should help her quell some of the thoughts and images racing through her mind.

She loved her new pod machine; a cup of English Breakfast tea brewed as swiftly as a cup of coffee. Mug in hand, she left the kitchen and came around the counter—and froze.

She wasn't alone in the house. There was someone sitting in the chair by the sofa.

A dark-haired young man in Colonial dress.

It was Julian Mitchell.

She blinked.

He was still there.

The cup fell from her hand. She heard it shatter on the tile floor.

Then she followed it down. She was vaguely aware that a few body parts hurt but not for long.

Mercifully, the world went black as she passed out cold.

4

Tyler stood in the attic of the Tarleton-Dandridge House looking at the disarray.

Someone had been searching—for what?

He wanted to straighten up the room; it was far easier to figure out what was missing when everything else was in the right place. He'd need to involve others with that, which he didn't want to do quite yet. He'd had offers from the board to come in and help, but he'd turned them down. He'd actually lied to Nathan Pierson, telling him he preferred to wait until he was sure the police were finished with their forensics before bringing anyone else in.

The police *were* finished. And after speaking with Detective Jenson, he knew they weren't expecting to find anything useful, unless by some unlikely chance they were to lift foreign prints—those not associated with the four guides or the board members, whose prints they'd already taken. If they were *really* lucky, they'd come up with prints belonging to someone with a criminal record.

He wanted to work with Allison Leigh for the obvious reasons. She was the one who'd found the body and who knew this house backward and forward, along with the history. He'd gone through the biographies and résumés of the employees and the board, and there was no one better qualified to help him than Allison. She was in denial right now; he assumed that would change.

So far, although he had a sense of being watched in the house, Tyler hadn't seen a single movement, felt a brush of cold air or even heard an old board creak.

The house was waiting—or those within it were. Waiting and watching.

He left the attic and walked back down to the second floor, taking a few minutes to go into every room. He'd been glad to hear from Nathan Pierson that there was no plan by the board to give up the house. It was on the national historic register, of course, so there was virtually no threat that it would be bulldozed. Meticulously restored, the Tarleton-Dandridge House was one of the finest examples of early Americana he'd ever seen. It would be a shame if it was closed to the public to become the offices of an accounting agency or a bank.

Tyler paused at Lucy Tarleton's room. He walked inside to look at the painting of Beast Bradley.

Here, as Tyler had observed before, he was portrayed as a thoughtful man. He appeared to be strong, but almost saddened by the weight of responsibility. He'd been a man with well-arranged features, handsome in youth.

Interesting.

Next he studied the painting of a young and innocent Lucy Tarleton, a woman as yet untouched by death and bloodshed. He noted that there was something about Lucy's eyes that made him think of Allison. There was definitely a resemblance, although it was true that many young women, dressed as Lucy, might look like the long-gone heroine.

Tyler stood very still, allowing himself to *feel* the house.

Again he experienced the sensation of being watched, but there were no sounds from the old place, nor did he see anything or notice any drafts.

He headed down to the study where he'd left his briefcase with his computer and the records Adam had arranged for him to receive.

They recorded many instances of normal life and death—many births had taken place in the house, although sadly two of the mothers had died in childbirth. A number of people had died in their beds of natural causes, one Dandridge at the grand old age of a hundred and five.

During the War of 1812, Sophia Tarleton-Dandridge and her husband had owned the house; they'd taken in a wounded soldier and he had passed away. He was buried with the family in the graveyard behind the stables. A family friend had come to the house after the Battle of Gettysburg. He was also buried in the family graveyard.

Sad and tragic deaths due to warfare, Tyler thought. Not unexpected and not the kind of thing that would produce anything terrible.

But then, Beast Bradley had been the terror that touched the house....

Looking further into the family history, Tyler saw that another death had been that of a young Dandridge girl in 1863. He wondered if she'd been in love with the Civil War soldier who'd died. She'd taken rat poison and killed herself soon after his death.

He shuddered. Hard way to die, rat poison.

And another hard way to die—a bayonet through the chin. He tried to imagine how it had happened. Julian had sat down, his musket held between his legs. He'd leaned forward and set the soft flesh behind his jawbone on the blade of the bayonet. Then he'd lowered his head with enough force for the blade to go through that soft flesh and his throat? It seemed almost impossible.

Unless he'd been helped.

Fascinating though the historical events were, Tyler was more interested in Julian's death and the deaths of people who had died closer to the present. There'd been several of those, starting in the late 1970s.

One of the docents, Bill Hall, had been found at the foot of the staircase. While closing up at night, he'd apparently tripped and fallen down the stairs, landing at an angle that had snapped his neck.

Eight years ago, a college student, Sam Daily, had told friends he was going to break into a historic house and rearrange a few items as a joke. It hadn't gone so well; he'd tried to dismantle the alarm and a wire had shorted out, sending electric volts shooting through him. He'd been discovered on the ground near the back door the following morning.

Tragically the joke had been on him.

Just three years ago, another of the older docents or tour guides, Angela Wilson, had been found dead in Tarleton's study. She'd been sitting in the same chair, in the same position, as Julian Mitchell. She had died of a massive heart attack.

One death from a fall, one from electrocution and one from what might well be a perfectly natural cause for someone of Angela's age, a heart attack.

And now a man dead of a bayonet shoved through his throat—as if he'd set his own chin atop it for the blade to run through.

Tyler drummed his fingers on the desk.

He was here because of Adam Harrison. Adam had a love of and connection to various historic properties. Technically, the Krewes were Adam's teams, so they went where Adam Harrison requested they go. Everything that had happened here *could* have been natural or accidental.

But Adam had a knack of knowing when things weren't right.

Add in the trashing of the small office in the attic....

Someone had been looking for something. What? And why?

And how did any of it relate to the fact that Artie Dixon was in a coma?

Tyler pulled out his cell phone and called Logan Raintree, one of his best friends, a fellow Ranger at one time, and now the head of their unit.

"Is it something—or nothing?" Logan asked. "Do you need the rest of the Krewe?"

"Something," Tyler said. "And yes. I'd like you to come here."

"Any idea as to what's going on?"

"Nope. But the house has been closed down for the interim. I think we should set up here."

"We'll be in tomorrow night," Logan promised him.

Tyler hung up and put through another call. When he reached Adam Harrison, he asked about keys to the attic.

"The board members all have a key, and so does Allison. There's also a key in the small pantry or storage room, where the employees have their lockers and keep their street clothing. It's always hung on a peg there."

"Is the pantry locked during the day?" Tyler asked.

"No, not from what I understand. The employees slip in and out when they have a break or need to get to their own belongings. No member of the public goes into the house without a docent or tour guide, and they've never had trouble before."

"I'll see if that key is still in place, but a lot of people have keys. They could have been used—or copied at a previous date."

"How are you doing?"

"I lost my guide," Tyler told him.

"I can call someone else."

Tyler hesitated. Maybe that was the right thing to do. Bring in someone who *hadn't* discovered a dead friend at the house. Someone who wasn't derisive of the investigation.

But he realized he didn't want anyone else.

And as far as her attitude was concerned... It didn't matter if you believed the world was round or not, because it was round regardless of what you believed.

Eventually, Allison would accept the fact that something existed in the Tarleton-Dandridge House.

And as Todd had suggested, *it liked her.*

"Thanks, Adam. I'll move along on my own for a bit, see if Ms. Leigh begins to show some interest. I'm sure her heart is in the right place. I'll give her more time. The rest of the team will be in tomorrow night, and we'll see where we are then."

Adam agreed with him and they hung up. Tyler immediately went to the guides' room; the key hung on a peg there, so access to the attic was ridiculously easy. He returned to the study, picking up the folders that held information on the board members. Pausing, he looked at the painting of Beast Bradley.

He'd been perceived so differently by the two artists.

He stood, fascinated by the painting, and walked over to it. A Plexiglas cover protected it and he saw that, apparently from the time it had been hung, it had resided on that wall to avoid direct sunlight.

He tried to read the signature of the artist and was surprised to realize that the name was T. Dandridge. He squinted to find the date; the painting had been done in 1781. The year the Colonies had finally achieved their independence.

He smiled. Yes, the artist of this particular likeness had truly loathed his subject.

Tyler left the study and went up the stairs, back to Lucy Tarleton's room, and looked at the painting there. The signature appeared to be Josiah Bell. The work was dated 1777.

Thoughtful, Tyler returned to the study once more. A truism in life was that everyone perceived others in their own way. Where one person saw kindness in someone, another saw weakness. Where one saw cruelty, another saw strength.

Perception. Always nine-tenths of reality.

He smiled. Sadly, he was certain, Allison Leigh saw him as an oversize quack. A pretentious hick.

Amused, he considered his own perceptions of her. A woman with a lot of pride and yet humility. A lover of truth and honor, but stubborn and determined. Stunning with her pitch-dark hair and bright blue eyes, but dismissive of her looks. The woman was a scholar, after all, and took her work seriously.

He hoped she'd come around. There was just something about her—something in the helpless look she'd given Todd, something that was kind and empathetic.

And despite the situation—despite her exhausted, annoyed and bewildered behavior toward him—he still found her...sensual.

The ghost likes her, Todd had said. Yes, sometimes

ghosts watched a person, and just as the living did, they knew who they liked—and who they didn't.

He stared at the painting. It didn't move, but Todd was right. The eyes had been well-painted, giving the illusion that the painting could watch someone moving about the room.

He leaned back in his chair. "I am here," he said softly.

He was greeted by silence. There were secrets in this house, but so far, the ghostly inhabitants were guarding those secrets.

Some of his coworkers had known from the time they were children that they had an extra sense, whether they saw it as a gift or a curse. They'd had grandparents or friends who'd appeared at their own funerals or talked to them in the middle of the night, or even showed up in other places.

Tyler, however, had no clue he had any unusual abilities until he'd done a stint in the service and then come home to become a Texas Ranger. He'd loved stories about the Rangers all his life; becoming a Ranger had been a dream. It was when he'd been a Ranger for a year that he'd first experienced the *unusual*. The situation had been especially poignant. Drug runners had kidnapped their mule's younger sister. The older sister had become a heroin addict, and when she hadn't been able to produce the money they'd wanted quickly enough, they'd killed her with an overdose. The younger sister had been left to rot at the bottom of a cistern out on the dusty Texas plain. A desperate, state-wide search had been instigated to find the seventeen-year-old. Tyler was standing in the middle of the sprawling ranch house where the drug runners were based when the older sister, pathetic, shaking and twitching, had appeared to him, begging him to help.

He thought he'd been drinking too much; he tried to tell himself that he wasn't seeing what he was seeing. She followed him. She was next to him even when he was with other officers. She didn't know where her sister was, but he had to help her, she said.

He was trying. He was trying so damned hard.

He stayed on his shift for several extra hours, searching the house, the barn, the stables, everywhere. He headed back to a bar for the night and discovered the dead woman on the stool next to him. He went home and she invaded his bedroom.

The next morning he got up and joined the search again, quizzing his ghost relentlessly about the property.

In the end, he found the younger sister in the cistern. He found her alive—shaken and dehydrated, but alive. His crying, grateful ghost left him, and for months afterward, he wondered if the pressure of the case hadn't made him delusional.

Then he'd walked into his office one day to see an old man sitting by his desk. No one else saw this old man, who wanted Tyler to find his murderer. Eventually he did.

The poor guy's son-in-law had figured he wasn't leaving the world soon enough and had helped him meet his Maker.

For a long time, he'd thought he was crazy. But as he and Logan Raintree worked together, they each learned that the other saw unusual things. That they *both* did. When Logan was approached by Jackson Crow, head of the first Krewe, and then Tyler was asked to join, as well, he felt it was the right thing to do. And it had been. They'd solved cases. Saved lives.

And they uncovered the truth.

He'd also learned that not all ghosts walked over to a man and started up a conversation. Some chose to speak only to certain people.

Just like the living did.

He shook off his memories and returned to the information on the four board members who ran the private Old Philly History Corporation.

Nathan Pierson, forty-five, real estate broker by day, financially comfortable with excellent stock investments.

Sarah Vining, fifty-one, philanthropist, wealthy due to an oil inheritance.

Cherry Addison, forty-three, a direct descendent of the Tarleton-Dandridge family on the maternal side, a former model and sometime actress with family money. Married to an artist of increasing renown.

Ethan Oxford, seventy-two, lawyer and politician.

He needed to meet them all. The best way to do that might be to call an impromptu board meeting.

Tyler realized he wasn't giving the attention he should to the folders. He rose and stretched. As he did, he thought he heard something from the rear of the house.

He left the study, looking at the rooms and the elegant entry as he walked to the front door. Nothing seemed to have changed. He strode through the rooms and then to the back door, unlocking it to step outside.

The moon was waning, but it still seemed to be full. And beneath that light, in the middle of the yard between the kitchen and the stables, he saw a horse. A majestic animal, huge, black and sleek.

He walked over to the horse and the animal gazed at him. He felt a cold sensation as a large black head nuzzled his chest. He stroked the cool air, seeing the animal's dark eyes and fine brow.

"Hey, fellow, still pounding the beat, eh?" he murmured.

The horse whinnied but couldn't answer any questions for him. A ghost horse couldn't speak any more than a living one could. But he was encouraged. If the horse was here, the house itself was opening to him.

He heard another sound—whining. He glanced down. There was a dog by his feet. a hound, large and tawny in color, with huge brown eyes that looked up at him trustingly. He hunkered down to touch the dog, feeling air, but aware that the hound knew it was being stroked. "Thank you, boy. Thank you for coming to me," he said softly. "If I can help, I will."

He was so involved with visions of the family creatures that he was startled when his phone rang.

"Montague," he said quickly, grinning to himself. The ghost hound had pushed him—nothing but a blast of air or imagination, but it had almost knocked him over.

"Agent Montague, it's Allison Leigh. I've, uh, had a nap. If you want to talk, I'm willing."

"I'll be right by to get you," he said.

Allison had managed to convince herself that she was totally sane; she was just under intense pressure.

And she was going to do the sane and intelligent thing. See a shrink.

Annette Fanning sat on a stool at the counter, looking at her with concern.

She was grateful to Annette. Her friend had arrived

just as she'd come to, and when she'd let Annette in and continued to run through her house searching for a sign that someone had been there, Annette had kept quiet and helped. Now, she stared at Allison.

"You're making more tea? What you need is a good shot," Annette told her sagely. "And if you won't have one, I will. You'd barely gotten off the floor when I got here. You could have hurt yourself! I still don't understand what happened. You *saw* someone in your house, or you *think* you saw someone?"

"I don't think anyone was really here. I'm sure I'm just mourning Julian, which is something I wasn't able to do before. I mean, I found him, and then the rest of the night I was with the cops and at the station and back at the house, and then we found the office trashed...."

"You need a good shot of whiskey," Annette said again, getting up and going to the cabinet.

"I don't want any whiskey. I just called that agent and said I'd go out with him."

"Now *that's* a plan. He's really hot-looking, Allison."

Allison frowned at her. "I don't mean *go out* in that sense. I'm going to answer questions for him and tell him about people. It's not a date."

"That's a pity," Annette said. She was tiny and blonde and struggled to reach the bottle shoved at the back of the cabinet. "You should get a real life, you know. You can't spend your life in the past."

"I don't spend my life in the past," Allison said, getting the bottle for her. "And I don't want a shot, really."

"I do—*really!*" Annette accepted the whiskey bottle and poured herself a measure. "You haven't gone out since you were dating Peter Aubrey, right? I thought you two were great together."

"When he was clean, we were great. I cared about

Pete and it was fun being with him. But I didn't have the power to change him. I picked him up from various gigs three times when his friends called to say he'd passed out and needed help. And I went back to him twice when he said he'd kill himself if I left him. I learned. It has nothing to do with me—he has to find a way to face his demons. I went to Narcotics Anonymous and learned that I can't change him. Only he can do that. If he ever gets cleaned up, goes into rehab and is serious about it, I'll consider seeing him again," Allison told her. "I'm not antisocial. I'm not lonely. And now is not the time to worry about my social life. Julian is dead, Annette, and the house is in the middle of some investigation...." She let her voice fade away; Annette's big brown eyes were moist again.

"I still can't believe it," Annette said. "I can't believe that Julian's dead."

"I'm sorry, Annette, I didn't mean—"

"No, no, I know." She let out a long sigh. "I called Nathan to find out if the board knew anything about funeral arrangements but no one's heard anything. The family wants the body shipped back to Indiana, but the morgue isn't going to release him until...until whatever, I don't know. There are still tests being done, I guess. Do you think he'd been drinking or that he was high or something? This is all so mysterious. Oh! Nathan did say he'd make sure we have a memorial in the next few weeks, no matter what. Julian had a lot of fans in the city."

"He was a decent musician and he had a great stage presence. I guess that's why he made a good guide," Allison said.

"When he showed up," Annette agreed. She walked back into the living room. "Hey, where's your broom?

I'm going to sweep one more time. You walk around barefoot—don't want you cutting your foot."

"Drink your whiskey. The floor is fine. I cleaned it over and over again," Allison said.

The doorbell rang, and Allison looked at Annette. "Not a word, okay? Not a single word."

"Not even 'hello'?" Annette asked. "And here I'd been thinking about adding something like 'nice to meet you'!"

Allison went to the door, flashing Annette a warning frown. Annette grinned.

Tyler stood there, so tall he nearly filled the doorframe.

"Hi," she greeted him. "Come in."

He entered. Allison quickly introduced him to Annette, who giggled, offering him her hand.

"You're *really* tall," Annette said.

Tyler nodded. "Yes, ma'am."

"Annette!" Allison whispered. "That's...rude."

"Not at all, Ms. Fanning," Tyler said with a laugh. "It's nice to meet you. I'm sorry it's under such circumstances."

"Yes. Julian." Annette shook her head. Denial would be with all of them for a long time, Allison thought.

"Actually, I'm glad you're here," Tyler told Annette. "I wanted to talk to you about the Tarleton-Dandridge House and about Julian."

"I spoke with a police officer, but I'm happy to talk to you, too. I last saw Julian at lunch. I didn't think about it much. I had to leave early myself. Root canal," she explained. "But I'm not surprised he ducked out for an audition. Music was everything to Julian. Oh, he liked his job and he was good at it. But he did want to be rich and famous. A rock star."

"Mind if we sit?" Tyler asked Allison.

She indicated the parlor. Her house, which had been built in the early 1800s, wasn't quite as old as the Tarleton-Dandridge. The original owner's grandson had sold it to her great-grandfather in 1890. Originally, the kitchen had been outside, and the counter had been put in somewhere around 1910, when the kitchen became part of the house. A lot of her furniture was pre-Civil War.

Her sofa, however, was a purchase she'd made just a few years earlier. It was plush and soft and nice, like the massive armchair to the side of it.

Tyler Montague took the chair; Annette sat close by, on the edge of the sofa, clearly fascinated. She rested an elbow on one arm of the sofa as she stared at him.

"What do *you* think happened at the Tarleton-Dandridge House?" Tyler asked her.

Annette blinked. "Do you mean about Julian—or someone trashing the office?"

"Both, either," Tyler said.

"I'm sad, of course, and horrified. We talked about Julian all the time. He knew it and didn't really care. He held on to his job at the house because he was good, very dramatic. But he wasn't responsible. We all liked him. It was hard not to. He was just…ambitious. He wanted to be a rock star, like I said. But he did love history." She paused. "And he loved to play online games—Words with Friends—all kinds of stuff. He acted like a blowhard sometimes, but he was very smart." Tears welled up in Annette's eyes. "It's sad. It's so, so sad. But it was an accident, wasn't it?"

"That's what we're trying to determine," Tyler said.

"But…he was alone in the house with Allison, wasn't he? She would *never* have hurt him. She won't even put out poison to kill rats.... I think she gives half her income to societies that save animals. Of course, it's true that people who love animals don't always love people, but to suspect that Allison could have hurt Julian in any way—it's crazy! Okay, he's made us so mad at times that she might have wanted to smack him. And he did try to pick her up when he first started working there a year ago. She was seeing Peter Aubrey back then, and besides, she isn't the type to play around at work and—"

Allison finally interrupted her rambling. "Annette. I think Tyler wants to talk about the house."

"All impressions are important," Tyler said smoothly. "So, you do believe Julian Mitchell was intelligent?"

"Julian was definitely smart," Allison replied. "He was brilliant with the English language." She hesitated and then admitted, "He and I did have a competition on Words with Friends. His ability was uncanny."

"I didn't even bother to play with him, I was so bad," Annette said.

"Would Julian have trashed the attic for any reason?" Tyler asked.

Annette and Allison looked at each other. "I don't know why he would—Julian had access to the attic. He could go up there whenever he wanted. But I don't understand why *anyone* would trash the attic. We never keep money there. Cash receipts and credit card payments are kept in the lockbox in the little pantry where we get changed. Every couple of days, one of us took the deposit to the bank. And there's never enough cash worth stealing. These days, reservations are mostly done online or with credit cards."

"So what *is* kept in the attic?" Tyler asked.

"Paperwork, records—copies of records. Everything

historically significant is in locked display cases," Annette said.

"What kind of paperwork?"

"The usual." Annette shrugged.

"Financial logs, schedules, events, reservations and some of the research we do," Allison explained.

"It's Allison's research. She's always writing some paper or other," Annette said. "She's a professor! And she's the best guide they've ever had, because she knows so much about the families and their history. Julian was interested in her research, but he wouldn't need to trash the attic. None of us would. Allison is always happy to show us her work."

Tyler watched her intently. Allison decided she was a little uncomfortable with Annette being so much of a champion.

"I write papers, yes, articles, on select periods of American history or focusing on a certain event," Allison said. "Eventually I hope to complete a book."

"But right now?"

"Right now I'm working on a paper about the British occupation of Philadelphia, focusing on the Tarleton-Dandridge House and Bradley's relationship with the family, especially Lucy. I'm also looking at Lucy's relationship with her fiancé, Stewart Douglas. There's a lot of mystery around her death. No one was called in to investigate and historians assume that's because Beast Bradley killed her and it was all shoved under the carpet. The British were evacuating at about the same time." She paused, impatient. "I'm hungry. I'm *really* hungry. Could we go somewhere for food?" She had groceries but wanted to bring this inquiry to an end— and wanted to escape her house for a while.

"Oh!" Annette said with dismay. "I have to get back.

I told Barrie I'd only be a few minutes, but I was so worried about Allison I forgot the time."

"You were worried about Allison? Why?" Tyler asked.

"Because it's been so traumatic!" Allison said firmly, giving Annette a warning stare.

"Ah, yeah, right. I wanted to make sure she was doing okay. I'd be in a loony bin if it'd been me who found Julian," Annette said. "Well." She stood as if loath to go. Tyler rose to his feet, as well.

Allison looked at Tyler, wondering whether she was stuck with him.

"Are you hungry, too? You don't need to come with me. You can find me here tomorrow," she said. She didn't know whether she dreaded having him come along, or whether she'd be disappointed if he didn't.

"Eating, yeah, I'm into it. Works for me a few times a day. I'll join you."

Annette offered him her hand and Tyler shook it. "Nice to meet you," she said. "Call me anytime."

"Thanks."

Allison got them both out the door, then hesitated, looking back, before closing it.

She thought she saw something move in the kitchen. *It's just a reflection,* she told herself. A reflection from the outside light on the shiny steel toaster. It was nothing....

She realized she was afraid to come home alone.

5

Allison Leigh did know and love her city, Tyler observed. Her home was on Chestnut, near a number of tourist destinations. When they left the house, she didn't have a place in mind; she told him the city was filled with wonderful restaurants.

They decided to leave the cars and walk down to Walnut, where a friend of hers owned a pub called Mc-Dooley's. His name really was McDooley and the pub was very old. Oddly enough, another McDooley—no relation—had owned the pub in the 1920s so there'd been no need for a name change when this McDooley bought the pub.

Tyler was surprised that her explanation regarding McDooley's ownership of McDooley's was given with such ease and charm. He hadn't imagined she was capable of being so lighthearted, but she had him laughing, and while they walked she mentioned funny or odd tidbits of history that kept him fascinated.

Her friend McDooley—first name Evan—was behind the bar when they walked in, a jovial-looking man probably around thirty, and probably fond of a pint or two, since he was showing the beginnings of a beer belly at his young age.

Evan McDooley started off smiling when he saw Allison, then quickly became grave, telling her how sorry he'd been to hear that a friend and coworker of hers had died. She thanked him and introduced him to Tyler. Evan's eyes widened. "I've heard of you!" he exclaimed. "Will this be like...a real ghost investigation?"

"Like a real investigation," Tyler told him. "We go through everything. Any possible structural problems, history, people involved with the house—everything."

"Wow," Evan said, his hands frozen on the glass he'd been drying as he stared at Tyler. "That sounds really cool. Oh, wait, no, sorry—the house is closed, right, Allison? People will be out of work for a while. Hey, I could use an extra waiter or waitress for the night shift, if any of you need some income."

"I'm fine. I'm researching a paper so I could use the time off," Allison said. "But I'll talk to Jason and Annette. One of them might be grateful for some work."

"There's a booth in the corner that's free if you want to take a seat and I'll have someone right with you. Can I get you a brew? We have a nice selection of beers on tap."

Allison asked him for a Scottish ale and Tyler chose a stout. Evan pulled the drafts before they walked to the table. Tyler hadn't expected her to drink with him, even a beer, but then he hadn't expected her to be so charming as they walked to the restaurant, either.

"Tell me about the paper you're writing now," Tyler said as they sat.

She waved a hand in the air. "I already told you."

"Tell me more."

"Okay, well, I'm an assistant professor of history. I'm sure you know we're expected to publish. So I write pieces that appear in magazines read by other profes-

sors who actually care about little incidents that occurred—along with the major events, of course. I'm
interested in the everyday, human dimension of history—social history you might call it. Domestic life
is a big part of that. That's why I focus on something
like the Tarleton-Dandridge House instead of the war."

"How many people know what you're doing?"

She made a face. "*Everyone* knows I'm working on a
piece about Lucy Tarleton and Beast Bradley, and that
I'm planning to write a book about everything that went
on at the house the year the British were in occupancy."

"Did you leave papers in the office?"

"Some of my research, but it's all copies of papers,
newspaper articles and letters I've gathered from librar-
ies and other institutions. Also copies of documents
held by the house. As Annette mentioned, the originals
are under lock and key. Oh, plus some of my notes. The
article's a work in progress." Allison frowned. "I don't
know why anyone would want copies of what I've got,"
she said. "Honestly, I don't understand what anyone
would want in that attic."

"Tell me more about your friend Annette," Tyler
said.

"You met her."

"For ten minutes."

"Ten minutes should do it. She's a bundle of energy, loves life, loves working at the house. She en-
joys working in the old taverns, too—she's on call at
one called the Bitsy Betsy House. The staff serve at
the tables and break into period song with a strolling
flutist now and then."

Tyler grinned. "Sounds like fun."

"It is."

"What's Jason Lawrence like?"

"Jason is a nice guy," Allison said. "Responsible and a good tour guide. Very entertaining when we go out to dinner together. Acts a little silly when he drinks, but who doesn't? He's smart, and he's been honest about the fact that he's heading back to NYU in a couple of years. He wants to do his doctorate in political science."

"You get along well with them? Both him and Annette?"

"Yes, we get along great."

"But no one really got along with Julian Mitchell?"

She lowered her head. "You have to understand. We all *liked* him. He was fun, and he was a terrific performer."

"What about the board members? How do you feel about them?"

"The board?" she asked, frowning again.

Tyler took a sip of his draft. It was good and very cold. "The board members who run the house."

"Oh, well, they're...fine."

"You don't sound like you're all that fond of them," he told her.

"No, you're wrong. I just don't work with them every day. I do like them. Not as much as my friends and colleagues, but that's a given, isn't it?"

"I don't know who your friends are, do I?" He smiled at her. "If I'd walked in here alone, would I have known you were friends with the owner?"

She grinned at that and raised her draft to him. "Ah, but you're an FBI agent. With all sorts of information in your dossiers and reports."

"A report can't really tell you how someone feels about others," he said.

"But you do know a lot about all of us, right?"

"Not as much as I should." He took another sip of

his beer. "This came up quickly. I drove here an hour after Adam called me, and I didn't get to my reading material until you ditched me today."

"I didn't exactly ditch you."

"That's *exactly* what you did."

"A colleague of mine died," she pointed out.

"Yes, I realize that," he said quietly. "But I hope you'll help me. I'm trying to find out why your colleague died. Of the board members, who's your favorite?" he asked.

"Hmm. I'm not sure. Either Nathan or Sarah. Sarah is the kind of woman who can remind you of a shelter dog—she looks as if she's afraid she's going to be beaten. I don't know why. She came from money, married money, never had children and is a widow now. Her husband was quite a bit older. Maybe he was a jerk. She doesn't talk about him or the time she was married at all. She's very sweet and hard to draw into a conversation. I always feel like I should help her or stand up for her—but I have no idea what I'd be standing up *against*. Nathan, on the other hand, is talkative and cheerful, and he really loves the house and the history. Ethan Oxford is quiet and dignified, and I don't know him very well. It's usually either Nathan or Sarah who talks to us about policy changes and so on. And Cherry... hmm. She has attitude. Or make that *arrogance*. The problem is that she isn't always right about historical facts, even when they concern the house. And if anyone tries to explain something to her, she gets angry and tells us she's a descendent of the family and we're not. But, in all honesty, I don't really blame her. She's married to a well-known artist who gets tons of attention, so...maybe it's her way of making sure she has her own identity."

"Interesting. I can't wait to meet her," Tyler said dryly.

"You haven't met the board yet?"

"I have a meeting with them in the morning."

"Where are you staying?" she asked him.

"At the Tarleton-Dandridge House," he said.

She seemed startled by that. "You're *staying* there?"

"Sure. It's best to be right where you're working. And I thought you didn't believe in ghosts."

"I don't," she said quickly. Too quickly? "But no one's ever stayed there—not in my memory. There are so many priceless artifacts in that house."

"I'm not going to throw a frat party."

She flushed. "We open the house and grounds for special events, but bring in extra security. It's just… well, paintings on the wall are irreplaceable. Knick-knacks set around the place are invaluable. Some of the lace doilies on the furniture are from the 1700s. You have to be so careful in there."

He leaned back, smiling. She was always so serious, it was rather endearing.

"What was high school like for you?" he asked.

"Why?"

"Brains and beauty," he teased. "Did you ever go to a football game?"

"Yes, I did. And I actually watch football."

"Really?"

"Well, now and then." She waved a hand in the air. "I throw a party every year for the Super Bowl thing."

He lowered his head, still smiling.

She continued, her tone that of a professor. "But as to the Tarleton-Dandridge House…things there truly *are* irreplaceable. We lose so much history every year.

We should preserve whatever we can for the ages, for our children and grandchildren."

"I won't do any damage to the house. The board knows I'm in there and they've approved. It was Adam's idea. When my Krewe arrives, they'll be staying there, as well."

"Lord," she murmured. "Please. You're going to tramp through the house with all kinds of ridiculous equipment?"

"We have cameras and heat sensors, but we don't *tramp*."

She sat back, frowning. "You really should be supervised while you're there."

He laughed. "Allison, think about it. We do what we do because of a man who respects history as holy ground. We've worked in some of the most historic and fragile and secretive places in this country. You're welcome to come back with me and see where I've set up," he told her.

Evidently, that suggestion didn't please her at all. She ignored the question and pointed to his menu.

"You should try their shepherd's pie," she said. "It's excellent."

He did; they ordered and their food was served ten minutes later. He was surprised that she seemed nervous as the meal came to a close. "I was hoping you'd be around during the day. You loved the house when you were a child, you've worked there as a guide, and you can supervise everything that goes on."

"Maybe," she said. "How do you know I loved the house when I was young? Oh, of course, you have information on me, as well."

"Of course."

"That's not really fair, is it?"

"I'm the investigator. I think that means it's fair."

"But what about you? Did ghosts talk to you as a kid?" she asked teasingly.

"Nope. I grew up in San Antonio, went into the service, got out, went to the University of Maryland for criminal law and became a Texas Ranger."

"How was high school for *you?*" she asked him. "Wait, don't tell me. You were a linebacker on the football team. Cheerleaders were entertainment for you, and you somehow managed to keep your grades up enough to stay on the team and get scholarships, but you were bred with Texas machismo and therefore it was necessary to join the army before going for your education. That sounds terrible—I'm sorry. I'm grateful to our armed forces."

"I joined the navy."

"And the rest?"

"I don't really remember the cheerleaders as entertainment."

"You dated one, though, right?"

He laughed. "No, never. I dated the same girl through high school. She's gone on to work for the Centers for Disease Control in Atlanta. We're still friends."

"Hmm," was all the response he received.

He asked the waitress for their check, only to find out that Evan had picked it up and wouldn't back down, even when Tyler tried to explain that as a law enforcement officer, he could be cited for accepting a free meal. "But Ally isn't a law enforcement officer, and she's the one I'm taking care of. Besides, you're her guest. And I won't tell if you don't. Come back with friends and spend more money," he told them cheerfully, waving away their thanks.

Tyler realized he was never going to get that check;

he thanked Evan, assured him they'd return soon and left their waitress a generous tip.

It was while they were on their way out that a slim woman in very high heels and a tight skirt came breezing through the doorway. She almost passed them, but then she noticed Allison and started to say something but saw Tyler, as well, and stopped dead.

"Hello, Cherry," Allison said.

"Hello, Ally." She glanced at Allison briefly, staring at Tyler, and then shaking her head as she looked at Allison again. "Oh, my dear, it's good to see you out and about. I'm so, so sorry about that charming young man, Julian." She didn't wait for Allison to reply, but turned to Tyler, extending a hand. "You must be with Adam Harrison's people."

"Yes, ma'am. Tyler Montague."

"Cherry. Cherry Addison. You're very welcome here. We adore the house and want any...difficulties resolved. I must admit I didn't think the idea of bringing your team in to stay was the best, but we made the decision as a group. And you certainly look as if you'll be capable of managing any situation."

"I hope so, ma'am," he told her. So this was the Tarleton-Dandridge descendent. She was an attractive woman, determined to retain the appearance of youth. Her hair was carefully cut at an angle, and her face was smooth. Unfortunately, its smooth perfection was indicative of cosmetic surgery or at least Botox.

"You're helping Agent Montague?" she asked Allison, who nodded. "Well, naturally, Allison knows her history. We're delighted to have such a scholar among our guides, but...of course, *I* know the history of the house as no one else does. So when you need my assistance..."

"Yes, of course. We're scheduled to meet in the morning," Tyler reminded her.

"Ten o'clock. I believe we'll be at Ethan's place." She shuddered. "I'm glad we're not meeting at the house. However, I look forward to speaking with you tomorrow. Needless to say, the board is anxious about the house. We take its preservation very seriously. Because of what's happened—so tragic—it seemed necessary to close for a period. But should you need my personal assistance in any way, don't hesitate to get in touch. I will make myself entirely available to you."

"That's kind of you, thank you," Tyler said. She still just stood there, staring at him.

"Well, good evening, then, ma'am. I'll see you in the morning."

"Yes, good evening. Allison, have the best night you can, my dear," she said, and moved into the restaurant.

Tyler held the door until she was inside. She looked at him again, gave him a lingering smile and headed to the bar.

When he closed the door, he saw that Allison was grinning.

"Well, that was the famous descendent," he said. "What's so funny?"

"She was ready to devour you."

"I don't think she expected to see either of us here."

"I don't think she could care less about seeing *me*. But you're a big boy. You can handle her...and her *assistance*."

"What does that mean?"

"She *is* a Dandridge descendent."

"She doesn't work at the house every day."

"Technically, I'm part-time."

He smiled and didn't reply. She seemed to be in a

good mood, still amused by Cherry Addison's reaction to him.

But as they walked, her smile faded. She moved more slowly as they left the restaurant behind.

He was surprised. She was trying to draw out their evening together.

Fine. He slowed his pace, as well, curious about her reasons.

They walked back along Market Street and the quiet of night made the experience of looking at the facade of Independence Hall seem even more hallowed. He tried to imagine how the hotheaded politicians of the time had managed to work together well enough to "make thirteen colonies chime as one."

"A penny for your thoughts," Allison said.

"A penny? With inflation? My thoughts are worth at least two cents."

She laughed. "I'm not sure I could afford them these days."

"I was thinking that it's a miracle we exist as a nation. Could you picture our Congress today cooperating to make that kind of decision?"

"Good point," she said. "Patrick Henry and Sam Adams were fierce and fiery orators, and they didn't always agree with each other. They made it work somehow."

"They had the same goal."

She laughed. "And they put aside their differences to achieve that goal. We can keep hoping! They realized that society would change over time. When you think about the past two-hundred-plus years, they didn't do so badly. Most of them knew the slavery question would arise, but they felt they had to create a country before dealing with such a serious issue. We've made mistakes as a nation and we'll continue to make mistakes. That's human nature. The American dream is one thing, while men and women are flesh and blood and real. All we can do is try to avoid those mistakes in the future. You know the famous quote about learning from history or else being doomed to repeat it."

He nodded. She was interesting, reasonable…and, yes, charming. Fun to be with.

He realized it wasn't a sudden desire for his company that had her stalling, dragging her feet, walking slowly. She seemed loath to go in the direction of her house.

"Is something wrong?" he asked her.

"No, no, nothing. I was thinking maybe I'd go to the Tarleton-Dandridge House with you now."

He arched a brow. "You're afraid the intriguing Cherry Addison will step in—and give me incorrect information. Or that she'll convince me the ghosts of her ancestors are running around and our investigation would make a great TV show."

She sent him a stern glare. "You wanted me to talk. You wanted my opinion on people there. You want to know about the history of the house. I'm too keyed up to sleep, so I'll come back with you, if you don't mind."

"Not at all. I'm a big believer in plunging right in."

He kept a smile in place.

He wondered what was going on with her. The last thing she really wanted to do, he thought, was to go to the Tarleton-Dandridge House with him.

She just didn't want to go home. Why?

She was surprised that he hadn't come right out and demanded to know what she was lying about.

But he hadn't.

She sounded like a liar to herself, and she was seriously worried about her sanity.

What a choice!

Home—where Julian Mitchell might suddenly appear to be sitting in the chair by her sofa. Or the Tarleton-Dandridge House with Tyler Montague.

Montague was alive. That meant he won.

The question was, how long could she pretend to be helping him at the house?

She'd already been through the crime scene. The idea of walking through it again just made her feel numb.

They went into the mudroom and then the foyer. The entry was large, which was convenient when they were doing tours. People could disperse and look into the different rooms so they weren't all trying to crowd into one area at the same time.

"Here we are," Tyler said.

"Where are you sleeping?" she asked him.

"The master bedroom. I'm the first one here, so I get first choice."

"That's a rope bed. The quilt on it is from the 1800s."

"The quilt is safely in a closet. I brought sheets and a blanket."

"What about the rest of your people?"

"They'll come with bedding, as well."

"As well," Allison repeated. "As well as cameras and all their *ghost-hunting* equipment," she said scornfully.

He stopped and turned to her. "I'm sorry you find us laughable. My unit has an extraordinary record of solving every case we've been brought in on."

"There really isn't a case here—I mean, not worthy of your effort. I can't see how there could be." She thought she must have sounded desperate and tried to calm her voice. "There is nothing in that attic. Nothing worth taking. I keep thinking that Julian had to be playing a prank and it got the best of him. Who knows, maybe he thought he'd create a mystery for us, and that I'd find him in the study playing Beast Bradley and he'd scare me."

"That may be the case," Tyler said mildly. "If so, we won't be here long. Look, Allison, there've been a lot of deaths in this house."

She unfastened the red velvet cord that sectioned off the period sofa and sank into it. "It's an old house," she said stubbornly. "People die."

"I'm not talking about the natural deaths, and you know it."

"The unnatural ones, like the poor kid who electrocuted himself?" Allison asked. "Sam Daily. That was eight years ago. I never met him. I was a college student back then, working occasionally on my breaks. There is no real protection against human stupidity. He started ripping out wires and got an electric shock. That's what happens." She winced, remembering. They'd shut down the house then, too. But only for a few days.

"You were here?"

"Like I said, I never saw the student—or the police or anyone. It was horrible, tragic. As tragic as when a spring-breaker gets drunk and goes over a balcony at a Florida hotel. Everyone felt terrible, especially for the parents. When we came back to work…it was uncomfortable. And still, there was nothing any of us could have done, and certainly nothing that any form of law enforcement could have done. He thought he could trip the alarm and play games in the house. A live wire killed him. That's all I know."

"I didn't say you should know more."

She lifted a hand. "The thing is, that kind of tragedy could have happened anywhere. There's no reason
to assume that ghosts are running around this house.
People can do crazy things, and sometimes they pay
horrible consequences."

"Sadly, that's true." Tyler took a seat next to her.
"What about the other incidents?" he asked.

She cast him a wry glance. "I wasn't alive when Bill
Hall fell down the stairs."

"Angela Wilson?"

She felt a little pang squeeze her heart. "I loved
Angie. She was so knowledgeable and she was the
grand matriarch here. I knew her from when I was
really young. She encouraged me to love history and
books and...she was a role model for me. She had a
wonderful career, wrote several fantastic historical nov-
els, married a great guy and had kids. She was seventy-
two—not old at all these days, and in great shape. But
she had a heart attack."

"I'm sorry," he said softly.

"Thank you," she murmured just as softly.

He rose. "I'm going to take a walk around the house
and make sure all the doors are closed and the windows
are secure and ready for the alarm, so I can go right to
sleep when I get back. Then I'll stroll on over to your
house with you and pick up my car. I'm exhausted.
You must be, too."

She nodded.

He stood up and started for the stairs.

Allison was dismayed to realize that she wanted to
call him back. She wanted to leap to her feet and go
with him.

She was terrified of being alone.

Somehow, she managed to stay seated.

As his footsteps disappeared up the stairs, she got up, too. She couldn't sit still—and she didn't want to go home.

Check into a hotel? That was ridiculous!

But it was better than going home. Thankfully, she knew some good therapists and she'd go see one first thing in the morning.

All she had to do was get through the night.

"Allison!"

She heard the whisper of her name, but denied it to herself.

The sound came again, more urgent.

"Allison, please!"

She turned and there he was, Julian Mitchell, still in period costume, in the doorway that led to Angus Tarleton's study.

She backed away from him. She backed up so far that she couldn't move any farther; she could feel the sofa against her legs.

Julian Mitchell came toward her.

Once again, it was too much.

This time, she didn't hurt herself. She passed out onto the period sofa that sat just inside the entry of the Tarleton-Dandridge House.

Tyler didn't think he'd taken *that* long to walk around and assure himself that the house was secure.

He must have been longer than he'd thought.

When he returned to the foyer, Allison was stretched out on the sofa, sound asleep. He gazed down at her for a moment. Maybe she'd awaken soon. He hated to rouse her when she'd been through so much and was so exhausted.

There was more work he could do in the study; he decided he'd get to it and wait for her to wake up.

He ran upstairs and got a pillow—one he'd brought himself, with a twenty-first-century pillowcase bought at Target—and slipped it beneath her head. On second thought, he went back up and returned with a blanket. When he'd covered her, he went into Angus Tarleton's study.

While he continued to read about the people involved with the house throughout its history, he found that he was continually distracted. Looking up at the painting of Beast Bradley, he knew why.

The portrait didn't bother him. It was the work of an excellent artist, someone capable of imbuing a painting with character. He'd shown a handsome man steeped in cruelty, a portrayal that was so different from the painting in Lucy Tarleton's room.

Granted, the one in the study had been executed by a Dandridge. Did that mean anything? Naturally, the Dandridges hated the man who'd caused the death of Lucy Tarleton, Sophia Dandridge's sister. And Bradley had probably brought so much misery to Angus Tarleton that he'd died years earlier than he should have.

So what exactly was the truth about Beast Bradley? Did his infatuation with Lucy turn him into a monster or had history been written by the victors—the patriots in this case? Maybe he'd been nothing more than human, having virtues along with his faults.

Then again, how did anyone forgive a man who'd cut the throat of a young woman in her own parlor?

The house seemed silent. Nothing even seemed to shift. He yawned, exhausted, then went back out to the parlor.

Allison Leigh was still sleeping soundly.

"Allison?"

He touched her shoulder. She didn't awaken.

She looked young and vulnerable lying there, and angelically beautiful. Her dark hair was sleek and lustrous against the crimson velvet of the sofa; her long lashes swept ivory cheeks.

"Allison?" He shook her slightly but she still didn't wake.

Perplexed, Tyler straightened, studying her for a minute or two.

It probably wouldn't look proper to leave her sleeping there. But…they were living in the modern world. He was going upstairs, she was downstairs, and he really didn't give a damn what people said. She lived alone, and he was pretty sure she didn't have to answer to anyone.

"Sleep tight," he murmured.

He walked the stairs up to the second floor, heading for the master bedroom.

He paused to glance at the other painting of Beast Bradley. Here, there was strength in the eyes, but not that expression of brutal cunning and cruelty.

"Talk to me?" he offered.

But the house was silent.

He went on to bed, open to the spirits who might roam the house.

That night, none of them chose to appear.

Allison woke with a start.

She sat up, feeling lost. Then she noticed the blanket around her and turned to see the pillow she'd slept on. She looked around, realizing she was in the foyer of the Tarleton-Dandridge House. She remembered seeing Julian and she remembered passing out.

She didn't want to be here. She'd *imagined* Julian last night; he was on her mind. She was near the place where he'd died. She had been an idiot to come here.

Now she had to go.

She rose just as Tyler Montague came walking through from the salon doorway, a cup of coffee in his hand.

"It's black. Hope that's okay. I don't use cream or sugar so I hadn't bought any yet. I didn't disturb anything historical. I made it in the pot you keep in your docents' room. You all might have cream and sugar in there somewhere? I didn't prowl through anyone's things," he said, offering her the cup.

She nodded and accepted the cup numbly.

"I, uh, slept here all night?" she asked him.

"Unless you woke up and went tearing around the historic district while I was sleeping," he said. "Enjoying the wild nightlife."

She ignored his attempt at levity. "You didn't see or hear anything...odd?"

"No," he said. "Did you?"

"Ah, no, no. I must've been so tired... I'm sorry. I need to leave now. I have—I'm going to have a doctor's appointment."

She gulped down a huge sip of the coffee, which was hot. She coughed but didn't scald her mouth, thank God.

"Hey!" Tyler took the cup from her while she caught her breath. "Are you all right?"

"I'm fine. Embarrassed. I was just so tired. Thanks for the pillow and the blanket. You should have woken me."

"I tried."

"Oh, I'm sorry."

"Don't be. You were out like a light," he told her.
You'll never know how much! she thought.

"I'll call you later." She took the coffee cup from him and drank more carefully, then pushed it back in his hands. "I'll call you later!" she repeated.

Allison tried not to run to the door. When she reached it, she remembered that an alarm was set. She keyed in the numbers to let herself out.

At the gate, she did the same thing. She didn't look back. She ran down the street, not sure at first what she was doing or even what time it was, just desperate to get away from the Tarleton-Dandridge House.

Eventually, she slowed her gait. She finally checked her watch and saw that it was still early—not yet seven. She'd go home and shower, then show up at the university's medical buildings and hope that a professor friend, a psychiatrist, would be able to see her.

At her house, she paused, fumbling in her handbag for her keys. She didn't want to go into the house alone.

But she couldn't go anywhere in the clothes she'd been wearing all day and all night. Determined, she slipped her key into the lock and went inside. Still, it took her a minute to go farther than the doorway.

She started talking out loud. "Julian, I'm taking a shower. There will be no crazy stuff going on now, okay? I do not see you and I will not see you. You are a product of my imagination."

She ran through the front of the house and up the stairs to her bedroom, looking straight ahead all the while. She showered as quickly as she could, dropping the soap several times when it fell through her trembling fingers.

She wasn't sure if her shirt matched her jeans and she didn't care. Besides, did it matter what shirt was worn with a pair of jeans? She was so terrified she just about fell down the stairs, but she was almost there, almost out of the house.

She had to try twice to get the door open. When she did, she turned back. She could see the top of a head above the upholstered wingback chair.

A hand rose.

She clearly heard Julian say, "I'll be here when you get back."

6

Allison drove directly to the university. Once she'd parked, she headed for the medical compound and found Dr. Marty Hanson, who was a practicing psychiatrist.

Marty said it probably wasn't the best thing to work together, since they were friends. But she was able to send Allison to a colleague she admired, Dr. Rudy Blount, who was a short, friendly man in his early fifties with wire-rimmed spectacles and a balding head. He asked Allison to make herself comfortable. No, she didn't have to lie down on the sofa but she was welcome to do so. She could also just sit and talk to him from an armchair.

Allison opted for the armchair and a conversational approach. Dr. Blount was personable. They talked about their mutual love of the city and discussed issues in the news. He asked about her daily life; he knew that, like Marty, she taught at the university. He assured her that anything she said was completely and totally confidential.

Finally, Allison released a deep breath and explained her problem.

She told him about finding Julian—and then seeing him in her house.

"Is it stress?" she asked him.

"What do you think?" he asked her.

"I think it's stress," she said.

"Then it's most likely stress."

"I've never believed in ghosts," she told him.

He folded his hands and set them in his lap. "Ghosts. Well, what are ghosts, Ms. Leigh? Maybe they're memories. Maybe they're images we create in our minds. Maybe they're reminders that we should have done something, but didn't. Tell me, were you feeling any guilt about your friend Julian?"

"No, I wasn't feeling guilty about Julian. He was always showing up late and we—the group of us—were always covering his ass!"

"Do you feel you need to defend yourself in any way over his death? Do you think you could have saved him somehow?"

"No, I'm not feeling defensive. I would've done anything to save him, but the second I saw him, I knew he was dead."

"Did you check for a pulse?"

"I never touched him. I called the police."

"As you waited were you frightened that something would happen to *you?*"

Allison shook her head. She hadn't felt that at all. "No, no…it looked as if he'd just sat down…wrong. You know how people rest their elbows on a table and their chins on their hands? Well, it's as if he thought he had a table and the bayonet was his hand."

"Very sad, and terrible for Julian, and for you. At this point, it has to be difficult to understand what you're feeling. Guilt is an interesting emotion. It was fine to be angry with him while he was alive, but now that he's dead, you may feel guilty about that anger without being aware of it."

"I really don't think I feel guilty. Whenever he left us in the lurch, we were always honest about it. He'd know we were angry because we'd tell him, and he'd apologize and promise not to do it again. He also said that when he made it big, he'd never forget us or leave us behind."

"Did you like the young man?"

"As a friend, definitely. When we were away from work."

"Have you ever had a feeling like this before?"

"A feeling like what?"

"That someone's still with you. Someone dead. A spirit—a ghost."

"Never." Allison shook her head. "But now...I'm afraid to be in my own house. I slept on a sofa at the Tarleton-Dandridge last night because I was afraid to go home. No, that's a lie. I didn't start out sleeping. I passed out. Because I saw Julian. I was with one of the FBI men—Agent Montague, who wants my help with the history and the people there—and when he went to check on the windows, doors, alarm system, all that, Julian suddenly appeared. And the next thing I knew I was sinking, the world went black, and then I woke up this morning feeling like an idiot."

"The agent didn't come to help you?" Dr. Blount asked in obvious surprise.

"He thought I'd fallen asleep. He gave me a pillow and a blanket," she said dryly.

"Didn't the police have crime tape around the Tarleton-Dandridge House? When the tragedy was announced on the news, the reporter said the place was going to be closed for a few weeks," Dr. Blount said.

"Yes, they've closed the house. But the police—or the directors or someone—brought in a federal team that's investigating the house."

"I see. That's why you were with an agent. A federal agent."

"Yes."

"Ah!" Dr. Blount said.

"Ah?"

"Do you have something against the federal government investigation? It doesn't sound as if you approve."

"I *don't* approve."

"Why not?"

"I don't want anyone making a mockery of the Tarleton-Dandridge House—with people running around and filmmakers making everyone's eyes look like those of a deer caught in the headlights. And going 'What's that? Did you hear that?' whenever a floorboard creaks. Please! Have you seen those shows? I think one of the educational channels used to do them with actors re-creating what happened in the past, and using lights to make a place seem spooky. Then they'll have people walk through the building screaming now and then. It's not fair to the historical integrity of the house!"

"FBI agents film their investigations with special lights?" He seemed puzzled.

"No."

"They publicize what they're doing?"

"No, no, it's just that I've read up on these particular agents. They're called in when there's something *unusual*. Unusual to them, from what I've read, means paranormal. And we're dealing with *history* here. Sacred ground. Old Philadelphia is the site of some of the most momentous events in our nation's past."

"I agree. But filming—for the public. Do you think these people are going to do that?"

"I know they're bringing in equipment to monitor the house during the night. And maybe during the day, too. I know that everything about this government agency is kept as quiet as possible, but information leaks out and other units of the FBI consider them 'special.'"

Dr. Blount smiled. "Maybe you *believe* you know all this but it's not quite what's going on. And maybe you resent these people so much because you're afraid of seeing something you don't want to see—like Julian Mitchell."

"Is that what you think? That it's stress over Julian's death *and* the fact that I don't really trust these people?"

"Is that what *you* think?" he asked.

"I don't know what I think! That's why I'm here."

"There's an old joke that a patient talks and a psychiatrist listens and asks over and over again if that's what he or she thinks. But the human mind is complex, and in the absence of actual mental illness, we rule our own thoughts. I can give you a medication—a mild one—that'll help you sleep until this is over. You probably need to come to terms with what's happening in your life."

"A friend died," she said softly.

He nodded. "That's hard enough to accept. You know the stages of grief, I'm sure—denial, anger, bargaining, depression and, finally, acceptance. We all go through these feelings. You found the young man and you were horrified and perhaps tried to deny that what you saw could be true. You're angry he's dead, and that may be manifesting in the way you feel about a government group coming into the Tarleton-Dandridge House.

Seeing this young man in your house may be your way of bargaining—he's not really dead if you can see him. And we're all depressed when we hear about the loss of someone young, someone who shouldn't have died. I think, once you accept what's happened, you'll begin to heal. But no one can really rush the stages of grief. We all go through them."

"So, I'm seeing Julian in my mind?"

"Is that what you believe?"

She burst out laughing. "Honestly, I want you to tell me that I *am* seeing him in my own mind."

"If you believe that, will it help you?"

"Immeasurably!"

Dr. Blount grinned. "Do you want to go it alone? Or would like a sleep medication?"

"I hate taking pills unless I have to."

"So you don't want a prescription?"

"No, I definitely want one!"

Allison wasn't sure what she felt when she left Dr. Blount's office; she knew he'd rearranged his schedule to see her, and she was grateful, but their visit hadn't really helped her.

She wished he'd just said, "Don't be ridiculous. Ghosts don't exist. It's all in your head."

And now, of course, the problem was that, once again, she didn't want to go home.

Julian had told her he'd be waiting.

Ethan Oxford lived in another historic house. His was on Walnut Street.

The board was ready to meet in Ethan's dining room. Originally, Tyler thought, the place had been designed so that it could also function as a ballroom. A large period table was in the center of the room, and the walls were covered with portraits of historic figures.

Dolley Madison held pride of place against the far wall.

Oxford was a dignified man. His white hair, beard and mustache were perfectly groomed. He was gracious as he answered the door himself, setting an arm around Tyler's shoulders as he led him toward the dining room. "I'll admit, young man, I'm the one who insisted we call Adam Harrison. He and I go way back. We've served on the boards of many fine charities together and I've known many people Adam has helped. Discreetly, of course. Now, I'm not saying the young man's death wasn't completely accidental, but what with that fellow being in the hospital, as well…I think the house needs investigation."

"Sir, it's usually worth some research when there've been a number of…accidents," Tyler agreed.

Oxford stood back, grinning at Tyler. "You're not what I was expecting. You actually look like a real lawman."

"Thank you," Tyler said.

"Well, come on in. The others are waiting."

He'd met Cherry the night before, of course. This morning she gushed over him as if they were long lost friends. Nathan Pierson seemed intrigued to meet him. Sarah Vining gave him a limp hand. He had the feeling that she wasn't one to create waves. He remembered that Allison had told him Sarah reminded her of an abused pup at a shelter.

"Coffee?" Oxford asked him. It was already set out in a silver carafe.

"Thank you," Tyler said.

He accepted a cup and the seat that was offered to

him. The others joined him at one end of the massive table.

"What have you discovered so far?" Oxford asked anxiously.

"So far, I'm studying the house and delving into what happened to bring me here," Tyler said. "I made a point of removing the reproduction bedding from the room I'm using, which we'll be careful to do everywhere. I understand how many objects in the house are priceless, and we will take extreme care."

"The house is haunted. You found that out, right?" Cherry said.

He smiled. "Remnants of the past always remain in a place where the passions of history ran high, Mrs. Addison. I don't believe that a ghost rummaged through the office in the attic or caused Mr. Mitchell to die. But we will find out what did, whether it was accidental or manufactured."

"Manufactured. What does that mean?" Pierson asked, frowning.

"Caused by a person or persons unknown."

"Oh, dear! He couldn't have been…murdered!" Sarah Vining cried.

"There, there, Sarah," Oxford said in a comforting voice.

"It's pretty unusual for someone to set his chin on a bayonet," Tyler explained. "And a few of the events that have occurred in the past definitely pose a unique challenge. Here's the thing," he said. "No one wants the public to start believing that the house is *dangerously* haunted. We all know that a good ghost story draws people, but they don't want to think there's something really evil about a house."

"There's nothing evil about the Tarleton-Dandridge

House," Cherry protested. "We have a poignant love story, and a beautiful woman who haunts the house. Why, the ghost tours would go out of business if the house were to blow away!"

Tyler doubted that; Cherry seemed to think the house was the most important building in the historic city. But he lowered his head.

"You don't need to worry," he said quietly. "My team can go through the house quickly."

"I hope so! The newspapers have gotten wind of that man in the hospital—and his son swears the portrait of Beast Bradley put him there!" Sarah spoke tremulously. "I hate this! If there's anything you can do to restore our wonderful piece of the past to total respectability, we'll greatly appreciate it!"

"I'll remind you, Agent Montague, *I'm* here to help if you need me," Cherry said.

"We're all here. We've asked these people in because of the gossip that was already going around the city. And now this," Ethan said, shaking his head.

"Gossip?" Tyler asked.

"I called Adam the second I heard what happened because of the other deaths in the house." Oxford shook his head again. "People are saying one event could be an accident, but…a docent? A college student? And now…a docent again. Or a guide, what have you. And on top of that, someone rummaging through the attic. Why, we were all there right before young Mr. Mitchell died—and right before that attic was raided. Will you be able to tell if Mr. Mitchell was distressed in some way…if there was a reason he might have torn the attic apart?"

"We'll certainly be looking into that. What I need to know from all of you is whether you have any idea why someone would be searching for something in that attic. And what that might be."

He surveyed the table. They all stared back at him.

"I can't think of anything," Cherry said. "The house has had a thorough history done, which was easy because it went from the original family directly into the hands of the Old Philly organization."

"An oral history," Tyler said politely.

Cherry sat up very straight. "Would you suggest my family were liars, Agent Montague?"

"Not at all, Mrs. Addison," Tyler assured her. "But oral history can be like the whispering game. Tell a friend, who tells a friend, and by the time they've told several friends, the story has changed. Don't worry, I'm not implying that's the case." He rose; he'd been hoping to learn something he didn't know or couldn't access in his files. They were all looking to him for answers when he'd just arrived and was still figuring it out.

"You don't think our guide—Ms. Leigh—might have, er, helped Mr. Mitchell die, do you?" Cherry asked.

Tyler was startled by the question. Maybe he shouldn't have been. Despite Allison's obvious grief at the loss of a colleague, the police had questioned her long enough.

He reminded himself that he barely knew Allison Leigh.

But he also had a good sense of people; he was seldom fooled.

"No, I don't. Julian Mitchell was a physically fit man. It's unlikely that even as a friend, joking around with him, she could have forced his chin down on that bayonet," Tyler said.

Nathan frowned. "Cherry, that was horrible! To say such a thing."

"However," Ethan said, drumming his fingers on the table, "whoever trashed the attic might have been looking for Allison's research."

"Ethan, don't be ridiculous," Cherry said, waving a beautifully manicured hand in the air. "Her so-called research sheds no new light on anything. She's found a few quotes and notations we didn't know about. She has nothing new." Cherry paused. "She did mention to me that she wanted to take a research trip to Valley Forge. She's been communicating with some professor there who claims he owns letters written by Lucy Tarleton. I highly doubt this and I warned Allison he's probably a fraud or the letters were faked, but I believe she still meant to investigate."

Cherry didn't exactly roll her eyes, but her opinion of the unnamed professor's research was evident.

Tyler stood and said, "Well, Mrs. Addison, here's the thing about history. It belongs to everyone and it's not immutable. History changes when new facts emerge or when attitudes change—views on slavery being an obvious example. So I assume Ms. Leigh will follow where her research leads. Thank you all for your time and your faith. We'll keep you advised of every move we make and, of course, anything we're able to determine."

Oxford and Pierson stood politely when Tyler did. He could tell they were going to talk about him when he was gone. That was all right; he'd learned from them what he could.

The rest of his Krewe would be arriving by nightfall. He returned to the house and did an inventory of the employees' work area, not wanting to infringe on anyone's private property, but figuring out the best way to make the place habitable. There was a small refrigerator, a microwave and a coffeepot. Not much, but it would do, especially since they were located in the heart of the historic district, which placed them in the middle of restaurant heaven.

Making a mental list of a few supplies to pick up, he left the house and walked over to Allison's, about half a mile away. Passing through the historic district, he listened to the sounds of excitement from parents, couples and children, all thrilled to see the famous Liberty Bell and walk through Independence Hall.

He understood Allison's deep passion for Philadelphia and its history. He often felt that the greatest achievement of American democracy had been freedom of speech and of the press, freedoms that could be abused at times and yet were necessary for a true government of the people.

With that thought in mind, he found himself thinking again of the two different paintings of Beast Bradley. It was remarkable what one man saw that another didn't. And each had the right to his own views.

He tried Allison's door; she didn't answer. He tried her cell phone next but got her answering machine. He left a message, asking her to give him a call.

After that, he stopped at the hospital. The children weren't there today but Haley Dixon was sitting by her husband's side, holding his hand. She didn't see Tyler at first and he felt a hard tug at his heartstrings—no relationship in the world was perfect, he knew that. But the love and tenderness in Haley's eyes as she watched her husband, her hand curled around his, was beautiful.

He prayed that Dixon would recover even as he wondered whether the man's condition could possibly have anything to do with the Tarleton-Dandridge House.

Haley Dixon must have heard him then because she turned toward him. Her eyes were damp, but she smiled. She gently released her husband's hand and walked over to join him at the door.

"Any change?" he asked.

She shook her head. "They're still waiting for the test results."

"How are the boys?"

Haley shrugged apologetically. "Todd's convinced that a ghost did this to his father. But he's also convinced that Ms. Leigh can do something about it, and he believes in you."

"I wish I could promise you that all we had to do was talk to a ghost and everything would be all right. But I *can* promise you that I have a team coming in tonight and we'll do everything possible to find out if there were any factors at the house that could have caused this."

She nodded. "All the other tourists and docents are okay—" She broke off and grimaced. "Except for the young man who died, of course. Do you think there could be some kind of toxin? Mold in the walls, lead, anything that might be responsible for this? Something Artie's allergic to, maybe, that doesn't affect most people?"

"Government regulations are pretty stringent, but you never know what might've been missed. We'll keep at it."

She suddenly stood on tiptoe to plant a kiss on his cheek. She flushed. "I'm sorry. It's just that a lot of people would think we're ridiculous for believing the house could have caused any of this, and I want you to know that I—we, all of us—are grateful for your concern and anything you can do."

"A kiss on the cheek is never anything to apologize for," he told her. "I'll check back with you tomorrow."

Leaving the hospital, Tyler headed to the police station. So far, the police had gained nothing from their forensic investigation of the house or the attic. The prints they'd lifted all belonged to those who worked there and, presumably, tourists. There'd been an abundance of prints with no matches in the databases. The medical examiner had yet to make a ruling on Julian Mitchell's death, and it might be several days before he was able to do so.

Detective Jenson looked sad as usual, a little world-weary, but like the faithful old bloodhound he so resembled, ready to take on the world. "I would've given you a call in the next hour or so. I'd asked the board of directors to keep everyone out of the attic until we'd processed some of our information, but now we need someone back in there. Someone associated with the house. It might just have been mischief, but the only way we'll discover who created the mess up in the Tarleton-Dandridge attic is to discover if anything's missing. Everyone I've spoken with is totally mystified. Nathan Pierson said he was pretty sure no one would find any illegal substances. Now, as I say, I'd like to get one of the historical staff back in there. To be honest, it wouldn't be much of a priority for the department if it weren't for the dead boy—and the fact that the medical examiner hasn't made any kind of statement." Detective Jenson paused for a moment. "I'm surprised they've got the feds on something like this, although I have heard a little about your group. Got to admit I don't quite understand it."

"Don't worry. Those of us involved don't always understand it, either, but we get results," Tyler said. He liked Jenson and liked dealing with him. The man didn't seem at all territorial and didn't argue with someone else taking care of a crime that *might* have been a prank and a murder that *might* have been an accident.

"I'll bring Ms. Leigh back in to start putting the attic in order. She's apparently more or less in charge of the other guides," Tyler told him. "She can decide whether to bring in her coworkers."

Jenson nodded. He glanced down, his expression strange, and then he looked up at Tyler again. "It was the damnedest thing. Finding that young man—it almost looked as if he was resting his chin on the musket except that the bayonet had gone through his chin and there was blood everywhere. His eyes were still wide open and he was staring at the wall. I have to tell you, I've seen a lot in my years on the force here, but that young man…" His voice trailed off and then he focused on Tyler and shrugged. "Nothing wrong with the feds taking over on this, not the way I see it."

Tyler thanked him for his help and left the station. He called Allison's cell on his way but she didn't answer.

She'd probably seen his name on her caller ID.

After going to the store, he'd stop by her place before returning to the Tarleton-Dandridge House.

Allison went to Starbucks and ordered a latte with two extra shots, since it might not be easy to stay awake today.

She hovered there, wishing she'd had the presence of mind to bring her laptop or iPad, anything she might

have played with so she could have joined those casually enjoying their coffee.

There was only so long she could linger. She felt
restless.

What she needed was a shot of courage, not just caf-
feine. She'd seen Dr. "What do *you* think?" Blount and
now she really had to go home.

But despite her stern resolution, she parked her car
in the driveway at her house and then wandered the
historic district, staying away from the walk down
Chestnut that would bring her back to the Tarleton-
Dandridge.

Hovering near Independence Hall, staring up at the
redbrick building that still brought her a little thrill
every time she saw it, she heard a teenage boy talking to another.

"Me! I'd be Patrick Henry, if I was a founding father!
He was cool. He was so fierce. He stood right in that
building and said, 'Give me liberty or give me death!'"

Allison winced, wondering if she should play the
eternal teacher and tell the boy that Patrick Henry had
indeed said those words but not at Independence Hall.
He'd spoken his fiery rhetoric to the Virginia Conven-
tion at St. John's Church in Richmond.

She was startled when the teen shivered as though
he'd felt a sudden blast of cold air. Then he turned and
stared at Allison, not as if he'd known she was there,
but as if he'd been searching for someone—anyone—
to be near him.

He seemed about sixteen, a handsome kid, the kind
teenage girls would definitely find appealing.

"Hi," he said, frowning as he looked at her. The
brother or friend he was with seemed troubled, as well.

"Hi. Where are you from?" Allison asked him.

He made a face. "Indiana."

She laughed. "What's wrong with Indiana?"

"I live in a cornfield."

"Well, we need corn. By the way, I was listening to you, and I'm a huge Patrick Henry fan, too. But guess what? Although I love Philly and I'd like to think most of our brilliant quotes come from speeches here, he said those words in Richmond, Virginia."

"Yeah?" The boy didn't seem angry about being corrected. "Maybe that explains it."

"Explains what?"

"The cold."

"The cold?" she repeated.

"Yeah, I felt something cold touch me when I said it. Hey, maybe Patrick Henry is running around here!" he said happily. "Maybe he's a ghost, and he didn't like that I'd made a mistake."

Allison shook her head. "He's buried at Red Hill, in Virginia, his family home, the last place he lived. It's beautiful there. If I were Patrick Henry and still running around, I think I'd be there. He really loved Virginia and, back then, they were 'statesmen.' The events at Independence Hall turned the Colonies into states and the states into a nation."

"I heard about that," the other boy said. "I heard the politicians fought back. That Thomas Jefferson had a hard time writing the Declaration of Independence and that he had to word it so all the representatives from all the colonies would be happy."

"Yup. Can you imagine trying to do that today? Back then, there were only thirteen states. Now we have fifty," Allison said. She was surprised the boys were listening to her, and she was happy they were old enough to be exploring on their own—and that they seemed to care about history. She also liked their companionship at the moment. She found she could even smile and say, "Hmm, maybe if anyone's running around here, it's Gouverneur Morris."

"Governor who?" the younger one asked.

"Not governor. *Gouverneur.* That was the man's name," Allison said. "He was born in New York City but he spent a lot of time here, helping to form the nation. While Thomas Jefferson was drafting the Declaration of Independence, Morris was busy working on the Constitution. He was an interesting man, if you want to look up one of the founding fathers who isn't as well known as Jefferson or Patrick Henry. He lost out a few times for trying to create a more centralized government. While many of the others were thinking mostly about states' rights, Morris already saw that we needed to band together to really make things work. He was antislavery, as were most of the founding fathers, but that was one issue they were afraid to touch just then. In his later life, he was a peg-legged old curmudgeon, but he was pretty remarkable."

"I'd like to be in government," the younger boy said. "First, I'd make a law that everybody has to be nice to everyone else, no matter where they came from. Because the United States is made up of people who came from other places, right?"

"Yes, and that's very commendable."

"Then I'd stop them from killing whales and wolves and baby seals, and I'd make people use their blinkers when they're driving!"

Allison started to laugh at that, but the laughter died in her throat. She blinked. Someone was strolling across the grounds, coming toward Independence Hall, wearing a period costume.

It was Julian Mitchell. She could see him plainly, just as she'd seen him in her home and at the Tarleton-Dandridge House.

He stood behind the boys.

"I really have to talk to you," he said. "Please, Allison."

She felt herself growing dizzy, darkness encroaching. She fought the feeling.

"You're not there," she whispered. "You are a product of my stressed-out imagination."

"Huh?" the boy said. "I'm right here. I'm Toby Gray. This is my buddy, Hudson."

The kids looked at her, visibly frightened.

Of course. There was a dead man standing behind them.

No, the kids were afraid of *her!*

"I'm Allison," she said, trying to be polite. "Nice to meet you."

She turned and hurried in the direction of her house. She felt the cold follow her.

Allison began to move more quickly. By the time she got home, she was running. She'd left the gates to the driveway and the front walk open, and she tore along the path, nearly tripping up the steps to her porch.

Her fingers shook when she put the key in the lock. She burst into the house, slammed the door and leaned against it. A sigh of relief escaped her as she looked toward the plush wingback chair in her parlor. There was no one there.

For several long moments she continued to lean against the door, breathing hard. As last, she walked toward the kitchen. Her hands were shaking when she took the bottle of whiskey from the cabinet. Pouring a shot, she drank it down in a flash.

And then she saw him again. He walked through the door. He didn't open it to come in; he just appeared inside, coming toward her once again.

She poured another shot. The whiskey dripped over her fingers and sloshed around in the glass. She managed to get some in, and swallowed the second shot.

"Allison, please."

"You can say *please* all you want. I don't see you! You are a product of my imagination, of your terrible death—what the hell were you *doing,* Julian? No, I don't see you. I can't see you. I don't mean to be cruel but you're dead and you're lying in the morgue and they won't even release your body yet."

"I know."

"So, quit talking to me! Get out of my mind. I was good to you, Julian. You were a jerk and I'm a nice person and I covered for you. We all did. I'm so sorry you're not going to live to be a rich and famous drummer and lead vocalist. Maybe you can do that in someone else's mind. Please, *please,* get out of mine."

"Allison—"

She poured another shot of whiskey, staring at him, gulping it down.

Ignore him. Just ignore him.

She walked out of the kitchen, stumbling against the wall. He only existed in her imagination, of course, but she gave him a wide berth, circling around him. Going over to her entertainment system, she turned on the television. She hit a Philly educational channel that was showing a reenactment of a meeting at Independence Hall.

The people in it were all dressed like Julian. She changed the channel, and then flicked it to music, playing a classic Beatles CD.

That done, she felt her knees grow weak. Her stomach was burning, her head spinning. She didn't drink that often and now three large whiskies were shooting through her with wicked repercussions.

Julian took a seat in the wingback chair again.

She looked at him and picked up a magazine. "I do not see you. You will go away."

She forced her attention onto the magazine. She felt a chill, a movement in the air, and something seemed to touch her knee. She finally raised her head.

Julian crouched in front of her, one hand resting lightly on her knee. Mesmerized, she gazed into his eyes. Julian had been a good-looking young man with deep green eyes and dark hair that curled over his brow—perfect for new-age rock music *and* for performing as a historical interpreter. When she wasn't annoyed with him, she'd always cared about him as she would a younger brother.

"Please, Allison, who else can I turn to? Please, see me. Help me."

Her tone was husky. "Julian, I can't help you. You're dead. I would've done anything. I was ready to perform CPR, but I could see from the doorway that…that you were gone. I could see the blood—oh, God, Julian, you hit a vein or an artery. There was so much blood. But you were staring at the wall. And you…."

She couldn't go on. Tears stung her eyes. Maybe that was it. She hadn't been able to really mourn a friend. Maybe she did feel guilty; maybe she felt she could have done more for him in life or prevented his death.

"Julian, how can I help you now?" she wailed.

"You *will* help me. I know you, Ally. Something in the house isn't right—and I *know* you'll figure out what it is!"

7

Tyler was surprised when Allison answered his next call, and more surprised when she said she'd go to the Tarleton-Dandridge House and start straightening up the attic whenever he wished. If he thought she needed help with that, she could call Annette or Jason or both.

She could have walked over but he was out, anyway, and had the car; he said he'd pick her up. She agreed.

He was a little shocked when he arrived at her house.

He tended to think of her as tall, elegant, classically beautiful, but reserved in many ways—as academics were often assumed to be. Of course, he'd first met her when she was costumed and in disarray and exhausted.

But tonight...

She opened the door with a strength that sent it banging against the wall. She watched it happen, then stared at him and grinned. "Whoops."

"Are you ready?" he asked her.

She looked all right. She was wearing jeans and a tailored shirt with a casual jacket; her hair was brushed—except for a few strands that seemed to be standing straight up on top of her head.

"I am so-o-o ready to get out of here!" she said.

"Okay." He nodded slowly.

"Oh! I should get my bag." But she remained standing there.

"Yes, you should," he said.

She turned to head back into the parlor. She bumped into the wall as she did.

He stepped inside, closing the door behind him.

"Allison, are you okay?"

"Fine. Oh, yeah, just fine," she said cheerfully.

He caught her by the shoulders when she'd picked up her purse and had come back to join him. "It's not that I know you well, but...you really don't seem to be *you* this evening."

"I'm the new me," she proclaimed.

It hit him then. Not the odor of booze, but rather the potent smell of a minty mouthwash.

"You've been drinking."

"We all drink. Water, staff of life. Wait, maybe that's bread."

"I think we should start in the morning," he said. "You should go to bed."

She shook her head. "No, no, I shouldn't go to bed. I should go with you. Too bad it's the Tarleton-Dandridge House—actually, too bad it's anywhere in Philly at the moment. But no, not staying here. Not tonight."

She was different. Very different.

Afraid.

He was thoughtful as she looked up at him hopefully.

"Really, I have to leave here. Now," she told him.

He didn't answer.

"Your people are coming tonight, aren't they? Your people!" She laughed. "I guess I made that sound as if you're all part of an alien nation or something. I didn't mean that. I meant, your coworkers are coming tonight."

"They're driving up. They'll probably get here late."

"I can't wait to meet them. Lots of people, right? Or several, at least."

"Yes, several people," he said. Tyler thought about the situation, somewhat amused. She wasn't exactly drunk, but she was pretty darned tipsy. He had a feeling it wasn't a condition with which she was really comfortable, and he wondered where she'd been or what she'd been doing to bring her to such a state.

She'd found a dead friend. That would do it for most people. She'd spent the night after finding Julian at the police station, being relentlessly questioned. Surely, her behavior now, her reaction, was quite normal.

"Yes, we'll go—first to a nice crowded restaurant with a coffee bar, and then to the house. How does that sound?"

She blinked and then smiled. "Restaurant, yes, that would be great. Food would be good. Oh, yes. Food."

He escorted her out onto the porch. "Allow me, please," he said politely, taking her keys to lock the house.

"Thank you," she said with great dignity.

"I have my car. I was shopping," he told her. "I'll have to stop by the Tarleton-Dandridge House to drop off a few perishables."

"Okay."

When he got to their destination, she was looking straight ahead.

"Do you want to wait in the car?" he asked.

She raised huge frightened eyes to his. *"Alone?"*

"Well, yes—if I'm leaving the car and you're waiting in it, you'd be alone."

"I'll come with you."

She stepped out of the car as he reached into the

backseat for the one plastic bag that held butter, milk, cheese and eggs.

She stared at the house.

"Ready?" he asked.

"Sure."

She followed him up the path to the house and waited behind him as he opened the door. She kept looking around nervously as if she expected someone to pop out from behind the closet door in the mudroom and shout, "Boo!"

Inside, he started to tell her he'd only be a minute. But she was right behind him, so close, in fact, that she was nearly touching him. When he walked into their employee room and bent down to open the refrigerator door, he nearly pushed her over by accident.

He reached out for her when she stumbled.

"You okay?" he asked.

"Just fine."

She was standing by him with her eyes closed.

"All right, we're leaving now."

"For the restaurant."

"Yes." He started to walk. She followed. She'd opened her eyes but only a slit—just enough not to crash into walls or furniture.

He decided to let it go for the moment. He felt her behind him—almost on top of him—as they exited the house. "You okay to walk to the restaurant?" he asked her.

"Of course!" she said with the indignant tone of one who wasn't really okay at all.

He took her arm. She didn't protest.

"There are so many places around here," he said.

"So many."

"Do you want to go to your friend's pub?" he asked.

She shook her head, flushing. "No, um, somewhere different tonight."

"Okay."

He knew it didn't matter where they went; she just wanted people to be there. He'd seen an Italian place that looked interesting down a side street and he headed toward it.

"Luigi's," she said.

"Is it any good?"

"Sure! Warm, friendly, always busy."

There were a number of people at the restaurant, but the staff seemed to handle the bustling activity well. They didn't have to wait more than a minute or two before they were seated at a table with a red checkered cloth.

He didn't give the waitress an opportunity to offer them a cocktail or wine. "Two coffees and waters please."

Allison didn't argue. She told him they prepared an extraordinary eggplant.

When the bread came, she was happy to devour a piece.

"Did you eat at all today?" he asked her.

She thought about it for a minute. "No."

"I don't want to tell you how to run your life or anything, but if you're going to swig booze, you really should add food to the mix."

She threw him an evil glare but didn't deny his words.

"What brought this on?" he asked.

"What brought what on?"

"Your apparent affair with a booze bottle."

She stiffened. "I'm twenty-eight, nearly twenty-nine. A responsible, voting citizen often charged with forming the minds of the coming generation. I am certainly entitled to a drink if I choose."

"Yes, you are. But I get the impression you don't drink heavily that often."

"I didn't drink heavily," she told him. "I drank quite casually and lightly."

"Alone?"

"Now that's rude and personal."

"So, all alone, you decided to get smashed."

"I am *not* smashed."

"True—I've seen worse. Actually, at various times in my life, I'm sure I've *been* worse. It just doesn't seem to be you."

"Ah, but you don't really know me!"

"The only thing I can tell you is that booze isn't going to make it go away."

"Make what go away?" she asked, frowning and intense.

Their server arrived; Allison ordered chicken with broccoli and ziti, while he chose the lasagna. He was glad to see that Allison quickly drank down the water. She set the empty glass on the table and picked up her coffee.

Tyler leaned toward her, placing his hand on hers. "It won't make the demons in your mind go away. They only get more vicious."

She jerked her hand back. "I have no demons in my mind. I lost a friend, okay? I was distressed by his death. I'm just having an off moment—or an off hour, or whatever. I'll be fine. And I don't know what you want at the Tarleton-Dandridge House. You can't change the past."

"No, you can't. But you *can* discover the truth about

it and sometimes the truth about the past can change the present or the future."

She sipped her coffee again, then pressed her fingers to her temples.

"After we've eaten, if you want, I can walk you back to your house and you can get some sleep," he said.

"No," she said firmly. "I want to be where you are." The last words were tremulous, and somehow, the tone of her voice seemed to seep into his bones, his bloodstream. She was a beautiful woman, tall, slim, elegant. The blue of her eyes seemed like a deep sea, sparkling as if it lay beneath a brilliant sun. He couldn't help being affected.

Tyler raised his brows, studying her. He knew he was attractive to the opposite sex, but he was sure she hadn't suddenly decided that she cared for him and would be lost without him by her side. Something had unnerved her.

And he realized that he yearned to help.

"Okay. You want to be with me."

She wagged a finger at him. "Your Krewe is coming."

"Yes, they are." He hesitated. "I think you'll like them. Logan Raintree heads up my unit. He's an ex-Ranger like me. He's now officially engaged to Kelsey O'Brien, who used to be a U.S. Marshal. Kelsey has a cousin on our Krewe, Sean Cameron, who's a whiz with cameras and special effects. We have Jane Everett, an artist, who can take a spoken description of someone and turn it into something that's almost an absolute likeness. And..." He shrugged. "Our last Krewe member is Kat Sokolov."

"She's an artist? A vocal recognition specialist? A forensics guru?" Allison asked.

"She's...a medical examiner," Tyler said.

"Will she see Julian?"

"Yes."

Their meals were put before them and Tyler thanked their server. Allison picked up her fork, pushing her food around.

"You really should eat," he told her.

"Yes, I'm eating, I'm eating!" she said, spearing a piece of broccoli as if to prove it. She was beginning to sound fine again.

When she'd finished—consuming everything on her plate—he offered her a few ibuprofen caplets to minimize the headache that seemed to be coming on.

She took them with a second glass of water and then sipped her third cup of coffee.

Again, he set a hand on hers. This time, she didn't pull away. "I can help you," he said.

She nodded. "You're a decent person, and I appreciate it. But I have to help myself." She sat straighter, appearing more controlled than she had been, her tone suggesting it was business as usual.

"Well, if you want any of us to help you in any way, just say the word."

She smiled—a real smile. A sincere smile. "Thank you. I do feel much better. You've helped me already."

"So, what would you be doing if we weren't investigating the house? If it was your day off?"

"Since I'm not teaching right now, you mean? Research and writing."

"About the house?"

"Academics need to publish."

"I know. You're working on the history of the house?" he asked.

"Not the house itself. Well, in a way. I'm doing a

study of the British occupation, and the social and political ramifications. The situation between Lucy Tarleton and Beast Bradley and his relationship with the Tarleton-Dandridge family are an excellent example of the complex political climate at the time. That we won the Revolution was pretty much a miracle, you know. The British had the finest fighting forces, on land and sea. Taking nothing away from George Washington's abilities—he had no money, deserting troops and he was facing horrendous firepower—we were losing more battles than we were winning. That's why I admire the founding fathers. Signing that declaration made you a dead man if you were apprehended, but so many signed it, knowing they were up against unbelievable odds. I wonder if I could have done it," she admitted.

"So the work you're doing is on Beast Bradley."

She picked up her coffee cup. "I started researching him more or less by accident. The story that we know has been handed down, more oral history and even legend than anything. Oh, the foundations are fact—Beast Bradley did take over the house, the Tarleton family did pretend to be Loyalist during that period and Lucy Tarleton was murdered there. But I couldn't find anything written about the event that wasn't secondhand. I realize Lucy couldn't have told the story herself, but Angus never wrote about it. The first person to put anything on paper was the first Dandridge to own the house—Sophia's husband, Tobias."

"There have to be more records somewhere, letters, something," Tyler said.

"I'm sure there are. They just have to be hunted down. I had figured I'd try to get to a few places where they've preserved letters and journals from the period. I'd thought about taking a trip to Valley Forge and maybe one to Saratoga. I was hoping I could find more information, particularly at Valley Forge. I've been in touch with an amateur historian there who's really interested in this period. We know Lucy went from the house to Valley Forge several times during the occupation. She must have been acquainted with a number of the men there. She was being a patriotic angel of mercy and brought through anything she could—shoes, bandages, blankets—things that were desperately needed. Of course, her main mission was to provide information, so what she could sneak through the barricades was limited. She must have been a truly heroic and sympathetic woman."

"I'm very curious about the two paintings," he said.

"The paintings in Lucy's bedroom and in Angus's study?" Allison asked. "They *are* very different. The one in Lucy's bedroom is rather surprising, but that's where the Dandridge family had it, and supposedly, it'd been there since the British occupation."

"Don't you think that's odd?"

"Yes, but we never really know why people do what they do," Allison said. "Unless they tell us, and even then…" She started to lift her cup; it clattered as it fell back into the saucer.

"What's wrong?" Tyler asked. She'd seen something behind him. He turned to look.

There were other diners, nothing more.

She stared down at the table.

"Allison?"

She shook her head, then picked up her cup again. Her fingers were long and elegant with silvery polish on the nails. She held her cup firmly, almost tightly enough to snap off the handle. "Can we go now?"

"Of course." He gestured at the waiter, then quickly

paid the check when it came. He escorted her from the restaurant with his hand on her back. She seemed to want to be touched; again, he wasn't lacking in self-confidence, but he didn't think she was dying to be in his arms.

As they walked, he began to smile. He'd seen it before—he'd *been* there before, right where she was now. *Seeing those he should not see.*

Allison was seeing a ghost.

If he suggested it, she'd deny it. She'd give him psychological explanations.

But she was afraid.

"I went to the hospital today," he said.

"Oh!" She flashed him a guilty look. "I should have gone by. How is Mr. Dixon? How's Haley—and the boys?"

"The boys weren't there. Mr. Dixon's condition is unchanged. Haley seems to be holding up fairly well."

"I do need to see those kids."

"Tomorrow, maybe. I know they'd appreciate it. But I believe Todd in particular will appreciate that you're going through the house. He's convinced you're the key to making his father better."

"But I'm not!" She looked at him earnestly. "Tyler, honestly, how could I help? Even if I were one of those crazy dial-a-psychic people and thought I could have a conversation with every soul who ever spent time in the house, how could that help Mr. Dixon?"

"Coma is a complex condition, and it can be brought on by so many things. Kat is our medical specialist, but she's the first to remind us all that, so far, science has shown that the human brain's capacity is far greater than we use. There may be scientific answers that coincide with a great deal of what we consider to be paranormal. Maybe just talking to Mr. Dixon will bring him back. I've heard of cases where someone's been in a coma for an unknown reason for years—and then come back. No matter how far we think we've gotten in our technological age, there are many things we have yet to understand."

"I just don't want to encourage Todd to believe I can create some kind of miracle for him."

"Just assure him that you'll try."

They reached the Tarleton-Dandridge House and Tyler opened the gate and the door, keying in the alarm. Allison followed closely behind him.

"So, shall we go up to the attic?" he asked.

"I guess we should."

She didn't want to look toward Angus Tarleton's study, and he didn't blame her. The police would be sending a crime scene cleanup crew in the next few days, but at this point her friend's blood still stained the floor.

They climbed the stairs to the second story. Tyler had been repeatedly drawn to the painting in Lucy's room; he saw that Allison lingered just outside in the hallway, studying it.

"He doesn't look so evil here," she said. "He looks… contemplative, or thoughtful, almost as if he's carrying a heavy burden and is sorry for what must be."

"A far kinder artist," Tyler agreed.

"Which image do you think is the real one?"

"I imagine a little of both. We all know that good people can do bad things, and people we consider to be *bad* can do good things. And every human being is a mixture of virtues and faults."

He was surprised when she grinned at him. "You're all right, you know."

He grinned back. "So you've said."

"No, really, you've been exceptionally kind when I was pretty argumentative or...or strange."

"Ma'am, my pleasure."

"Were you a cowboy?"

"My family might have owned cows at one time," he said, "but I never had any. I can ride like a demon, though, and I love horses."

"Straight shooter?" she teased.

"My aim is damned good, if I do say so myself."

They continued to the attic. For a moment, they paused in the doorway, examining the wreckage. Then Tyler stepped in, first lifting up the printer and computer and moving papers so they'd have a place to start.

Allison went down on her knees, trying to gather up the slew of papers that covered the floor. He knelt beside her, collecting other ones and giving them to her to sort. "I think these are some kind of reservation sheets," he said.

"They are. If you can look for those, I'll try to gather the research papers. Oh, and that journal can go back on the desk. It's petty-cash payouts. Lord! The tiny scraps all over are receipts for cleaning supplies, coffee... Things the employees pick up but that the corporation pays for."

"I'll get all of that stuff. The research is mostly yours?"

"Mostly. But everyone who works here—or worked here," she added, "loved the history and was interested in it. If my coworkers came across an article or theory regarding the family or the house or even the British in Philly, they made a point of sending me the link or getting me a copy."

Tyler found sheets ripped from an educational magazine. The headline read Lord Brian Bradley. True Beast or Passionate Loyalist?

He sat down to read the article. It began with the basics: Brian Bradley was from a noble Yorkshire family with ties to the Royal House of Hanover. His service to the British military and the Crown started when he was barely out of his teens. He'd been promoted to the rank of general soon after the beginning of the conflict with the Americans and he'd been ordered to the city of Philadelphia to control the intelligence slipping out— and gain it for the British. Angus Tarleton's house was considered one of the finest in the city, so it was natural that an important figure in an occupying force should take the mansion. The Tarletons professed their allegiance to the Crown and were allowed to host the general and several members of his retinue. It was likely that the family did resent the fact that the general took over the master chamber; Susannah Tarleton, Angus's wife, had died in 1774, but Angus was asked to vacate his chamber and move into another room in the house. He was said to have done as requested graciously.

As he read Tyler realized that Allison had grown quiet. He looked over to see her staring at the door.

"What is it?" he asked her.

She didn't hear him at first.

"Allison."

She glanced at him, startled.

"What do you see?"

She shook her head. "Nothing."

"Are you okay?"

She managed a weak smile. "Fine."

Tyler frowned, but he couldn't drag anything else out of her. He returned to the article.

"While popular legend had it that 'Beast' Bradley

took suspected patriot spies out to the woods and executed them," he read, "there is no record or proof of this action. When the British fled the city and victory was at last proclaimed, twenty citizens were charged with treason and two executed, but by the patriots, not the British. While Bradley was required to interrogate prisoners, there is no known record of any of his interrogations causing the death of those questioned, nor does legend name any names. Whether Bradley did or didn't murder Lucy Tarleton in her own home is up for debate, since the story seems to be part of family lore. Therefore, this researcher finds the popular accepted version of her death suspect. Lucy Tarleton is buried in the family cemetery on the grounds of the Tarleton-Dandridge House and, not surprisingly, has been seen 'haunting' the property."

Tyler felt an unnatural stillness around him; he looked up again. Allison was frozen, staring at the entrance, where the stairs from the second floor came up to the attic.

He looked in the same direction. There was nothing there.

He set down his reading, rose and walked over to her, reaching down for her hands, urging her to rise.

She took his hands, gazing up at him blankly and then with a question in her eyes.

"Break time. How about a walk outside? I haven't seen much of the grounds."

She stood, her knees wobbly.

She nodded. "We can get out for a few minutes," she said. "It's pretty out there. At one time, of course, there were acres and acres. Now there's just the kitchen, the stables and the cemetery. The cemetery is nice, and the family vault is beautiful. There are other burials and entombments out there, too, and if family members die, they can still be entombed in one of the above- or belowground vaults. The specs for it are held at the offices of Old Philly History."

She seemed to need to speak; she was going on and on about the property. He set a finger against her lips, looking down into her eyes. "What is it you're seeing?"

He thought he heard something. A man's whisper.

"Tell him. Just tell him!"

Allison groaned.

"Allison, you see someone. I can hear him. Who is it?"

She looked beyond him, to the doorway. Her words were anguished as she spoke to the person Tyler had yet to see. "Stop it! Stop it, please stop it, Julian. You're a figment of my imagination, not *his*."

Tyler turned to the doorframe. Slowly, he began to see the figure of a young man. Julian Mitchell had been good-looking with a cocky flair to his appearance. He leaned into the room casually but in life, Tyler thought with some amusement, he'd probably practiced his stance in the mirror.

"Allison, come on. I can't do much about who does or doesn't see me. I tried knocking the hat off a nasty old lady who was giving a waitress grief at that restaurant tonight and it didn't work—although I did give her a bit of a chill. But I *know* you see me clearly, that you hear every word I say," the ghost told her.

"Yes, don't you get it? I see you. I'm feeling guilty— though I have no idea why! I covered for your sorry ass a dozen times, and I always tried to show up when you had a performance. We were good friends, Julian, you know we were!" Allison said. Then she clapped a hand over her mouth and turned to face Tyler.

"I am so sorry. I don't know what's wrong with me. I went to a shrink this morning, and he told me I'm creating Julian in my mind. Because I think I should have saved him, or that I might have been a better friend, or...I don't know. He's like a plague! He won't go away. He was at my house, then he was here, then he was at Independence Hall.... He's everywhere! I can't get away from him."

She was so distressed, so fragile and, seemingly, so broken. Tyler pulled her into his arms and said, "It's all right. It's really all right."

He spoke to the young man standing in the doorway. "Surely, there's a better way to do this! Allison was a good friend to you, and now you're doing *this* to her?"

Julian Mitchell's ghost had the grace to look apologetic.

"I have to, don't you see? I have to, because I don't know what happened, and I'm walking in this new world—this world of death!—alone. But I didn't kill myself, and it wasn't an accident."

He left the doorframe and walked toward them.

"I need help!" he said, an edge of desperation in his voice.

Allison frowned at Tyler. "You see him? You don't have to humor me!"

Tyler smiled and stroked her cheek. "You didn't want us here because you said we were ghost busters. You thought we were all about sensationalism and cheap thrills. That's not it, Allison. We try to help the living—*and* the dead."

"And you have to help *me,*" Julian said. "I was murdered."

"Who did it?" Tyler asked.

"That's what you have to find out!" Julian Mitchell shook his head irritably. He sank down to the floor in his period dress. "I don't *know* who or how—all I know is that it has something to do with that god-awful painting of Beast Bradley in Angus Tarleton's study."

8

Allison wasn't sure whether or not she felt reassured. According to Tyler, she wasn't going crazy....

But now it seemed that on the day Julian Mitchell died, she'd stepped out of anything resembling a normal life—and straight into an episode of that old TV show *The Twilight Zone*.

In the few beats of silence following Julian's dramatic statement, they were all startled by the loud and strident ring of Tyler's phone.

He fumbled in his pocket and found his cell. "Montague!...Yes, yes, I'll be right there." He clicked off the phone.

"The Krewe members are here," he said. "I've got to run down and open the gate and let them into the house."

"Krewe members?" To Allison's astonishment, Julian began to vanish into thin air.

"They're like us, Julian," Tyler said quickly. "They know. They see."

"Are you sure?" Julian asked, his image fading in and out.

"I have to go let them in," Tyler said again.

"I'm coming with you!" Allison told him, staring

wide-eyed at the place where Julian seemed solid and then not, there and then not.

"Ally!" Julian said, using her nickname in a broken plea. "Ally, I don't want to hurt you. I just want help."

"We'll *all* go down," Tyler said with an exasperated sigh. "Might as well make the introductions—all of them."

He headed for the door; Allison started to follow and then stopped for a minute. Julian was suddenly the same man he'd always been to her. A little brother, someone with whom she was often frustrated and still cared about a great deal. He was in costume, a performer as always, in death as in life. Selfish—he just was!—but not cruel or evil or even aware of the trouble or aggravation he caused others.

He'd come to her for help a thousand times in life.

It wasn't so unusual, perhaps, that he had done so now.

"Julian, come on, let's meet the others. From what I understand, these are the people who can help you."

He looked at her and seemed solid again. He nodded. They might both have found courage at the same time.

Tyler had gone down the stairs. With renewed composure, Allison followed him. Julian, she felt certain, was behind her. She could *feel* him.

Allison waited in the grand entry while Tyler went through the mudroom, leaving the front door ajar while he hurried out to open the gate. She heard easy conversation and the sound of luggage and bags scraping on the brick walkway and then Tyler's team started to come in. The first through the doorway was Tyler; next was a tall, striking dark-haired man of mixed Native American and European descent, then a tall blonde woman, a tiny blonde woman, a slender dark-haired

woman with a stunning face and another tall man with
sandy hair and light eyes. Tyler began the introductions:
Logan Raintree, their team head, was accompanied by
the tall blonde, Kelsey O'Brien, once a U.S. Marshal.
The tiny blonde was Kat Sokolov, medical pathologist,
the tall man with the light eyes was Sean Cameron,
computer and camera expert, and the pretty brunette
was Jane Everett, forensic artist.

Allison shook hands with all and greeted them. They
seemed very normal. The introductions were so pleasant she might have been meeting them at a casual party.
She thought they were a group she would have *enjoyed*
meeting at a party.

"Sean, the big case is the camera equipment?" Tyler
asked.

"Yes, I figured we'd put the computers and the
screens somewhere central, like here in this hallway. I
can set up the cameras in whichever rooms you want,"
Sean told him.

"Have you discovered anything? Can you bring us
up to speed?" Logan asked.

"Wait, wait, please!" Kelsey O'Brien held up one
hand. "Ms. Leigh, can you show me the restroom? It's
been a long drive."

"These guys don't like to stop once they're on the
road," Jane Everett said.

"I would've stopped!" Logan protested.

"If he'd actually noticed that one of us was speaking." Kat smiled at Allison. "Logan gets into think-
mode the minute we're on our way anywhere."

"A public restroom was put in right there, beneath
the stairs," Allison said, directing Kelsey. "There's also
a small restroom in the break area—used to be a pantry—and there's a shower stall in there, too. That's

it—oh, except for another small restroom out by the stables. We only have the one shower. But, of course, any of you are welcome to spend time at my house for a longer shower or a better night's sleep, if necessary."

"That's very kind of you, Ms. Leigh," Logan said. He looked at Tyler, slowly arching a brow. "There's one introduction you haven't made. Is Ms. Leigh aware…?"

"Of Julian Mitchell?" Tyler asked. "Julian, I'm pretty sure you just heard all the intros. Want to become a little more visible?"

To Allison's amazement, she heard Julian's voice, almost like a distorted echo—and almost shy.

Julian! Suddenly shy.

"I'm not that good at this yet," he said. "But, um, yes, how do you do? And welcome to the Tarleton-Dandridge House."

"Hello," Logan murmured, and the others did the same.

"You've been perfectly good at showing yourself to me and scaring me out of my wits and sanity," Allison said. "Please," she told the others, "don't get the impression that Julian is any kind of shrinking violet."

"Ally!" Julian said. His form began to appear.

"You were killed here, Julian?" Logan asked quietly, glancing at Tyler.

"Julian and I met just before you arrived," Tyler explained.

Logan nodded. "Five-minute bathroom break," he said. "Everyone back in here, and we'll talk to Julian and get set up."

"Ah, the one benefit!" Julian now appeared fully before them all, still in his Colonial splendor.

"What's that?" Sean Cameron asked.

"I don't need a bathroom break anymore." Julian tried to say the words jokingly. It didn't work.

There was such sadness in his voice that they were all silent. Tyler stood close to him, setting a hand lightly in the air where Julian's shoulder seemed to be. It was evident to Allison that Tyler had known the dead before. His movement was in no way awkward; his hand didn't sit there lamely, but really seemed to touch the spirit of the dead man. "The human body is fragile, Julian. And with it comes frailty and pain. The soul is on a higher plane and yet it can still feel the torture of grief and loss, but there's a place of peace and beauty, too. We've learned that, we've seen it. And we'll get you there."

"Please, yes," Julian said softly. Then he grinned and stepped back as if embarrassed by his weakness. "Bathroom break! Then I'll tell you what I know!"

"You know who did this?" Kelsey asked him.

"Yes—no. I heard a voice and I saw—"

"You saw what?" Tyler broke in.

"The painting. It was Beast Bradley. I saw him come alive in the painting, and I heard him speak to me."

Paintings don't speak! Allison longed to cry.

But she remained silent.

"What did he say?" Tyler asked.

"He said, 'It's time for you to die, boy. It's time for you to die.'"

Tyler's team was efficient. After Julian spoke, they moved about, Kelsey running for the restroom, Sean opening equipment and Tyler himself directing the others so they could rearrange the foyer in a way that would allow them to gather there. He thought Allison seemed tense as they shifted things around; Logan noticed and assured her that they were being very careful.

She laughed. "We're trying to solve the death of a dear friend and I'm worried about historical preservation. I *am* crazy."

"We respect that," Logan said with a glimmer of a smile.

Allison, Tyler was glad to see, had relaxed. She'd accepted the fact that she did see Julian—and that others saw him, too.

That was kind of a pity, he mused. It was nice when she'd seemed to need him for strength. Now, she had her *self* back. She was confident again. Maybe this was the best scenario; she'd lost the hostility she'd had toward him and his crew. She was part of the investigation now, and that was good. They needed her.

Still, it *was* really nice when she'd clung to him!

He shook off the thought. Sean had nearly completed their setup of a video monitoring system. And a place where they could all talk had now been arranged. The sofa Allison had slept on was part of the circle, along with a few of the chairs brought in from the dining room and a big wingback that stood near the stairway. Julian Mitchell had chosen that chair. He was either being courteous or playing his part as a colonist; he waited until the women were seated to take his own chair.

Logan nodded toward Tyler, since he was the lead investigator here.

"Julian, what exactly happened? I went to check out the painting. It's a strange portrait, done by Tobias Dandridge. He must have been an accomplished artist, and he also hated Beast Bradley, that's for certain. But I didn't find anything about the painting that would make you think it was alive or that it had moved," Tyler said.

"I'm telling you, the eyes were looking at me. Of course, the way the damned thing is painted, it always seems to be looking at you. But that afternoon when I sat down, it was...more than that. He was *staring* at me. And then I heard him speaking," Julian said.

"Where the hell had you been all day?" Allison asked.

He shrugged apologetically. "Okay, so there was an audition to open for a major concert coming to Philadelphia. They wanted a local band, and we'd made it past the first auditions. I didn't know until that morning, I swear!" he told Allison. "So I snuck out after lunch. I came back in at the tail end of your last tour, and while you were with one of the kids, I went up to the attic to wait until it was over. I heard everyone leaving and I knew you were locking up, so I slipped down to Angus's study to talk to you and apologize and suck up. If I could get you to forgive me, the others would, too."

Tyler saw that Julian gazed at Allison with yearning and hope, praying she'd forgive him, even now. Apparently, she was always the "nice guy," the one the others turned to, the responsible one.

"Everyone's forgiven you every single time, Julian," she said quietly. "This time, of course...well, everyone wants to tell you how sorry they are."

Julian let out a little sound that was like a sob.

Allison reached over to touch him, but she wasn't accustomed to ghosts and her hand fell—heavily—through the air. She flushed and said, "We do love you, Julian, no matter what. And remember, none of us is meant to stay on this earth forever."

"What then, Julian?" Tyler asked.

"I was sitting back in old Angus's chair, just waiting, and I saw something in the painting. The eyes were *alive,* and then the painting spoke…. That was when I felt my chin go over the bayonet and I felt this raw agony. My head felt like it had been hit by a hammer. I remember trying to scream but it was impossible. I was cold and then I realized that I was staring at myself and that I wasn't actually *in* myself anymore… The room was silent and I looked at the blood on the floor and I knew it was mine. Then everything went black." He paused for a minute, inhaling on a deep breath. "I heard Ally scream. And I watched as she sank against the door. Then she fumbled in her pockets for her phone and called 9-1-1 and just sat there, crying."

"Did you see anyone else?" Tyler asked. "After your chin fell on the bayonet and you started bleeding to dea—" He stopped abruptly. "Was there anyone else in the room with you?"

Julian was thoughtful. "Bleeding to death. I'm dead. No way out of it. No, I didn't see anyone. It was as if I couldn't look away from the painting." He frowned. "Wait! I think—I could be wrong—I think I sensed some kind of movement. Someone…skirting around the desk to the door into the music room. There *was* someone with me!"

"Any idea who it was?" Logan asked him.

Julian nodded. "Well, I guess it had to be Beast Bradley, right? I was looking at his picture."

"Pictures don't kill," Allison insisted.

"Nor do the spirits of those who haunt a house," Tyler said. "They can create ill will, they can make a place uncomfortable, but they can't come out of a painting and force your head down on a bayonet. Not that I know of."

"In our experience," Logan explained to Julian, "it's human beings using ghost stories who do the killing."

"There was *something* about that painting," Julian said stubbornly.

"Let's get the painting," Allison suggested.

Tyler looked at her, surprised that she was going to condone taking down a historic piece of art.

Then again, sitting next to a ghost could change a person's mind on what was the right thing to do.

"I'll go get it," Sean said. "Carefully," he added, smiling at Allison.

He disappeared into Angus Tarleton's study and quickly reappeared, holding the painting gingerly. He set it against the sofa and hunkered down to look at it.

"Good piece," he said.

"But there's nothing unusual about the painting, is there?" Tyler asked. He stood beside Sean, studying the work. He knew he was the best shot in their crowd, that he could bail them out in a melee and that, thanks to his college years, he also comprehended a fair amount of science and the preservation of evidence.

But Sean was their expert on visual tricks, film and computers.

Sean shook his head. "It's excellently done. The artist was a master at capturing expression and especially at painting eyes. But…it's a painting."

"I'm telling you, it moved—and it talked," Julian said. "Or Beast Bradley did." He turned to Allison. "I'm irresponsible and I've been an idiot lots of times, but you know I don't lie or make things up. The man in this painting moved."

"Could the painting have been switched?" Tyler mused.

"I don't know how," Allison said. "The board was

here most of the day. They left when I was doing the last tour."

"Yes, I was back in the house when they were leaving," Julian said. He laughed dryly. "I didn't even have my musket and bayonet when I listened to them leave. I went to the closet to get it. I wanted to be in full character when I tried to cajole you into forgiving me," he told Allison. "I thought you'd find that charming," he said sheepishly. "Or proof of my sincerity. Or...something."

"All right, so the board was here—the four of them—in the attic office. They left. You were on the second level?" Logan asked.

"I was on the second level, yes, dodging between the two tours. I followed Jason's tour into the house and went upstairs while he was in the grand salon. I was in Lucy Tarleton's bedroom while I waited for the board members to go downstairs. After that I was up in the attic for a while. By the way, that's great stuff you're doing on Lucy and her movements during the war, Allison. Anyhow, when the last tour went out and Jason and Allison were over in the pantry area behind the dining room, I snuck into Angus Tarleton's study." He paused, eyes widening. "Weird! I felt like someone had gone up to the attic after me, kind of like I was being followed."

Allison shook her head. "There aren't any secret panels, hidden rooms or anything like that here," she said.

"Yes, but I was running around the house with a couple of dozen people in it, and you didn't find me," Julian reminded her.

"That's true," Allison murmured. Then she looked up at them and said, "There *is* one other way to get from the ground floor to the second—through a servants' stairway beyond a door in the pantry. I don't know if anyone's ever taken it or not. We never used it. You can only access it through the pantry, which is our employee area, and guests aren't allowed in there. The door on the second floor opens just beside the master bedroom."

"Shall we take a look?" Tyler suggested.

"We can do that now," Logan said, glancing at his watch. "Then we should finish unloading and setting up, have something to eat and let Allison go home and get some rest."

They rose, but Julian sat stubbornly.

"You're not going to let this slide, are you? Decide that I was stoned or something and tell everyone it was an accident? I was *murdered.* I'm not lying. My head was pushed down on that bayonet. It happened while I was staring at the painting. I was murdered."

"We have a long way to go here," Logan said.

"*Were* you stoned?" Kat asked him. "I'm sorry, but I'm a medical examiner, and I'll be checking out your autopsy report tomorrow. And your remains."

Julian stood, looking at Kat. "I had a few tokes of pot. Hey, I was at an audition! I wasn't drinking or any-thing." He frowned. "*You're* an M.E.?"

She nodded.

Julian shrugged. "Well, I guess if someone's going to be playing around with my body, I won't mind so much if it's you."

"Julian!" Allison chastised. She turned back to the others. "I'll show you the back stairway."

She told them that once a week a cleaning crew came in—a carefully selected cleaning crew—to dust the fragile historic pieces.

But when they followed her through the pantry,

which was a tight squeeze with the seven of them and the spiritual remains of Julian Mitchell, they discovered that the servants' stairway was extremely dusty.

"They haven't been in here for a while," Allison said. "We'll have to go one at a time. It's narrow and has a sharp angle."

Tyler brought up the rear as they climbed up. The servants' stairway led to a very small landing by a door, which opened into the hallway next to the master bedroom.

"This hasn't been disturbed," Logan said. "Well, we're on the second floor. We might as well decide on bedrooms."

"I've been in the master," Tyler said. "But I'll get my stuff out. There's more room in there for you and Kelsey. In fact, if no one has a problem with it, I'll move into Lucy's room."

Allison seemed tense as she watched them choose their rooms. Sean said he thought maybe he'd just take his sleeping bag up to the attic. Jane and Kat opted to stay together in Sophia Tarleton-Dandridge's bedroom.

"How are you?" Tyler asked.

"Fine."

"She's scared." Julian was standing behind Allison as if protecting her in a brotherly fashion.

"I was scared of you!"

"I don't think you should be alone," Julian said.

"Why? I just told you—*you* were the one scaring me. Now that I know you're real—well, not *real,* but real in terms of being a ghost—I'm not scared anymore."

Julian placed his hands on her shoulders. Tyler saw her jump slightly, feeling the strange physical sensation of being "touched" by a ghost. "They'll let you stay here. There are two bedrooms left on this floor. Allison, whoever killed me might be after you."

"Why would anyone be after me?"

"Why would anyone have killed me?" Julian demanded. "Well, sure, you probably all said at one time or another that you wanted to kill me, but you didn't mean it. Think about it, Ally—why would anyone kill me? It wasn't my voice or my guitar playing, I swear!"

Tyler was glad to see her smile at that.

"This is a historic property, Julian. In two of the bedrooms, the mattresses can't even be used. They're kept so visitors can see what the rope beds were like and how people had to tighten the ropes now and then. The mattresses on them are made of straw."

"We carry bedrolls wherever we go," Tyler said. "Are the ropes on the beds original?"

Allison shook her head. "No, they've been replaced dozens of times through the decades—centuries. The rooms themselves went through a number of changes over the years, but when the house became the property of Old Philly History, the decor was brought back to what it had been during the Colonial era. The bed frames *are* original, but nothing else. Except that some of the quilts are from the eighteenth century."

"We'll carefully fold up the quilts," Kat promised her.

"There's one dingy little shower down in the pantry," Allison said. "I can't stay here. I don't want to take room away from all of you."

"Your life—or a shower?" Julian muttered.

"Hey, may I remind you that you were killed here?" Allison said to him.

"You shouldn't be alone," Julian repeated stubbornly.

"And," Tyler added, "here's what we know so far. Julian was up in the attic reading research papers. He felt that someone was watching him. He came downstairs. The attic—where he'd just been—was trashed. And when he went into the study, he was killed."

"Ms. Leigh," Logan said, joining the group, "or Allison if I may call you that. I don't have the authority to tell you what to do. But if Julian was killed because of something he knew about this house, or something another person *believed* he knew, you might be in danger, as well. It would be smart to stay in a house with six trained agents."

Allison looked helplessly from one to the other.

"You don't have anywhere else you have to be," Julian said. "You could sit right here and work on your paper with all your precious Tarleton-Dandridge pieces surrounding you. *And* be safe."

"You're the one who's going to be helping us, Allison," Kat pointed out. "It would be wonderful to have you here."

For a moment, Tyler didn't think she'd be persuaded.

"Better safe than dead, and trust me, I know," Julian said. "Please, Ally. I was a jerk to you, and you were my friend. Let me be your friend now. Please, do what I say?"

She threw up her hands. "All right."

"I'll walk Allison over to her place so she can pack a bag," Tyler said. "We'll be back soon."

It was easier to accept the strange invitation from the Krewe than Allison had expected.

That was because she was scared.

She didn't *want* to be scared; she wanted to be a rational and independent adult. She liked her home.

It had been her home all her life. She'd been excited to leave for college, but when her parents had talked about selling their house, she knew she wanted it. And they hadn't really wanted to sell, so her slowly buying the house from them had made sense. She loved living there.

She told herself that she was going to be staying just down the street...and just for a little while.

It was unnerving that someone might want to kill her. She still couldn't grasp that fact—and it might not be a fact at all. Julian might've been killed for an entirely different reason. Or he might have imagined that the painting had talked to him, and he might have imagined that he heard things—old houses creaked all the time. He might even have imagined that someone had pressed his head down.

As they walked to her house from the Tarleton-Dandridge property, she asked Tyler if that might be the case.

"Just because Julian's a ghost doesn't mean he knows everything, right?"

"No, of course not. He only knows now what he knew when he was living," Tyler said.

"I can't believe I'm asking you about ghosts."

"No one does," he said lightly.

"Do you always see ghosts? When you're in the historic district, say, do you see our founding fathers walking around the Liberty Bell?"

He laughed. "A ghost can only be in one place at one time, and not all souls stay grounded to this earth. Of those who do stay, some are here to help others and some for justice. Some appear to many people, and some just to a certain few. Some remain shadowy figures for the time they stay—too shy or locked in their own worlds to make contact with anyone."

"If there were other ghosts in this house, would Julian see them?"

"If they chose to be seen."

"Do you think there are other...entities at the house?"

"Possibly," he told her.

She shivered. "And if there are...could they move around, too?"

"Most likely."

She felt another shiver rip through her. "I don't know how you do this," she said.

He shrugged. "I didn't really choose it. It chose me. I could have decided to become a roaring alcoholic—which did occur to me at the time—or accept that I was seeing things and hearing things that others didn't." He paused, reflective. "But I worked with Logan, and we eventually realized that we shared certain...abilities? And we were thrown into working with Kat often enough, and Jane—and even Sean. That's when we were in Texas."

"And Kelsey?"

"Kelsey was a U.S. Marshal, as you know, and she was transferred to Texas specifically to meet Jackson Crow, the head of the first unit."

"And she's—wow, this is nosy. She's with Logan now?"

"They're engaged. They're just waiting for a break between cases to tie the knot."

"Oh! They met on a case?"

"Yep."

"Julian might still have imagined what happened," Allison said, returning to the previous subject.

"Hey!"

She nearly jumped a mile high when the voice came from behind them.

She swung around. She could see Julian walking a few feet to her side.

"Don't do that!" she scolded.

"Don't do what? You know I'm here," he told her.

"You don't need to follow me like a shadow."

"I'm worried about you."

"Julian, I'm with a federal agent. He carries a gun. He's a big Texan. You should be at the house in case they need your help."

"I'm here now. And it shouldn't take you long to get a few things together."

Allison sighed with aggravation.

Tyler grinned. "I can't beat him up and tell him not to hang around."

"I'm not intruding!" Julian protested. "I don't follow people into the shower or anything. Hmm, that's a thought."

"Julian!" Allison said.

"Just kidding. I was a jerk, not a peeping Tom!"

When they reached her house, Allison left Julian and Tyler in her parlor and hurried up the stairs to pack her bag. Luckily, it was a short walk between her house and the Tarleton-Dandridge. It would be easy to come back and forth for what she needed or wanted—like a long hot bath now and then. Of course, Julian had been teasing, but she found it uncomfortable to think that a ghost *could* follow her anywhere she went.

She glanced in the bathroom mirror. Her eyes were way too wide. She looked like a cartoon character who'd stuck her finger in an electrical outlet.

Because she saw a ghost.

She couldn't think about it; she didn't dare think about it. She had to hold on to Tyler's words. *I could have decided to become a roaring alcoholic...or accept that I was seeing things and hearing things that others didn't.*

She could just imagine explaining this situation to some of her academic colleagues!

She understood why the Krewe kept quiet about what they did and why information about them could only be surmised by reading between the lines.

She thought about Adam Harrison, and how kindly and *sane* he had always seemed.

He *was* sane. He just knew what other people didn't, that a lot lay beneath the surface of their daily lives, that the soul did exist and, sometimes, it lingered.

Allison gathered what she needed for a night or two, and hurried down the stairs.

Tyler stared up at her as she descended. Julian stood behind him, his tension unmistakable.

"What?" she asked suspiciously.

"I'm glad you decided to stay with us," he said.

"Why?"

Julian stepped forward. "Mrs. Dixon—Todd's mother—called Tyler from the hospital."

"Did Mr. Dixon come to?" She couldn't hide her anxiety.

"Yes," Julian said.

"Thank God—he's out of the coma!"

But Tyler shook his head grimly. "No, he fell back into it. He came to for about twenty seconds, sat up in bed and spoke one word."

"What was it?" she asked.

"Allison," Julian said.

"What?"

"That's what he said," Tyler told her quietly. "He said one word. *Allison.* He said your name."

9

Tyler watched as Allison sat by Artie Dixon's bedside. Unnerved, she'd been convinced that Haley Dixon had misheard what her husband said. *Allison* could have been *a reason* or any other combination of words.

But he'd noted right away that she cared about Todd and Todd's family, and because Haley had asked that Allison come to the hospital, she had. Now she sat on the bed, holding Artie's hand and talking to him. She kept telling him she was fine and he didn't need to worry about her. He needed to wake up and be with his sons, who loved him and were worried sick, and his wife, who adored him. Bad things had happened, she said, but a wonderful federal unit had arrived to sort everything out.

The ghost of Julian Mitchell had accompanied them at first. He and Tyler had stood outside the room, watching through the glass. After a few minutes, Julian had looked at Tyler with a pained expression. "I've got to get out of here. I'm going to take a walk back to the house. Maybe if I just keep hanging around there, I'll see something the living can't."

Tyler had merely inclined his head. Todd was with them, and he didn't think the boy needed to wonder what invisible being Tyler was communicating with.

Tyler and Todd continued to wait and watch. Tyler rested his hands gently on Todd's shoulders. Meanwhile, Logan and Kelsey were with Haley Dixon, going over everything that had happened when they'd taken the tour at the Tarleton-Dandridge House and later that night in the hotel room. Kat was reading to Jimmy Dixon and coaxing him to tell her what he could remember about that day, and Sean was searching for Dixon's doctor.

Tyler doubted they'd learn anything new, but sometimes, one tiny bit of information could make all the difference.

"His hand moved!" Todd said suddenly. He gazed up at Tyler, eyes huge. "I saw it! My dad's hand moved. He squeezed Allison's hand—I'm sure of it!"

"Maybe he did, Todd," he said. "Let's see what happens now."

They waited longer. He could hear Allison's voice, filled with warmth and reassurance. She wasn't going to give up easily.

But eventually, Sean found Dixon's doctor, who walked past them and into the room. Allison rose, squeezing Dixon's hand, telling him she'd be back.

When she joined them in the hall, Todd nearly jumped on her, he was so anxious. "My dad moved, didn't he? I know he heard you. I saw his hand move."

The doctor had followed Allison out. "That might just have been a physical reaction. It doesn't mean she reached his mind. It doesn't mean she didn't. But don't be discouraged, Todd. Your father's vital signs are strong and the scans reveal he hasn't suffered any kind of permanent brain damage." The doctor turned to Allison. "Thank you for coming in and trying to talk to him."

"I'm glad to," Allison said.

"Did you hear Mr. Dixon when he spoke?" Tyler asked the doctor.

"No, but Clare—the nurse who was with Mr. and Mrs. Dixon when he spoke—is still on duty. I'll call her for you." He smiled at them and departed down the hall.

"Don't look so shaken," Sean said to Allison. "It could be a perfectly logical thing. You were one of the last people he saw before he lost consciousness, so..."

"I just wish I could help," Allison mumbled.

"I wasn't with my dad. I was with my aunt, getting chips from the machine," Todd said. "I wasn't there. He spoke and I wasn't there!" Todd felt the anguish of a child who blamed himself for choosing something insignificant over being with his father.

"Don't fret about that, Todd," Allison said, smoothing the boy's hair. "Your dad knows how much you love him, and we all believe he'll be okay."

"But why doesn't he wake up?" Todd asked.

They were spared from having to answer when a young platinum-blonde nurse came walking over to them. She nodded at the group and told Todd, "It's a good sign, you know. I heard your dad speak plain as day. It's a really good sign!"

She offered her hand to Allison and Tyler. "I'm Clare. I was with Mrs. Dixon when Mr. Dixon sat up and said 'Allison.'"

"I guess you just answered the question we had for you," Tyler said, introducing himself and Allison in return.

"Maybe he said the word *malice*," Allison said hopefully. "Or something like *talk to me, son?*"

Clare shook her head. "No." She smiled sympathetically. "I guess he's worried about you, Allison. Wherever his mind might be right now, he's worried about you. I'm glad you came in to see him. We've learned through our experience with other coma patients that they do remember things they heard or that happened before they were in that state. And there's evidence that they can understand what's said to them."

When she left them, Todd looked at Allison. "You'll keep coming to see my dad, won't you?"

She nodded. "I promise."

It was late when they got back to the Tarleton-Dandridge House. Allison seemed exhausted and distracted. Kelsey, Kat and Jane chatted with her, trying to make her feel more normal, as they made tea and then went up to bed.

The entire crew was worn out, but Tyler spoke to Logan and Sean down in the entry. Sean had finished setting up the computer to record anything caught on the cameras he'd placed throughout the house.

"Did Haley Dixon say anything I might not have heard already?" Tyler asked Logan.

"She was upset about the painting. She said that Todd felt there was something funny about it, and his father said it was the weirdest damned thing he'd ever seen. He felt the painting was somehow alive—like a special-effects painting."

"We've looked at the damned thing. It's a painting, believe me. I'd know if there was anything that'd been altered on it," Sean insisted.

"Well, let's give it up for now and get some sleep," Logan said.

"Good plan," Sean agreed.

They went up to their rooms. Tyler had just crawled into bed when he felt a weight shift the rope beneath the mattress and his bedroll. Tyler still didn't know

all the "rules" that went with being a ghost, but he did
know that they could learn to move things and that they
could be *felt* if not really touched. Maybe they could
tell when someone tried to touch them with warmth
and good intentions.

Julian was perched at the foot of the bed. Tyler almost groaned aloud; it had been a long day.

"Hey," Julian said.

"Hey," Tyler responded tiredly.

"I think I'm going a little crazy," Julian said.

Crazy? You're dead.

Tyler refrained from saying the words.

"Why?"

"I couldn't pinpoint it, and I've been through the
house and the grounds since. But when I got back here,
I had the feeling that someone had just left."

"We'd all just left. We went to the hospital."

Julian shook his head. "No, that's not what I mean.
We'd already been gone a while. There was some...I
don't know, residual energy? Something that made me
feel convinced that someone had been here."

"Did you see anyone?" Tyler asked. "See a car leave?
Anything?"

"No, I was walking along feeling sorry for myself,
trying to sidle up next to people I passed on the street.
I think I gave a few of them chills," he said, chortling
to himself.

Tyler rolled his eyes. Most personalities didn't
change when they became ghosts. Julian was the same
prankster he'd been in life.

He rued the fact that Sean hadn't set the cameras to
record until they'd returned.

However, the call about Dixon had come quickly.
Sean hadn't actually had a chance to ensure that they

were set up for the night or to see what went on in the house when they were sleeping.

"The board members still have keys," Tyler said. "We can ask. Maybe one of them came by for some specific purpose."

"You need to get those keys from them," Julian said.

Tyler shrugged. "We can get the keys, but if any of them are guilty of something, they've had plenty of chances to make copies. I think we should just set up our alarm system to see if someone with a key does come and go. Sean will take care of it."

Julian started to rise as if Tyler would automatically join him.

"In the morning," Tyler said. "I really don't expect anyone to come into a house filled with agents. Whoever it was knew we were going out this evening—although I have no idea how."

"In the morning," Julian repeated. "For now, I'm going to go down and be the alarm system. I'll be on the sofa in the entry."

He left. Tyler prayed for sleep.

But an hour later, he still lay awake in Lucy Tarleton's room, staring at the painting of Lord Brian "Beast" Bradley. He looked so different from the Brit envisioned in the painting below.

There had been other instances, probably in every war, when men on one side or the other had carried out covert executions. During the Revolutionary War Nathan Hale had been executed by the British. John André had been executed by the patriots for convincing Benedict Arnold to sell out. But for the most part, murder during conflict was not the norm, unless war itself was considered the greatest form of murder.

The story associated with the house was almost a

fairy tale, a very romantic one about love and the price paid for love. It had a dashing heroine, Lucy Tarleton, and a patriot hero, Stewart Douglas, Lucy's true love, and it had an ogre, as well—Beast Bradley.

But the man depicted in the painting in Lucy Tarleton's bedroom did not seem capable of the vicious and cold-blooded murder of a young woman in her own home.

Tyler rolled over.

Even with his bedroll over the straw mattress, he wasn't very comfortable. That didn't really bother him; he'd spent many a night on the cold ground in Texas. What bothered him was the case.

First, *was* there a case?

Allison could have a reasonable theory—that Julian Mitchell had imagined he was being followed. He'd imagined the painting doing terrible things to him and had set his own chin on the bayonet and died.

Except that the attic office had been trashed. And Julian *claimed* he'd been murdered.

Tyler rolled over again and punched his pillow, still troubled by the fact that Julian suspected Allison could be in danger.

And Artie Dixon had come out of his coma long enough to say her name.

She had to know *something*. She didn't know she knew it, but that was the only reason someone might search the office in the attic and kill a man who'd just been up there.

Still, the painting in the study... Sean had inspected it. There were no trick lights or cut-out eyes. It was a painting, nothing more or less.

He was glad Allison was sleeping directly across the hall. She'd chosen one of the family guest rooms, and to the best of his knowledge, nothing had ever happened there.

With a groan, he rose and threw on his robe. He was worried about her. He had Julian to thank for that— Julian, and the man in the hospital who'd woken just long enough to say her name.

The house was quiet. He could hear the old grandfather clock below in the entry clanging out the hour. Two o'clock.

Tyler walked across the hall. Allison's door was ajar. He tapped lightly, but she didn't answer. He opened the door farther and saw that she lay there, sleeping peacefully.

He left her door ajar and started to walk back to his own room but paused. He had a sudden feeling that something about the house wasn't quite right.

He walked to the stairway and heard another door creak. He turned silently, but it was Logan, who'd come out of his room. He joined Tyler at the landing, looking down the stairs.

"Did you hear anything?" Logan asked him.

Tyler shook his head. "I think I'm just restless. Worried. Maybe our ghost does have me concerned that someone's out to hide something and may think that Allison has knowledge regarding whatever it is. Did you hear anything?"

Logan, too, shook his head. "No, but I was awake. I had the same feeling. That strange *something is moving in the darkness* feeling. Want to check out the first floor?"

"Yeah, I guess I do," Tyler said.

They walked down the stairs together. There was a greenish glow from the computer with the different screens Sean had set up. They studied them, but there was nothing to be seen. The ghost of Julian Mitchell was sound asleep on the sofa. Julian didn't rise or acknowledge him. Tyler smiled inwardly. So much for Julian as a watchdog.

Logan checked the front door and the alarm.

"I'll take the salon, dining room and pantry. Can you look into the study, the ladies' room and the music room?" Logan asked.

"Sure," Tyler said. "Meet you in the back."

He went into the study first; night-lights glowing softly in the corridors led the way.

He saw nothing there, but in the shadows, the painting of Lord Brian "Beast" Bradley seemed more cruel and cunning than ever before. Tyler stared at it for a moment, then went to the doorway leading to the ladies' room and, after that, the music room. He found nothing in any of the rooms.

Nothing that wanted to be found, at any rate.

Julian wasn't even stirring. He certainly wasn't watching over the house where he'd died.

When Tyler met Logan, who was checking the lock and the alarm on the back door, he asked, "Anything?"

"Nope. But we both needed the walk-through. Strange, I just had a feeling," Logan said. "Our imaginations can come into play."

"That's true, but...sometimes it *is* something."

"Well, there's still some sleep to be had," Logan said.

"Yeah, let's get back up."

As they walked upstairs, Kelsey was coming out of the room she shared with Logan.

"What did you find?" she asked anxiously.

"Nothing. Sorry I woke you," Logan said.

"I was awake, anyway. It does feel as if...as if there's something or someone in the house."

Logan slipped an arm around her shoulders. "If so, we're not the ones they want to talk to."

"Good night," Kelsey told Tyler, but she paused. "Make sure you leave Allison's door open. And your own."

He smiled at her. "That's the way I was planning it."

Logan and Kelsey went to bed, and Tyler did the same, keeping his door half-open.

If anyone moved in the hall, he'd hear it. He was a light sleeper.

If anyone made a move toward Allison in any way, he'd know it.

Comfortable at last with that thought, he lay down again. He grinned, thinking about their ghost. He would've been impatient with Julian's lack of responsibility in life, but he would have liked him.

Julian had been intense when he'd spoken with Tyler at Allison's house, while she was packing. He'd charged him fiercely to ensure that Allison was safe.

"She's amazing, you know? There's no one like her. She has a great sense of humor, and she makes everything work and everyone get along. And she's so smart and beautiful and...you have to watch her every step, okay? We can't let anything happen to her."

"We won't," Tyler had assured him.

"Man, I was into her," Julian said sadly. "But she wanted...well, something I wasn't. I couldn't help her or be there for her when I was alive, but now...now, I'm a ghost! A bunch of air, a cold breeze. So it's gotta be you. You understand?"

"We know how to protect people," Tyler had said.

"From *this?*" Julian had asked. "From paintings that

move and someone who can creep around behind you? You've got to be wary—every second. Every single second."

And then the phone call had come.

Dixon had woken up and spoken one word.

Allison.

Tyler groaned, tossing in bed again. He had to sleep or he'd be no good to anyone tomorrow.

He must have finally dozed. He dreamed about a giant black horse, rearing and snorting in the yard, carrying a beautiful young woman. Lucy Tarleton.

In his dreams, Lucy's face was Allison's.

When Allison awoke, she heard the others downstairs in the entry.

She felt good; she'd slept extremely well.

When she went to bed, she'd been afraid she'd be plagued by dreams all night long or that she'd wake up to see another ghost sitting in the room.

But she'd felt safe. Ridiculously safe. Tyler was across the hall, and there were five other agents in the house.

Until this was over, she knew darned well *she* wasn't leaving.

She hurried down the servants' stairs, delighted to find that the bath was empty. Showering quickly and dressing, she came out to join the others. Kat wasn't there, nor was Jane. But Kelsey, Logan, Sean and Tyler were together.

They were gathered around the bank of screens Sean had set up.

When she arrived, they turned, almost as one, to stare at her.

She stood still, looking back at them. "What?" she

asked. Her feeling of serenity from the night of undisturbed sleep began to evaporate.

"What?" she repeated.

"You need to see this," Tyler said.

She walked over to the screens, which showed six views of the house. One camera was in the upstairs hallway, one in the attic. One showed Angus Tarleton's study and another showed a view of the salon. The fifth displayed the front of the house.

The last camera was set to monitor activity in the entry.

She could see their group on the screen as they all watched the computers.

"Hold on," Sean said. "I'm rolling back."

There was a timer set in a black margin at the top of each screen. Allison saw the hours roll back. She noticed something, a splinter of light, and then Sean slowed down the reverse, stopped and moved it forward.

She saw Tyler come out of his room and silently check on her, and then she saw Logan emerge, as well. They could be seen on the various screens as they came down the stairs and walked through the house, walked back up the stairs and met Kelsey on the second-floor landing.

"You woke up and checked out the house. That's a good thing," she murmured.

"Wait," Sean said.

At the foot of the stairs, a figure began to appear. It was that of a woman. She was hazy at first, but it might have been the low night-light that made her look as if she'd arrived like a wraith.

Then again, she might have *been* a wraith.

She seemed to gather substance.

She moved from the stairway to the door that led to Angus Tarleton's study, and she paused there. Sean pushed a key on his computer board and they saw a close-up of the woman.

Allison's throat tightened. She would have gasped aloud—if she hadn't felt that she was choking.

The woman was beautifully gowned in a Colonial-era dress; her stomacher was blue with white embroidery, her skirt was blue and the sleeves on her gown were white. Her hair, a soft brown, was tied back but curling tendrils escaped to frame her face.

Her face...

Allison had already accepted that a good friend she'd seen murdered was now a ghost.

Why was *this* terrifying her so much? Because it made her feel as if she was a ghost herself?

Really, how could things get worse? Her friend was a ghost who believed she could discover the truth about his death. A man in a coma had called her name, and now she was seeing an image of a ghost, a ghost who looked just like her!

She backed away from the screen. "What is this?" she asked, fear making her tone sharp. "Some kind of trick photography?"

Tyler laid a hand on her arm. "Allison, it's not a trick, but it isn't anything that should upset you."

She jerked away. "What, are you crazy? Are you creating footage for one of those stupid ghost shows?"

They were all silent, not replying to her accusation. She realized how brittle she sounded.

Mean, bitter and nasty. That wasn't her personality. And what she'd accused them of wasn't what they were doing, and she knew it, but...

"You might have been related to her. Somehow," Sean said, clearing his throat.

"I wasn't! She didn't have children. She died." Allison shook her head. "I've seen paintings of her.... She *didn't* resemble me. Not that closely, anyhow."

"Well, you didn't come downstairs, dress up and wander around the house last night, did you?" Kelsey asked.

Allison turned around with a sharp retort but it never left her lips. Kelsey was looking at her with empathy and understanding.

These people dealt with things like this all the time. None of it surprised them. Nothing surprised them.

She was still in denial. But she had a right to be! First, Julian. Now...this.

"It's a strong resemblance," Logan said. "However, that doesn't really mean anything."

"Yeah. Her hair is nowhere near as dark as Allison's," Sean added.

Tyler wasn't speaking. She'd moved away from him, and he was watching her.

"It's not me, it wasn't me, and I'm no relation to Lucy Tarleton," she said. "I'm not a descendent. I can't be."

"Of course. It's just a resemblance," Logan said.

Allison felt that her knees would go any second. This wasn't fair! She'd felt so safe, as if the situation would really be solved, as if Julian's killer would be discovered and her life could go back to what it had been.

"I don't think I can do this," she said. "I'm not geared up for this kind of thing."

Kelsey told her, "Hey, I understand. I always wanted to be a law enforcement officer, so finding out I had a few abilities that would help me with that wasn't...well, wasn't so hard to take. You're a professor, a scholar—

an academic. We can all understand how upsetting it must be, how frightening."

"I'm not a coward!" she protested. But she was, and it was evident in her swift denial.

"I'll get you some coffee," Kelsey offered, leaving the salon for the pantry.

"We can't stop you from going home, if that's what you'd like to do," Tyler said.

"No, we can't stop you, but…" Logan turned her to face him. "Allison, it's becoming very clear that you're the key to whatever is going on here. You can really help us. And if you decide to go back to your own house, we can't be there to protect you."

"We can have police cars patrol around your house, though," Tyler said.

"But the cops only have so much manpower. It'll be hard for them to watch you," Sean pointed out.

Kelsey returned with a cup of coffee for her. "When it's morning, no matter what the trauma, coffee makes it better."

"Where's Julian?" she asked.

"We told him not to, but when Kat and Jane went to the morgue, Julian went with them," Logan said.

Allison took her coffee and sank down into one of the chairs by the bank of screens. "I haven't really been threatened," she said. "Not by anyone living. Or anyone…not living. Julian is just worried. I don't know why he was killed. But there's no suggestion that whoever killed him would want to kill me."

"Should we wait until there's a bayonet through your throat?" Tyler asked harshly.

"Tyler," Kelsey murmured.

"Run that image again, Sean," Tyler said, and his voice sounded tense.

"I saw it the first time!" Allison said.

"Well, see it again."

The image leaped to the screen again. Allison gritted her teeth.

Tyler hunkered down before her, his face just a breath away. "You're in danger. If you don't see it, you're the most idiotic academic I've ever come across. Quit fighting it. If you want us to help you, accept the fact that someone in this house is trying to reach you, because someone *outside* this house is planning to kill you. Please—trust me. Trust my experience. *You* are the catalyst here. The key and the answer. Accept it, and maybe you'll survive."

10

Allison tried to remain completely stoic and not let Tyler or any of them see the emotions sweeping through her.

She stared down into her coffee cup. She couldn't meet his eyes any longer.

They were right about one thing. She didn't want to die!

As she gazed into her coffee, she felt a sensation of strength slowly begin to fill her veins. She looked up; Tyler was still there, his face just inches from hers.

"I'm here, aren't I?" she told him softly. "Alive…"

Something in his expression changed. Something she was afraid to see. He cared. He had spoken harshly to her, but he really cared. She didn't know what had passed between them, but he was there to be her guardian.

"Please, admit that what's on that screen is unnerving!" she said.

He nodded grimly.

She'd dressed up for years in the manner of Lucy Tarleton, and hosted tours through the house as if it were her own. She was young; Lucy had been young. There'd been jokes about her resembling the young patriot many times before, but it was also true that she'd never seen such a *strong* resemblance. And no one had ever suggested she was a spitting image of the long-dead heroine.

But it was just a resemblance. Maybe it had always been there.

Even if that was true, a ghost had shown up on film!

A ghost had been in or around the house, day after day....

And she had never known it.

"It's so much to take in, to get used to," Kelsey said gently. She nudged Tyler. He rose and stood near her, still watching intently.

"I'm sorry for sounding so cowardly. I'm usually not the type of person who jumps at shadows or..." Her voice faded away. She almost laughed and said, *Or believes in ghosts and things that go bump in the night.*

She didn't just *believe* in ghosts now.

She *knew* they existed.

She clenched her teeth tightly together.

Trying to run away from what was happening would only make it worse.

Allison squared her shoulders. She looked up at the group and said, "I don't suppose it would help for me to go home. If I'm the key to this thing as you say, then I guess Tyler was right. I'd better start figuring out how to solve it. Where do we go from here?"

"It's not that you have to go anywhere. It's that you have to open your mind to what you see and hear, and discover what the messages might be," Logan explained.

"But we're supposed to be *doing* something, aren't we?" she asked.

"We are doing things," Logan assured her. "Kat and

Jane are down at the morgue. We've been studying the film we've taken overnight. Sometimes, when the spirits don't reach out to us, we can see them on film, so at least we know they're there."

"But...that's it?"

"It's only ten o'clock," Kelsey said. "If it was as easy as stepping inside and demanding that everyone who remained in the house show themselves and tell us what's up, we might be done already." She sat down next to Allison and continued. "The ghosts in this house may not have seen any more than you did. But they might know a great deal more about the past, and that could help us with the present."

"Oh. But..."

Logan stood up. He glanced at Tyler and then at her. "Listen, Allison, we've gone over the house, the locks, the alarm system and every possible entry. Julian heard something and saw something. Someone was here. Someone living." He hesitated and looked at Tyler again. She realized he was trying to tell her something she wouldn't want to hear.

"Whoever caused Julian's death has to be someone you're close to, Allison," Tyler said. "Whoever was in the house is someone who has access to it."

"Julian is dead, so that would leave Annette and Jason." Allison shook her head. "No, no—I don't believe it was either of them. I *know* Annette was in agony from that tooth that needed the root canal. And I was with Jason. I watched him leave before...before I found Julian."

"We've confirmed that Annette had a root canal done," Logan said.

"You checked out her story?" Allison asked.

"We check out everything."

"There's also the board of directors," Tyler said.

Startled, Allison looked at him. "As in Ethan Oxford? He's not a small man. I can't see *him* trying to creep around this place! Julian, yes, he was young and spry and in excellent shape. But—"

"There's also Cherry Addison—" Tyler began.

"Cherry! We'd have heard those spiked heels of hers a mile away," Allison interrupted.

"And Sarah Vining and Nathan Pierson," he finished.

"I just can't imagine our dignified board tiptoeing around the house to shove Julian's head down on a bayonet and then somehow traumatize Artie Dixon and send him into a coma," Allison said. "Have you *met* our board? Well, I know you met Cherry, but—"

"I've met them all," Tyler told her. "We'll need to spend some more time with them. And, I'm sorry to say, with Jason and Annette, as well."

Allison started to answer but fell silent as they heard a commotion at the door. Logan frowned and raised a brow at Tyler, who shrugged.

"We have to knock. People are living there now!" they heard.

It was a feminine voice—one Allison knew well.

"You won't have to wait for the board. A few of them are already here," she said.

"Did you know they were coming?" Logan asked Tyler.

Tyler shook his head as he walked to the door, unlocking it. Sarah stepped back in shock as the door opened; she had a hand on Nathan Pierson's arm. Nathan still held his key, ready to use it, and Cherry Addison was standing impatiently behind them.

"Hello," Tyler said.

"Agent Montague." Nathan spoke casually, grinning. "We've come to see if you're settling in all right."

"Oh, good God, Nathan, tell them the truth. We came to make sure you weren't putting garlic around the windows or doing anything to destroy the integrity of the property," Cherry told him. She smiled, though. Cherry really seemed to like Tyler.

"Come and meet the rest of the Krewe," Tyler said. "And no, I guarantee that we don't put garlic around the windows."

As they filed in, Tyler began the introductions to Sean, Kelsey and Logan. When he'd finished, he asked, "Where's Ethan?"

"Ethan's been friends with Adam Harrison for a long time. I believe they're at a fundraiser now, some kind of breakfast," Nathan said. "I'd thought Adam would be the head honcho here," he added.

"Adam puts things together. He's the organizer. We're the workers," Logan explained.

Allison noted that Sean had hit a key on the computer; the scenes depicted on all the screens were of the present.

Cherry Addison turned to her. "So, Allison, you're still showing the Krewe around. That's so kind of you, dear. You could be taking this time to hole up in your little room on campus and do your brilliant academic work."

Cherry had a way of speaking. Her words were benign enough, but her tone often contradicted them, with a sarcastic or disbelieving inflection that suggested the opposite of what she said. She seemed to be saying that Allison belonged in a stuffy university office or library.

"Cherry, you know how I love the house!" Allison said.

"Ms. Leigh has been extremely helpful," Tyler put in.

"Of course, the house and its history are near and dear to us all." Sarah smiled at Allison. Bless Sarah; she was so like a nervous terrier, but her intentions were always the best. "And I just can't believe that anyone— anyone!—would purposely hurt that young Mr. Mitchell. He was such a talented man," Sarah said sadly.

"And a showoff, not to mention a goofball." Cherry's voice was caustic. "What's most troubling is the type of story that keeps coming out in the media about that man—Artie Dixon. They've practically turned his coma into an alien invasion!"

"Cherry, that's one of the reasons Ethan was so keen on inviting this unit of law enforcement to come in," Nathan said. "They'll bring our historic property back into historic perspective." He shrugged. "But, even if that doesn't happen, everyone loves a good haunted house, huh?"

"As long as people stop dying in it," Allison said.

She was surprised that she'd spoken. She stood, uncomfortable with the words that had escaped her. A silence descended on the room.

Nathan looked at her. "You're right, Allison. As long as people stop dying in it. Well, we'll leave you to your work. We just thought we should drop by and see if you needed anything. Oh, as to the office. I can arrange to come and help you put things back in order, Allison."

Allison smiled at him. "Thanks, Nathan. I can do it on my own, but it's up to you."

"I suppose I could help," Cherry said, sounding reluctant. "But not today. Oh, my husband is having a gallery showing tomorrow evening. You must all come."

"Cherry, they're here to work," Sarah reminded her.

"All work and no play…" Cherry gestured expansively. "They need to breathe once in a while, Sarah.

Please join us. The gallery is farther down on Walnut. Take a break and come by."

"Have you discovered anything?" Sarah asked the group. "Is it possible that Julian trashed the office before doing himself in?"

"We've really just begun, Ms. Vining," Kelsey said. "But we will do our absolute best to find out the truth."

Sarah nodded. "Yes, I'm sure you will."

"I have a luncheon date," Nathan said. "I need to get moving. But we do want you to let us know if you need anything. Anything at all."

"Thank you," Logan said on behalf of the group.

"I have to go and supervise some hangings," Cherry said. "Of paintings and art pieces!" she added quickly. "Oh, of course, the gallery owner hangs the painting, but I need to be there to see that everything's just right."

That drew smiles. Cherry seemed glad.

"I could stay now if you wanted," Sarah told Allison.

Tyler answered for her. "We were about to go out for a late breakfast. But if you're worried about any of the papers or materials that are out of order or might have been compromised, please feel free to come back."

"I'll do that," Sarah said. "I'll help you, Allison. You and I are both so careful about our research. I'd really like to find out if anything was taken."

"Of course, Sarah," Allison said.

"Well, then, we're out of here." Nathan paused and smiled at Allison again. "Thank you, Allison. Thanks for all you're doing for the house."

"It's my pleasure," she responded. "I love the house and the history."

"Of course you do, dear," Cherry said, but somehow she made it sound like a reproach.

Tyler walked them all to the door. After another chorus of goodbyes, they were gone.

"They can enter this house at any time," he said as he returned.

"We could have asked for their keys," Allison told him.

"No, we don't want them thinking they're under suspicion. What we do need is an alarm system that'll alert us if anyone tries to enter with a key. Can you work on that, Sean?"

Logan turned to Allison. "On the day Julian died, did you see them all leave?"

"Yes, as my last tour was coming in."

"But Julian came into the house, and you didn't see him. So one of them could have doubled back," Tyler said. "Annette was at the dentist, but where were you when Jason left? The house couldn't have been locked until he was out and you closed up, right?"

"Did you see Jason leave the house?" Logan asked her.

"I heard Jason shut the door, but I didn't actually *see* him go. I did notice the board leaving, but..."

"One of them could've come back in, and you wouldn't have known it."

"That can't be," she said, and she knew her tone sounded desperate. "Annette, Jason and I all got mad at Julian, but none of us would have killed him. And I can't think of any reason that a member of the board would have killed Julian. They could simply have fired him!"

"They could fire him—but that wouldn't help if he knew something he shouldn't," Kelsey said.

"Breakfast," Logan announced. "Or nearly lunch if you prefer. Hungry investigators don't concentrate well. Let's get something to eat and stoke up for the day. Then we'll get started in earnest here."

"Let's just walk to your friend's restaurant," Tyler suggested. "What time does it open?"

"You mean Evan's place? McDooley's? He opens at eleven," she said. "You don't suspect Evan in this, do you?" she asked, her tone wry.

"No, I suspect a board member, Jason or Annette, and I'm sorry, because I know that hurts you. And after the way she just insisted on going into the office with you, I want to know more about Sarah Vining."

"Sarah? But she's..." Allison began, not sure how to say what she meant.

"Because she looks fragile, sweet, eternally nervous and innocent?" Kelsey asked. "Never trust appearances."

"We're all speculating right now," Logan said. "Sean, can you quickly rig up an alarm for us?"

"Yep, got the camera aimed at the door and a zip connection to my phone."

"Then let's go," Tyler said. "McDooley's was a great place and I'm hungry."

They all agreed. Still shaking inwardly, Allison wondered how they could forget what they'd seen and think about something as mundane as food. But they were obviously used to bizarre occurrences....

Evan beamed delightedly when Allison walked in with Tyler, Kelsey, Logan and Sean.

"Hey, thanks! You did come back with friends," he said to Tyler.

"We need a hangout." Tyler grinned. "Allison, introduce Evan around, will you?"

She did so, and then her eyes widened as she saw

Jason walking up to her. He was wearing a McDooley's polo shirt and jeans.

"Hey, Ally, oh, Lord! How are you? You poor girl, finding Julian like that... And I'd just been bitching about him. I wish I'd at least been with you when you found him."

"It's horrible, yes, and we're all devastated, but..." She tried to smile. "But you're working. Evan told me to get in touch with you and Annette. I just hadn't had a chance."

"I called him right away. I figured he'd lend a hand. I desperately need to work, since I still have to pay for school." Jason kissed her cheek. "Thankfully, Evan said he could use the help." He stood back, smiling curiously and waiting to meet the others. "I'm really pleased you're here," he told the Krewe. "I admit... I was mad as hell at Julian. He seemed to believe he was a star and that our little lives didn't matter next to his. But you couldn't help liking him. We're all reeling after his death." He looked at Allison. "You holding up okay? The police came and gave me the third degree, but I heard you were at the station all night."

"I'm glad they grilled us. We owe it to Julian to figure out exactly what happened," she said.

Jason frowned. "What do you mean? Julian was messing around the way he always did, right?"

"Probably," she lied. She assumed the Krewe didn't want others knowing about their suspicions. "These people are going to find out what—if anything—is going on at the house."

He still seemed surprised. "I heard about your unit coming in. I'm just not sure what this can do for Julian. Well, nothing can be done for Julian now, of course. But, anyway, sit. I'll get your orders and you can tell me anything else you think I need to know. Or ask me anything you want," he told the Krewe members.

Jason escorted them over to one of his booths. He made suggestions, and they ordered their meals and five glasses of iced tea.

"So that's Jason," Tyler said as he watched him leave.

"He's a good kid. And it wouldn't have made any sense for him to do anything to Julian," Allison said earnestly. She was seated next to Tyler. Kelsey was between Logan and Sean on the other side of the booth. "Jason wants to keep going to school. You heard him. He needs an income."

Kelsey reached across the table and squeezed her hand. She said, "I admire your loyalty to your friends. During a case in San Antonio, I learned the hard way that we never know another person as well as we think we do."

"Yeah, but you got *me* out of the deal, right?" Logan teased.

Allison was touched by the closeness between them, and yet when they worked together, you wouldn't know they were a couple.

Everyone in the Krewe seemed close to and dependent on one another. Their easy manner didn't interfere with their professionalism and only seemed to enhance it.

"So, you all met on a case?" she asked them.

Logan said, "Yes, we did. Kelsey was the outsider."

"The rest of us are from Texas," Sean explained.

"But you work out of Virginia?" Allison asked.

Sean nodded. "Now we do. And the way we work… works, somehow. Will Chan, one of the original Krewe members, was involved in our last case. He's back with his crew while Kat, who was lead on that investigation, is back with us. They're fortunate, though. They became a couple and found a great place in Arlington to call home when we're on base."

"Sean isn't so lucky," Kelsey said, punching his shoulder lightly. "The love of his life actually has his old job in California. She's with one of the premier special effects studios in Hollywood. So they have to get together when they can."

Sean looked at her with a grimace and lifted his glass of iced tea. "It can work—if you want it to. We do."

"My poor cousin!"

"I'd forgotten you're cousins," Allison said.

"You don't see a family resemblance?" Kelsey asked.

"I wasn't really looking for one, but yeah...the eyes."

"Genetics can be unpredictable. Certain characteristics can skip generations and reappear. Luckily, sometimes that happens with inherited diseases, too. Sometimes they'll skip enough generations for cures to be discovered," Logan said.

Allison realized that Tyler was studying her. She felt a rush of warmth; he was probably thinking about the image of the wraithlike Lucy Tarleton—and just how much she and Allison resembled each other.

She also realized she liked being where she was. There was something about Tyler that evoked trust. The man was six-four-plus and built of steel, and that surely led to a feeling of safety. But she liked the feel of him, the clean scent of him, his deep voice....

She didn't *want* to think about him in any kind of physical way. She was a tool for him and his team, and they were providing her with a safe haven. To suddenly enjoy the presence of this particular man was not wise.

Especially since her taste in men hadn't proven to be at all that reliable in the past.

Apparently, his thoughts didn't quite match hers because he asked, "Can you trace your ancestry back to the Revolution? You're a historian, so I imagine you know your own family history."

Allison nodded. "My dad's family, yes. They've been in Philly since the 1700s. I lose count of the *greats,* but I have family buried at Christ Church graveyard—not all that far from Benjamin Franklin. In fact, I think the monument is close enough for pennies to fall on great-great-great-whatever granddad."

"Pennies? Why?"

"Local tradition has it that tossing pennies on Ben's grave brings financial good fortune."

Logan grinned. "Well, that kind of contradicts that proverb of his—a penny saved is a penny earned."

They all laughed. Tyler asked, "Did you have a great-great-great-whatever fighting in the Revolution?"

She nodded again. "William Peter Leigh. He survived the war and lived to the ripe old age of eighty-seven. He's at Christ Church with his two wives, several of his children and their children. My mother's from a more recent wave of Irish immigrants. They came to New York during the Famine and then made their way over to Philadelphia."

"It would be interesting to find out more about your family," Logan murmured.

Allison shook her head. "I know what you're trying to do, but as Tyler said, I'm a historian, and I'm familiar with my own family background. I am *not* related to the Tarleton or the Dandridge families. The Philadelphia Department of Records has my dad's family history generation by generation—and a lot of what's in the Department of Records can be verified by church records. Same with the Tarleton family. Angus Tarleton had two children, Lucy and Sophia. Lucy died, and you can trace the Dandridge family, as well. The name died out with Cherry Addison's mother." She sipped her iced tea. "But I'm not sure why this is relevant. You tell me that what was done to Julian wasn't done by a ghost. So how can the past matter so much?"

"It might and it might not," Logan said vaguely. "We'll see."

"When we get back into the office, I'd like to keep going through the papers and records that were thrown around up there." Tyler smiled at her. "I'd also like a better tour of the property."

"You mean the stables and the graveyard?" Allison asked.

"Yes. I looked around quickly when I first arrived, but there's nothing like a good tour—with a knowledgeable guide."

As he finished speaking, Jason and a few other servers appeared with their meals. "Careful if you're driving out on the highway," he told them. "There was a massive accident on US1."

"That's awful," Allison said.

"They're just showing it on the television up at the bar," Jason was saying. "It looks like at least ten cars are involved and two trucks have turned over. I'm afraid there are going to be some fatalities."

Allison slid out of the booth and followed Jason over to the bar. A reporter was at the scene of the crash, and she saw a twisted mass of steel on the road. One car had flipped and fallen on another. One truck was on its side, another stretched across the road, forming a barrier.

Staring at the tangle, she gasped. "Jason, that car—it's a blue Volvo."

"Yeah," he said.

They were thinking the same thing.

Sarah Vining drove a blue Volvo.

"Let's not jump to conclusions," Jason said. "There must be a lot of blue Volvos in the Philly area."

"Sarah said she'd always drive a Volvo because it was the safest car on the road," Allison whispered.

"Yes, and it is a Volvo, so even if Sarah's in that car, I'm sure she's going to be okay."

Allison noticed Tyler standing next to her and saw that he had his phone out. He was speaking to someone who could zero in on the license plate and pull up the vehicle records.

She and Jason waited anxiously as he spoke. He grunted replies, finished with a terse "Thanks," and snapped his phone shut. He looked from Jason to Allison.

"The car does belong to Sarah Vining," he said. "From what the police have determined so far, Sarah was the one who caused the accident."

11

While Logan spoke with officers at the accident scene, Tyler found the ambulance bearing Sarah Vining to the hospital. After showing his I.D., he was permitted to join the EMTs. The siren was blaring but he could make out what they were saying behind him.

The EMTs were troubled, speaking urgently with doctors while en route, doing their best to save the woman.

The Volvo she had so depended on had stood her in good stead; she had slammed into one of the trucks and her air bag had inflated to protect her.

But while cars continued to slam into one another around her, Sarah had done the unthinkable—she had stumbled out of her car. She'd been hit by another vehicle and hurled several feet in the air.

Sarah lay bruised and broken with an IV in her arm—unresponsive to anything that was said or done to her as the medical techs strove diligently to keep her alive.

When they reached the emergency room, she was immediately wheeled in.

Tyler wasn't allowed entry, but he identified himself to the emergency room doctor and told him he'd be waiting for any information or any possibility of talking to the woman. While the doctor seemed surprised that a federal agent was so determined to see a vehicular accident victim, he agreed as he hurried off.

Tyler paced the waiting room. He'd been suspicious of the woman just before this happened. And he was still suspicious—although no longer of Sarah herself.

He wanted to know what would cause the woman to lose control of her vehicle as she had. And why in God's name would she crawl out of the car?

More victims from the accident arrived at the hospital. It was controlled chaos as those with the severest injuries were treated first and the triage nurses worked at a record pace to see that everyone was taken in according to need.

Tyler followed one of the EMTs outside, where the man had just leaned against a wall to draw a deep breath.

"Is everyone in?" he asked.

The EMT nodded. "Twenty-four people. I'm praying they all make it. One guy was bleeding like a sieve. There were a few children...but I think they're going to be okay. A broken arm, a few bumps and bruises, trauma from air bags. It's been a rough day." He offered Tyler a weak smile. "No one at the morgue yet, though, and we thought we'd see a lot of dead." His eyes narrowed. "You have a family member involved?"

"A friend," he said. "I'm glad to hear that, so far, everyone's hanging in."

He went back to the emergency waiting room and sat down beside a woman with her arm in a makeshift sling, hoping for a chance to ask her what she'd seen without looking like an ambulance chaser or a voyeur.

He didn't have to worry; she just started talking.

"It was unbelievable!" she said, turning to him with wide eyes. "The woman in the blue Volvo was in front of me, driving, and then she threw her arms up and started screaming. A few seconds later, she veered into the next lane, crashing into a truck and spinning into me! Then another car hit the truck and another car hit me.... Why on earth would she suddenly do that? Oh, my God, I'll never forget the sound. It was awful, just awful...the screeching of brakes, the cars all slamming together. Were you there?"

"No, I wasn't. I'm so sorry for everyone who was hurt," Tyler told her.

"I'm alive!" she said. "It's a miracle."

"But you did see the woman driving. And she was fine at first, and then..."

"It was as if she went crazy. As if she was struck by lightning or possessed by a demon or something. I knew to get away from her but it was too late—it all happened so fast!"

Tears appeared in her eyes. Tyler placed a comforting hand on her arm. "Thank God you're all right," he said sincerely.

He saw the doctor who'd been with Sarah Vining when she was wheeled in.

Tyler excused himself, stood and walked over to him.

"I'm sorry to tell you this. Ms. Vining was declared dead about four minutes ago," the doctor told him.

"Her injuries were that extensive?" Tyler asked, feeling deep pity for the woman, and a sense of loss. He also felt the tension of needing to find out how she'd died.

He knew she hadn't just "gone crazy" and caused

the accident. Waiting to hear what had happened was like waiting for a hammer to fall.

"Snakebite," the doctor said.

"What?" Tyler asked. "Snakebite?"

"The EMTs were at a loss because they couldn't see the bite. There must've been a snake in her car. A copperhead? They'll know for sure when they've finished the autopsy. She was bitten. The bite probably caused her to lose control of the car. Her other injuries led us astray at first, and between the trauma of the accident and the poison...Ms. Vining succumbed."

"Thank you. Where will she be taken?" Tyler paused. "You're sure? She was bitten by a snake?"

"Look, I still have people here to see, but check it out for yourself." He nodded to one of the nurses in the hall. The young man came forward to direct Tyler into the room where Sarah Vining lay on the operating table.

Tyler touched her—she was still warm. But she looked dead. Her face was ashen and gray, and bruises were beginning to show on her flesh. She'd been a tiny woman; she now looked shrunken, almost as if she were being mummified with each second that passed.

"Bite is just above her knee on the inner thigh," the nurse told him.

Tyler moved the sheet. There was no doubt that she'd been bitten by a snake. The wound had begun to blacken and go raw before she'd died.

"Thank you. She will go to autopsy, right?" Tyler asked.

"It's the law."

"Of course."

He left the hospital and returned to the Tarleton-Dandridge House, suddenly anxious to be with Allison again.

He knew there was a killer now. A killer who had procured a copperhead—easy enough in the woods nearby, or even in barns and basements—and put it in Sarah's car.

The killer had taken chances. Sarah might have seen the snake. If she'd been able to speak long enough, she might have told the emergency rescue personnel she'd been bitten. And if they'd given her the antidote along with their other life-saving techniques, she might have survived.

No, this killer had taken a chance. He'd injured scores of people in that accident—just to kill Sarah Vining.

When he opened the door, he saw Sean watching the screens by himself.

"Where's Allison?"

"She's in the attic with Logan and Kelsey, going through papers," Sean said. "I'm guessing it's not good news."

"Sarah Vining is dead."

"The crash killed her?" Sean asked.

"That—combined with a copperhead bite."

Sean sat back. As he did so Allison came running down the stairs. She knew from his face that the news was bad.

Logan followed her down more slowly.

"Well?" he asked.

Tyler shook his head.

Allison stopped at the bottom of the stairs. "She's dead? Sarah Vining is dead?"

"I'm sorry."

Shaking, she sank onto a step. "But it was an automobile accident. We saw it on the news. It couldn't have anything to do with what's happening here."

He walked over and sat beside her. She wasn't crying; she just stared ahead, dazed.

"Allison, it wasn't an accident."

She looked at him. "I saw it. I saw it on TV. Dozens of cars and people were involved."

"There was a snake in her car."

"A...snake?"

"She was bitten by a copperhead."

"Yes, but you can survive a snakebite! People survive them all the time."

"Allison, between the snakebite and the trauma of the crash, she died. She caused the crash—because she'd been bitten by a snake. That's not an accident."

"I've never heard of a copperhead being in anyone's car, but I *have* heard of people finding them in their basements or garages," she said. Then she gasped, taking in the reality of another death. "Oh, poor Sarah. She was always such a sad little creature."

"Julian and Sarah. Three days apart. We need to be vigilant. Someone is trying to keep some kind of information from being discovered," Logan said. He walked around in front of Allison. "I'm so sorry. I know you've lost a friend, and now another coworker. This is far more painful for you than we can begin to understand, but the harder we work at learning the truth, the better our chances of saving others."

"You think someone is trying to kill everyone associated with the house?" Allison asked him bluntly.

"Only people who might know something," Tyler said. "Of course, we're speculating, but we're pretty good at sorting things out. This morning, Sarah was talking about getting back into the office. Maybe she came across some kind of information in there the day Julian died. The board was meeting up there, right?"

"Yes."

The word sounded like a sob. He put his arm around her shoulders, thinking that she might well push him away again—but she didn't. "Allison, you've been hit with a lot. Two friends dead, the ghost of a friend, the appearance of a ghost that looks like you and a man in a coma saying your name. It's too much to take in. We understand. But I believe *you* are on to something about the house that someone doesn't want the world to know. Someone who didn't care who they killed in that accident." He paused. "It has to be an employee— or one of the board members."

"And we're down one board member and one em- ployee," Logan said.

"What about the tour groups that were in the house?" she asked. "We might have had someone on one of the tours who was just crazy, or had some bizarre agenda? We can't watch every person every minute they're in here. Someone could have slipped away. And that per- son could have gotten out, too. I hadn't set the alarm when I found Julian's body."

"It's possible," Logan told her.

"But unlikely," Sean said from behind the screens. He came over to them and spoke to Allison. "From what I understand about the boy whose dad is in a coma, the kid's convinced that the ghost of Beast Brad- ley likes you, Allison. I think we should try to coax either Lucy Tarleton or Beast Bradley into appearing to you. If you can get close enough to one or even both of them, they might be able to help. You never know what a ghost might know."

The door opened; Jane and Kat had returned. They were followed by Julian, who was arguing with Kat.

"That was horrible—and completely undignified!" he said.

"Julian!" Kat set her handbag on a side table and turned to him. "If I hadn't asked that they shave your head, we wouldn't know that you'd formed a hematoma. A bruise. Someone had cracked you on the head to get your chin into that blade."

"I *told* you what happened," Julian said. "Good Lord, doesn't anyone listen to me?"

"We all listen to you. And we believe you, Julian," Jane said, trying to calm him down. "But we can't go into a courtroom and tell a jury that your *ghost* told us what happened!"

"As if it wasn't bad enough to see myself with that... that Y incision!" Julian moaned.

"I told you not to come with us," Kat said.

Julian saw that the others were watching him. "Okay, so I shouldn't have gone. But I felt I had to."

"And," Kat continued, "we've proven that what you said is true. If I hadn't done what I did, the medical examiner might still be thinking it was an accident."

"You asked him not to let anything out to the press yet?" Tyler asked.

Kat nodded. "Of course."

"A sound and decent guy?"

"The M.E. on Julian's case was a woman. She's about sixty, and I believe she'll be extremely discreet," Kat said.

Julian walked over to Allison. "See? I told you I was murdered."

"I didn't disbelieve you," Allison told him.

"We're going to solve this," Jane assured Julian. Then she paused, looking at the others. "What's wrong? Did something happen?"

"I called you. Didn't you get my message?" Logan asked.

Jane fumbled in her pocket. "We didn't have our phones. I didn't think to check for messages."

"There was a huge pileup on US1," Logan said. He went on to explain that he and Tyler had gone to the site, and that Tyler had accompanied Sarah to the hospital.

And that Sarah had died.

And the *way* she'd died.

"We have to move fast on this," Jane murmured.

"You'll have to get me in to the autopsy," Kat said urgently, addressing Logan.

"Sarah is...dead? Too?" Julian asked. "And it was made to look like another accident. With a snake. Lord, someone's pushing it. I'm really sorry about Sarah. I'm still really sorry about me."

"My condolences, Allison," Jane said. "But...we need to figure out what's going on. I can play with the different paintings and pictures, and see what I can learn by doing that."

"Are you going to get started now?" Logan asked Jane.

"Yes, unless you need me for anything else?"

"No, I'd like to see what you discover."

"What do you *think* you'll discover?" Allison asked.

"The truth," Jane told her.

Allison smiled at that. "The truth about..."

"The past owners of the house and those who dwelt within," Jane said. "You'll see, and I'm sure you'll find it fascinating."

"Do you need help setting up?" Sean asked her.

"You can grab the box with the printer and scanner," Jane said. "I'm going to set up shop in the grand salon." She turned to Allison. "Please don't worry. I have protective covers for the table."

"You know, I'm not worried about artifacts anymore," Allison said.

"I'm going to do some sketches, photos and comparisons of the paintings in the house. If anyone wants me, that's where I'll be." She shrugged, smoothing back her hair. "Well, whether you want me or not, that's where I'll be."

"Kat, get Kelsey—she's out in the yard. If we're lucky, you can reach the records office before they close and at least start seeing what you can dig up. I'll spell Sean at the screens so he can get some rest." Logan looked at Tyler, and Tyler looked at Allison.

"We have to get back into the office and sort out those papers," he said. "But before it's too late and too dark, I'd like to see the rest of the grounds—through your eyes. I've been wanting to do that and circumstances keep getting in the way. Let's do it now. I'd like you to show me the stables and the family graveyard."

"All right," Allison said slowly.

Julian shuddered. "Graveyard! I think I'll sit with Jane for a while."

"As long as you don't drive me crazy!" Jane warned him.

Julian grinned at Allison. "I woulda had a big crush on her!" he said. He spoke lightly, but she saw the sadness in his eyes. She wanted to give him a warm hug filled with comfort but, of course, she couldn't. And he bent down instead as if he was trying to hug her. "It's going to be okay, Allison. Maybe Sarah...maybe she'll be like me. She'd love to stay in this old place forever. She adored the house."

"That's not helping me, Julian," Allison said.

"Whoa, I'm sorry, not the right thing to say. Okay, well...hmm. I guess I'll go 'haunt' the gorgeous Jane."

"You were gorgeous yourself, my friend," Allison told him. "You were."

He smiled wistfully at her and turned to head into the salon. Sean stood and stretched, and Logan took over his seat.

"Shall we see the property now?" Tyler asked.

"Yes," Allison said. "Give me a minute. I want to rinse my face." She drew in a deep breath. "We'll hear from the rest of the board soon, I imagine. They'll want to arrange something for Sarah."

Tyler nodded. He watched her rise stiffly and walk toward the pantry.

She hadn't been as close to Sarah as she had to Julian.

But she'd lost someone, and everyone deserved a few tears.

"I'll be right back," she promised.

Allison was true to her word. She just needed cold water on her face and a moment alone to breathe.

Now Sarah was dead, too.

But these people, the Krewe, were here to help.

So she was going to help them by doing whatever she could.

She met Tyler back in the salon and motioned for him to follow her.

The narrow hallway in the foyer led straight to the back door; the Tarleton-Dandridge was, despite its grandiose styling, still a shotgun house. The hall had allowed the breeze to sweep right through on hot days.

"The back can be accessed through the pantry and the music room," Tyler noted.

"It's the same door, but the music room and the pantry lead toward it from either side of the house."

"No other doors? Nothing we might have missed?"

She shook her head. "There's a fire escape out of Lucy Tarleton's room. If you look out the right-hand window, you'll see it. It's a legal requirement," she said.

Tyler stopped at the twenty-foot expanse between the house and the stables.

"What?" she asked him.

"I saw the horse," he said. He looked at her. "And the dog."

"Firewalker and Robert?" Had he *seen* them or had he *imagined* them?

"The horse was beautiful, a huge black stallion, about seventeen hands tall," he told her.

"And the dog?"

"Big old hound or maybe some kind of hound mix. Huge and tawny."

"He was a wolfhound mix," Allison said.

"Nice dog," Tyler said. "I wouldn't mind a dog like that. Of course, I guess back then, he had lots of room to run. He wouldn't really make an apartment dog."

"You live in an apartment?"

"For the moment." He scanned the property as they spoke and then his eyes settled on her. "I lived most of my life in San Antonio, but as you know, our main office is in Arlington, Virginia. Our permanent homes are there now. I want to get a house, and there's still plenty of land around us. The closer you get to the Capitol, of course, the harder it becomes to have much of a property. But I'd like to have a horse again, and a dog—something like the ghost dog, an enormous old hound, loyal to the core."

"Also furry, muddy and dirty," Allison said.

"Ah, you're not a dog girl."

"I love dogs! I'll have you know that my little mutt lived to the ripe old age of nineteen. I got him when he was six weeks old and I was four, and we didn't lose him until I'd graduated after my first stint at college." She hesitated. "I wasn't ready for another dog after him, I guess."

He looked out over the property, glad that she seemed to be speaking calmly, that she wasn't in shock the way she'd been after Julian's death.

"Robert must have been a great dog," Tyler said. "I suspect he went everywhere with Lucy Tarleton and that she had to convince him to stay—maybe with her sister, maybe she got a servant to lock him up—every time she made one of her rides down to Valley Forge." He pointed across the stables. "How do you suppose she pulled it off? The family groom must have been loyal to her, and she had to be an excellent rider to slip through the British military that surrounded the city at the time."

"She was passionate about her cause. She'd grown up here and knew the area well, while the British were on foreign soil. I think you're right—the groom knew what she was doing and helped her. If she was caught, she could act the part of a stricken woman, just trying to reach a wounded cousin or friend. She probably played the 'I'm just a woman' card many times. We can't know the details." Allison paused, shrugging lightly. "We get history in one big package, all tied up with the outcome known."

"That's true—and it's human nature to invent or embroider some of those details. We do know she died, but no one was there when it happened—except her father, according to what I've read. There could be no torture worse for a father than seeing his daughter killed."

Allison nodded. "That was the outcome. I like to think about her before the end. Lucy Tarleton didn't *know* she'd get caught when she was riding through the night. But so many people took huge risks, even though they knew the punishment for what they were doing could be death. It's strange, you make me think of the colonists' day-to-day life in a way I haven't for a while. And about Lucy. She was like any other woman of any other time. She loved her dog, and her dog was fiercely loyal and loving to her." Allison shivered. "I can only imagine the day Beast Bradley caught her. She was returning from one of her spy missions, but I don't believe he ever *proved* she was spying. I think he found out about Stewart Douglas—that's how the story came down to us, anyway."

"A girl with a dog and a horse," Tyler murmured.

"The dog was killed, you know. According to the legend. I'm hoping he ripped his attacker to shreds before he went down."

"I'm sure he fought tooth and nail," Tyler said. "Maybe he stays around because he's looking for Lucy."

"But the horse wasn't killed," Allison told him. "Actually, the fate of the horse is a curious one. The British took him when they evacuated Philadelphia. But he wound up back here—he's buried in the graveyard, too. So is the dog. There's an area toward the rear for family pets."

"Let's go see it, shall we?"

"Okay." Allison smiled at him.

There'd been something about their conversation here that was wistful and poignant. Allison wasn't sure what she'd thought about him before, other than that unmistakable attraction, but they seemed to be drawing closer.

Maybe she needed to back away. She'd lost friends. She was learning all about the world beneath what was seen, and she was coming in contact with *entities* that were uninvited.

But it felt as if Tyler had now been part of her life forever, although it had just been a few days. She was becoming dependent on him. He could be harsh, but only to make her see.

He was definitely an imposing person.

Maybe any time a tall man with a gun came from Texas, the rest of the world automatically assumed *cowboy*. He was tall, extremely well-built, and now that they'd shared a quiet moment thinking about the *lives* of others rather than their deaths, she knew she liked his mind and the way he thought. She suddenly knew that he wasn't just attractive, he was...sexually appealing. For the past few months, she'd refused to even consider a relationship with anyone, not after her last fiasco....

Another person had died. And here she was, thinking about this man.

"Yes!" she said, turning away from him. "The graveyard! The family plot. Well, let me get into tour guide mode here." She moved past him. Allison wondered if, when this mystery was solved, he would go back to Virginia, or on to another city to solve another problem. She would always remember this moment, standing in the yard, reflecting on the life of a long-dead woman and the simple human fact that she had loved her dog. This moment, because it was when Allison discovered she was intrigued and excited by being near him. She wondered what it would be like to really touch him....

She launched into her talk. "The stables, as you see,

are to your right. There's actually work space in the old servants' quarters over the stables. There are stalls for eight horses, a tack room and a little office. The watering trough is still there—it's the original stone trough. The stalls themselves are wood and have been repaired over the years, but the circular carving on the gates to the individual stalls is original. As we pass the stables, we come to the family graveyard. It was a huge property back then, so it was natural that household members were buried here. During the yellow fever epidemic, the family moved out of the city and came back afterward. They were blessed. None of the Dandridge family died." She paused. "You probably know that a yellow fever epidemic swept through Philadelphia in the summer of 1793."

"I've been reading up." He smiled at her. "I don't know as much as you do, but yes, the then-capital city had a population of about fifty-five thousand. Dolley Madison lost her first husband and two of her children during the epidemic."

"Well, the Dandridge family was smart—they got out. They weren't here when the criers went through the town saying, 'Bring out your dead, bring out your dead!'"

She looked at the stables; she went through them so often. Cleaned out now, as they'd been since the turn of the twentieth century, they still smelled of leather, horses, cigars and polish. The upstairs had been converted to caretaker apartments long ago, before the house was bequeathed to Old Philly History.

"Graveyard now?" Tyler asked. "Or are you stalling?"

She laughed. "Why worry about a graveyard? A

ghost appeared to me in my living room. What else is there to fear?"

"From the dead, usually nothing. Although…"

"What, the dead can be evil?"

"I wasn't involved with the cases, but a few times, when someone really evil died somewhere—that somewhere being a place where they'd killed and tortured others—there was a remnant of evil that lingered. But the *ghosts* didn't kill. Sometimes, maybe evil attracts evil."

"I don't believe the Tarleton-Dandridge family was evil in any way, so the family graveyard should be safe," she said. "And thankfully, it is broad daylight."

She started walking ahead, leading him past the stables.

The old family graveyard had the right aura. There were several vaults dedicated to the family, and there were plots with large angels and obelisks, memorials to other family members.

"A lot of people found a last resting place here," Tyler commented.

"They often had big families back then. Sophia and Tobias Dandridge had seven children, and those children went off and had more children, and that was over two hundred years ago, so…"

A small brick wall, about three feet high, surrounded the burying ground. There was a little picket fence at the entry, and stones had been laid out as walkways.

"I take it you're looking for Lucy first?" Allison asked Tyler.

"Yes, I'd like to see her grave. But I'm guessing it's in the chapellike vault over there—center, toward the rear. The one that says Tarleton."

"Yes, she's in there. Lucy, her father, her mother,

her father's parents, one aunt who never married and an uncle who'd been an Episcopal priest," Allison told him. "A few of the family who came before Angus are there, too, but the vault was constructed while the Revolution was being waged, so the others were reentombed. At least I assume so."

They skirted angels and cherubs and two smaller vaults to reach the largest and finest of the vaults, which was guarded by a metal gate and a wooden door. Allison thought Tyler was surprised when she pulled open the gate.

"It's not locked?"

"No. It's actually a nice little chapel, as well. It has an altar, a few benches and a stained-glass window in back. Lucy's uncle James is buried under the altar. There's a pretty monument to her aunt Cecilia toward the front, and we believe she's buried there. You'll see monuments on the other walls, and those are to Angus's parents and a few other family members. And Lucy, Angus and Susannah—Lucy's mother—are in marble tombs just behind the altar, beneath the stained-glass window. They're really striking—reminiscent of Renaissance tombs."

Allison wasn't sure why, but when she entered the vault, she bypassed the old stone benches and walked around the altar to come to the middle of the tombs at the rear. Light was streaming through the cut-glass windows high above, casting dancing rays upon the effigies of the three Tarleton family members.

Lucy was in the middle. Sculpted out of marble, she seemed beautifully at peace. Her long hair crowned her head and face; she held a bouquet of flowers in her hands. Her mother's tomb was similar—flowers seemed to be the object of choice for the sculptor when it came to women—while Angus was holding a book.

"Wow, impressive tombs. They must be the only ones like this in the city."

"I haven't seen many like them. Seriously, they look as if they belong in Notre Dame or Westminster Abbey."

"Exceptionally fine."

"Were you expecting to find Lucy rotting away in a shroud, entombed in a wall?" Allison asked him, a note of teasing reproach in her voice.

"Honestly? Yes. Not that it really matters what becomes of the body once we're gone. Unless, of course, you do remain behind and have to watch," he said thoughtfully. "Has she ever been disinterred?"

"Goodness, no! That would be akin to blasphemy."

"I'm just curious. We take for granted that the history that came down to us was true—that Lord Bradley killed her."

"So far, there hasn't been much reason to doubt it. From all accounts, the Tarleton family was a loving one. The history comes from Sophia and her husband, Tobias Dandridge. They loved Lucy, they were patriots—and there was no reason for them to lie about what happened," Allison said. "We might not have completely firm and unimpeachable evidence, but I've always believed their version. I'm not sure why you think it's a lie."

"I'm not saying that. I'm just questioning the telling of this particular tale."

"Why?"

"For one thing, the paintings of Lord Brian Bradley. They're so different."

"Two different artists."

Tyler shrugged. "Speaking of different artists—where is Tobias Dandridge?"

Allison told him, "Outside, to your right facing the house. It's a pretty little vault, too, but more like you'd expect. It's a typical small mausoleum."

They went outside the Dandridge vault and followed a little pebbled path around the graveyard's various sections. Allison always found it sad to see the Colonial- and Victorian-era markers for children. So many died so young.

The Dandridge vault had a bronze plaque above it that trumpeted the family name. It was about the same size as the Tarleton vault, but the rows of etched markers outside announced many more names.

"Lots more Dandridges," Tyler said.

"Well, the Tarleton family name died out with Angus," Allison reminded him.

They didn't enter the tomb; here the gate and door were locked. There was nothing for tourists to see.

"Back there. I'll show you where Robert the dog is buried," Allison told him.

There were a number of markers for pets. One of them, recently imbedded, was dedicated to Bibi the cat.

"She was here when I was a teenager," Allison said. "The guides fed her. Everyone loved her. And here, just a few feet away—there's Robert."

A very handsome stone statue of a dog had been carved to sit atop the grave. The hound must have been close to two hundred pounds.

"He must have been something to wrestle with," Tyler commented.

"I imagine that's why he was killed."

"Was he shot, stabbed—taken down with a rifle butt or a bayonet?" Tyler asked.

"I don't know. You can read the memorial stone—we have a group from the university that comes out to clean and repair these all the time. It says, 'Robert, a fine patriot who died in defense of his beloved mistress, Lucy Tarleton.'"

Tyler paused to read the memorial and then he looked up at her.

"Do you ever *feel* Lucy out here, or any of the family? Anything, like even the brush of a cold nose against your fingers?"

"No," she said a little harshly. Had she ever felt such a thing? She wasn't sure.

She'd never believed in ghosts before. If she *had* felt something, she would've thought that the chill of winter was coming on....

"No," she repeated, suddenly eager to leave the graveyard. "Well, let's go back to the house. It is heading toward fall, you know. It's getting cool."

"You're welcome to my jacket," he said, starting to shed it.

"Thanks. But let's just go back."

She walked ahead of him, hurrying toward the house. As she neared it, she glanced up—and nearly tripped.

She caught herself. And froze.

There was someone upstairs, looking out Lucy's window. Allison told herself that it might be Jane. Or maybe Kelsey had returned.

But she knew better; she'd seen the image on screen.

It was frighteningly like looking in a mirror.

For a moment, it seemed as if Lucy Tarleton had defied the ages and stared down at her, sadness and yearning on her face.

And then she faded as if she'd never been, and Allison wondered again what might be real to a sixth sense or on a different dimension, and what might be a trick of her tortured mind.

"What is it?" Tyler asked her.

"Nothing," she said. But as she entered the house, she felt something touch her fingers.

Like the cold, wet nose of a very large dog.

12

Tyler realized that Allison had hung back, but when he reached the foyer and the bank of screens again, she was right behind him.

"Where is everyone?" he asked Sean.

"Logan has gone off with Kelsey to continue searching through old records, and Kat's at the morgue. Jane is still working in the salon."

"We're going up to the attic," Tyler said. "I could be wrong. But I believe there's something in the research papers—or maybe in papers that were stolen—that may be the clue to all this."

Sean nodded.

Allison touched Tyler's arm. "Should we go to the morgue first?" she asked him.

Tyler hesitated. "Can you take it?"

She looked at him with clear, level eyes. "I can take anything, I think."

He raised his brows.

She shrugged with a half smile. "A ghost, phantoms on a screen…what's one more ghost?" she asked dryly.

"All right—if you're sure that's what you want to do."

"I'm sure. I knew Sarah best."

"The autopsy is scheduled for tomorrow," Sean told them. "Logan was hoping that—"

"He was hoping that Sarah remained behind," Allison said. "Right? And that's the thing. She may speak to me where she wouldn't speak to others."

"Fine. We'll go," Tyler said.

To his surprise, Allison seemed calm and rational during their drive.

The morgue was a comprehensive and up-to-date facility. As they walked to the entry, he saw that she'd turned a little pale.

"You're *sure* you're all right to do this?" he asked.

She offered him a weak smile. "I've never been here. This is my city, and in all these years, I've never been here."

"Not many people make a habit of hanging out at the medical examiner's offices," he said.

As they continued into the building, Tyler called Jane. She told him not to worry. Adam Harrison had greased the wheels and there'd be no difficulty getting them in.

The medical pathologist who'd been given Julian Mitchell's case was also on Sarah's; that had been arranged by Adam. Her name was Dr. Ana Grant, and she came with Kat to meet them in the vestibule. Slim with short graying hair and an easy manner, she spoke in a well-modulated voice that held empathy as well as professionalism.

"Dr. Grant has been very helpful," Kat told him.

"Sarah Vining's body just arrived," Dr. Grant said after the introductions. "I was showing your associate the snakebite marks when you called. We came out to escort you back—I'm afraid she's in a freezer room with other…guests. Her autopsy is scheduled for tomorrow morning, but her body has been cleaned in prep."

Tyler had been in many a morgue. He wanted to put a protective arm around Allison's shoulders, but held himself in check. She was still pale, but she didn't look as if she was about to pass out or collapse in horror. Of course, the outer offices of the medical examiner's office were neat and orderly in appearance.

But as they entered the hallways, he thought he could detect the chemical odor that hinted of death and he kept a sharp eye on Allison.

She moved up next to him. "Do people ever think you're mentally ill when you want to touch the dead?" she asked him in a whisper.

"We do it discreetly," he whispered back.

A few minutes later they were staring down at Sarah Vining's body, covered with a sheet.

Sarah looked small, skinny and gray.

"The bite mark is on the inner thigh just above the knee. She was driving when the snake panicked and struck her. I assume it had somehow gotten under the seat."

He watched as Dr. Grant showed them the bite marks but then he looked at Allison. She was almost as gray as Sarah Vining.

She stepped forward, saying softly, "She was a friend."

"I understand," Dr. Grant said.

Allison touched Sarah's hair. Tyler thought she'd step back quickly, but she didn't. She stayed there, gently touching the dead woman and gazing down at her.

Dr. Grant spoke quietly to Kat and Tyler. "I don't think we'll find anything we don't see here when the autopsy is performed," she said. "I'll know better what organs gave out when, but I have an educated hunch that between the bite and the trauma of the accident, her heart failed her."

"Have you ever heard of such a thing before?" Tyler asked.

"People dying after a bite like that?" Dr. Grant shrugged. "Copperheads are dangerous and can be vicious when they're threatened. But we do have antidotes for the bites, and these days most people survive. But elderly people, small children, those who are ill when they're bitten—they're in the greatest danger. The heart can fail under stress and trauma. That's what I believe happened to Sarah. And in the midst of that massive accident, I'm sure no one expected her real problem to be a snakebite."

"Thank you," Tyler said, glancing from Dr. Grant to Kat.

Allison hadn't been listening. He saw that she was staring down at Sarah Vining, her fingers still resting lightly on her hair.

"Allison?"

She looked up at him. "I'm ready," she said.

Kat stayed behind; there was evidently more of a medical nature that she wanted to discuss with Dr. Grant.

Tyler led Allison out. "Anything?" he asked her as they reached the car.

"Sorrow and confusion," she told him.

"I can only imagine how you feel," Tyler said.

She shook her head. "No. Yes, I mean, of course, my heart bleeds for both Julian and Sarah. They were murdered, their lives were stolen from them. That's what I got from Sarah. She doesn't *know* why she's dead. She doesn't understand. She doesn't remember anything except for a sudden and excruciating pain—and then the air bag blowing up in her face. She remembers stumbling out and being thrown several feet while the world seemed to explode around her in horrible screeches and bangs while the other cars crashed into one another."

"So she *is* there?" he asked incredulously. He grimaced. "You felt her—heard her—and neither Kat nor I did?"

Allison nodded. "I felt as if her eyes opened and she looked at me. And it was as if I could hear her." She was quiet for a minute. "She doesn't mind that she's dead. She said she has incredible faith and she's…she's waiting to go. Oh, and she wants to be buried or entombed at the house. Do you think our friend Adam has the clout to arrange that?"

"We'll see," he said, climbing into the driver's seat. "But," he added as she joined him, "Adam does seem to have the power to make the earth move—no pun intended. I'm sure he can do something." He put the car into reverse and turned to drive out of the lot before he spoke to her again. "You're okay?" he murmured.

"I'm fine. I came because I'm the 'key,'" she told him with a self-conscious shrug. "I'll admit I've been frightened out of my mind. But that all started the moment I saw Julian dead in the study. It got worse when I saw him as a ghost. And then Lucy. And then the whole thing with Mr. Dixon… But I'm tired of being terrified. I want to get to the end of this, no matter what it is. I don't want anyone else dying, and I don't understand why Julian and Sarah are dead. And why a man who visited the house is in a coma. Whatever is going on, right now I feel like saying 'come and do your worst' because I'm…ready to fight back." She turned to look at him with an awkward smile.

He nodded slowly. "It's a terrible thing to go through life frightened."

"I just... I don't get it. I really didn't believe in ghosts. I actually think I *wanted* to believe in ghosts, because then I'd know there was something beyond this life. But...why now?"

She twisted in her seat to face him as he drove. "What about you? Supposedly, if you're going to have second sight, you're born with it."

"Not me. My first reaction was like yours."

"How? What did you do?"

"Drank," he said. "Like I told you before." She gave him a frown and he laughed softly, then launched into his story about finding the younger sister of the dead heroin dealer in Texas, the woman whose ghost had appeared repeatedly to him. "After that," he concluded, "it seemed as if a door had opened. And I worked with Logan, who's one of those people who *saw* things at an early age, but he has Native American blood and I often think Native Americans have a far greater understanding that the world is more than what we see. But even Logan was always careful. Maybe this second sight or extra sense comes to people when it's necessary. We— and by *we* I mean our Krewes—don't have any real answers and we don't pretend to. We've just learned that the dead may be out there—and that they have reasons for their presence and they may be able to help."

He was surprised to see a smile curving her lips.

"What's so amusing?"

"With my new power, maybe I can summon all the old statesmen and leaders and wives I've wanted to meet. Dolley Madison must have been an incredible woman. And how I'd love to meet Lincoln—and Robert E. Lee!"

"I wish it worked that way," he told her. "Most of the time, people do move on. Good thing, or the streets would be so crowded with specters that none of us would be able to take a step." She laughed, but he grew serious as he said, "I think that when a soul is finally at peace, it does move on."

She seemed more comfortable with him than she'd ever been. And she seemed stronger. He knew he'd met her at a time of crisis in her life—but that she had an inner strength and real courage.

"Another favorite historical heroine of mine has always been Lucy Tarleton," she said. "And we *know* she's stayed behind. We've seen her on the screens, walking around the house in the middle of the night."

"We have to coax her out," he said.

"Why won't she just come to us and say, *Listen, here's the way it really was?*"

"We don't have all the answers, I told you that. Certain spirits will talk to certain people. Some never learn how to be seen and heard."

She smiled at him, then sobered. "I shouldn't be smiling. Two colleagues are dead—and speaking to me. But the reality is they're dead. And that fact is still devastating."

He reached over to squeeze her hand, once again wondering, as he touched her, if she'd draw away. But she didn't.

They returned to the Tarleton-Dandridge House. Sean had left; Logan was in his place, with Kelsey at his side.

"Anything?" Logan and Tyler said at the same time.

"I'll answer first," Logan said. "We found records with birth and death dates, family trees—nothing we didn't know. But it's good to investigate, to make sure we're not assuming something is obvious, only to find out we're wrong. What about the morgue?"

Tyler was surprised when Allison gave a full report on her exchange with Sarah Vining.

Logan nodded. "So she didn't know anything at all—except that she was suddenly in pain and then staggering out in a melee of cars colliding?"

"Nothing. She doesn't know why she's dead. All she knows is that she is. And she's oddly at peace with it," Allison told him.

"Some people just are," Logan said. "We're on earth for only so long, and I believe that peace comes to some people when they've died." He was thoughtful for a moment. "But Sarah's still here."

"Maybe because she's part of this...whatever it is," Tyler said.

"Maybe," Logan agreed. "It's really late, you two. There are sandwiches in the pantry, sodas, beer, some wine... Coffee, too, but I'm not suggesting that now. It's about time to get some sleep."

Allison turned to Tyler. "You wanted to look through papers in the attic."

"It can wait until morning," he said.

"I think we should go back now. We've gotten started. Let's give it an hour."

Allison had undergone a complete change, he realized. He smiled. "Rome wasn't built in a day."

She obviously wasn't impressed with his cliché. "But two friends have died in a matter of days," she said.

"You're right. We'll grab a sandwich and head on up."

Thirty minutes later they were back in the attic. Allison made piles, gathering financial papers to put with financial papers, bookings for private events with bookings for other private events, and research materials with other research materials. He offered to help her but she suggested he read; she knew what she was doing.

He came across a number of articles on the people of Philadelphia at the time of the Revolution and found himself fascinated by these snippets of history. He'd assumed that, with the exception of the Civil War, their own era was the most contentious in American history, but now he recognized that the founding fathers hadn't had an easy task. Nor had the patriots and their families. There were cases in which sons were determined on the Revolution while their fathers were adamant that they pack up for Canada—the British colonies—"until the foolish fighting and dying was over." There were sad human-interest pieces on daughters who'd married into patriot or Loyalist families when their parents were on the opposite side.

As he read through newspaper, magazine and other articles printed from online sites, he noticed that Allison had finished gathering most of the paperwork together but seemed troubled. She looked at him.

"May I?" she asked.

He was seated on the floor, back against the wall, his pile of research materials before him. She indicated the pile. "Of course," he told her.

"I was thinking about a certain article. It was written by a man who'd been a high school history teacher in Maryland and then moved to Valley Forge and had his own tour company. He knows quite a lot about generals, including Washington, and even the enlisted men."

"I was looking at it the other night," Tyler said, producing the article he'd been reading about Beast Bradley just before he'd made Julian's acquaintance and the others had arrived. "It's by Martin Standish. Is this it? 'Brian Bradley was born to Lord and Lady Bradley in Yorkshire, England, in 1750. His family could easily trace their lineage to the Royal House of Hanover— literally, he was born with a silver spoon ready for his mouth.'"

"Yes—I mean, no," she said. "That was the first of two articles he wrote. I'd been planning to drive down to see him. He's a brilliant man. The first article focused on Bradley. He wrote another on Lucy and her patriot lover, Stewart Douglas—and that's gone missing. I remember that he focused on the Tarleton family and their social situation and standing as the crises came to a head. It's assumed that both Bradley and Douglas were killed during the war—but there's no proof. They were presumed dead. Neither of them appeared to claim their property afterward, and because of who he was, it was assumed that perhaps Bradley's own men did him in and that's why there's no record of it. And of course hundreds of men died on battlefields and were never identified."

"I'd like to see that second article," Tyler said. "Can't you just bring it back up online?"

"I'm sure I could."

"But why would someone take it?" he asked.

"I don't know. He quotes from letters he has in his own possession and they make her patriot lover sound like a bit of an ass. Maybe that's what someone didn't want anyone taking seriously?" Allison suggested.

"He's not even buried here, is he? Stewart Douglas, I mean. Do you speak about him on the tours?"

"Sometimes. We would've spoken about him a lot more if he was buried here, but he isn't."

"Was he supposed to have killed Beast Bradley in retaliation?"

"We don't know. I guess that's one theory. All we know is that neither of them came home after the Revolution—to Philadelphia or England—so the assumption is that they were both buried in a mass grave at some battlefield. Although historians know what happened to a lot of rank-and-file soldiers. Those two just seem to have disappeared."

"Have you spoken with this fellow—Martin Standish?"

"I've emailed him a few times. He appreciates my interest—he thinks it's great that people at the house aren't just ignoring him. I guess he tried to make contact years before and he was shut out. I can call him." She gave him a puzzled look. "Do you think he can help?"

"Maybe." Tyler stood, yawning. "Okay, I've got to call it quits. That means you have to call it quits. The rest of the house has called it quits."

"I can keep going—"

"No. I want you across the hall. I want to jump out of bed like a lightning bolt if I hear the slightest sound coming from your room."

She sighed. "I *am* tired."

"Then we definitely call it quits. No one'll be coming up here until we come back. No one can get in the house without us knowing it. No one—dead or alive—can move around downstairs without appearing on one of Sean's screens. Bed," he said firmly.

She lowered her head for a moment and then nodded. "Fine."

He didn't turn out the attic lights; he wanted anything that happened up there clearly visible on the screens.

They went downstairs to the second floor.

Julian—or Julian's spirit—was slumped against the wall by Allison's room. For a ghost, he seemed to need his sleep.

"Good night," Allison whispered to Tyler.

"Good night," he said. "Leave the door cracked. If anything happens, scream like a banshee. I'll be right with you."

Men were supposed to have the minds that resided in gutters, Allison told herself.

But when Tyler had said that one word—*bed*—her mind had immediately leaped to other thoughts.

As she lay down to sleep, she realized that her opinion of him had changed drastically. When they first met, she'd considered him a tall, good-looking shyster who was going to turn this house into a gawker's showcase. She'd imagined ridiculous lights and people caught in them with wide, reflecting eyes while they shouted, "Did you hear that?" or, "Yes, there's a ghost here, I can feel it…."

But she knew differently now.

Now, he was tall and good-looking and exceedingly…

Attractive. Sensual. Yes, the word *bed* had made her think of quite another way that a bed could be used.

She had to stop thinking like that. He was with five other agents. He was kind and protective and sincere in his efforts to help her—and be helped by her.

She wasn't an object of attraction or sexual interest to him.

She was a *key*.

But she couldn't stop remembering the way it felt when he touched her. His hand on hers, electricity shooting through her. There was something about him....

The machismo of a Texan, a cowboy.

Except he wasn't like that. Well, he was a Texan, but he didn't seem to think a man had his place and a woman had hers. He was just strong by nature—and he was there whenever she felt confused or vulnerable.

Transference. That was it. He was her rock through all of this. She wasn't *really* attracted; she was just leaning on him. That wasn't true. Yes, it was. She was leaning on him.

But she *liked* him. And she hadn't trusted herself since she'd ended it with Peter Aubrey. She'd understood that Peter had loved her, but he was an addict and he wasn't going to change for her *or* for himself. What she'd done was right, and she could only hope that Peter would live long enough to find his way.

So, yes, this stirring was fantastic. This longing, this...

Bed.

She found herself imagining him naked. His body was long, sleek and hard—she knew that. He was probably beautiful when he was naked.

She groaned, tossing in bed. This was ridiculous. She'd been better off when she'd considered him a ghost-busting sexist.

She had to sleep. She had to stop her mind from going in this direction. She had to remember that Sarah Vining was dead. Dead. Someone was killing people, and they were here to figure out why.

She closed her eyes and prayed for sleep.

Eventually, it came.

She didn't dream in the night; she awoke suddenly. When she did, she saw someone at the foot of the bed.

She would have screamed except that the scream died in her throat, and while she was gasping for breath, she saw that it was the woman who'd appeared on Sean's footage the night before.

Lucy Tarleton.

A woman she resembled to an uncanny degree.

Fear nearly strangled her.

The ghost of a friend slept outside her door, and she had spoken to the corpse of another that afternoon. There was no reason to feel such terror at this point, especially since she was certain the woman had not come to hurt her.

Lucy raised a finger to her lips. She looked around as if afraid she'd be seen. She walked out of the room, then returned, hovering by the doorframe and beckoning to Allison.

Again, as it had earlier that day, Allison's terror receded.

She reminded herself of what she'd determined earlier—she wasn't going to live in fear. Whatever this was, she was seeing it through.

She rose from her bed, letting the spirit know that she meant to follow. As she trailed behind Lucy, the ghost began moving more swiftly. Allison was halfway down the stairs before she heard Tyler calling her.

She paused but didn't stop. Tyler would follow her; she didn't want to lose the ghost.

Lucy swept down the stairs and turned into the central hallway, heading for the door. When Allison reached it, Tyler was right behind her.

"Allison!"

"It's Lucy. She just went through the door," Allison explained. "I have to get out there. I have to see where she's leading me."

Tyler didn't question her. He keyed in the number on the alarm and opened the door.

They both stepped out.

Lucy was mounting Firewalker, the great black horse. The dog, Robert, was barking and running around excitedly. Firewalker reared up, and Lucy spoke affectionately to the dog, ordering him back to the house.

The dog obeyed, but stood by the house barking.

Then Lucy leaned forward, speaking to the horse and nudging him with her heels.

The horse broke into a canter.

And Firewalker and Lucy raced into the night.

Allison felt Tyler's hands on her shoulders. "Did you see that?" she whispered.

"Yes."

"What does it mean?" Allison asked. It was chilly outside; she was dressed in a blue flannel nightshirt. Behind her, Tyler wore nothing but pajama pants. He had to be cold, but it seemed that he came closer to warm her. She felt the length of his body.

It was distracting.

Even more distracting than a ghost who'd come to her bedroom and lured her down the stairs.

"When did you see her? How did you see her?" Tyler asked.

"I woke up. She was at the foot of my bed. She wanted me to follow her," Allison said.

What *she* wanted was to lean back in his arms. She wanted to trust him. She wanted to forget everything that was going on and even herself—to relish the feel of him and forget the world and indulge in nothing but sexual passion and pure carnal pleasure.

She heard him swallow behind her. He stepped back.

Had he been thinking along the same lines?

"She wanted you to follow her, and she came out here—and mounted her horse and rode away," he mused. "She still wants you to follow," he said after a moment.

Allison struggled to keep her thoughts where they should be.

"I can't. I don't have a ghost horse—or any horse—of my own, and if I did...I don't know how to ride."

She turned and saw that he was smiling.

"Where did she go when she left here?" he asked.

"You know where she went—she carried secrets to the patriots at Valley Forge."

He nodded. "And where is that writer you've been emailing?"

"Valley Forge," she said, frowning.

"Lucy wants you to go to Valley Forge," he said.

"Hey, what's up?" Logan had come down. He was wearing a robe—and he was armed and ready.

Tyler quickly explained. Logan nodded. "Sounds like a field trip to me. But it's three in the morning. I think you should wait until a normal hour and then go. That is, Allison, if the writer's willing to see you. If he's there. You don't know, do you, if the man still lives in Valley Forge?"

"We communicated not long ago. I don't think he leaves that often, although he does participate in battle reenactments," Allison said.

"Call him around nine," Tyler suggested. "And if he's agreeable, we'll see him tomorrow. And even if he's not...Lucy wants you to follow her. She rode to Valley Forge. That's what we have to do."

"The two of you can leave tomorrow. Jane can continue working with the likenesses and Kat will attend the autopsy. We'll keep working the records from this angle, and Sean can monitor the house to see what goes on here in your absence. That is, if you're willing to do all this, Allison?" Logan asked.

Road trip! Alone with Tyler.

Not a good idea. But necessary.

She felt strangely weak and strong at the same time.

"Allison?" Tyler prompted her.

She had to force herself not to smile. There was nothing to smile about. Two people were dead. They were just going on a research mission.

"Yes, of course," she said primly. "I'll do whatever it takes."

The rest of the household—including Julian, who managed to look sleepy even though he was a ghost—had come outside.

Allison noticed that all the other Krewe members were armed. Everyone moved back into the house and gathered in the entry around the screens.

"Ally?" Julian sounded concerned.

"I'm fine," she assured him.

"I didn't hear you move!" Julian said. "Am I supposed to sleep like that?"

"Did you love to sleep when you were alive?" Kelsey asked him. "Did you keep late hours?"

"Yeah, well, I was always burning the candle at both ends," he said apologetically.

"I'm fine, really. I followed Lucy of my own accord, and I ran the way I did because I didn't want her to disappear," Allison explained.

"Still, you should have gotten me first," Tyler said.

"You were right behind me."

"Yes, but you shouldn't take off without me."

"You didn't bring your gun," Allison pointed out.

She thought he flushed slightly at that; he should have been armed.

"That's why you should get me instead of making me bolt out to catch up with you," Tyler grumbled.

"It's important that none of us go off on our own from now on," Logan said firmly.

Jane yawned. "I could use some more sleep. Okay if I go back to bed?"

Logan nodded. "Go on up."

"I want to see what we caught on our digital film," Sean said, walking over to take his seat by the screens.

He hit some keys on the computer keyboard, and they saw the film in reverse. Seconds later, it moved forward.

Lucy appeared at the foot of the stairs as she had before. Then she looked into Angus Tarleton's study.

She left the study and hurried up the stairs, where she entered Allison's room.

She reappeared a moment later.

And then they saw Allison running out and, within a split second, Tyler bursting out of his room to follow her.

"You do have good hearing," Allison murmured.

They watched as Lucy, followed by Allison and Tyler, raced to the back door.

Sean reset the cameras. "The resemblance is really uncanny," he commented.

Allison sighed. "I'm not a Tarleton or a Dandridge. My records prove it. I wasn't adopted. In fact, my mom had me at the same hospital where Artie Dixon is now."

"Yes, of course," Tyler said thoughtfully.

"You thinking what I'm thinking?" Logan asked him.

Tyler nodded, studying Allison.

"I *wasn't* adopted," she said, shaking her head. She wasn't angry, just amused. They were so determined to find a reason for the resemblance.

"No," Tyler agreed. "*You* weren't adopted. But I'm willing to bet someone in your family was."

"We'll look for any possibility when we study the records while you're gone," Logan told them.

"Adoption is wonderful, but I know that neither of my parents was adopted, either. One of my best friends in school was, and my dad used to tell her how fortunate she was that her parents had chosen her and loved her so much," Allison said.

"I wasn't thinking about your parents," Tyler said. "I'm thinking further back. *Much* further back."

"What do you mean?" Allison asked him.

"I mean back to Lucy Tarleton."

13

"You can't go to Valley Forge today," Kelsey told Tyler the next morning as he walked into the pantry to pour a cup of coffee after he'd showered and dressed.

"Why not?"

"Because we have an invitation," Kelsey told him.

"To what?"

"It's easy to understand why you've forgotten," Kelsey said with a wry grin. "Cherry Addison. Remember, yesterday, before all hell broke loose? She invited us to her husband's showing. You could go to Valley Forge and we could go to the show, but I believe all our suspects will be there."

"Valley Forge is only about twenty miles north of the city," Tyler said. "It's a day trip for a lot of people visiting Philly."

"Yes, but what if you do find something there?"

Tyler frowned. He wanted to get to Valley Forge, but seeing all the suspects in one place at one time was too good an opportunity to miss.

"Are they still having the show?" Tyler asked. "Sarah Vining died yesterday."

"That's not enough to stop this, with the gallery set up and all the invitations sent out. Even if it conflicted with a funeral, which it won't, I'm not sure the Addisons would have stopped it," Kelsey said. "And at Kat's request, they're holding Julian's *and* Sarah's bodies for at least a few days, so..."

Kelsey handed Tyler a cup of coffee. "Your call."

"What time is the showing?"

"I called Mrs. Addison this morning. Cocktails and hors d'oeuvres at six. Her husband, George, the artist, will be there, of course, to meet with his adoring fans."

"I understand he's good."

"We'll find out, won't we?"

"I guess so. Kat's going back to the morgue, right?"

Kelsey nodded. "I'm going to watch the house with Jane and Sean. Jane's still working, but you'll want to see the images she's come up with so far. I've spelled Sean a few times. He's equally convinced we've got to pay attention to the cameras—"

"We do," Tyler interrupted.

"Logan is going to the records office to see what he can discover."

"All right," Tyler said. "I'm heading down to the police station to talk to Jenson. When Allison wakes up, will you tell her what's going on?"

"I will. Anything else you want her to know or do?"

"Yes, ask her to print out the missing article—she believes she can find it online," Tyler said. "And ask her to call Martin Standish and see if we can set something up for tomorrow."

"Okay. See you later, then."

Jenson wasn't the officer investigating the accident that had injured two dozen people—several still in critical condition—and killed Sarah, but he offered any help Tyler and his Krewe might need. He also asked for an update on anything they'd discovered.

"We believe, beyond a reasonable doubt, that the death of Julian Mitchell was engineered. But we don't know why someone was rummaging through the attic, or if the same person tore apart the attic *and* killed Mr. Mitchell," Tyler explained. "We also believe yesterday's accident was maliciously planned with the intent to kill Sarah."

"I've heard there was a snake in Ms. Vining's car," Jenson said. "That's a far-fetched way to commit murder. The snake *might* just have crawled into the vehicle."

"How did a snake happen to crawl into *her* car?" Tyler asked in turn.

"It's not impossible."

"That snake was planted there," Tyler insisted. "Oh, has anyone found it yet?"

Jenson shook his head. "No one was looking for a snake. The car was towed to the impound. Of course, as soon as the PPD heard about the snakebite, we warned the men and women working the car to be careful and on the lookout for a snake. Thing is, that snake might be long gone by now."

"Or it might still be hiding in the car," Tyler warned.

"That's true. I don't think the vehicular people have examined the car yet. I'll make a call as soon as we're through." He paused, his expression puzzled. "The real question is, why would anyone risk the lives of that many people to kill one?"

"To make it look like an accident."

"I don't buy it," Jenson told him, clearly not won over. "Are we talking about insanity here?"

"So far, Sarah's is the only death, but a few others are critical," Tyler reminded him. "And I'm not suggesting that whoever's doing this is insane. I just think the agenda this person has precludes caring about any collateral damage."

"What can I do at my end?" Jenson asked. "If we find the creature—well, it's unlikely a snake is going to talk."

Tyler was surprised; Jenson did seem to have a sense of wry humor.

"No, but what you can do is check to see if any have been sold lately. Our murderer *might* have purchased the snake."

"Agent Montague, this is Philadelphia. We've sent out an alert, but I doubt we'll get anything. Copperheads are easy to find in the woods that surround the city," Jenson said. "They show up in basements and garages. We've also contacted Philadelphia's animal control, but they haven't had anyone call to ask *for* a copperhead. But you're right. We'll follow every angle."

"Whoever is doing this is extremely clever. These murders have taken calculation and planning and they've required a certain level of risk."

Jenson hesitated. "You're *sure* they're all murders?"

"I'm positive Sarah's is. And there's evidence of a blow on Julian Mitchell's head. That proves someone shoved him down on that bayonet. So, yes, I'm sure."

Jenson still didn't seem convinced, but he wasn't argumentative. "What do you want from me?"

"Have your men keep an eye on Ethan Oxford, Nathan Pierson, Cherry Addison, Jason Lawrence and Annette Fanning," he said.

"That's a tall order and a lot of manpower. This is a big city. We have our share of crime, I'm afraid."

"I know you can't have your officers tracking them every minute of every day. Ask them to keep an eye out for suspicious activity," Tyler said. "Drive by their houses, check to see that they are where they're supposed to be."

"What about Ms. Leigh?"

"She was with us at the house yesterday, both before and during the accident," Tyler told him. "Three of the board members were there shortly before the accident, as well."

"Then we'll take a closer look at the board members." Jenson lifted his hands. "They're dedicated to that place. Why would any of them want to commit murders—bizarre murders that are bound to cast a bad light on the house?"

"If we can figure out why, we'll know who," Tyler said.

"Listen, I'm going to see whether we can find out if one of them has taken a nice walk in the woods lately. I don't believe our killer purchased the snake. And if they find the creature, maybe an expert can tell us more about it."

"We'll work that angle, too, but since you're local, you're in a better position to pursue it," Tyler said.

As he was about to leave, Jenson's phone rang. He raised one hand, asking Tyler to wait.

Then he hung up. "They've found your snake."

There was something about Adam Harrison that drew people to him.

After taking a cold shower—the hot water supply had run out—and getting dressed, Allison was surprised to see Adam at the house, seated in their little enclave around Sean's computer.

She'd sensed that he usually put one of his Krewes on a case and withdrew himself.

But when she arrived downstairs, he was there, together with Logan and Sean. When he saw her, he quickly rose.

"My dear," he said, coming toward her. He took both of her hands. "I'm delighted to see you looking so much better. I'm delighted, as well, that you've chosen to assist my unit."

"And I'm delighted that your unit is anxious to save my life," she said, meaning it.

"Naturally, our purpose is to save the lives of all we can."

"You're still here," she said. "Is that usual?" She smiled. "From what I understand, you're all over the country, involved with law enforcement...and philanthropy."

"Yes, well, Ethan and I go way back. He's an old friend. Actually, he was my son Josh's godfather. I felt this was a situation I should be here for, just in case I was needed."

"I'm happy to see you again," Allison said. "Well, I guess I'll be leaving soon."

"No, you're not," Kelsey said, sweeping into the room with a cup of coffee for her.

"Oh?"

"The trip to Valley Forge is postponed, because of the art showing tonight."

"And 'all the king's men' will be there," Adam murmured.

"Oh." Allison tried not to show her disappointment.

She'd looked forward to spending the day with Tyler, hoping for more—much more—than they'd experienced so far. Even if it couldn't last...

"In the meantime Tyler has a couple of requests," Logan told her. "He's asked that you contact Mr.

Standish and see if you can arrange an appointment for tomorrow. And would you look for that article online? The one that seems to be missing from the attic."

"Of course. Tyler isn't here?"

"He's checking in with the police."

"I understand that one of the resident ghosts is trying to reach you." Adam spoke in a low voice.

"I believe *I'm* a resident ghost now, and *I've* reached her just fine!"

She hadn't heard or seen Julian until he suddenly spoke behind her. She jumped, and Adam frowned. She realized he couldn't see the ghost.

"*Another* resident ghost," Kelsey said, rolling her eyes.

"We have someone present?" Adam asked.

"Julian Mitchell, my friend who was killed here," Allison replied.

"Ah." Adam wasn't sure where to look, but he ventured a question. "Mr. Mitchell, have you been able to contact any of your fellow ghosts in this house?"

"Tell him I've seen the ghost of Lucy Tarleton just like you've seen her—a wraith running away," Julian said.

Allison repeated his words.

Adam turned thoughtfully to Logan and then to Allison. "My Krewes have seen so much and learned so much, and there's still an infinite number of things we don't understand. It's impressive, I think, that Mr. Mitchell has so readily appeared to you. Was he an outgoing man in life?"

"Painfully," Allison said.

"Hey!" Julian protested.

"He was a performer," Allison said, feeling guilty

about her earlier comment. "A very good performer," she added.

Adam nodded. "Lucy Tarleton has been in this house for over two hundred years now. When she was alive, she was secretive by necessity. You may have to draw her out, and pay careful attention to every appearance she makes." He smiled sadly. "I just see one soul here on earth—my son, Josh. It took a very long time, and then one day...one day *he* broke through to me. He is still the only soul I'm able to communicate with, but I ask nothing else. It's through you, those who do have the gift, that I can try to help others. It's a remarkable world when you have a greater vision," he said.

"Adam, we believe Lucy is saying something. And Allison will figure out what it is," Logan assured him.

"Right now," Allison said, "I'm going to the office to pull up that article and I'll call Martin Standish."

"I'll go with you," Kelsey told her. When Allison looked at her sharply, Kelsey shrugged. "We need to take every precaution."

Adam had already turned to speak with Logan and Sean as Kelsey and Allison started up the stairs.

"The shower must've been freezing," Kelsey said. "I'm sorry. I should have warned you."

"It helped me wake up." Allison laughed, and Kelsey joined in. The more she was with members of the Krewe, the more Allison liked them. They were like a family, trusting in one another and all working together at whatever task they were assigned. Of course, Kelsey and Sean *were* family, and Kelsey and Logan were a couple. The others had all known one another in Texas.

She was glad of Kelsey's company.

"If I'm not heading to Valley Forge today," Allison said as they reached the attic office, "I'd like to stop by my place for a few more things, if someone can come with me. And, maybe, a long, *hot* shower."

"I'll walk over with you."

"Thanks." Allison sat down at the computer and keyed in a search for Martin Standish articles. She found the second one he'd written on Lord Brian "Beast" Bradley and printed it out. Then she called Martin, but had to leave a message.

"I'll have to wait for him to call back," she said.

But even as she spoke, her phone rang. She was surprised that Martin Standish had called her right back—and that he was angry. "Allison Leigh, from the Tarleton-Dandridge House!" he spat out. "If you're calling to tell me you plan to embarrass me with some kind of news story or sue me for slander, you're full of it!"

"What?" Allison said, stunned. "No, no, Mr. Standish, we've only corresponded on email. Do you remember? I admire your research very much. I'm eager to see you and learn more about the letters and information you have."

There was a distrustful silence on the other end. Then he asked, "You didn't call me and threaten me?"

"Never! I swear it," Allison said. Kelsey was looking at her, perplexed.

"Mr. Standish, I take it that someone did call and threaten you, but it wasn't me. When did this happen? Do you know who it was?" Allison asked.

Kelsey was watching her, trying to hear both ends of the conversation.

"It was a woman. I thought she was you," Standish muttered. "She said she was with the Tarleton-Dandridge House and she was appalled by the traitorous slant I was putting on the patriots of the house. And if I didn't stop, she'd see that I did."

"Mr. Standish, I'm sorry. I guarantee that call didn't come from anyone with the right to make it or to say such things. You and I have corresponded, and you know I'm intrigued by your information and theories. Actually, I was calling because I was hoping you'd take a few minutes to see me tomorrow," Allison said. "You have to believe me. That was no official stance taken by anyone at the Tarleton-Dandridge House."

He sniffed over the line. "Well, I didn't *think* it was you—not based on our email correspondence. I hear you're having all kinds of trouble there. A guide killed himself on a bayonet like an idiot, and one of your board members died in that awful accident yesterday."

"We need your help, Mr. Standish," Allison said simply.

"Everything I've written is online."

"Yes, but your letters aren't. And I'd like to see the other objects in your collection."

He was silent a minute. "All right. Two o'clock. I'll give you the address to my shop and my little museum," he told her. "Be on time, or forget it."

Once she'd hung up, Allison repeated the conversation to Kelsey.

"He said it was a woman who called?" Kelsey asked. Allison nodded.

"Sarah Vining is dead."

"Yes. That leaves Cherry Addison," Allison said.

"Or Annette Fanning," Kelsey reminded her. But she didn't press it.

Officer Alfred Crosbie from animal control had the snake in a terrarium.

A big terrarium.

It was a big snake.

"I'm sorry to say we'll have to kill the creature and do a necropsy if we're going to tell you anything about it. Not that I can tell you much—just what kind of food it's eaten, such as wild catches or pet-store-bred mice or rats. I do believe, however, that we're looking at a copperhead someone managed to catch in the wild," Crosbie told Tyler. "See, look at the snake closely. The skin's a little rough. An animal kept for research or as a pet—don't know anyone who keeps a pet copperhead, but some people are crazy—wouldn't be as beat-up as this."

Crosbie looked mournful at the idea of killing any creature. But by now, the police had concluded that there was something suspicious about the snake being in the car.

"Where did you find it?" Tyler asked him.

"Coiled tight under the driver's seat," Crosbie said. "We're lucky he didn't get out and slither away in all the commotion. But a snake has instincts, and he just hid. That's what creatures do. Shame to kill this one, but I'll let you know as soon as our vet gets the necropsy done."

Tyler thanked him. As he left the impound area, he started back toward the house but then paused.

He made his way to Ethan's grand old mansion. Oxford's housekeeper showed him into the study and he waited there for Ethan to arrive.

The older man wore a casual sweater, apologizing for his appearance. "Forgive me. I've been on the phone. I'm devastated by Sarah's death and, I'm afraid, she had no family. She asked me ages ago to be the executor of her will. Her body's still at the morgue, but I've been receiving calls about the legal status of her property."

"I'm so sorry, Mr. Oxford. And actually, Sarah's death is why I'm here to see you."

He sat down at his desk, suddenly looking very old and confused.

"Sarah died in an accident," he said. "She nearly killed dozens of people. I can't begin to imagine what happened to her."

The hospital had not released the results of Sarah's death. For once, it seemed, there'd been no leaks.

"Sarah caused the accident and died because of a snakebite," Tyler explained. "And I'll ask you not to share that information."

Oxford looked even more confused. "A snakebite?"

"Yes, sir. There was a copperhead in her car. And we believe it was put there intentionally."

Oxford stared at him as if he were speaking another language.

"You and the board members are friends, obviously, since you're handling Sarah's estate," Tyler said.

Oxford nodded, waving a hand in the air. "We have many similar interests. We all love the house and Philly and…art, music and so on." He sighed. "When I agreed to be Sarah's executor, I never figured I'd outlive her."

"What do you think of your fellow board members?" Tyler asked.

Oxford was offended. "I think they're fine human beings! I know I'm the one who asked Adam Harrison to bring in a team, but you're way off base if you believe any member of the board might have anything to do with this. I've known them for years."

"And they're all fine, upstanding citizens of Philadelphia, ardent supporters of the history of the city and the city itself," Tyler said mildly.

"Yes!" Ethan exclaimed. "There was a tour going

just before Julian Mitchell was found dead. You need to be looking at outside sources."

"We are. But outside sources don't know the house the way your board members and guides do. If you're right, you can help me clear those people, and then maybe we'll find another direction to go in." There was no other direction; he knew that. Oxford didn't.

Ethan let out a long sigh. "What did you want to ask?"

"Is there anything you can tell me about the board's activity in the past few weeks?"

"Activity?"

"Yes. Such as, has anyone been on a hunting or hiking trip out in the woods? Has anyone become involved with a magic shop or illusions of any kind?"

The man's face seemed to grow red as Tyler spoke.

"Yes," he said, "actually, someone has been on a hiking trip."

"Who?"

"Me," Oxford told him.

Kelsey tended to be soft-spoken, but Allison was pretty sure she had a strong, tough edge, since she'd been a U.S. Marshal before joining the unit.

She wished she was as strong.

"I think I'm going to take shooting lessons," Allison said as they left the attic.

Kelsey grinned. "It's not a bad idea to be acquainted with firearms, but it's a skill that came along with what I wanted to do. Hopefully, the world isn't so horrible that we all need to spend our days at a shooting range."

As they headed along the second floor landing to the staircase, Allison said, "I hear you're engaged. Congratulations. Is it hard working with Logan?"

"Thank you, and no, we work well together. We've had a few bumps along the way, of course. I remember thinking that I wasn't happy about the 'unit' situation when it first came up, but then...things happened. When we're working, we're working. Our private time is private. But we're kind of like the marine corps in our philosophy. No man—or woman—left behind. So we're all protective of one another. Logan and I...we manage."

"What about the others?" Allison asked. "How do *they* manage their relationships?"

"Sean was in special effects before he joined the unit, so he and Madison have a great deal in common—and they can both sleep on a plane. Which is good, since they've been a continent apart. Things are easy enough for Kat, since she and Will have an apartment in Virginia."

"Jane?"

"Jane was in love with a cop who was killed in the line of duty a couple of years ago. She dates casually, but I think it'll be a while before she's ready for another serious relationship. She's seeing a suit in Washington now."

"A suit?"

"Another federal agent—but he's in the tax division," Kelsey said, grinning.

"Oh. How does that work? I mean, does he have your...skills?"

"No. We don't say much when we're around him," Kelsey told her.

"So, you all live a pretty normal life?"

"I wouldn't call it normal. But I will say, I like that we're together. It's nice to be *unusual* together." Kelsey paused. "You didn't ask about Tyler."

"Oh. Yes, well, what about Tyler?" Allison tried to sound casual. But she fumbled with the switch as she turned on a hallway lamp, lighting their path to the stairs.

"Tyler is a great guy. He was one of Logan's best friends before we started this. They were both Texas Rangers."

"Yes, I knew that." Allison nodded.

"Everyone looks at Tyler and thinks, 'Hmm, tough guy. He must get anything he wants and be as hard as a rock.' He's not like that at all."

"He's very courteous."

Kelsey laughed. "That's what you think, is it?"

"What do you mean?"

"It means we can see sparks when you're with him," Kelsey said.

Allison felt her face heat with a fiery blush. "I don't know anything about his life or his...relationships."

"Does he go out? Yes. Is he in a relationship? No, not that I'm aware of, and I believe I would be. He's very private. He's kept what he knows, sees and does from almost everyone around him. I don't think Tyler could form a relationship with someone who wasn't... *unusual,* as well. He couldn't live a lie. Anyway, that's my two cents on the matter."

Allison realized she'd paused to stare at Kelsey when Kelsey said, "Maybe you should give Tyler a call now, and tell him about your talk with Martin Standish."

"Yes, I should do that."

Kelsey smiled and walked down the stairs.

Allison called Tyler. He listened to her gravely and asked, "He's sure it was a woman?"

"He sounded sure," Allison said. "I guess that would suggest Sarah, Annette or Cherry Addison."

"Sarah's dead, so..."

"She still might have called him. She wasn't dead then."

"In that case, you could ask her."

"You want me to go back to the morgue?" Allison asked.

"You were the one she talked to."

"Kat's there now, right?"

"Yes. Maybe she's made contact, but according to Kat, ghosts don't usually like to be around when an autopsy is being done on their remains. We'll go there sometime today."

Allison agreed. She wished Sarah was more like Julian—and that she wasn't haunting the morgue, of all places.

"I'll see you soon," he said, and hung up.

When she came downstairs, Adam Harrison was gone. He'd see them later at the gallery. Sean was adjusting a camera, and Jane beckoned them into the salon where she'd been working. Allison told the others about the phone call.

Logan, as usual, was pragmatic. "It's not conclusive that the same person called this man and then attacked Julian, but it's certainly a lead," he said. "And if it was a woman..."

"Do you think Annette Fanning will come to the art show?" Kelsey asked Allison.

"I assume so," Allison said. "We—the guides—supported the board members whenever we could. And vice versa."

Julian was there, staring down at prints Jane had made from the work she'd been doing.

"It's uncanny!" Julian breathed as Kelsey and Allison came into the room.

Logan smiled at Allison. "You really need to take a look."

"I took the picture of you off your Facebook page," Jane told her apologetically.

"Tyler is on to something," Logan said. "Check out the transparencies Jane's been working on."

Jane worked with mixed media, some of her examples done by transferring images on the computer and others using her own sketches.

Allison was a little afraid of what she was going to see.

But when they showed her what they were talking about, it was chilling.

Jane had juxtaposed pictures of Allison and paintings of Lucy Tarleton. When their faces were at the same angle and transparencies were placed on either image, they melded almost completely.

"You really do resemble her," Julian said. "I always thought so, but back then any pretty dark-haired, blue-eyed young woman could look something like Lucy."

She stepped back. "But I don't understand what this means. I'm *not* Lucy Tarleton come back to life. We've seen her ghost."

"We need to learn what the relationship is," Logan said. "It may matter."

"I think I know what it is."

Allison swung around. Tyler had returned, standing in the doorway of the grand salon.

"What?" Allison asked him.

He smiled. "I think your father's family did adopt a child. Not recently. I think they adopted him or her during the Revolution. I'm willing to bet that Lucy Tarleton had an illegitimate child—which her family would have covered up at the time—and that child was taken in by the Leigh family."

"But how could Lucy have done everything she did, carry on with her espionage, even walk around Philly, pregnant?" Allison demanded.

"Supposedly queens and nobility managed to hide the births of their lovers' offspring throughout history," Tyler said. "That would explain why Lucy's trying to get through to you. She's afraid for you and she believes the only way you'll be safe is if you find out who's killing people at this house—and why."

"An interesting theory," Jane said. "Allison, don't look so stricken. It's a good thing—if it's true. It means Lucy will do whatever she can to protect you."

"Which, I'm afraid, isn't all that much." Julian grimaced. "I'm a ghost and what can *I* do? Hope to sound an alarm? Blow cold air at someone?"

"You moved paper today," Jane reminded him brightly.

"It took incredible will and practice," Julian said.

"Ah, but Lucy's been around for over two centuries," Tyler pointed out. "She's had time to learn. We don't know what she's capable of."

"*Not* talking to her fellow ghosts, I can tell you that much," Julian said with a sniff.

"Let me show you what else I've come up with," Jane told them. "I took pictures of the paintings and worked with them. I made three-dimensional head shapes—the same as I did with Lucy and Allison," she said. "And here's what I have of Beast Bradley."

Allison walked over to the end of the table. Jane had devised a picture that blended the two images of Beast Bradley, the one from the study and that from Lucy's bedroom.

The person she'd portrayed was a new man. He was older than he appeared in the study painting, but the eyes were those from the painting in the bedroom. What they saw was a serious man, worn with the rigors of life, but thoughtful rather than cruel.

"Great image, Jane. It combines the two images into what's probably closest to truth," Tyler said.

"So...where are we? I might be a descendent of Lucy's illegitimate child, and Beast Bradley was human. That doesn't tell us who killed Julian," Allison said.

"No, but we're getting there."

Logan nodded slowly. "It was a woman who spoke to Martin Standish, and the one who has the most to lose—being the last descendent of the Dandridge family—is Cherry Addison. We'll see if we can trip her up tonight."

"Phone tap?" Tyler suggested.

"I'll speak to Adam."

"I need to go back to my house," Allison said. "I guess now would be as good a time as any."

"I'll walk you over," Tyler offered.

"Kelsey said she didn't mind..." Allison began.

"No, but I could use a walk. Helps me think," he said. "We're going to stop by the morgue, as well, remember? So on second thought, we'd better drive."

Allison nodded, feeling excitement sweep through her veins. She turned quickly, not wanting anyone to see.

She was even willing to go back to the morgue for time alone with him. Well, *sort of* alone...

When she'd first met Tyler, she'd never imagined she could feel about him the way she did.

As much as it thrilled her, it scared her, too. Maybe,

subconsciously, she felt she had to sabotage the possibility of the two of them being together. Maybe her last affair had been such a fiasco that she didn't trust her own instincts.

"Anyone who wants to shower or shave or get ready in a real bathroom with lots of hot water is welcome to come to my house," she said.

"Thanks," Logan called to her.

No one else responded. They were already talking again, working again.

It wasn't right to feel this way about a man she'd just met.

But she did.

14

Even Dr. Grant, who'd spent a great deal of time with Kat, knew Adam and had been as patient as a saint with them, was perturbed when Tyler told her they needed to see the body again.

She didn't deny his request, but looked at him very strangely.

"Dr. Sokolov was here with me during the autopsy. I assure you, everything was done correctly and thoroughly," she insisted.

"You know she was killed by a snakebite. We believe that snake was purposely put in Ms. Vining's car to kill her," Tyler said. "Did her heart give out?"

Dr. Grant nodded absently, clearly somewhat confused. But she allowed them to go back into the freezer and pull out the corpse. Tyler distracted her with questions about the autopsy, while Allison touched Sarah's face. She'd closed her eyes and was completely still for several minutes. Dr. Grant began to stare at her, so Tyler distracted the doctor again with news about the accident.

"By the way, animal control found the snake. It was coiled up beneath the driver's seat."

"Her driving must have disturbed the creature," Dr.

Grant said. "Ms. Vining had several contusions, and a broken rib—from the air bag and struggling out of the car. I've confirmed that the toxin, combined with the trauma of being hit by another vehicle, caused complete failure of her heart."

"Thank you for bearing with us," Tyler said. "We really want this solved. And, Dr. Grant, everything about this case is being kept quiet."

"Of course. We don't have leaks here, Agent Montague."

He was glad to see Allison was stepping away from the corpse.

"Thank you," he told Dr. Grant a second time. "We'll try not to bother you again."

"Mr. Oxford wants to make arrangements with a funeral home. He said he doesn't expect a large turnout, and that he and several other people associated with the house were her closest friends. But he's been asking me about releasing the body, since he'd like to have a service for her."

"She always said she wanted to be buried or entombed at the Tarleton-Dandridge House," Allison murmured.

"Really?" Dr. Grant seemed surprised. "I thought Mr. Oxford said she was to be cremated."

That was a surprise to both of them.

As they left the medical examiner's office, Tyler already had his phone out. Allison glanced at him quizzically.

"I'm calling Adam. I don't want Sarah cremated."

"I know she wouldn't have wanted that, either," Allison said.

He nodded. When he'd finished speaking with

Adam, Tyler hung up and looked at her. "Well?" he asked. "What did you learn from Sarah?"

"She emphatically denies that she called Martin Standish to give him a hard time. In fact, she swears she never even talked to the man."

"I didn't think it was Sarah, but now we're sure of it."

"The dead never lie?" she asked.

"The dead are like the living. Was Sarah a liar?"

"No, not that I know of," Allison replied.

"Then why would she lie now? Did you ask her why she was so eager to help you sort through the stuff in the office?"

"Yes, she said she was worried. She didn't know why everything was messed up like that, and in light of what happened to Julian, she thought she could help figure things out."

They walked to the car. "Do we have time for a quick stop at the hospital?" she asked. "I hate to disappoint a child and I promised Todd I'd go to see his father."

"Of course."

Yes, the hospital. It was right to go there; a child depended on them. But, in reality, was it going to change Artie Dixon's condition if and when they solved the murder?

And what the hell was the matter with *him?*

He was better off when he and Allison weren't alone.

When there were others around to ensure that he kept his distance.

"Of course," he repeated.

At the hospital he discovered that Haley Dixon maintained her constant vigil. She sat by her husband day and night; her sister brought the children to see their father, and then took them home, trying to keep their lives somewhat normal.

Allison convinced Haley to let her sit with Artie, and Tyler talked her into taking a break and going down to the hospital cafeteria with him.

He bought Haley a coffee and they sat at a table. She looked terrible. There were huge dark circles under her eyes and she was gaunt, as if she hadn't eaten since her husband got sick.

"Has he woken again?" Tyler asked. "Even for a few seconds?"

Haley shook her head. "I don't understand it," she said. "They've PET-scanned him, CAT-scanned him, you-name-it-scanned him, and they can't find the reason. The doctor said it was as if a door had just shut in his brain, the door that gave him access to the outside world. Everyone here is so nice, but they've already talked to me about places that provide extended care. They're at a loss."

Tyler murmured his sympathy.

She reached across the table and gripped his hand. "You're my only hope! Please, you and Ms. Leigh— you're my only hope. You can't give up on us. You can't give up."

"We won't," Tyler promised her.

"He seems better after she's been here. That sounds ridiculous, doesn't it? He's in a coma. But it's as if he breathes easier, as if...as if there's sunshine in the room." She sighed. "I know other dreadful things are going on. I heard about the accident. My sister said she barely missed being in it. Oh, my God! If my sister had been there...if my kids...I think I'd lose my mind completely."

"Your children weren't in it and neither was your sister," Tyler said in a calm voice.

Her eyes focused on his. "But that woman... I never met her, but that woman who was killed—*she* was on the board for the Tarleton-Dandridge House. I read about her in the paper. She caused the accident and now she's dead. She was from that awful, awful house."

"The house didn't kill anyone, Mrs. Dixon."

"No, the painting does this stuff," she said earnestly. "The painting of that heinous man, Beast Bradley."

"Paintings don't kill, either. There's someone real and alive who's doing those things, and we're going to find out who it is. You have to protect your own health for your husband's sake—and for your children."

She nodded, and almost smiled at him. "You're right," she told him. "It's just...there was something about that painting. I was creeped out by it. So was Todd. Of course, it wasn't in the room with us when Artie slipped into the coma, but...I don't know. I can't help thinking there's something wrong with it. Maybe Artie realized that before he went into the coma."

"We'll look at it again," Tyler said.

She let out a soft sigh. "Thank you. It was good to get away for a few minutes, but we should head back now."

Allison had run out of things to say, but she kept talking, holding Artie Dixon's hand. She wasn't afraid...she even whispered to him that she was looking forward to spending more time alone with Agent Montague.

She paused when she thought she heard him speak. She went completely still, staring at him intently. He hadn't moved. Nothing about him had changed.

But it was as if he'd spoken....

"The painting," he told her. "There's something wrong with that painting. Maybe if you can tear it apart, you'll discover what it is."

For a minute, ice filled her veins.

She'd recently learned she could speak with the dead.

Was Artie dead?

She managed not to jerk her hands away. She hadn't breathed in that moment of shock; now she inhaled deeply. She could see his heartbeat on the monitor.

She heard Mrs. Dixon and Tyler in the hallway, returning to the room.

Squeezing Artie's hand, she said, "I'll have them look at the painting again. I'll have their special-effects person tear it apart. We'll find out. I can hear you, and if I can hear you, you're in there and your family wants you well. Please—come back to us," she whispered urgently.

When Mrs. Dixon and Tyler stepped back into the room, Allison released Mr. Dixon's hand and stood.

"Thank you." Haley Dixon hugged her gratefully.

"Anytime. I mean that," Allison said. "Please give the children our regards."

"I will. Todd will be so happy you were here."

They said their goodbyes. As they drove to her place, Allison asked, "Could Sean be wrong about that painting? *Could* there be something wrong with it?"

He glanced at her. "Funny, that's what Haley was just saying to me. She's convinced the painting is evil."

"What do you think?"

He shrugged. "Looked like a painting to me," he said. "Sean is really good at what he does. He would've seen any trick in it."

"But we should examine it again," she said.

"We will."

They arrived at her house and got out of the car. She felt awkward when she let him in; she'd wanted to be alone with him so badly and now here they were—and she didn't know what to do.

"I'm going to take a hot shower," she said. "I got a cold blast this morning, and then I was at the morgue and...do you mind?"

She turned to look at him. He'd leaned against the door, watching her.

"Do you mind?" she asked again.

He shook his head.

"You're welcome to take a shower, too." The words tumbled from her lips. She didn't know whether she sounded serious or facetious.

A slow, rueful smile curved his lips. "With you?"

She gazed back at him. She tried to think of something clever to say. A charming quip that would make her seem sophisticated and...

Not desperate.

Nothing came to her. Nothing at all.

"Um, that would be great," she said.

"Pardon?" He stiffened against the door, brows furrowed.

She flinched. She felt gawky and...pathetic.

"I...I'd love it if you took a shower with me," she managed at last. "Actually, I'd like a great deal more than a shower with you."

He left the door, reaching her in a single stride. Then she was in his arms, and she felt her knees begin to tremble. In fact, her whole body was trembling; she could hardly remember how it felt to be held like this. He raised her chin and kissed her, and the pressure of his mouth was instantly erotic. She reveled in the searing heat of his tongue against her lips, then teasing its way into her mouth.

She kissed him feverishly in return. She felt something hard and steely and realized it wasn't him—it was his gun.

He drew away from her, shrugging out of his jacket, pulling off his gun clip.

He made a move to pull her into his arms again, but she backed away and he looked at her, puzzled.

"Shower, please? I've...envisioned this moment and I never thought I'd smell like formaldehyde if and when..."

He smiled. "You've envisioned this moment?"

Blushing, she nodded.

"I have, too," he told her. "What about protection?"

"I'm on the pill."

He nodded, and she turned to go upstairs. She didn't hear him following her and she looked back, but he was only gathering up his jacket and gun and holster.

She hurried into the bathroom, silently thanking the powers that be—her bathroom was spotlessly clean. She wondered if that was something men noticed. Then she forgot about it. She started the hot spray of the shower, and as she turned, she ended up in his arms. "Your lips don't smell like any chemical at all," he said. "I'm not sure that's a romantic thing to say, but..."

She smiled, pressing against him. Their lips touched again and they began pulling at each other's clothing, kicking off shoes, skimming off their jeans.

She'd been right.

He was beautiful naked.

Later, she barely remembered stripping and helping him strip and stepping into the shower stall. She felt the delicious wet heat of the water, along with the stroking of his hands. They kissed again under the warm cascade, and she felt the full length of his body against hers.

Beautiful, and scarred. She knew he'd been a Ranger and he'd fought, bringing down criminals. And he was still in law enforcement. She didn't know what had caused the scars that lay white against the bronze of his flesh. She traced a white scar line on his lower abdomen and kissed it gently.

"Knife wound. I didn't move quickly enough against a drug dealer in San Antonio," he told her.

"Thank God he didn't kill you!"

"He's doing twenty-five to life."

She looked into his eyes and he grimaced. Her fingers rode over another scar on his arm, with the steamy water following her touch.

He pulled her to him with a shrug. "Dodged a bullet outside Houston."

There was a third scar low on his abdomen. She eased against his body, feeling his heat and vitality along with the slickness of the steam. Her fingers traced the clean white line. "This one?"

He grinned, drawing her up. "Appendectomy," he said, and she smiled, and they kissed again.

She didn't think she'd ever been so stirred or felt such hunger and urgency. She wondered if they would make love in the shower stall.

But they didn't. Tyler lifted her up, leaving the shower, wrapped her in one of the bath towels and caressed her body as he dried it. She shivered at his touch, just savoring the feel, then growing more confident and pressing against him, forming her mouth to his, feeling the pounding of his heart and hers as their excitement began to soar. She nearly tripped on the towel; they both laughed and he swept her into his arms. The feel of his arms was a promise in itself....

Falling down on the bed, smelling of soap and steam, they began to make love in earnest. His kisses traveled the length of her, teasing and intimate, and she lay still, feeling luxurious and then writhing and arching and returning every touch. When he rose above her and met her eyes and thrust with excruciating care into her body, she thought she'd explode in that instant, but he withdrew and began a slow, intense movement, his eyes locked with hers. The world didn't seem in the least real, and yet she could feel the softness of the bed and the cool cotton of the sheets. But most of all she could feel the strength of his body. Everything that had happened in the past few days evaporated as sheer sensation seemed to lift her into a realm of ecstasy. She clung to him as waves of sensation rolled over her, as the climax seized her, and as she drifted in an aftermath that seemed a little like dying...and coming back to life.

When they lay silently, she stroked the rich, tawny fall of hair from his forehead, gazing into his eyes.

"I feel so right—and so wrong," she whispered.

He smiled and pulled her toward him. "Living is right," he told her. "Hurting others is wrong, but living...and finding something you've longed for in life isn't."

She realized again *why* they knew each other, as reality came crashing back upon her.

"I feel so bad for Julian and Sarah," she whispered.

He drew her close. "Allison, we can hurt for others.

But you're doing everything you can to help them. Taking a breath yourself isn't wrong. Life is precious and fragile, and we live it while we can."

She didn't dare get too comfortable. She nestled against his chest and started to speak. But then she trembled. "Your life is filled with people who are ready to take on any fight," she said. "And when you met me, I was a basket case at the police station. You know so many women who are heroines in real life, and I've been...pretty much a sniveling coward."

His fingers threaded into her hair and he smiled, not with amusement, but with wonder. "Have you never heard?" he asked her. "Courage isn't about not feeling fear. Courage is when you're terrified—but go forth, anyway. I think you're one of the bravest women I've ever met."

There was something in his words, something in the way he spoke, and she felt her muscles begin to relax as she curled up again.

He smoothed back her hair and teased, "All right, the first time I saw you, you *were* a sniveling coward...."

She laughed and started to rise. "The art showing," she began.

"We'll get there."

"It's late."

"So?"

His lips found hers again.

"We can make love quickly," she whispered against his lips.

"Um, not too quickly. But we'll shower again and dress for the occasion with all due haste."

When his fingers traveled seductively down her spine, she could only agree.

* * *

Cherry Addison stood at the entrance to the gallery as if she were royalty greeting her subjects.

Her manner was gracious—and affected, in Tyler's opinion.

He wasn't sure he wanted to be at the showing, after all. He would've liked a night with Allison, never getting out of bed. A night in which he described the good, the bad and the ugly in his life, and learned more about hers.

Except, of course, people had died. And it was important that they be here.

Cherry welcomed them as they came in. She was standing with her husband, George, who smiled and seemed to be a genuinely warm man. The gallery owner was there, as well, directing people toward the food and drink and telling them they mustn't miss the collage.

On their way to get some appetizers and a glass of wine, they walked down the gallery, looking at the paintings. George Addison was very good. The works on the wall depicted images of modern life: a mother holding a newborn, her eyes filled with exhilaration and exhaustion, a child watching a balloon disappear into the sky, a construction worker on a girder, happy as he opened a lunch pail high above the world. The details were contemporary but the emotions were enduring, universal.

"I can actually say I love his stuff!" Jane said, coming up behind them.

"Take a look at the other wall," Logan suggested, joining them, too.

Tyler set a hand on Allison's back as they walked toward the other side. Here, George Addison had done similar work but these included historical scenes and people. Tyler thought the paintings on this wall were even finer, more unusual, than the others.

One depicted a tree with a worn-out, dirt-smudged Union soldier on one side, and a bleeding Rebel on the other. A lone World War I soldier huddled in a trench with dead men and dead horses around him.

He had painted the Tarleton-Dandridge House with a woman in front.

Lucy Tarleton. She stood there with strength evident in her expression, her stance—and sadness in her eyes.

Glancing down at Allison, Tyler saw that she was staring at the image, the same sadness in her own eyes. She looked up at him and flushed. "She's so conflicted."

"It was a time of conflict," he reminded her. He lowered his voice. "And, if I'm right, she had the problem of a hidden, illicit child to worry about!"

They studied the rest of the paintings, all of them imbued with a similar life and humanity.

Finally they made their way over to the bar. Annette Fanning and Jason Lawrence were there, looking a little lost. Allison greeted them both with a kiss.

"Nice showing, with Sarah dead on a morgue slab!" Annette whispered sarcastically.

"Can't stop the mighty wheels of…art showings," Jason said.

"If I understand correctly," Tyler told them, "it was impossible to cancel the gallery and undo all the setup at such a late date."

"I guess so. And George didn't know Sarah all that well," Annette said. "He's a nice guy. No idea how Cherry rated him. Oops!" Her eyes went wide. "I didn't just say that!"

"But I'll say this." Jason lifted his glass, smiling

at someone across the room. "It's a pity it was Sarah, and not Cherry."

"Jason!" Allison said, horrified.

"Sarah was nicer. A lot nicer," Jason muttered.

"Julian and Sarah are dead," Annette said. "This all seems so wrong."

Allison nodded. "And here *we* are—the three guides who remain, huddled together. And there *they* are, the three remaining board members." She pointed across the room. Ethan Oxford and Nathan Pierson had arrived and joined Cherry.

"Excuse me," Tyler said. "I have a question for Cherry."

He left them and walked over to the gathering of the board. Ethan eyed him warily; Tyler knew that even though he'd done his best to be polite during their conversation earlier, Ethan had taken offense. He knew Adam had been to see him again after that, but he wasn't sure how warm Ethan's greeting would be.

Tyler said hello to the two men, both of them friendly in their response. Obviously, Ethan had decided that any disagreement had no place in a social situation of this kind. Cherry smiled benevolently.

"Cherry's husband is talented, isn't he?" Pierson said.

"Very," Tyler agreed. "He makes me think of the paintings at the Tarleton-Dandridge House. Both of those oils of Beast Bradley were painted by men with real skill."

"George loves those two paintings," Cherry said. "You have to tell him you see something similar in his work."

"Just curious, but I'm sure you read in the paper that the young boy whose dad is still in a coma believes Beast Bradley came alive in that painting in the study," Tyler said. "Have you ever felt or seen anything unusual about it?"

"It reveals a lot of bitterness," Ethan said. "But then, it was painted by Lucy Tarleton's brother-in-law, who had reason to hate Beast Bradley. Apparently, Tobias had been an up-and-coming artist before the war, but that was his last painting. He was injured in the right arm by a musket ball just before the battle of Yorktown. That painting was done immediately after the British left Philly, and he never painted again. There are a few of his prewar pieces in museums, mostly in New York."

"But it's just a painting," Cherry said. "I was saddened to hear about the man and his son. When something terrible happens, there has to be a reason, even if we don't understand it. To a young impressionable boy, I can easily imagine it might be that painting."

Tyler nodded and changed the subject. None of them seemed convinced that the painting was evil. He thought they were genuine; he could usually sense an outright lie.

"Cherry, do you know Martin Standish?" he asked.

She flushed slightly. "Who?"

"A historian named Martin Standish."

"I've never met him," she said.

"Have you ever spoken with him?"

The others were glancing from Cherry to him in confusion.

"Yes, I've spoken with him," she said defiantly. "He writes dreadful articles about the Tarleton-Dandridge House and my family. I've called him and warned him to stop."

"Cherry!" Ethan admonished.

"Ethan, the man is a fruitcake. He has some deluded

idea about being an expert on the Revolution and he writes a lot of nonsense with no evidence whatsoever." She faced Tyler. "Why?"

"Oh, I was just curious," he told her. "I've read a few of his articles."

"They're trash. And lies," Cherry insisted.

He smiled at her and turned back to the others. "Did you know that Sarah was actually killed by a snake?"

Ethan Oxford looked at him gravely. Of course he already knew.

"A snake?" Pierson seemed skeptical.

"What are you talking about?" Cherry asked. "And please, hush, this is uncomfortable as it is. We should have canceled tonight, but we couldn't."

"There was a snake in Sarah's car. It bit her. That's why the car went out of control," Tyler said.

"A snake—in her *car?*" Cherry shuddered. "What kind of snake?"

"A copperhead. And yes, please keep this quiet. The police aren't letting out any information about the cause of the accident yet. It's still under investigation."

"Copperheads are plentiful in the woods," Nathan Pierson said, shaking his head. "I've heard of them getting into people's homes, but a car? How unusual."

Cherry shuddered again. "The poor dear! I can't imagine.... Oh, I'm so sorry."

With a quick farewell, she walked away. "Have you ever had an encounter with a copperhead?" Tyler asked the men.

"Yes," Oxford said stonily. "I've told you. I'm a hiker."

Pierson laughed. "Me? No. If I found a snake, I doubt if I'd even know what kind it was. I'd call the animal experts in a flash!" He sobered, looking at Tyler.

"Poor Sarah. She was such a timid little creature. It's even more horrible to think about how terrified she must have been before she died. Excuse me. I'm going to go and say hello to that group over there."

As he left them. Ethan Oxford frowned at Tyler with open hostility. "My friends don't go around planting snakes in people's cars!"

"I apologize if I've offended you, Mr. Oxford. But you did call Adam in."

Ethan sighed. Tyler walked with him as he moved toward one of the paintings; to a casual observer, it would look as if they were discussing it. "Yes, I called Adam in," he said quietly. "But I thought you people could...perform an exorcism or something."

Tyler shook his head. "We don't perform exorcisms, so I don't know what you were really hoping for. Truth? Well, it's hard to fathom what's happened in this house. The first 'more recent' death occurred in the late seventies. Accident? Who knows? A man fell down the stairs and broke his neck. But eight years ago a college student was electrocuted by a system that should never have failed the way it did. Three years ago, you had a guide die in the study, someone who died in *exactly* that same place as Julian Mitchell. And now a man has fallen into a coma after visiting the house. There's a pattern here and it has to be stopped."

Oxford turned to him. "It's the ghosts, don't you understand?"

Tyler was startled, taken aback by the man's desperate appeal.

"The ghosts there kill people. They do. I've heard from others...who've told me the painting of Bradley is *evil*. I couldn't say that in front of Nathan and Cherry. And I certainly couldn't tell it to the regular cops. But you *know* the ghosts are there, and you have to…make them go away."

"Mr. Oxford, the ghosts may be there. I pray they are, and that they help us. Because a ghost didn't go out in the woods, capture a snake and put it in Sarah's car. And a ghost didn't smash Julian Mitchell's head down on a bayonet. Someone living, probably in this room right now, did those things. And we'll find out who it is."

Tyler nodded politely and excused himself, walking back to where the guides were gathered with members of his Krewe.

"I wish Sarah was here. I'm going to miss her," Jason Lawrence was saying. He raised his plastic wineglass. "To Sarah."

"To Sarah," they all repeated, raising their own glasses.

As they spoke, Tyler noted that Julian, a ghost still clad in Colonial attire, was in the gallery, wandering in their direction. Allison saw him and smiled.

"And Julian," Allison added.

"And Julian," they all chorused.

"An entertaining guy, even if he was an irresponsible ass," Jason said.

Julian frowned. He waved a hand, which went right through Jason's glass. But he tried again, and this time, Jason's champagne spilled on his shirt.

"Wow, that was clumsy!" Jason said.

"Julian!" Allison remonstrated.

The ghost grinned. The others stared at Allison.

"Julian, uh, he was a good guy," she said.

"Yeah, and maybe he really would've gotten us all backstage passes to some really great musical acts," Annette said.

"I can't believe I'd just left the house when Julian died, and that I was walking around with a tray of beer mugs when I saw the news about Sarah on TV," Jason said. "It all seems so…hard to grasp. That I missed Julian's death by minutes and that I was doing something so…ordinary when Sarah died."

"I was asleep, mourning my lack of work," Annette told them.

"It's a wonder no one else was killed in that accident," Logan said, "and a blessing."

Adam Harrison arrived then. Tyler noticed that he spent most of his time with Ethan, although in typical Adam fashion, he moved around the room and seemed to make everyone in it feel comfortable.

Tyler's mind raced. Cherry had made the call to Martin Standish. Ethan had been in the woods.

Jason had been at work. But how long had he been there? Had he just started his shift? He wasn't going to ask Jason; he'd ask Evan McDooley.

Nathan Pierson denied any knowledge of snakes.

Annette didn't have an alibi; sleep had never been one.

Allison and the Krewe went back to the Tarleton-Dandridge House, where they discussed the evening, pointing out the merits of the various suspects.

It came time for bed at last. Tyler reminded Allison to keep her door ajar so he could hear her and watch out for her.

Kelsey gave a loud sigh of exasperation.

"What, you think we're all blind?" she demanded. "Keep Allison *really* safe—stay in the same room. Don't bother with this pretense. Lord, please, spare us from those who think we're idiots and don't know what's going on!"

Tyler looked at Allison.

She laughed. "I don't think any of you are blind *or* idiots. I'll get my things," she said to Tyler.

He felt like a college kid. But Sean had already waved good-night, and Jane and Kat had gone into the room they were sharing.

"See you in the morning," Logan said, shrugging as if to disavow any connection with his fiancée's outburst.

He walked into Lucy Tarleton's room. A moment later, Allison joined him.

And all he could do was smile.

15

Allison caught herself humming as she went down to shower the next morning. Everyone knew where she'd been all night, but they all seemed pleased that she and Tyler were happy in each other's company, or they didn't consider it any of their business.

She met Logan in the kitchen after her shower. He brought her a cup of coffee and asked, "Allison, what's in the second article by Martin Standish?"

"I printed it out after I talked to him yesterday," Allison said. "It's an interesting piece on the conflict of loyalties in the colonies. Many people wanted to stand up for their rights—no taxation without representation—but they *didn't* want to split from the mother country. Of course, most schoolchildren know that a lot of those Loyalists either returned to England or went to Canada. The article talks about the way we tend to think of Philly as a city that was occupied. We forget that there were people here who accepted it, saw it as a done deal. They gave up their loyalty to the fledgling United States and welcomed the British. Angus Tarleton was no spring chicken when they occupied the city. According to the Standish article, he was old and tired and wanted to live out his life in peace. Most of their friends tended to sympathize with the patriot cause, and, whether it was official or not, Lucy had been with an ardent patriot, Stewart Douglas, who'd left to fight with the American forces. But, as Standish points out, there's no mention of Stewart Douglas having been at Valley Forge. Some historians suspect he was going in and out of Philly, stealing supplies, listening for information and secrets. But whether or not he saw Lucy before her death, no one knows. The article hints that Lucy might not have been *pretending* her affection for Beast Bradley. There's no question that she started out using him for whatever information she could gather for the forces, but she might have fallen in love with him and suffered serious conflicts because of it."

"Until he killed her," Tyler suggested from the doorway. "That doesn't bode well for an affair. Remind me of the exact date Philly was occupied," he said as he walked into the pantry to pour himself coffee.

"September 26, 1777," she answered. "There'd been a lot of jockeying between George Washington and Howe, but Howe got around Washington after a few skirmishes. Usually, in war, when a capital city is taken, the war is over—but the British didn't count on the patriots continuing to fight. The British general Cornwallis surrendered on October 19, 1781, at Yorktown. There were skirmishes after that, but it was the last major battle, although the Treaty of Paris wasn't signed until September 3, 1783, officially ending the war."

Tyler and Logan looked at each other, grinning.

"Hey, I teach this stuff," Allison said. "In fact, I do a course on the history of American government, comparing the Revolutionary era to our modern politics. Not that much has really changed since those early days. They all had different opinions back then, too. Not everyone worshipped the ground Washington walked on. He had his critics."

"Okay, but the British got here on September 26, 1777," Tyler said. "And when did they leave?"

"On June 18, 1778. That's when they evacuated Philadelphia."

"And Lucy Tarleton died on what date?" Logan asked.

"It's believed she was killed just before the British evacuated. According to the stories we have, Beast Bradley murdered her in the grand salon hours before leaving the city. Angus was apparently found cradling his daughter's body by Tobias Dandridge, the man who would later marry Sophia—and the artist who painted the likeness of Bradley in the study."

Logan and Tyler looked at each other again.

"What?" Allison asked.

"September to June. Nine months—give or take a few weeks," Tyler said.

"Are you saying—"

"Suppose history has it wrong," he went on. "What if Beast Bradley moved in and Lucy fell for him right away? Or, even if she wasn't in love with him, what if she was willing to use him for information, as you said? And willing to sleep with him to keep her family safe? According to all the stories, she played at being attracted to him. So, what if she had a child with him— and she was killed because of that child?"

Allison groaned. "And one of my ancestors was that child? I don't know—they would've had to begin their affair immediately. And the child had to have been born just before she died. And if *she* was killed, why would someone let the child live?"

"I imagine it's easier to kill a woman who's angered or betrayed you than a helpless infant," Logan said. "The murder might have been because he was furious, a crime of passion. *If* Beast Bradley killed her."

Allison was thoughtful. "Okay, wait," she said after a moment. "You think maybe Lucy *did* care about Beast Bradley, and that she had an affair with him—and a child. So someone else killed her. Who? Angus? Because his daughter had, in his view, betrayed him and her country? And, of course, the baby was innocent, so he asked the Leigh who would've been my ancestor to take the baby in?"

"It's possible," Tyler said. "And I think it's a theory we can investigate when we go to Valley Forge. I want to hear what Martin Standish has to say."

"Allison, did he come to his theories and conclusions because of letters in his possession?" Logan asked.

"Yes. But it's difficult to prove those theories because the letters might not be signed. Or they're signed with initials or just a term of endearment. This would be for the protection of both the writer and the recipient." Allison paused. "The war was a hard, sad time for many. Some letters were written by soldiers and sent out. Others were written by friends and relatives and smuggled in to them."

"Valley Forge is only twenty miles northwest of Philly," Tyler said. "But our appointment with Standish is at two this afternoon. Since we don't know what we'll find out or how long it might take, I suggest we plan on staying overnight if need be."

"I wouldn't mind being out of the city for a night," Allison murmured.

"You feel you need to get out of this house for a while?" he asked her.

"Yes, but I also have a feeling there's something in Valley Forge we need to know. Maybe you're right and we have the history all wrong," Allison said. "We'll have to do some cajoling to get Martin to really help us. He was pretty angry about that phone call of Cherry's."

"And who more than Cherry would receive a comedown if it was proven that *Allison* is a descendent— not just of the house, but of Lucy Tarleton," Logan remarked. "What's your feeling about Cherry?" he asked Tyler.

"I agree that she stands to lose the most," he said. "But I don't know...."

"Martin Standish is passionate—and possessive!— in regard to his letters," Allison told them. "He admits there's no way to *prove* who wrote them, but according to the article, he believes they belonged to 'heroes and heroines who dared not write their names.'"

"How did he get hold of these letters?" Tyler asked.

Allison shrugged. "He hasn't said. It can be big business, you know. There are many letters from all periods of history in private hands. Sometimes people don't even realize they own them. They find them when they're cleaning out an attic or a basement. Anytime you go to a reenactment, you'll generally see collectors buying and selling historical items and letters. There's nothing illegal about owning them. Sometimes, what happens is that children inherit collections or letters, guns, even articles of clothing—and they don't have a real appreciation for those objects." She gave another shrug. "So they might have them appraised and sell them. That's how some of them came on to the market. In Martin Standish's case, he's a true lover of the era, and his collection is precious to him."

"You think he's just going to let us rummage through everything?" Tyler asked her.

She smiled. "Not *rummage*. I think, if I approach him in the right way, he'll let us study his documents. You do realize they won't be in a stack on his desk. He'll have done everything necessary to preserve them."

Tyler clapped his hands. "Road trip. Let's get started." He turned to Logan. "We keep coming back to that painting of Beast Bradley in the study. With the overlays Jane's done, we probably have a truer image of the man. But that doesn't help with what we've heard about the painting—from Julian, from the Dixon family, from Ethan."

"I'll get Sean on it again," Logan promised.

They took their time driving to Valley Forge.

Tyler enjoyed the trip. Being with Allison was like being with a personal guide; she pointed out landmarks along the way and memorials to events that had taken place. The patriots hadn't just abandoned Philadelphia. The British had won the Battle of Brandywine. There'd been a rain-out, basically a draw, at the Battle of the Clouds.

They stopped at the site of the Paoli Massacre and spent an hour walking around the pristine grounds where the British had routed Anthony Wayne's troops on September 20, 1777.

Looking out over the beautiful countryside, just touched by the gentle breeze of the late-summer day, Tyler found himself seeing the era that had given them their country through Allison's eyes.

"You told me once that courage wasn't about not being afraid," she said. "I still marvel when I think about the fight these men waged. Every man who put his name on the Declaration of Independence knew that doing so made him a traitor, and if the war was lost and he was captured, he could be executed. They *had* to be afraid. Only an idiot wouldn't be. The British had the most powerful fighting forces in the world at the time, and those men—Washington, Jefferson, all the others—still signed that piece of paper. Washington's army faced near-starvation, a lack of supplies, lack of clothing...and, of course, some did desert. But whenever I think about it, I'm in awe that we have a country. They were routed again and again, but they prevailed in the end." She smiled mischievously. "And there *were* a few victories in there! The Americans did win against the British general Burgoyne during the Battle of Saratoga. And once Lafayette arrived and Pulaski helped whip our men into fighting shape, the army was in much better condition."

He slipped his arms around her, pulling her close. "You make me see the world in a whole new light," he whispered.

She leaned against him. The sun was shining down on her hair, which made it look as dark and glossy as a raven's wing. He had to remind himself that they weren't on a date—or sightseeing.

"So, there's action all around Philly, even after the British occupy the city," he said pensively. "When they do, our Lucy, who's friends with a number of fighting men, immediately begins her flirtation with Lord Brian Bradley. Whenever she gains information, she rides out. Sadly, I guess neither she nor any other patriot spy reached this particular battlefield in time. Sounds like it was a horrible massacre."

"The Americans repulsed the British at Whitemarsh," Allison said. "Lucy might have been able to get information to someone about that."

"Washington retired with his forces to Valley Forge in December, right?" Tyler asked.

"December 19," Allison replied. "We should move on. You can see some of the landscape around there before we meet up with Martin Standish. The old stone farmhouses that were used as headquarters still exist and they've built replicas of the wooden huts the soldiers used to survive the winter. You've never been there? On a school trip or a family vacation, maybe?"

He shook his head. "No. But I can tell you the story of the Alamo with every detail and every argument about the deaths of our Texas heroes."

"'Don't mess with Texas!'" she said, smiling.

They made the drive to Valley Forge, and once they arrived, Tyler was even more impressed. There had been no fighting at Valley Forge; there were still fortifications and cannon and all manner of defenses. At the time, the Americans hadn't known the British wouldn't chase them to the valley.

But despite the lack of fighting, there had been many, many deaths. Two thousand had died from the harshness of that winter and the diseases that riddled the troops.

They stopped to see George Washington's restored headquarters, and Tyler felt humbled as he studied the general's maps and other artifacts. From beyond the little house and the hill on which it sat, he saw an exceptional view of the Schuylkill River.

At quarter to two, they came to an old corner brick building, where a small sign announced Standish House: Open upon Appointment.

Tyler had barely knocked when Martin Standish opened the door. He was a wizened little man with Ben Franklin glasses, wispy white hair and a round belly.

Indeed, he looked like an older Ben Franklin.

"Come in, come in," he said, hustling them inside and locking the door behind them. "No one followed you, did they?"

Tyler was surprised. "No one knows we're here, Mr. Standish," he assured the man. "This is Allison Leigh. You've spoken to her online and on the phone. And I'm Agent Tyler Montague, with the FBI. Why are you afraid we were followed?"

"I received several calls this morning, from people asking to see my collection."

"What people?" Allison asked.

"Young lady, if I knew that, I wouldn't be so worried. But considering everything that's happened, I don't trust too many people. In fact, after you two leave today, I'm going out of town for a while. This is all making me very nervous," he said.

"You feel threatened?" Tyler tried to take in the little museum as he spoke. It was really the man's downstairs living area. But there were display cases on tables throughout; he had remnants of clothing, vests, caps, belts and a number of powder horns and flintlock muskets. The walls were adorned with maps and sketches of generals and the rank and file of the Revolutionary armies.

Standish was watching him and shaking his head. "What, sir? Agent or not, what are you, stupid?" Standish demanded rudely. "You've got corpses at that house. And I've got that woman calling me first, and this morning I get three calls, and oddly enough, although the voices were similar, each claimed to be from a different place—supposedly researchers out of Virginia, New York City and Vermont! And what's happening in Philly around the Tarleton-Dandridge House? That's scary. Coincidence that a woman dies in a car accident after a fellow stabs himself to death with his costume bayonet? No, I don't think so. I don't believe in coincidence, no sirree. I'm getting out of here and not telling a soul except my daughter where I'll be."

Tyler glanced at Allison. "Could you tell whether the caller today was a man or a woman?"

"Couldn't tell at all."

"I'd like your permission to check your phone records. We can find out where those calls came from," Tyler said.

Standish raised his brows. "Sure. If you can do that, great."

"It only takes a phone call."

Standish seemed to like him then.

"I don't understand it. Someone's worried that the story about the Tarleton-Dandridge House might not be entirely true," Standish said. "We need to admit our mistakes. I'm referring to the things we *did* wrong and the stories we *got* wrong. It doesn't mean we're not a great country if we do. Lord, there's power in seeing the past clearly." He looked at Allison. "You teach history to our young minds. You know it's wrong to pollute the past by pretending that the men who came before us were without fault. The media today puts every indiscretion, big or small, out there for the world to see. But can anyone in our society be foolish enough not to realize that men of power have *always* held a sexual attraction for those around them? And that they're frequently willing to exploit it?" He made a scornful sound, shaking his head. "Thomas Jefferson! We worship the ground he walked on, but he had an affair with his slave Sally Hemings. Everyone back then talked about it and his mixed-race children—everyone except Jefferson. The man just kept mum." He wagged a finger in the air. "But the interesting thing is that Sally Hemings was already Jefferson's sister-in-law. She was the daughter of Jefferson's wife's father. People talked about him back then, but he still came down in history as a great man. But scandal isn't new, is it?"

"No, Mr. Standish, scandal isn't new at all. I don't think most people are alarmed when politicians are human. I think we're alarmed when they lie and make bad decisions. When we see that a politician lied about an affair and covered it up, we wonder what else he might lie about," Allison said.

Tyler cleared his throat. "What's the lie that surrounds the Tarleton-Dandridge House, Mr. Standish? If we can discover the truth, maybe we can prove that someone doesn't want history changed—and we can make sure no one else is killed." He took out his phone and put a call through to Logan, asking Standish for particulars as he requested Logan to get Standish's phone records pulled.

"Now, as to Lucy Tarleton! Let me show you...."

Standish had been ready for them. They weren't going to have to sort through anything.

He brought out a safety deposit box. "I keep the museum at a constant temperature of about sixty-eight degrees," he told them. "You don't go laminating precious things like this. You don't cover them with any substance and you don't use paper clips or the like. And you handle them as little as possible. I have copies, but..." He turned to Allison. "For you, the real thing."

Allison thanked him with a grateful smile that seemed to make his day.

Standish brought over a magnifying glass. "Helps to read that old cursive style with the glass…and there's a light on it, a mild one. Harsh sunlight and artificial light can play havoc with such valuable pieces."

Standish removed a letter from the box and laid it out on a clean glass surface. "There, my dear!"

Allison didn't touch it. Standish held the glass and she read aloud, "'My dearest friend and confidant, my…prayers are with you for your safety always. My father and sister fare well and my own disposition is excellent. The dreary days of pain go on, but I must tell you that nothing puts us in distress. There are galas, which I of course attend; they are the greatest source of pleasure for one such as me, and from them I gain my strength. Do not fear for me or my family. The emotions that tug at the heart are one matter, while the truth of the day is another. I remain, most and always, faithfully, your best friend.'"

Allison looked up at Standish. She smiled and quoted, "'…they are the greatest source of pleasure for one such as me.'"

"Greatest source of pleasure," Tyler said. "Because those parties were where Lucy got her information."

Allison spoke excitedly. "If Lucy did write this, she was writing to a friend in the patriot forces. She wanted him to know she wasn't suffering and she hinted at what she was doing for the American cause. *If* Lucy wrote it."

Standish smiled. He went to one of the display cases and brought out a framed livestock bill. "This is a copy, but it's a bill that was signed by Lucy Tarleton. You see her signature and her notation that she would like ten more laying chickens. Look at the writing, and then look at the letter."

Allison and Tyler both did. The handwriting was almost identical, down to the curlicues on her capital letters.

"There's an *S* on this side of the sheet. I assume she didn't have access to an envelope. But I suspect Lucy gave this letter to a friend here at Valley Forge and the friend was to give it to S—Stewart Douglas," Standish explained.

"She wanted him to know she was doing well," Allison said.

"She wanted him to know she was collecting secrets and living in comparative comfort," Tyler said. "But... it doesn't sound like a letter one would write a lover."

"No!" Standish seemed pleased.

Tyler was glad. His last remark had apparently improved the man's estimation of his intelligence.

"Here's the second!" Standish said, producing a second safety deposit box. He did love his letters. There was a case for each.

Allison read again. Once more, the letter was addressed to "My dearest friend and confidant."

"'You may have heard the rumors concerning my health. I am well, no matter what is said. Because you know me, I am certain you will understand. Know I have not and will not betray our cause or that which is expected of me. And if you fail to understand, you will nonetheless have pity and forgiveness for me. We all play our role in the human drama set before us, with its treacheries of flesh and feeling that may become a small part of the tragedy that wrecks our world. Pray, understand. I am a true friend to you and to all that is our dream. However, when you hear about wolves that howl at night and tear at man and creature, do not be deceived. Rumor must start when there is an enemy, even though that enemy be nothing more than human. I pray for your health; beware the diseases that ravage. Stay low, my dear brother, and keep your powder dry,'" Allison read.

"Yes, yes?" Standish prompted.

"So, Stewart Douglas *wasn't* the great love of her life. She was trying to explain that she set out to seduce Brian Bradley's secrets from him, playing a role, but she found she enjoyed her role too much—she really cared for the man," Tyler conjectured. "He wasn't a beast."

"Yes!" Standish said with great delight. "There's one more letter that bears examination," he said, bringing out another of his safety deposit boxes. "This one," he told them, "is from S to L. It has to be from Stewart Douglas to Lucy."

Tyler stepped forward. This time, he read aloud. "'My dearest friend and sweetest confidant, little sister mine. I laugh sometimes when I think of the roles the world would have us play and the roles that Fate gives to us instead. I pray for your safety above all else, because it is a dangerous stage upon which you perform. I had heard they noticed the anxiety upon your beautiful face. Whatever the future may bring, wherever it will take you, do not let it steal away the smile you used to wear. We are but a speck in the grand scheme of God's great plan. While you may play true to your design, remember that war will end.'"

"Stewart Douglas wasn't angry with her. It doesn't even sound as if he was—or had ever been—in love with her," Allison commented.

"You're the professional historian," he said, smiling at her, "and I'm just an amateur. But I do know that marriages were frequently arranged at the time."

"Yes, of course. They were good friends and perhaps the families expected her to marry Stewart. But he wasn't out for Bradley's blood for having taken his fiancée. He understood what she was telling him." Allison sighed. "But this doesn't mean Bradley didn't kill Lucy Tarleton."

"The comments regarding her health might have referred to a pregnancy," Tyler said.

"Why, yes! That's possible," Standish agreed.

"But if Lucy was pregnant with Bradley's child," Allison said, "why would he have killed her?"

"Maybe in a fit of rage," Standish suggested.

"I don't think he did kill her," Tyler said.

"If he didn't, then who did? It doesn't sound like it would have been Stewart Douglas. The way these letters read, it's more like a sister and brother writing to each other," Allison argued.

"I made copies for you. You may take them," Standish said, as if presenting them with the crown jewels.

"That's extremely kind of you, Mr. Standish," Allison said.

"Yes, indeed, thank you." Tyler felt the buzz of his cell phone in his pocket, excused himself and answered it.

It was Logan, and he already had a report on the phone records. "There were seven calls made to Mr. Standish this morning. Four of them were from Ms. Mia Standish of King of Prussia, Pennsylvania."

"Mia's your daughter, I assume?" he asked Standish, who nodded.

"And?" Tyler returned to Logan.

"The other three were made from a prepaid cell. It was purchased with cash on Saturday from a Quickie Mart, so no one knows who bought that particular phone. But tracing the satellites, we know the calls were made from Philly."

Tyler thanked Logan and assured him they were making headway. He hung up and explained to Standish that they couldn't trace the calls more precisely because they'd been made from a prepaid cell phone.

"I didn't think you'd get the info on that." He looked at Tyler. "You're an agent, for real?"

"I am."

"Good. Then you can see me to my car and follow me for a few miles. I'm going north to a cabin I have up in the woods with some old hunting friends. I'm not sticking around to die."

"The danger seems to be in Philly," Allison said gently.

Standish snorted. "You know, that guide dying in the late seventies might have been an accident, but the rest of the deaths associated with that place? The kid being electrocuted, the heart attack in Angus's study. And now…another dead guide and a dead board member? Someone is killing people. And I'm going into hiding."

"I think you're doing the right thing," Tyler said.

Allison nodded in agreement. Standish gave her copies of the letters and she thanked him again. He locked his place and went into the garage, where he got into a pickup truck with a shotgun on the front seat.

They followed him for an hour.

There was a chain hotel on the way as they headed back. Tyler suggested they stop there for the night.

When they entered their room, he immediately pulled her into his arms.

She responded with a fiery, passionate kiss, her fingers playing with his waistband and the buckle of his belt. He disarmed himself quickly, fumbling as he unfastened her shirt.

She pulled back, breathless. "This case is all...falling into place.... Perhaps we should be more, um, try to figure it out."

He reached for her again, letting out a groan as his naked body came into contact with hers.

"I *am* trying to figure it all out."

"No, you're not. You're kissing my neck," she told him.

"Yes, and if you keep running your fingers along my spine like that..."

"I should stop."

"No," he said huskily, taking hold of her face and staring into her eyes. "What better way could there be to figure out—" he paused to kiss her "—what was going on in the minds of a pair of lovers...than to *be* a pair of lovers?"

"I like your logic," she whispered. And proceeded to show him just how much.

16

Tyler had just opened his eyes, feeling the warmth of the morning sun through the motel-room drapes, when his phone began to buzz on the bedside table.

He scrambled to answer it.

Logan was calling him. "Hey, did I wake you?" he asked.

"No, I was waking up. Has something happened?"

"No, but Sean thinks he has the solution to the painting."

"Really?" He sat up. Beside him, Allison stirred underneath the sheet. He smiled at her, setting a hand on her hip to reassure her that nothing else—like another horrific accident—had taken place.

"So what is it?" he asked Logan.

"It's not the painting."

"Pardon?"

"He looked at the painting from every angle with his special lights. Studied it in every way he could without ripping into the canvas—which is just canvas—or taking the whole thing apart. And when he was done, he said he had the answer. There have to be two paintings. Someone has a *second* painting, and there's light for the eyes and perhaps some kind of recorder to terrify people or divert their attention. He believes that whoever is doing this somehow manages to switch the paintings."

Tyler rubbed his eyes. "We'll hurry back."

"No rush. Yesterday was uneventful. We went through all the records we could find on the Leigh family—Allison's branch—and there was no mention anywhere of a baby having been adopted. But there *was* a son listed as having been born to one of the young Leigh wives in June of 1778, around the time Lucy Tarleton was killed and just before the British evacuated Philly. We can still disinter Lucy and do some DNA testing, but I'm sure we're right on the money in suspecting that Allison is a descendent."

"I don't think we should let Cherry know," Tyler murmured. Allison was looking at him, and he smiled reassuringly again—or he hoped it was reassuring—but didn't explain.

"What did you learn?" Logan asked.

"We're discovering there are a lot of holes in the history that's been taught. We don't have the whole picture yet, but I do think Lucy was pregnant—and she had Brian Bradley's child, not Stewart Douglas's. What we haven't figured out is who spirited the baby away and who killed Lucy Tarleton. It doesn't make any sense for Bradley to have done it."

"Unless he was afraid of being branded a traitor by the British."

"Not to be cynical, but remember, having an illegitimate child would have been par for the course on the male side, especially for an aristocrat. The female would be branded the whore. If a British officer, who held power in Philadelphia at the time, had a child with a patriot woman, it might've been seen as a ho-hum event. Or even a feather in his cap."

Allison was frowning at him, but then she smiled. "It's true," she whispered. "No one would have thought badly of him. As for Lucy..."

"Regardless of which side he was fighting on," Tyler said, "I believe he was a good soldier and I don't believe he was a 'beast.' By military standards, it was a sound tactic for the British to take Philly. I see Bradley as a military man. I don't see him as the kind of man who would kill a woman he loved—a woman who had just borne his child."

"What about her lover?" Logan asked. "Stewart Douglas."

Tyler shook his head. "I doubt she and Stewart Douglas were ever really lovers, although they were likely engaged," he said. "We have copies of the letters. I don't think Stewart Douglas killed her, either, but I don't know enough about him. By the way, Martin Standish is a good guy—and a scared one. He left his place for a cabin in the woods. He didn't tell anyone where he's going except for his daughter, and we saw him out of town. No one followed him," Tyler said. "I'm still uncomfortable with the whole situation, though. The office was trashed and Standish received those strange calls yesterday, the ones from the prepaid cell phone. He's worried. I'm thinking maybe he has reason to be and we should take some action."

"Can you have Allison try to reach him? Maybe she can persuade him to allow a few agents to watch over him up there. I can send Kelsey and Sean. Bring Allison back to the house. By the way, not a ghost has stirred here. Well, except for Julian Mitchell. He's 'keeping guard' by haunting the entry—and falling asleep on the sofa. That is, when he's not following Jane around."

"I'll have Allison call Standish right away," Tyler said, "and then we'll get something to eat and head back to Philly."

He ended the call and as he looked over at Allison, he felt a tremor streak through him. He hadn't realized how much he'd like waking next to her. Against the hotel's snow-white sheets, her hair truly was the color of a raven's wing, so dark it was touched by a cast of blue. Her eyes were as bright and clear as the sky—and seemed as deep as a sun-kissed sea. It wasn't just that he found her arousing, which he did, but that being with her seemed so *right*. She was like someone who'd been missing from his life, and even the good relationships he'd had—the relationships, not the casual nights—didn't compare with the way he felt now. He couldn't remember not having her beside him and he would never *not* want her beside him; he didn't want to envision a morning without seeing her eyes on his when she woke, or feeling her warmth.

They really had just met. That seemed to mean nothing. He felt like he'd known her forever...or been waiting to know her forever.

She was looking at him expectantly, and he asked her to try calling Standish. She nodded and rose, searching for her handbag and her cell phone. She moved so naturally and easily, comfortable with him in her nakedness.

Yes, he felt like he'd known her forever, but not so long that he didn't feel an immediate stirring in his groin as he watched her.

Sitting on the foot of the bed, she called Standish's cell.

"He's not answering," she said.

Tyler leaped out of bed, grabbing his clothes. "Call Logan and get Standish's daughter's number. Ask her for a location. And have her check with his cronies up at that cabin and see if he's just gone out with them. I'm going to find him."

Allison quickly did as he asked; meanwhile, Tyler hurried to throw water on his face and run a toothbrush over his teeth.

He'd just finished when Allison was in the bathroom beside him. "I'm not staying here," she said.

"I want to go see if—"

"And you're not leaving me here. It's not safe, is it?"

He paused.

"I can shower later. Logan is calling Standish's daughter. I'll be ready by the time we have an address."

He looked at her, shaking his head slightly. But she was right. She shouldn't be alone.

Even if a murderer couldn't be in more than one place and even if the only person who knew where they were was Logan...

"Let's do it," he said.

They were both ready in less than five minutes.

He was disappointed to leave the room behind.

There would be no leisurely morning.

But he found he was more taken with her than ever. When it was time to move, Allison didn't hesitate.

As Logan drove, Allison keyed the coordinates of the cabin into the satellite navigator in the car. Logan had gotten the address from Standish's daughter, who'd been upset but quick to understand and give them the directions. She hadn't been able to reach her father that morning, either.

Sean was driving up with Kelsey, but Tyler and Allison would get to the cabin first.

It was about a thirty-minute drive for them. Tyler could have kicked himself for not realizing yesterday that Martin Standish might prove to be a major target for the killer, who now seemed determined to protect a lie.

The countryside was beautiful, rolling hills, forests and farmland. They climbed higher into the foothills; as they neared the cabin, the road grew narrow. A mist settled over the land, soft and lovely—and yet it was the last thing Tyler wanted right then.

A concealing mist.

Eventually, they climbed a rough stone path with the car protesting all the way. They'd arrived at the cabin, a small log structure surrounded by trees.

"There's his truck," Allison said, pointing out Standish's small Ford.

She climbed out of the car. He did the same, drawing his Glock and warning her, "Stay behind me."

"This killer isn't going to shoot it out with you. He's not particularly brave, just devious," she said, and he was glad of the anger in her voice.

"Stay behind me," he repeated.

They walked up to the cabin, with Tyler keeping a keen eye on the woods.

He banged on the front door. Standish didn't answer. When he twisted the knob, the door opened and they went in.

It was just a small cabin, consisting of two rooms and a bath. There was a coffeepot on the counter; it was still hot.

"He's not here," Tyler said, stating the obvious.

"There's his cell phone." Allison pointed to a rough-hewn table by an old wingback chair in front of a wood-burning stove.

"So he made coffee and walked out of the cabin, leaving his cell phone behind. He doesn't seem like the kind of man who has to have it every second, so maybe that's not unusual."

"Or maybe he went fishing," Allison said hopefully. "Lots of streams in this area. And these guys come up here to go hunting. I don't see his rifle, and I didn't see it on the rack of his pickup truck."

"He's not fishing," Tyler said. "He left because he heard something outside. He took the rifle with him." He strode back to the door. There'd been some rain in the area recently, and he could make out what might be Standish's footprints leading into the copse of trees to the rear of the cabin.

"Stay close!" he told Allison.

She followed him as they moved into the woods. The mist that hovered in the foothills grew thicker, and the sun couldn't cut through the high canopy of pines. It felt as if they were in a realm of shadow where the pines could come to life and the low-hanging branches could reach out like fingers to snare the unwary.

"Allison?"

"I'm close," she said, crashing into him as he stopped.

He nodded and kept going. He could hear a brook and they walked toward it. He paused every so often, listening. There was no breeze so the mist seemed stagnant; they heard only minor rustling when small forest denizens scurried about. Still, he found himself moving very carefully. He suddenly felt certain that someone with malicious purpose *had* been there, and recently. Whether that someone had fled or not, he didn't know.

As they neared the little stream, he heard Allison cry out. "There! Oh, Tyler, there he is!"

She rushed around him and he chased after her, instinctively searching the perimeter. He could see no one.

Allison was already in the stream and down on her knees by the fallen form of Martin Standish. He was headfirst in the water, and she rolled him over.

She leaned against him. "He's not breathing, Tyler!"

"Call 9-1-1. Get them out here as fast as possible."

He hunkered down, checking Standish for visible wounds. Despite the icy water of the stream, he was still warm. Tyler pulled him from the rippling water onto the shore and started performing CPR, counting as he listened to Allison make the call.

She knelt down on Martin's other side to help. Tyler instructed her, breathing into Standish's mouth as she held his nose, and he applied pressure to the man's chest, counting.

He was about to give up. They'd tried long and hard, and he was afraid he'd broken one of Martin's ribs despite his best efforts to exert pressure at the perfect level.

Then Standish breathed. He gulped in a huge swallow of air and began coughing violently.

Allison looked up at Tyler. "He...he might make it!"

Tyler nodded, feeling for the man's pulse. It was faint and irregular, but it was there. He ripped off his jacket, covering him.

Standish opened his eyes. He stared at Tyler and Allison, and seemed to recognize them.

"Voices," he said hoarsely. "There were voices in the woods...ghosts. There were ghosts in the woods."

His eyes closed. Allison and Tyler frowned at each other.

Tyler wanted to search the woods, but he wasn't leaving Standish and Allison alone.

"What should we do?" she asked.

"We wait," he said. He pulled out his cell phone to call Sean first and then Logan.

Allison watched him, her blue eyes grave. Then she looked out at the surrounding trees. "This just happened, Tyler," she said. "If we hadn't come when we did, he would have drowned."

"He may still have a long haul ahead of him."

"Voices in the woods," she repeated. "Ghosts."

"There were no ghosts in the woods," Tyler said, gritting his teeth.

"Listen!" she said.

He heard it. From somewhere down in the rugged terrain of the foothills, a motor was being revved.

"Whoever it was took a different path," he said, feeling angrier.

They never should have left Standish.

It seemed like forever before he heard Sean shouting for them. He and Kelsey came bursting through to the stream, armed and wary.

"Over here!" Allison called, although they'd been seen.

Tyler rose. "EMTs should be here any moment," he said. "Kelsey, stay with them. Sean, I'm pretty sure our killer has fled, but I want to get into the woods."

Kelsey crouched down by Martin Standish and Allison. Tyler, with Sean flanking him, walked back into the woods.

The mist lay everywhere among the trees.

But someone had come here. Someone who knew

about Martin Standish and had been interested enough to learn his habits—and where he spent his leisure time. Someone who'd been watching the activity at the Tarleton-Dandridge House and had known, or surmised, that he and Allison had come to see Standish.

Tyler walked through the woods, away from the cabin, calling out to Sean, who was following the same path but thirty feet closer to the main road below. When he was near the edge, he came across a pine with a large broken branch. He dropped down to the earth and he could see the dirt and needles that had been disturbed. Just beyond the broken branch, the forest began to dwindle and an overgrown embankment led down to the road.

Their quarry had indeed fled.

He saw Sean break through the trees.

"He was here," Tyler said.

Sean joined him. "Find anything?"

"I found out how he got away."

"Did Standish say anything? Did he see anything?" Sean asked.

"Yeah, voices in the woods. Ghosts in the woods."

"This guy is using technical devices," Sean said. "I believe he has a copy of the Beast Bradley painting, and he substitutes it for the other when he's stalking his prey. He has some kind of mechanism to throw his voice. I'll bet he lured Standish to the water that way. He's not stupid—Standish had a shotgun. If we're lucky, our guy dropped something. I'll have Logan see if we can get a crime scene unit to go through these woods."

"We'll *need* a unit. It's almost impossible to see in here with the canopy of branches and the mist."

Sean rested a hand on his shoulder. "We can't protect everyone who ever walked into the Tarleton-Dandridge House," he said.

Tyler couldn't shake his anger with himself. "I should have known. Hell, someone called him three times, and he felt enough anxiety to head out. He said no one knew where he was going except for his daughter, but...this person knows the area, Sean. This is someone who's read everything that's been written about the house. The board and the other guides were aware that Allison was working on a paper—and that she'd studied what Standish wrote."

"Tyler, quit beating yourself up. We couldn't have known that Standish would be in danger. And it looks like you got to him in time," Sean told him.

"Barely, and I don't know if he'll make it. He's not a young man."

"He'll make it," Sean said. "I can hear the sirens now."

Allison stepped aside when the EMTs arrived with their medical bags and stretcher. She looked on as they set up an IV and took Standish's vital signs.

"CPR?" one of the young men asked her.

"Yes, he wasn't breathing at first."

"Has he spoken?"

"Briefly."

The EMTs didn't care about voices or ghosts in the woods; their only concern was for the injured man.

"He was in the water?"

"Yes. Facedown. We don't know how he got there, if he was injured, tripped—pushed. We don't know," Allison said.

She watched, stricken, while the team worked on

Standish. Then one of them glanced up at her and smiled.

"I'm an EMT, not a doc. But I think he's going to be okay. Thank God you came along when you did."

She smiled back weakly.

It was a shame she'd ever contacted the man. She'd unwittingly put him in danger.

Sean and Tyler returned from the woods, their expressions grim, as Standish was placed on a stretcher. It was decided that Kelsey and Sean would go to the hospital and guard Martin Standish there. Logan seemed to think it was important that Allison be at the house.

She and Tyler waited, standing by the beautiful little bubbling stream, as the EMTs moved out. "It's my fault," Allison couldn't help saying.

Tyler shook his head. "No. I was the fool," he said harshly. "I should've had someone watching him from the minute we found out about the missing article."

Allison was afraid that he felt his interest in her might be keeping him from making the best judgments.

"No," she said, "you don't understand. If I hadn't gotten it into my head to publish another paper on the house, maybe none of this would have happened."

"Allison, it's no one else's fault when someone commits murder. It's the work of the bastard who believes his life or agenda is greater than the lives of anyone else. And I don't think the killing started with your paper. I think it started before. Obviously, no one living now was responsible for the death of a Civil War soldier or the suicide of a distraught young woman— things that took place years ago—but as to the kid who was electrocuted, and the guide who had a heart attack in Angus's study...I think we may be looking at the same perpetrator." He turned away suddenly, and she realized he'd heard movement from the trees.

"Crime scene techs are here," he said. He walked away to greet the team, and she could hear him explaining the situation succinctly, including a chronicle of the actions they'd taken since they'd come.

Allison walked closer to the stream. She stared down at the water. It seemed to glitter. As the water skipped over pebbles and rocks, it reflected rays of sunshine, which shone like scattered diamonds.

Something caught her eye and she cried out.

Tyler spun around, his face anxious.

"I see Standish's rifle," she said. "There—it looks as if he threw it. As if he was hit from behind, and then threw it."

Tyler and the crew of techs walked over to her.

"Good eye," one of the techs said.

He sloshed through the stream to collect the rifle and then glanced at Tyler. "We'll comb this part of the woods," he said. "We'll get back to you with anything we have, down to gum wrappers if there are any."

Tyler thanked him, then led Allison back through the woods to his car, parked in front of the cabin. "Let's get back to Philly," he said.

She was hesitant as they drove. "Tyler, maybe *I* should go away. People around me, even people I hardly know, seem to wind up dead or in the hospital."

"What? Go back to your house? No. Don't you see, Allison? That would mean one or two of us having to patrol your house to make sure no one's figured out a way to break in. Besides, you've been around all these people for years. Any one of our suspects could have a key."

"I meant fly away somewhere," she said.

"If that would keep you safe, I'd have you do it in a second. But this person is a step ahead. He'd find you, Allison. He'd go after you. He found Standish."

"I just feel that…"

He reached out, squeezing her hand. "Yeah, I know," he said huskily. "But we need you where you are. I need you with me—where I know I can keep you safe."

She smiled at that. "I like being…safe," she told him. "But I can't stop feeling that I'm a catalyst for others being hurt. And killed."

"What will solve this is finding out the *who*. That will prevent more people from being hurt or killed. I think we're just about onto the *why*. Our killer knows that, and it's making him desperate. And when a killer gets desperate, he gets careless."

She leaned back in the passenger seat, closing her eyes.

When they were a little more than halfway back to the city, Tyler's phone rang. He asked her to pick it up.

It was Sean, and she put the phone on speaker.

They both listened as Sean told them that Martin Standish was going to make it. "He's conscious again and clear in his mind. He was knocked out by a massive blow to the head. He would have drowned if you two hadn't come along when you did."

"I'm so thankful we did," Allison said.

"He's going to have some tests done because it was a pretty nasty blow," Sean continued. "He says he heard voices calling to him from the woods. At first he was afraid it might have been his daughter, that she'd come up and gotten lost and was wandering through the woods. Then he heard voices that seemed to come from a number of directions. As if the woods were filled with ghosts. He heard another noise and got angry, so he followed it to the stream, thinking he'd be safe. The man is good with a shotgun, from what I've been told."

"And then?" Tyler asked.

"The next thing he knew, he felt a sharp pain against his skull, and he fell into the water. That's the last he remembered—until he felt Allison 'kissing' him," Sean said.

Tyler smiled. "That must've been nice for him."

"Yeah, the guy has quite a sense of humor for an old coot. You're not going to believe this. He's still in pain, but he seems happy now. He says someone's finally paying attention to him, and he thinks his research is going to change history."

"It will—but only in our small corner of the world," Allison said.

"Anyway, Kelsey and I will hang out here," Sean finished. "It's not a huge hospital and their security is pretty flimsy. One of us will be in his room at all times. And could you look for that other painting?" he asked. "I know it exists."

"We'll do that," Tyler promised.

When they reached the Tarleton-Dandridge, Kat was at the morgue, going through the autopsy reports on everyone who'd died at the house.

Jane and Logan were in the salon, where the antique dining table had been turned into a workstation. Julian was with them, trying to move a piece of paper.

He stood, relieved to see Allison. He tried to give her a hug.

She tried to hug him in return. With limited success.

Then she went to take a quick shower and Tyler planned to do the same as soon as she was out.

Logan listened to his report on what they'd discovered, then said he was going to keep searching through the records they'd amassed. "I think you should give Detective Jenson a call. The local police were going to keep tabs on Oxford, Addison, Pierson, Fanning and Lawrence."

Tyler agreed and made the call. Jenson told him, "Oxford left his house in the ten minutes between my patrol car's drive-by. Lawrence's car hasn't moved. No one's seen anyone come or go from the Addison house. Pierson had a meeting at a bank downtown. He left his place about twenty minutes ago." Jenson paused. "I'm not sure how much any of that will help you."

Tyler thanked him, saying, "It helps." He related everything about the trip he and Allison had taken to see Martin Standish and what had happened that morning.

"I can double the patrol," Jenson said. "But it's hard. We're not allowed overtime with the current budget cuts."

"We appreciate whatever you can do."

It was growing late. Logan ordered food. When Allison was done with the shower, Tyler went in. The hot water felt wonderful; he hadn't realized how cramped and stiff he was from getting soaked in the cold stream. Fortunately, the water stayed hot just long enough.... When he came out, he felt invigorated.

He knew Allison was with Logan and Jane. Logan was questioning her, once again, about the people she'd worked with at the house.

He went back to the entry and sat down at the bank of screens, rolling through the images quickly to watch the hours since they'd left.

Late in the middle of the night, Lucy Tarleton had appeared. She'd gone to the study and looked in, then hurried through the house to the back.

He wondered if, night after night, she repeated that same circuit. If so, he assumed it meant she was sneaking out of the house, heading over to the stables to get Firewalker and take off into the night, carrying her information to the patriots at Valley Forge.

There had been no other activity.

He felt a touch on his shoulder. "Give it a rest," Logan said. "Start over in the morning. Standish survived and he has two of the best guards around. Get some sleep."

Tyler nodded. "Thanks," he told Logan huskily.

Allison was already upstairs in Lucy's room. He found her in bed, wide-eyed and waiting for him.

"Should I be here?" she asked.

Tyler felt the day's tension, his own self-reproach, fall away as if he'd shed an irritating coat. She had that effect on him. It wasn't that she made him forget; she made him see more clearly.

"I'm grateful you are," he said, "and there's nowhere else I think you should be."

He stripped off his clothing and lay down beside her. He touched her hair softly, looking into the deep blue of her eyes, getting lost in them. "So, the last man you were seeing was something of a rock star, huh?"

"It was a while ago now," she said.

"What was he like?"

"Good guy, nice guy, but for the longest time, I thought there was something wrong with *me*. He'd plan to pick me up and wouldn't show. At that point I knew about the alcohol but not about the drugs. Later on, I went to a few Narcotics Anonymous meetings. And I knew he cared about me, but he refused to acknowledge the addictions. I ended the relationship. I don't know what he's doing now. I pray he's alive."

He stroked her hair. "It's a terrible thing, addiction," he told her, drawing her close.

She lay against him for a minute in silence, a silence that seemed relaxed and comfortable. Pulling her closer he kissed the top of her head.

She stirred, and he kissed her again. He felt her naked body slide against his, and her slightest touch was instant arousal.

He loved the fact that she could make the world go away. And that she could so easily return to it. He found himself wondering if she'd ever leave her beloved Philadelphia. Virginia wasn't that far, but...

He forgot the past and future as they made love.

And then they slept peacefully together.

In the middle of the night, he felt her move. He woke as she slipped out from the covers and stood there for a moment, framed in the pale moonlight that filtered through the drapes.

She walked away from him. Tyler rose quickly, watching her; she wasn't awake, he thought. She wasn't aware of him.

For a few seconds he was afraid she'd take off through the night stark naked. She didn't. She went to the foot of the bed and pulled on her robe, although she didn't bother with slippers. She hurried across the room to the wall where there was nothing—nothing that he could see. She bent to pick up something, cradling it tenderly against her body. She paused, head bent, as if she was praying, and then hurried to the door.

He grabbed his own robe, throwing it on. Allison opened the door and eased through. In the hallway she paused again, as if listening for others in the household.

She walked carefully down the stairs and went to stand in the entrance to the study, looking into the darkened room. Then she ran down the hallway to the back door. The alarm was keyed; she wasn't going to stop to put in the code.

He realized that to Allison, at that moment, there was no code. She was seeing the house through the memory of another woman.

Lucy Tarleton.

He slipped ahead of her, tapping in the alarm code just in time. Allison opened the back door and stepped into the night.

She moved forward and handed whatever she was carrying to someone who was invisible to him.

A second later she stepped back, tears in her eyes.

Tyler felt as if a rush of wind swept by him.

Then Allison burst into tears and sank to the ground.

17

By then, the others were up. Tyler bent down beside Allison, drawing her to her feet. He brought an arm around her.

"She gave the baby away. She carried her baby out in the middle of the night and she gave him away," Allison said.

"I know. I saw," Tyler told her.

She looked baffled. "It's true. It's really true. She gave the baby to the Leigh family, my family, and all these years, none of us had any idea."

"As we've said many times, history is always told by the victors," Tyler said. "I suppose Lucy's patriot family didn't want it known she'd had a bastard child—especially since the baby's father was one of the enemy. It ruined the romance and drama of her heroism in their eyes."

"But what about Bradley? He must have known. Do you think that's what sent him into a frenzy—why he killed her?" Allison asked.

"Hey, let's get inside. It's cold out here," Jane said.

Kat was just inside the door. "Do you suppose that's why people have been killed through the years?" she asked. "I studied those autopsy reports inside and out.

The deaths *look* like they were accidental, but...faulty wiring caused the college student's death? At a historic property that's inspected all the time? Or tripping down the stairs?"

"Could *this* be the reason?" Tyler gestured at Allison. "I think we're looking for a truly obsessed killer who is devious, as well. And if——" He paused, aware that everyone was watching him. "And if it's because Allison really is a descendent of Lucy Tarleton, *she's* the one who matters. That would point to Cherry Addison. Not to mention the fact that her husband is an artist and she could have gotten him to paint a replica portrait."

"Then we announce tomorrow that we suspect Allison Leigh is a descendent of Lucy Tarleton's," Logan said. "We make an announcement to the media——and see what crawls out of the woodwork."

"Will that make the killer more desperate?" Jane asked. "Or will it just mean that the truth is out——and he'll disappear and we'll never know who he is?"

"Maybe we should make the announcement to the surviving guides and board members first," Kat suggested.

"Yes," Tyler agreed.

"Okay, we'll set it up for tomorrow night," Logan said. "During the day, we need to watch the board. Whoever was in the woods with Martin Standish is going to want to know if he survived or not. I left word with the hospital to report his condition as critical. We'll keep an eye on the board——and on Jason and Annette——and plan on having them over for after-dinner coffee. We'll present this information to them and see what kind of reaction we get."

"I don't think that's the motive," Allison said, wiping

her face. She shrugged. "I mean, I don't believe people were killed because of Lucy's baby. There's another possible spin to this story. Maybe the baby wasn't Beast Bradley's child, but Stewart Douglas's. I can't tell anyone, other than you, that I *saw* and acted out what happened the night Lucy gave her baby away. She sensed danger in the house. If she was afraid Beast Bradley would kill not just her but the child, as well, that would make her actions *more* heroic."

"So, the only person who might be distressed by the evidence that Lucy did have an illegitimate child would be...Cherry," Kat said.

"If that's not the reason for the murders, what is?" Tyler asked, frustrated.

"I say we tell the world we're going to have Lucy disinterred so we can do DNA tests on her and Allison, and prove it to all and sundry," Logan said. "I'd like to see how Cherry takes the news."

"We don't really have to dig her up, do we?" Allison asked.

"I think that'll be your choice in the end," Logan told her. "For the moment, it's a carrot...dangled in someone's face." He smiled. "If you're game to try it."

"I guess I'm game for anything at this point."

Julian had been standing by Jane. "Thank you," he said quietly. "I need to know the truth, Allison. I don't want to hurt anyone, and I don't want anyone else hurt. I don't know exactly what it is, but I need..."

"Justice," Tyler said. "We seek justice. For the living—and the dead."

Allison was nervous the next morning but she called Jason Lawrence and Annette Fanning while Logan phoned Cherry, Ethan Oxford and Nathan Pierson.

They explained that they were going to talk to those most closely associated with the house before giving new information to the press. Annette and Jason both sounded curious and nothing more.

Tyler suggested they go to the hospital and check on Artie Dixon's condition. Tyler sent Jane and Kat on a drive out to Valley Forge to meet with local police—and to check that nothing at Martin Standish's little museum had been touched.

At the hospital, Haley Dixon looked more worn than ever. Once again, Tyler coaxed her into coming to the cafeteria with him, while Allison sat down and held Dixon's hand.

A young woman poked her head in and introduced herself as Dixon's nurse for the day, telling her the LPN's name was on the board, if she needed assistance. "We monitor the vitals at all times, of course, out at the nurses' station, but hit the button if you need us." She rolled her eyes. "We've had all kinds of codes going today—reds and greens. Those are hostile or combative patients. You wouldn't believe how many people come in for help and then want to knock out their doctors and nurses!"

Allison smiled sympathetically and thanked her. As she sat down, she heard the warning, "Code green!" over the loudspeaker. Nurses and orderlies were running down the hall.

Allison concentrated on Artie Dixon, talking to him quietly and earnestly, asking him to speak to her with his mind. He did, but he was still obsessed with the painting. "Lies—what we see is all lies," Dixon told her.

"We believe there are two paintings, Mr. Dixon. And one of them is a false image, used to distract or perhaps hypnotize the watcher. Someone changes the painting."

"No," Dixon seemed to whisper. "The painting. I believe it is false. I believe it's all lies."

A nurse came into the room. At first, Allison was so intent on Artie Dixon that she didn't pay attention. Then, as the person in the scrubs began to flick a needle of medication to insert in the IV, Allison noticed that the nurse was wearing a cap and had a large air mask over his or her face.

A feeling of unease crept over her.

She rose abruptly. The nurses didn't usually come in dressed as if they were entering a surgery or intensive care.

"What is that?" she asked.

She screamed when the "nurse" turned, the needle raised—ready to shove it in her chest.

Allison panicked and pushed at the bed. It was heavy, but she pushed it far enough to catch the person in the thighs.

"Help!" she screamed at the top of her lungs.

The hospital seemed eerily silent.

The "nurse" was regaining his or her balance, but Allison had nothing with which to fight—other than her handbag. She slammed it across her would-be attacker's face and flew out into the hall.

The hall was empty. She could hear her attacker, heavy-footed, coming after her as the loudspeaker announced, "Code Red, Code Green. Code Red, Code Green, Neuro Section twelve!"

There was no one else around because they were all answering the code calls. And Allison had a feeling that those calls were rigged.

She paused in the hall. Which way? Where should she go?

She started toward the elevators and then turned

back; the person in the surgical garb was standing outside the room, dripping needle held high in a gloved hand.

She didn't know what was in the needle.

She was sure it was lethal.

She ran toward the elevators, aware that the person was running behind her.

Allison reached the elevator bank and slammed all the buttons. She didn't care if she went up or down—just so long as she could go *somewhere*.

She turned back. Her attacker was gaining on her.

She slammed the buttons again. An elevator door opened.

And Tyler stepped out. She threw herself in his arms, hysterically trying to explain that someone was behind her.

"Where, Allison, where?" he demanded.

"Artie!" Mrs. Dixon, who was beside him, cried out.

Allison swung around. There was no one behind her, no one at all.

Tyler didn't doubt Allison's word. He contacted a guard and had the hospital locked down, but he knew full well that in a hospital, it was easy for someone clad in the right uniform to simply disappear—hiding in plain sight.

And Allison, try as she might, couldn't describe her assailant. "Tall, I think. Maybe not, but at least my height," she said. "I don't even know if it was a man or woman," she told him.

Artie Dixon was fortunately unharmed. Tyler made arrangements with Jenson to send local officers to watch over his room from that point on. Haley Dixon remained hysterical for a long time after the incident and had to be sedated.

Security officers and police who had gone through the hospital reported to Tyler that they'd found no one answering the description hiding in lounges or in patients' bathrooms.

Tyler hadn't expected they would. The moment he'd stepped off the elevator, the perpetrator had been managing his or her escape. Strip off the cap and mask, walk calmly and briskly into a patient's room, perhaps even direct a cop to a different location. Slide out of the uniform and walk out like a visitor.

When they were finally leaving, he heard Allison gasp.

"What?"

"Annette! There's Annette."

Annette Fanning was hurrying through the parking lot to her car. Allison touched Tyler's arm. "Let me see what she says when I catch up with her. I want to see her reaction to me being here. But Annette *can't* be our killer. Really, it can't be Annette."

Allison ran ahead of him. He slowed his pace, watching carefully. Allison caught up with Annette, and the other woman turned to her, a look of surprise on her face.

"Hey! My God, I'm glad to see you. I don't know what was going on here, but I came to see my cousin in the maternity ward. And suddenly there were bells and bongs and security and cops all over."

Tyler could hear Annette speaking; he could also tell that she was reaching into her oversize handbag for something.

A needle? The needle she'd failed to thrust into Allison in Artie Dixon's hospital room?

No more taking chances.

Tyler sped across the parking lot and tackled Annette Fanning. He slammed into her, twisting so he didn't throw her onto the pavement but took that punishment himself.

Annette cried out. Tyler rolled, pulling her to her feet. He grabbed the bag from her.

"What the hell?" Annette demanded angrily.

"Tyler?" Allison said, as if she, too, thought he had lost his mind.

He ignored them both and searched Annette's bag. There was nothing in it more incriminating than a hairbrush and a box of tampons.

He thrust the bag back at her. "What's your cousin's name?"

"Judy Hall, and she had a baby girl last night at 10:03," Annette told him. "Check it out!" she added angrily.

"We will."

"What's the matter with you people?" Annette shouted.

"Allison was just attacked. In Artie Dixon's room," Tyler said.

Annette gasped. "And you think that I—that I... Don't be absurd! It couldn't have been me!"

"Why should we infer that it couldn't have been you?" Tyler asked.

"For one thing, because Allison is way stronger than I am!" Annette said.

"She's right," Allison agreed.

"You don't need much strength to shove a needle into someone." Tyler shook his head. "I'm done taking chances."

"No, no, it wasn't Annette—I *know* it wasn't Annette," Allison said.

"You can't just assume," Tyler began.

"I'm not assuming on the basis of friendship. But the attacker was taller. Annette's too small."

Annette groaned. "Thanks. Thanks a hell of a lot!"

When Allison and Tyler returned, Logan was alone in the house. He was seated in front of the screens, glancing at them now and then, and going over papers and folders, eternally patient while he searched for what he wanted.

He knew what had happened because Tyler had spoken to him.

"Jane and Kat are with the police at Valley Forge," he said. "There was an attempt to break into Martin Standish's house last night. With Standish's blessing, they're transferring some of his papers to a bank vault."

"That's a good idea," Allison said. "Are we still expecting the others tonight?"

"We are," Logan said.

"Including Annette." Tyler grimaced. His apology had been minimal, and Allison felt guilty, since they hadn't really learned anything from the encounter. So Annette's distress had been for nothing. Tyler had told Allison they couldn't afford to take any chances, and she understood that, but...

She looked around. "Where's Julian?"

"He went with Jane and Kat. He's decided you don't need him—and they might," Logan said, smiling. "What a pity they met at completely the wrong time! He's so courteous toward Jane, and while she pretends he's a pest, she really likes him."

"Yeah, talk about the *ultimate* bad timing," Allison murmured.

"Oh!" Both Logan and Tyler turned to her. "With everything that happened, I forgot to tell Tyler what

Artie 'said' to me. I don't think he was denying there
could be a second painting, but he wanted me to understand something about the painting in the study. He
kept saying it was a lie."

"I'll bet he means the painting itself is a lie," Tyler
said. "We know that when Tobias Dandridge painted
it, he despised Bradley. Bradley and the British troops
had left Philadelphia. Tobias was probably feeling a bit
inadequate, since the Colonial forces didn't defeat the
British here. The British abandoned the capital just as
the patriots had."

"Interesting. The history of the house and the family came down to us through Tobias Dandridge and his
wife, Sophia," Tyler said. "Lucy's sister."

"So, he painted the picture of Bradley as a monster and left that image of him for the world." Allison
sighed. "And now we know it's probably unfair."

"Let's go look," Tyler suggested. "See if we can find
the second painting."

"But...say there is such a painting," Allison said,
"would the killer leave it here?"

"Maybe not, but maybe we'll find a clue as to
whether or not it actually exists."

Logan checked his watch. "You have about an hour,"
he told them.

"Let's get on with it," Tyler said.

Allison thought they should trace the path someone
might take through the house and discover how easy it
would be to slip from the study to other rooms—and
then leave the property entirely. As they moved through
the study into the ladies' salon and the music room,
she could see how someone could have crept through
the various rooms without being seen by her, the lone

remaining guide, on the night Julian was killed. The house alarms didn't extend to the fence in front of the property or the wall that surrounded it.

She opened every cabinet and every drawer, looking for a place where a painting might have been hidden. They didn't find one, but toward the end of their search, Allison opened a cupboard where musical instruments had been kept during the Revolutionary era. It still contained a couple of fifes, carefully displayed on shelves.

"Wait!" Tyler said.

She'd been about to close the door. He stepped past her and ran a finger over the top shelf. He lifted the finger—and there was a slight smudge on it.

"Paint?" she asked.

He nodded. "We'll get a sample to the lab."

"But if there was a painting here, it's gone now."

"The more we know—or think we know—the better off we'll be."

"Hey!" Logan was standing in the doorway to the music room. They turned to see what he wanted.

"Showtime!" he announced. "They're arriving."

Allison followed Tyler out to the narrow hall and down to the entry. Ethan leaned on his cane, Cherry stood next to him and Nathan was just coming in. She walked forward to welcome them all, her heart beating fast, but behaving as naturally as she could.

"Let's adjourn to the grand salon, shall we?" Logan invited. "We can sit around the table."

"Ohhh!" Cherry said with dismay. "Look what you've done to this table! It's over two-hundred years old, you know!"

"It's covered with a plastic tarp that lets nothing through," Logan reassured her. "Not to worry. Please, have a seat. Coffee, tea—anything?"

They heard a key in the door. "I'm here!" Jason called from the entry.

"This way!" Tyler called back.

"Ethan, I just don't know if it was such a good idea, bringing this unit in. Sorry, you all, but really. You people don't seem to have any answers," Cherry said.

"This will be solved." Ethan spoke in a low, confident voice.

"I'm curious. Evidently, you've discovered something," Nathan said cheerfully. "I, for one, am agog to hear!"

Annette arrived just after Jason. She acted as if she didn't want to be in the house; she was hostile and whispered to Allison, "I'm not coming back to work here. I don't want to wind up like Julian or Sarah. And I don't want to be accused of hurting anyone, either!"

"Sarah had an accident," Cherry murmured.

"Now that we're all present... If you'll sit down, we'll tell you what we believe we can prove," Tyler said.

He remained standing while the others took chairs. "First," he began, "take a look at these likenesses."

He passed out copies of the computer images Jane had devised, melding Allison's face with the images of Lucy Tarleton.

Annette let out a little gasp. She stared across the table at Allison. "Oh, my God! That is *uncanny*."

"We don't think it's uncanny. We think its heredity," Logan said evenly.

"That's ridiculous!" Cherry snapped. "Lucy didn't have children."

"We believe she did, and we can prove it," Tyler said. "We want to do DNA testing."

"What?" Cherry gasped.

"Why not? Cool!" Jason said.

"I don't know... Disturbing the dead?" Ethan asked haltingly. "I need to speak with Adam."

"You may do that, of course, Mr. Oxford," Logan said. "I'm afraid he had to go back to D.C. yesterday, but you can call him, and of course, we'll bring him out again. We've concluded that someone is afraid of the discovery that Lucy did bear an illegitimate child. That someone is so obsessed with history, he or she doesn't want the truth known."

"About a possible descendent?" Nathan asked. "But...that's not logical, is it? That makes the story all the more appealing! It means we have a flesh-and-blood replica of our beautiful Lucy!"

"Wait a minute," Cherry protested. "Just because you can play with a computer and make Allison look like Lucy? I repeat—ridiculous!"

"That's not the only aspect of our theory, Cherry," Tyler said. "Martin Standish has letters in a safety deposit box that appear to have been written by Lucy. Reading between the lines, they indicate she was never in love with Stewart Douglas, that they were very good friends, and there was no reason for either Stewart Douglas *or* Brian Bradley to have killed her."

"Well, *someone* killed her. She ended up very dead!" Cherry said.

"So, we'll find a way to do the DNA testing." Logan cleared his throat. "I don't know how many of you are aware of this, but Allison was attacked at the hospital today. Someone dressed up in hospital scrubs came after her with a needle. A lethal dose of some kind of drug, I'm sure. So, where were you all today?"

"What?" Cherry demanded, rising.

"You're accusing *us?*" Nathan burst out.

"Well," Tyler said, sitting on the edge of the table,

"we know it's one of you. It has to be. We just have to figure out which. You're the only ones who know the house well enough. So, if we can trace your movements today?"

Jason raised his hand. "Hey, call Evan McDooley! I was working all day."

"I've already been accused," Annette said. "And I'm too short!"

"This is ridiculous," Cherry muttered again. "Fire them, Ethan. Get rid of them!"

"Cherry, you do stand to lose the most, you know," Tyler said in a reasonable voice. "No longer being the star of the history center—I mean, hey, a real live descendent of Lucy Tarleton?"

"That's not what a murder is committed for!"

"No, it's not, is it, Cherry?" Tyler asked.

"I'm going to the bathroom," Annette said abruptly. "You'll have to excuse me."

She got up to leave the room but asked, "Do I need a guard?"

No one spoke and she headed toward the back.

"So?" Tyler asked. "Who's next?"

"I was in my house all day. My housekeeper can vouch for me," Ethan said indignantly.

"Stockbroker and business," Nathan said.

"Oh, please. I was at the gallery," Cherry said.

As Cherry's words died, they suddenly heard a high-pitched scream. Annette was yelling in a panicked voice. "Help, help! Oh, my God!"

Allison jumped up, ready to run. Tyler was ahead of her, thrusting her behind him as Logan dashed toward the rear of the house, the others following him.

Allison slammed into Tyler when he stopped at the

door to the bathroom. "It bit me!" Annette screamed. "It bit me!"

Logan dialed 9-1-1; Tyler stepped past him.

There was a copperhead coiled behind the trash basket. As it started to strike again, Tyler pulled his Glock and shot the snake, then crouched down by Annette.

It was while he bent to minister to her that Allison felt the pinprick in her leg. She opened her mouth to speak, but no words came. She felt someone's arms around her, dragging her back. She tried to blink to see clearly; Logan and Tyler were involved with Annette. She saw Cherry's face, filled with concern. Jason Lawrence had knelt down beside Annette.

She didn't see Ethan Oxford or Nathan Pierson.

But she knew one of them was behind her. He'd drugged her and was dragging her away, and she couldn't speak or blink, and soon, everything was black.

18

The snake had been a fairly small copperhead, but Tyler didn't believe for a minute that it had just made its way into the house—any more than a copperhead had *just* made its way into Sarah Vining's car.

He knew the emergency crew would arrive shortly, but he fastened a tourniquet created from Jason's tie beneath Annette's knee.

She was crying and screaming all the while, and he knew the others were rushing around, trying to get her water, trying to help.

With the tourniquet in place, he looked at the wound; there was no need to try sucking out the poison and spitting it out himself. The EMTs would deal with it much more efficiently than he could ever manage. Copperhead bites were common enough in the area.

"I'm going to die!" Annette cried.

"You're not going to die. Put your arms around my neck. I'll carry you out to the sofa. When the EMTs get here, they'll give you an antidote. You'll spend the night in the hospital."

Cherry Addison came running up, her high heels clicking away, as he brought Annette to the sofa. Logan was still on the line with the 9-1-1 operator, taking her directions and nodding to Tyler that he'd done the right thing.

"I hate this house!" Annette sobbed as he set her down. "I hate this house. It's evil. It's evil, evil, evil. And now, I'm going to die in it. Oh, no. Oh, my God! I'm going to become one of the ghosts of the Tarleton-Dandridge House!"

Jason knelt down beside her. "Annette, come on! The house isn't evil."

"I don't ever want to see it again. I hate it!"

Tyler could hear the sirens; the emergency crew would arrive any minute. He stood, leaving Jason at Annette's side and Cherry standing close by, the glass of water in her hand.

He looked around. Ethan Oxford, his complexion gray, was right behind him.

But he didn't see Allison.

Or Nathan Pierson.

"Logan!"

"Yeah?"

"Where's Allison?"

Logan, too, looked around. "I'll take the upstairs," he said urgently.

"Nathan?" Tyler turned to Ethan. "Where is he? Where did Nathan go?"

Ethan shook his head, looking old and defeated. "I...I was watching Annette," he said.

Tyler raced to the front, letting the emergency crew in. They came from their vehicle with "poison control" bags in their hands.

"Back there," he said briefly. He ran outside, but there was nothing to see. He pulled out his phone and called Jenson at the local station, telling him to get some officers out, that the area had to be searched immediately. They needed an emergency canvas.

He rushed back in, grabbing Oxford by the shoulders. "Nathan Pierson. Did he drive here?"

"I don't know."

"Yes," Annette said weakly. "Yes, he drove."

Walking toward the hallway, Logan pulled out his phone again and asked Jenson for an alert on Pierson's car. He ran out the front door again, anxious to see if Nathan was trying to wrest Allison into his car.

But as he raced out, he felt something—someone—behind him.

He turned.

It was Lucy Tarleton. And she beckoned Tyler to the back of the house.

Allison was perfectly aware of where she was and what was happening.

She was in the apartment above the stables, stretched out on the floor. That faint scent of oiled leather, hay and horses still remained, wafting up from below.

Nathan Pierson was kneeling beside her. He looked amused—and sad.

"Ah, yes, in a few minutes, they'll come searching for you. They'll check the crypt, because they'll be sure that you were spirited away to die on top of Lucy's tomb. That would be poetic justice, but...I don't want them finding me. They won't think of anything as simple as the stables. What's that you say?" He laughed, knowing very well that she couldn't answer him. "They'll search for you everywhere? Yes, they will! Everyone loves you. In fact, I've actually been in love with you for years. You knew that, didn't you? A love-hate relationship, I'd guess you could say. Keeping alive the image of Lucy as a true heroine and not a slut hasn't been easy. Still, what a sweet, bright young woman you proved to be. Of course, I've watched you. I suspected you had to be a descendent, but we had historic records and that baby of Lucy's was so quickly swept away from all danger that your family remained above reproach. Oh, dear girl! For many years, you were like a beauty on a pedestal that I admired from afar. You loved the house and you told the stories dutifully. And what a scholar! Brains and beauty, Ally. Brains and beauty."

She would have answered him—if she'd been able to. She could see him; her eyes could move but it seemed that her body was incapable of obeying her brain.

Why? she wanted to ask him.

"Ah, why, you ask?" he said, smoothing back her hair.

He was thoughtful for a moment. "I never wanted to kill you, but since you've ruined everything, it seems only right that I explain. I am an American, Lucy. I am a patriot. I grew up going to every reenactment. Now, there are idiots who claim Washington was just a man and Lincoln had his faults. They like to talk about the way the founding fathers owned slaves and fought with one another. We have to stop that kind of talk, Allison. At the Tarleton-Dandridge House, we were true patriots. Lucy was a real heroine—along with her sister, her brother-in-law and the man who should have been her husband, Stewart Douglas. But you— and some of those others—wanted to ruin the image. Don't go thinking I'm crazy. I'm not. I'm a patriot. A true patriot. All those years ago, that kid. That stupid, stupid kid! He wanted to break in to steal the portrait of Beast Bradley. We need that portrait. It shows the

truth—that the British were our enemies. They stole
our freedoms and they wanted to kill us. Tobias Dandridge painted that portrait because that was the man
who came to destroy his life."

Allison was able to swallow and work her mouth.
She tried to dampen her tongue; the effort was nearly
useless but she discovered she could croak out words.

"Tobias. Tobias Dandridge."

"What?" Pierson demanded. He smiled. "The drug's
wearing off. I didn't give you enough. Oh, it's not going
to kill you. I'm afraid I'll have to stab you to death.
Like poor Lucy Tarleton. That's true poetic justice."

She was glad she couldn't feel anything. Despite everyone's determination that she not be alone, she *was*
alone. With a man who meant to slice her to ribbons.
And she could hardly blink. She tried to fight the terror. She needed courage.

To do what? Die when she couldn't move?

Courage wasn't about not being afraid. Courage was
being terrified, and going forth despite the fear.

She struggled. She could move her lips. "Tobias,"
she whispered. "Tobias Dandridge was the one who
murdered Lucy. That's what you're afraid I was going
to figure out. We've had it wrong for years. Lucy gave
the baby away to hide from Tobias. She was afraid. The
British were leaving and she knew it. Bradley couldn't
take her with him—and she wouldn't have gone. She
was in love with him, but she really was a patriot. You
do her a tremendous disservice, hiding the truth. She
was in love with Bradley, but she still carried information to the patriot troops. Dandridge killed her—and
convinced her father that Bradley had done it. And he
painted the portrait so the world would believe it, believe that Bradley was a monster. He also killed Lucy

because it meant Sophia would inherit the house and everything Angus Tarleton possessed—and he was going to marry Sophia. But Sophia suspected the truth, and that was why the other painting was kept in Lucy's bedroom. I imagine she hid that painting while he was alive. Sophia believed Lucy's spirit deserved a righteous image of the man she had loved."

"That's just a theory," Nathan said irritably. "The same as any other."

She was surprised that he could hear her, since she could barely form the words. He leaned close to her—so close. "But I believe it's the truth," she told him. "And others might believe it, too. I'm living proof that Lucy had a child. And if she'd had her supposed patriot lover's child, the baby would have been loved and cherished—even if *she'd* been killed."

"You would have written that filth!" Nathan said.

She didn't respond.

He paused for a minute. "Listen." He raised his head. "Listen. The sirens are blazing in the night. They're going to save Annette. But they can't save you because they don't know you're here. They think I've kidnapped you and taken you somewhere, and they'll comb the city. But you're *here*. I know this house, I know everything about it. I know how to slip in and around it, how to hide in it. They'll be searching the city and they'll think of the graveyard, but never the stables. This is so fitting, you see. Down there—in the stall below us—is where Lucy kept Firewalker, and where she came when she was about to ride out to the patriot camp. This is where she came when she was still loyal. And, Allison, it's where you'll die. You'll die—like Lucy. You're talking nicely now, but you can't scream. I'm going to make sure you can't scream. I really am sorry. I'm going to

spill your blood on this property. It's so fitting," he said
again. He started to reach into his pocket and she knew
he had the needle there, ready to shove into her flesh.

"And what will happen when I'm dead? They won't
stop until they find you."

"Foolish girl, I've been getting rid of those who were
disloyal for years. I will get away with all of it. I've spent
the past days—when I wasn't silencing a few people—
at my bankers'. My money is now in foreign accounts.
You can't imagine the number of countries that don't
honor extradition to the United States. I'll lie low for a
few years, and then all will be fine. Don't worry about
me, my dear. So nice of you to think of me at a time like
this, though. I do appreciate your concern."

"How did you kill Julian?" she asked. Her fingers
almost moved. "And *why?*"

"Oh, Julian! That's easy," he said. "I left the house,
walked back in right behind him and returned to the
office and then down the servants' stairs. I have a very
special copy of that painting of Bradley. I'd switched
the paintings during the middle of the board meeting. I
had a copy of the original done ages ago and a magician
in San Francisco did a little altering for me. Seriously,
if any of you had come in on me, what would you have
said about a board member adjusting a painting?" He
shook his head. "Old Angela—I tested it on her three
years ago and…well, what can I say? It worked. But Julian, that narcissist! He was so busy posing in the chair
he didn't hear me—not until I had the painting 'speak'
to him. He never saw me. I was behind the chair by the
bookcases. He was so involved with himself that he
never heard me, even when I pushed his head down."

"No, he didn't see you or hear you. But why—"

"I was afraid of what he'd learned reading your so-called research. I couldn't trust him. And I didn't like the way he acted around you."

"But—"

Nathan Pierson had the needle out. "We can't chat here any longer. I'm sorry to do this to you and sorry you can't scream. I believe Lucy screamed when she was executed for her disloyalty to the cause she claimed to love. But I can't have you heard up at the house. Think about it. All that commotion inside—and here you are, dying…bleeding out in the stables and they'll hate themselves, but—"

"They see you, Nathan," she said.

"Who sees me? We're alone. They'll rush to the tomb. Then they'll decide I took you off the property. By the time they run around like ants you'll be dead and I'll be long gone."

"Lucy sees you."

"Lucy is a ghost story."

"Lucy is a ghost—not a story. She's watching you now."

She made him turn; he dropped the needle and had to reach down to get it.

Then Allison saw that Lucy really *was* there. She'd slipped into the doorway, and Tyler was behind her.

He was ready, she thought. He had his Glock out as he walked into the room.

Nathan Pierson heard him at just that moment. He rose, drawing Allison's body against his. She flopped in his arms, twitching in an attempt to regain some motion.

"Let her go, Nathan," Tyler said calmly.

"You can't take a shot," Nathan told him. "You could

shoot Allison. Shoot her and kill her, and her death would be your fault."

"Lucy isn't going to let that happen," he said.

"Lucy! There is no damned ghost! What the hell is the matter with you people? Ghost busters, it's a joke."

"Not true. Lucy is here—and Julian is, too. I'm sure he hates you even more than Lucy does."

"There are no ghosts!" Pierson shouted. "Now you... you back up and let me leave with her or I swear I'll plunge this needle straight into her heart. It's filled with a Norcuron mix—I stole it from the hospital. In her heart? It'll kill her in a flash."

Allison reminded herself that courage was about being terrified—and going forth anyway!

She managed to open her mouth.

She had one chance and she knew it. She prayed that her drugged muscles would work.

She bit Nathan Pierson. Bit him as hard as she could.

He screamed. She was nearly dead weight.

He didn't drop her, but it was enough. Tyler used those split seconds to speed across the room, leaping over the trunks in his way, and tackle Nathan Pierson, bringing the three of them down to the ground. Pierson fought him desperately, reaching for the needle. But Tyler smashed his arm and grabbed the syringe and the two of them rolled, crashing into the wardrobe against the far wall.

Allison couldn't see what was happening. She willed herself to turn. Inch by inch...

By half inch.

She made it just in time to see the needle rise into the air.

And she saw Tyler lift his arm, slam Pierson's arm

against Angus's old wardrobe—and send the needle flying.

With a right swing he caught Nathan Pierson in the jaw.

That was when Pierson gave up the fight. Tyler scrambled to his feet, racing over to Allison.

For a moment, as Tyler took her in his arms, she saw Pierson lying on the floor, Lucy Tarleton standing above him.

Her ghostly form kicked him. She saw then that Julian had come forward to do the same thing, kicking him and kicking him. Whether Nathan felt it or not, she couldn't say. But he must have *sensed* their hatred.

Lucy Tarleton set a hand on Julian's arm. He turned to her, and their eyes met, and Lucy smiled at him, taking his hand.

Tyler picked Allison up and wordlessly began to walk down the stairs that brought them to the first level of the stables, where the horse stalls remained.

Logan burst through with Sean, and they dragged Nathan Pierson to his feet and read him his rights.

Cherry was standing outside the stall. "The bastard!" she cried. "He doesn't deserve any rights."

"He does," he said to Cherry, holding Allison in his arms. "They might figure out what it means to be a patriot—an American. Those men fought and died for our rights. So did Lucy Tarleton. But he forgot all about freedom of speech and freedom of the press—and our freedom to know the truth and learn from the truth."

Tyler walked with Allison, taking her outside beneath the moonlight shimmering over the property. She wished she could put her arms around him. She knew she was headed for a waiting ambulance, but she wanted to say something to him.

She didn't know what. *Thank you...thank you for my life. Thank you for being you, for believing...for finding me.*

He carried her into the ambulance and laid her down on the stretcher.

He smiled, then took her hand and kissed it. "True courage, my dear patriot!" he told her.

"I think I love you," she said.

"A true patriot, a remarkable woman, the woman I love—and a ball-breaker with wicked teeth! I could never, ever want anything more."

Once arrested, Nathan Pierson wasn't going down alone. He talked; he bargained. He played crazy and tried to pretend he'd been seduced and coerced into his actions.

When Allison was released from the hospital the next morning, Tyler told her the sad truth and they went to Annette's room together. She was still being dramatic, still pushing the nurses around.

Tyler let Jenson cuff her to the hospital bed. "Annette Fanning, you are under arrest..."

He went on to chronicle her crimes. Nathan Pierson had done the most damage, but Annette had put the copperhead in Sarah Vining's car and she'd been the one to steal the Norcuron mix from the hospital, where her cousin had really had a baby. She'd also allowed herself to be bitten by the small copperhead she'd smuggled into the bathroom, in order to give Nathan a chance to get Allison out of the house. They'd taken a lot of risks, but they'd almost pulled it off.

Annette could also solve one of the biggest mysteries in the case—Artie Dixon's coma. They would have known eventually when all the blood tests had been completed. Dixon had been a victim of argot poisoning; Annette had gotten it into his food when he and his family had gone to the Colonial tavern for dinner. She sometimes worked there, and it had been easy to mill around with her fellow workers in the kitchen. She'd never seen the Dixon family, and they had never seen her. But Pierson had described them to Annette, asking her to do something that would get the family talking about the ghosts in the house, specifically Brian Bradley. If others talked about the ghosts, it would only make Julian Mitchell's suicide—or accidental death— appear to be the work of the evil Beast Bradley's spirit, ever residing there.

They hadn't expected the coma. That had been an added benefit.

Annette was proud of her own brilliance. Her reward?

"Money. Lots of it," she said, and turned away with one word. "Attorney!"

Allison was deeply depressed and hurt by her friend's betrayal, but while Annette screamed that every person couldn't be her—with degrees, able to work anywhere, do anything—she walked quietly out of the room. She looked as if she'd break down, except that Logan was waiting for them outside.

"Artie Dixon has come out of his coma. He wants to thank you. He says you've spent hours and hours with him, trying to convince him that everything would be all right."

So she didn't break down. They visited with the Dixon family, and Todd kept taking Allison's hands and telling her she was the best, the coolest, the most wonderful.

She looked at Tyler and smiled. She'd been there

with Artie, yes. But not for hours and hours as he'd claimed. She and Tyler both had a feeling that Lucy Tarleton had found Dixon and stayed by him, eager to help a man who needed help—a family man.

She promised Todd they'd stay in touch. Haley Dixon hugged Allison and kissed Tyler on the cheek, and they left behind a very happy family.

A search of Nathan Pierson's house produced the trick painting he'd exchanged for the historical image of Beast Bradley in the study. It was fitted with empty eye sockets that could be lit up with blinding lasers, and tiny speakers that could be wirelessly attached to a small, voice-altering mechanism Pierson had used to terrify his victims or lure them into danger—Julian to his doom with his own bayonet, and Martin Standish out to the woods and the stream beyond.

That night, Allison ordered flowers and had them brought to the Tarleton tomb. Tyler joined her there. When she'd set them all around the family mausoleum, they walked back to the house.

The spirit of Lucy Tarleton was just coming from the stables. She led Firewalker, and the dog, Robert, pranced joyously at her side.

Lucy paused, staring at Tyler and Allison, and then she smiled. She lifted her fingers to her lips and blew them a kiss.

Tyler hadn't realized that Julian was with them. He saw Lucy beckon, and Julian walked over to her.

She leaped up on Firewalker, and then reached down a hand to Julian.

He looked back at Tyler and Allison.

Allison said, "Julian, go. A beautiful woman is trying to take you with her."

"But…"

"Surely, they need rock stars wherever she's going," Tyler said.

Julian grinned. He took Lucy's hand and jumped up on the massive steed behind her.

The sun was setting. They rode toward the burst of gold in the west.

Robert barked with excitement as he followed the riders, who disappeared into the light.

"They're at peace." Tyler spoke in a quiet voice.

"Thank God!" Allison said fervently.

"And we're free."

"And out of here—for the night, at least. I know this glorious, modern, five-star hotel in D.C. where docents get special rates. They have these wonderful Jacuzzis in every room, and a lovely old bar with cushioned seats in front of a charming fireplace."

He shrugged. "That'll do—for tonight."

She studied his eyes. "For tonight?"

"I was thinking about a warm beach with white sand. All the huts have every modern amenity. It's my turn for a vacation. Of course, when you want to work and write, they have Wi-Fi. When you don't…they have pristine private coves, snorkeling, diving—and no ghosts. Nope, no ghosts. The place I'm thinking of is in Jamaica, and it's brand-new. I don't want to stay there forever, but I was thinking of a week."

She kept staring at him.

"Are you in?" he asked.

"I am."

"And then…well, it's not that hard to get to Philly, not really. Unless the Krewe's across the country, I can get here easily."

"You won't have to," she said.

Heather Graham

His heart thundered. He tried not to show it, and held his head at a stoic Texas angle.

"I won't?"

She smiled, stood on her toes and kissed his lips with a very seductive and insinuating passion.

"We're not going to make it to that hotel," he murmured huskily. He gently pushed her away. "Back to the question. Why won't I have to come to Philly?"

"Because Virginia and the D.C. area are full of colleges...and I'll be just fine in Arlington," she said.

He kissed her. It was a wet, steamy kiss that made her tremble against him. "I told you I thought I loved you," she teased.

"No thinking about it, ma'am," he said. "I *know* I love you."

She closed her eyes and leaned against him. There was so much they still needed to learn about each other.

But none of it really mattered.

He'd been looking for her all his life.

And now he'd found her.

* * * * *